A Spy Like Me

KIM SHERWOOD is a novelist and a lecturer in creative writing at the University of Edinburgh. Her debut novel, *Testament*, won multiple awards, and Kim was short-listed for the Sunday Times Young Writer of the Year Award. Her latest novel, *A Wild and True Relation*, was described by Dame Hilary Mantel as "a rarity—a novel as remarkable for the vigor of the storytelling as for its literary ambition. Kim Sherwood is a writer of capacity, potency, and sophistication." *A Spy Like Me* is the second in an acclaimed series of Double O novels expanding the world of James Bond.

kimsherwoodauthor.com

ALSO BY KIM SHERWOOD

A Wild and True Relation
Testament

DOUBLE O NOVELS

Double or Nothing

A Spy Like Me

A Double O Novel

Kim Sherwood

HARPER LARGE PRINT

An Imprint of HarperCollinsPublishers

FIRST HARPER LARGE PRINT EDITION

ISBN: 978-0-06-335980-2

Library of Congress Cataloging-in-Publication Data is available upon request.

24 25 26 27 28 LBC 5 4 3 2 1

For my sister Rosie, my partner in (art) crime,
who is always there to walk and talk

I shall use my time.

—Ian Fleming, *You Only Live Twice*
(after Jack London)

PART I

Detonation

One
Breaking News

London

Moneypenny's worst fear is not being on time. It keeps her up at night: that as the Head of the Double O Section, she might have before her the cogs, the wheels, the pins, and yet fail to visualize the whole machine. At 1:25 p.m., a bomb will explode at BBC New Broadcasting House. She might not be on time to stop it, just like she didn't stop the Egyptian embassy bombing last month, or the shooting at the synagogue in Paris the week before that, or the hack on the International Monetary Fund two months ago. She knows the bomber's name is Jason Kent. He is twenty-five years old, white, unemployed; he has been arrested and charged repeatedly with domestic abuse; he is connected to international far-right extremist groups, where MI6's involvement began, leading to this partnership with MI5 on home soil. She knows *all* this and yet it's quarter past one and 004 and 008 have yet to ID the bomber on-site.

Moneypenny leans on the back of Aisha Asante's chair, peering over Aisha's head at the screens sifting surveillance footage. Beyond the wall of screens, the glass chamber containing Q seems thick to her with invisible electricity as the quantum computer works the datasets, its golden rods like the tendrils of an octopus pressed to some task. In reality, the tuneless hum is coming from Ibrahim Suleiman, who is monitoring the audio streaming from 004's brain-computer interface, installed—if one could use that word—in Joseph Dryden's skull after he suffered traumatic brain injury while serving in the Special Forces. The blast lacerated the vestibular nerve beneath his right ear, leaving him sensorineural deaf on one side, while the shock wave damaged the language center in the brain. The hidden microphone embedded in his ear canal by Q Branch, coupled with the brain-computer interface, bypasses both the cut nerve and the damaged tissue, and serves to link 004 to Q. But his ears aren't picking up anything useful today.

"No matches," says Aisha, more to herself than

to Moneypenny. She's pushed the sleeves of her hot pink blazer to her elbows. "How can there be no voice match? No facial recognition match?"

"Maybe Jason Kent decided against mass murder for today," mutters Ibrahim, messing up his already wild hair with a frantic hand.

Moneypenny stretches to hit the comms button. "004, 008, report."

Joseph Dryden's voice blooms into the underground chamber. "I know M ruled out evac to avoid spooking the target into early detonation, but we're running out of tarmac here, ma'am."

Moneypenny longs for Mrs. Keator's sharp tones, but the bastion of Q Branch retired after Bill Tanner was revealed to be a traitor and hanged himself four months ago. She raises a phone to her ear—the line is open to M at Vauxhall, and to Vallance at MI5. "Moneypenny here—recommend evac."

Vallance's voice is crisp: "Agree."

M's is soft: "Agree."

Moneypenny stabs the comms button. "008, start the evacuation. 004, keep hunting."

Dryden says, "Yes, ma'am."

Dodger Macintyre—Roger to his parents, Dodger since his schooldays at Wideawake Airfield on Ascension Island—has only recently moved from the role of Intelligence Officer at MI6 to Double O. A pilot and a language graduate, he spent most of his life abroad, from childhood to university to operating. He expected that trend to continue as 008, not to find himself working with MI5 and Scotland Yard to evacuate the BBC.

New Broadcasting House was designed with transparency in mind, a glass-fronted curve swishing between the original 1932 building and the East Wing to create an atrium the shape of a running teardrop. The idea of transparency—a BBC funded by the people, belonging to the people, seen by the people—continues inside. Audiences glimpse the four-thousand-square-meter news floor sitting in the glass well of the building in the background of daily broadcasts. There are transparent meeting rooms decorated with photographs from *Doctor Who* and *EastEnders*. Breakout spaces glow red beneath Perspex lights. That's a lot of glass to go boom.

008 gathers people from the back-to-back booths lining the atrium, where the cyclorama of the London sky promises nothing but rain. He ignores padded doors calling for silence to tell presenters to get off the air *now*.

"Maintain calm, look like you're simply stepping out for lunch."

He expects panic from the six thousand staff members

but gets none, the broadcasters switching to backup programs without question. Each desk is a habitat, whether it's a lipstick-stained KeepCup or a swivel chair with a scrap of paper taped to the back that reads *Helen's Supplied by HR—DO NOT Remove*. Hot desks flap with wearied Post-its: *In Use* or *Back in 5 minutes*. Journalists grab coats or phones and follow 008, exchanging grim chatter, some clustering uncertainly beneath banners that instruct, red-on-yellow, *People Gathering Point*. This is where they've been trained to seek safety in case of a bomb threat, well away from the glass façade. But Dodger ushers the journalists on, telling them to ignore the glass lifts sheathed in orange steel, and instead file through the doors leading to the 1932 wing.

All the bright lights and gleaming screens of the twenty-first century disappear, replaced by cold stone and a brown dado that follows the Art Deco curves of the stairwell. Dodger is gambling that, by avoiding the main entrance and exit, he can avoid spooking the bomber. "Keep going, keep going, keep going"— Dodger hopes his intent doesn't show as he scrutinizes each passing face, searching for the washed-out, almost invisible features of Jason Kent.

The busy hush of New Broadcasting House reminds Joseph Dryden of a Forward Operating Base. People show up here to get the job done. There is solidarity to the snaking workspaces, a sense of belonging to the same rare club, something sacred even, but held lightly, with an eye roll at the whimsical puzzle-piece sofas. Now, the thrum goes up a few notches. Dryden can smell violence in the air. It's coming. Will the bomber wait until 1:25 p.m. as planned or detonate early? Dryden strolls past the Middle East desk, then the neighboring section devoted to reporting on jihadism. He nods to the journalists scooping up their Tupperware and hurrying out, footfalls absorbed into thick gray carpets. He takes the spiral staircase down to the news floor.

It is surreal to stand behind the glass backdrop. BBC *News at One* is still broadcasting. Dryden can see the presenter's legs under the desk jiggling up and down—they've been alerted to the threat through their earpieces, but told to keep broadcasting until the last possible minute. The journalists around Dryden, who feature daily in the background of the news, are rigid at their monitors, watching colleagues evacuate out of shot of the cameras.

"We should evacuate the news floor," he says. "We're getting too close."

"If the news stops," says Moneypenny, "he'll know

he's caught and detonate early. We've told them to cut to packaged footage. As soon as that happens, people in the background can leave. But the presenters have to stay put for as long as possible."

Dryden says, "008, you got anything?"

Dodger Macintyre's voice burrs in Dryden's skull, patched through his neural link. "Negative, sir."

A small smile makes it onto Dryden's face. "004 is fine. I'd even stretch to Joe if you ID this son of a bitch for me."

A nervous laugh. "Yes, sir."

In the periphery of Dryden's vision, a lift starts to descend from the top floor. Lifts are only to be used in an evacuation by disabled staff members. The screen flashes that the lift's destination is the news floor. Evacuating staff wouldn't come down to the ground floor, where there is no exit onto street level. The lift is transparent on three sides. Inside is a white man with red hair wearing a combat jacket. Not Jason Kent. Wrong man. But that doesn't make him right, either.

"Descending lift," he says. "News floor."

Moneypenny holds her breath as Aisha pulls the security feed from the lift, which is playing BBC Radio

Asian Network, according to the poster above the panel of buttons. The man is carrying a messenger bag with the logo of a reputable delivery company—easy to fake, and the mailroom is nowhere near the news floor.

"Running his face now," says Ibrahim.

"What do you think?" says Moneypenny.

"I'd cross the street," says Aisha.

"Mm-hmm. He's getting fidgety—he's watching people leave."

"They could be going for lunch," says Aisha.

Moneypenny bunches her fists, remembering: "They play radio in the lifts. Has it gone quiet?"

Aisha flips her braided hair, picking up headphones. "BBC Radio Asian is still playing."

Moneypenny says, "004, I thought you evacuated the broadcast studios. We're still hearing radio."

"Yes, ma'am," says Dryden. "They've switched to backup."

Moneypenny takes a breath. She knows that. She knows the BBC never stops broadcasting. The day the radio goes quiet, that's when you know you are in real trouble.

"How can 004 get into that lift?"

"He could climb the shaft, it's all steel girders. But it's coming to him. At alarming speed."

"Got the ID!" calls Ibrahim. "Grant Bishop. He plays that social media terror game, points for attacks on minorities IRL. Multiple contacts with Kent."

Moneypenny raises the phone to her ear. "Vallance? Anything on Kent?"

Vallance says, "Still nothing since he alighted from the Tube at Oxford Street."

"How's that possible? How can a terrorist disappear from our surveillance?" says Ibrahim, before answering himself: "It's not possible."

Moneypenny swears. Another jab at the button. "004, the man in the lift poses a lethal threat."

Joseph Dryden says, "Understood," and walks with long, easy strides through the anxious journalists toward the lift. No time for aerial heroics, though he likes Aisha's faith in him. He doesn't think the target will blow himself up inside the lift alone—he'd get structural damage, sure, but no fatalities. He figures the target will step out onto the news floor, in sight of the running cameras and surrounded by journalists. Dryden moves just feet from where the lift will open. He sits on a desk and takes out his phone, as if idling while waiting for a colleague to meet him. He crosses one leg over the other. Allows his foot to tap. Three floors. Two.

"008, monitor the street," he says. "This may be a tag team."

One floor.

008 says, "Good luck"—but Dryden isn't focusing on voices anymore.

The lift doors sigh open.

Dryden stands up and draws his gun from his shoulder holster, training it in one fluid motion on the man, who takes a tentative step from the lift and freezes, blue eyes wide as overly pumped balloons.

Grant Bishop registers the reality of this six-foot-four Black man in a three-piece suit with cropped hair, carrying fourteen stone of muscle, who could be an actor or a big shot producer, but is in fact holding a real weapon and saying loudly but levelly as people dive beneath desks, one muffled scream amongst them— "Police, hands up."

Bishop squints, then his hand darts inside the messenger bag.

Dryden fires.

Brain matter splatters in a red mist to the back of the lift. The doors ding shut and the lift rises, carrying forensic evidence to the floor above.

"Everybody stay down," says Dryden, his voice warping in his own ears, swallowed by the fearful quiet. He harnesses his weapon and kneels by the corpse. A hole the size of a five-pence piece through the forehead of the skull leads to a two-pound coin crater at the back. He delicately wraps his fingers around the target's thin arm and lifts the flap of the bag.

It is empty. The fool was playing out a deadly bluff fatal only to himself. But that means . . .

Dryden shouts, "Dodger, it was a decoy! Evacuate!"

He sprints up the spiral staircase, racing past a model of the TARDIS. He's just paces now from the glass doors leading to the plaza. Outside, journalists form orderly lines beyond the security bollards around All Souls Church. Dryden picks out Dodger talking with a huddle of MI5 agents and police. He sees, but cannot hear through the glass, a police dog bark at what looks like a drain.

"008," he says, "come in, 008—"

Dodger Macintyre doesn't hear his radio over the buzzing mobile phones and the journalists talking to camera—breaking the news. Then he realizes a dog is barking, and remembers what three barks means. He pushes through officers congratulating him on 004's success. He bumps into the back of the dog's handler. The dog is pawing at a grated ventilation shaft in the paving, which would connect with the Tube.

"Get back!" shouts Dodger. "Everyone back!"

But the bollards are up, and traffic is shooting by, penning people to the spot, and the crowd is too big to corral. Dodger checks his watch: 1:25 p.m. He hauls the grate open.

The bomb is duct-taped to the roof of the tunnel. He swallows—he can hear himself swallow. It is a big enough IED to bring the floor of the plaza and everyone standing on it crashing down into the Tube. He has to get the device away from the public.

They've evacuated All Souls.

Dodger rips the bomb from its silver straps.

"Bomb! Move!"

He is sprinting toward the church, past the luminous yellow jackets of policemen and the distraught frozen faces of journalists and the blinking lights of cameras—into the tranquility of All Souls. He lobs the bomb down the nave and it explodes midair, thrusting him out through the doors, hurling policemen off their feet, spraying stained glass, caving columns, ringing bells.

Dryden is running with the dead man's blood on the soles of his shoes, leaving a long streak as he skids to a halt in the lobby. The glass doors of the building turn to sand, knocking him down. He hugs his head, inside of which Moneypenny's voice clamors for a report. Dryden swallows dust. He stands up. Runs through the smoke toward the steps of the church.

Moneypenny presses her hand to her mouth, nails digging into her cheek. She wasn't on time.

Two
Vibrations

London

Aring road outlines the heart of London. The northern boundary of this heart is Euston Road, a malodorous, raging bypass pushing traffic inch by fuming inch. Anybody who walks the pavements hurries, bent against the din of eternal construction and choking engines. Nobody stops to consider University College Hospital; it's best ignored, the subconscious says; push on by foot to the hush of the British Library, or seize a green light to escape the congestion of orange cones. Only, tonight is different. London's heart has faltered somewhere between faith and failure. The teal façade of the hospital is crisscrossed by the headlights of ambulances and press vans. Lorry drivers linger.

Pedestrians bound for a night shift or returning from a party stop to peer up at the hundreds of illuminated windows, beacons of the worst kind, and the best.

Behind one of those windows, 008's life is on the line. Behind another, 004's conviction is on the far side.

Joseph Dryden tells the doctor he cut himself shaving. She has the grace to laugh. He lies with a sheet protecting his modesty while the Scottish junior doctor who misses Glasgow and finds London too impersonal tweezes glass from his body and maintains this soothing small talk. When Ibrahim arrives to test his implant, Dryden tells him to go check 008's hearing. Ibrahim bites his lip, rocking from foot to foot, and then leaves with his shoulders hunched. The doctor purses her lips but says nothing.

Dryden studies the waiting-room TV, visible through the glass door. If he never sees a glass door again, he'll be happy. It is switched to BBC *News 24*, showing the explosion on a loop: the flying masonry, gray mushroom, and then the camera knocked skyward, peering tremblingly up at clouds that seem to swing like a child's mobile. Captioned politicians—addressing the nation with ashy faces—describe the calm reaction of the journalists and public as "the Blitz spirit." Dryden's skull is ringing like the bells of the church. Not because the implant has failed and his brain is scrambling his words—the improvements Aisha and Ibrahim made after a knockout punch disabled the device last year fixed that—but because he is too angry.

When the news switches away from London, the doctor notices every muscle in his body jump. She searches his face, then turns to the TV, seeing the coverage is now Afghanistan. The footage shows the Taliban driving triumphantly through Kabul. Approaching a year since the pullout.

"Did you serve?" she asks.

"Yes," he says. "For all the good it did."

The doctor says, "You did a lot of good today."

He snorts. "You ever feel like you're fighting a losing battle?"

"I work for the NHS. What do you think?"

For the first time, Dryden notices the silver bags beneath her eyes. "Workers of the world, unite."

The doctor mimes bumping his fist, leaving an inch of space around his bloody knuckles. "Amen."

The sign reads, *Used walking sticks.* The sticks lean in a jumble in the corner of the hospital corridor. Aluminum and plastic, flaked and flecked with time and pressure, scuffed at the base from poorly paved roads.

The sign isn't really a sign but a strip of masking tape holding up a scrap of paper. Moneypenny waits in a row of hard chairs, wondering if 008 will need a walking stick.

If.

To an observer, she might be a mother worried about the outcome of a child's emergency, her curls pulled flat, hands buried in her amber trench coat, the laces on one of her oxblood brogues untied and unnoticed, her stare—usually direct and cool—empty as a dry well.

When she hears her name, she snaps back to herself.

Another walking stick has moved into view, this one polished beech with a gold collar and an ivory head, gripped in M's red fist. A recent addition. She raises her chin. The neon hospital light plays on the bald dome of his head. His short white beard is bristled, like a cat stroked backward. His coat is buttoned wrongly. She's never known Sir Emery Ware to have so much as a loose thread to his appearance. Now, he could be a patient here. She says, "I suppose the PM wants my resignation."

"The PM wants your head and my balls, and he's not particularly fussed in what order," says M good-naturedly. He sits beside her, hitching his trousers.

"What did you tell him?"

M peers down the corridor, empty but for security officers, who drop back to give them a thirty-foot radius of sacred silence. "I reminded him *respectfully* that two dozen injuries are better than two dozen deaths, our NHS surgeons are doing what they do best, and a beloved British institution was saved—sparing some glass—thanks to the bravery of our agents."

"That's not good enough," says Moneypenny.

M raises an eyebrow. "Are you doing his part of the conversation too?"

She returns his gaze levelly. "We don't know what the body count is yet."

M glances at the clock.

"008 has a collapsed lung."

"And enough loose bones for a fortune-teller's trick. I know." He rubs his nose. "You wanted the job, Penny. This is the job."

She shakes her shoulders loose. "Yes, sir." She weighs her blank phone. "I don't see how Kent was able to move into the Tube's service shafts without CCTV picking him up."

M lays a hand on her arm. "Give it time. MI5's search of the bomber's home revealed much of what you'd expect. A small cell of far-right, homegrown extremists connected to international neo-Nazis. They targeted the BBC because they believe the organization stands for a 'fake news agenda supporting the liberal elite,' which they are intent on destroying. Speaking as a liberal elite, I will admit to having had better days. Still, one doesn't like to give the bastards the satisfaction, hey?"

Moneypenny can hear the whomp-whomp-whomp of military helicopters passing over London, joined by a siren. There is no other sound—no shouting, no panic-induced riots on the street. This is her experience of terror on British soil. The quieter things get, the worse they are.

M cocks his ear, too, saying, "I must get back to COBRA. Of course, the threat level has been raised to critical and will remain there while the cell is rolled up. There will be hand-wringing and soul-searching, all the harder when there is no foreign flag to target, simply unlooked-for questions about the rise of fascism amongst our own. There will be recriminations against us and MI5, of course, for letting one get through. But we'll let the politicians deliver the speeches. We work best in the dark. Call 000 home. Put him on this with 004."

"You know he and 004 don't play well together," says Moneypenny.

M shrugs. "Conrad Harthrop-Vane is arrogant

and cold. So was Bond. That's what makes them good weapons, for heaven's sake."

"So *was* Bond?"

M clears his throat. Doors swing open, letting in the noise of a fresh wave of emergency victims. "You know what I mean. A man must believe he's the best to take the risks this job demands. And he's got to do it with ice in him if he's going to make the kind of sacrifices philosophy candidates sweat over at Oxbridge interviews. Granted, 000 doesn't always display modern niceties. He doesn't need to. He's charming, fills out a suit, and has the brains to go with it. Conrad was dealt raw cards as a boy and he's turned them into a winning hand for his country. I'd back him any day of the week. To the hilt. I have."

Moneypenny nods. *Raw cards* is one way to put it. 000's father came from an aristocratic line that lost it all, leaving Conrad Harthrop-Vane the First hovering somewhere between con man, diplomat, and spy, a contact for MI6 in the criminal and political underworlds. Divorce and a gnawing custody battle were swiftly followed by cancer taking Conrad's mother's life. The psychiatrist at Shrublands said it was then that two key tenets were embedded in young Conrad Harthrop-Vane the Second. The first was a belief that the world isn't right, it isn't fair, there's no justice, and no point in trusting anyone. The second was perhaps more a question than a belief: If he'd been a better son, could he have kept his mother from dying?

Of course, orphans are MI6's bread and butter. The psychiatrist noted that unmourned grief turns to rage, and this is what happened after Conrad's mother died and his father placed him in boarding school, where he had to toughen up, channeling an iced-over fury into beating other boys at boxing, running, and fencing, receiving medals and applause. In the summer holidays, however, Conrad wasn't the big fish in the little pond; he was a minnow in his father's piranha pool.

In Conrad's first term at Cambridge, his father committed suicide. Abandonment, rejection—and, if he'd been a better son, could he have kept his father from dying?

There was one safe presence in his life: M, an old school chum of his father's. After Conrad Harthrop-Vane the First died, M threw the son a lifeline, and MI6 reeled in the broken boy. Alone in the world, angry, desperate to shine and eager to please. The perfect recruit.

Of course, temperamentally and socially, he is the direct opposite of 004. Moneypenny says, "You're right that we need all our talent on this, but I'd sooner pair 004 and 003, and let 000 work alone. It's what he does best."

M's phone buzzes. He says with a frown at the screen, "I need not remind you, Moneypenny, that Johanna Harwood isn't cleared for active duty."

"We just had our transparent face punched in, live on the news for all the world to see," says Moneypenny. "I don't care what Shrublands says. When I punch back, I'm going to do it with a heavyweight in the ring."

"Boxing and poker," says M, as his phone chimes again. "Have you noticed that when we employ imagery for the Great Game of espionage—itself a metaphor—we always use sports that require only a single actor? It was Kipling who said: *When he comes to the Great Game he must go alone.*"

"What's your point?"

"This isn't a team sport. Not everyone gets to play."

"You know the rest of that line?"

"Hmm?" M clutches the black box with its song of death.

"*When he comes to the Great Game he must go alone—alone, and at peril of his head.* Personally, I'd rather have someone watching my back."

"Be that as it may," says M, "sometimes a head is what's required. And this time, I fear it may be my own. Not that I expect or invite sympathy. Only that a man knows when he's played out. An attack like this happening on our own turf. Vallance and MI5 will be obvious candidates for the chopping block. But I can feel it in my bones, as my mother used to say. I'm growing too old for this game."

Moneypenny notices his hand trembling on the head of the cane. She brushes his cold fingers. "You're not playing it alone," she says. "And neither am I. We need you, so don't offer your head too readily."

M catches her fingers, planting a kiss on her knuckles.

Moneypenny snorts. "What I want to know is where this far-right cell got the funding, training, and weaponry. And who 004 needs to shoot next to stop another detonation."

The squeak of trainers on linoleum. Ibrahim Suleiman clears his throat. He is twisting his hands in a pouch formed from his oversized T-shirt. He says, "Q has something."

Aisha Asante is gray with adrenaline fatigue, but when Moneypenny asks her to explain it again, she wets her lips and points to the quantum computer dangling in the vacuum behind her.

"Q has identified a pattern," she says. "I fed in the data from today's"—a glance at the time—"yesterday's attack along with all other terror attacks in the last twelve months. I coupled it with significant financial transactions in a month's window of the attack. Six days prior to seventy-five percent of the attacks, a sale was made at Sotheby's worth over a million pounds."

M says, "Surely they make sales like that every day."

"They do, sir," says Aisha. "But the objects sold within a six-day window of the attack all moved through the same two free ports, one in Heraklion, Crete, and the other in Venice, Italy. Given the number of tax-free ports in Europe, it's a statistic that stands out."

Vallance, the director of MI5, appears on Aisha's screen as a silhouetted head in a video call box. "The neo-Nazi group we're investigating for the BBC blast doesn't seem organized or wealthy enough to be tied to regular art sales."

Moneypenny says, "We could be looking at one larger organization funding distinct groups through the sale of art, antiquities, and other high-value items to carry out attacks." She turns to M. "Rattenfänger."

M shakes his head. "Rattenfänger is—or was—a private military company involved in coups, conflicts, and civil wars. And we have their top man in our jail."

"Rattenfänger was also implicated in embassy bombings, kidnapping, data breaches . . . We've never discovered where they get their funding, who controls them, or how deep their tendrils run. Since we detained Colonel Mora, terror attacks have only increased globally. Perhaps Rattenfänger has shifted toward sponsoring separate terror groups."

M crosses his arms. "And they're doing that through selling shiny baubles?"

Moneypenny leans on Aisha's chair. "Were these items all sold by the same person?"

Aisha says, "It's hard to know, because sellers often use agents. Sotheby's do perform background checks to verify provenance, however, so we might discover more of a pattern with access to their files."

Vallance says, "Do they vet buyers?"

"To a point, sir," says Aisha. "Sotheby's verify that buyers have the funds in place to make the purchase. It's not their business to find out where the money came *from*. They've lost a lot of business, for example, since Russian oligarchs suddenly found their assets frozen. It was never Sotheby's job to make a moral judgment call on those oligarchs' bank accounts." A glance at M. "It was ours."

"All right, all right," says M. "I get enough of this from my granddaughter."

Aisha grins. "Q has run a check on regular Sotheby's buyers from the last year. One name stands out because she's currently under investigation by the National

Crime Agency, as an adjunct rather than a target. Marilyn Aliyeva, the mistress of Valentin Wiltshire. He's the target."

"Teddy Wiltshire?" says M, bumping his stick against the ground.

Ibrahim is just entering the room. "Watch out for vibrations."

M looks waspish. "Are you concerned I might tickle Q, young man?"

"Yes," says Ibrahim frankly, before sitting down at his console and pulling up a file.

M and Moneypenny share a smile.

"What have you got, Ibrahim?" says Moneypenny.

"The NCA have just sent over Wiltshire's record. Born in Turkmenistan in 1970. Moved to the UK in 1995, where he changed his surname from Kerimov to Wiltshire because, he said, he felt a spiritual connection to Stonehenge. Full name Valentin Eduard Wiltshire, known as Teddy."

"Lives up to the name, too," says M. "Crossed paths with him a few times at fund-raising events, parties where everyone has too much money and no idea how to spend it, but they *would* like to bend my ear if only I don't mind *terribly*. Teddy always struck me as a playboy run to fat. No bite to him."

"Well, he must have had teeth in his head at some

point, because he bit off a thirty-million-pound house in Tite Street, Chelsea, a couple of years ago," says Ibrahim, "where he lives with his wife, ironically named Chelsea, and their daughters Virginia, Adelaide, India, and Paris. Son Jordan is studying business at NYU."

"He collects places as well as antiques, then," says Moneypenny. She points to Aisha's screen. "What sort of things does Marilyn Aliyeva buy on Teddy's behalf?"

Aisha scrolls. "No real pattern. Dinosaur skulls. Art. Wine. Furniture. Ancient masks. Statues of gods. Anything very rare and very expensive."

"Where has all this money come from?"

Ibrahim says, "That's what the National Crime Agency want to know. His background is shipping and banking, but his taxes don't add up. The NCA is investigating him under an Unexplained Wealth Order in accordance with the Proceeds of Crime Act."

"When did Marilyn last make a purchase?"

Aisha clicks on one of the endless tabs. She turns to lock eyes with Moneypenny. "Six days ago. Something called a blind man's watch. She hasn't collected it yet."

"Why not?"

More scrolling. "Because she was arrested last week for causing a scene in some shop. She's being held while the NCA try to strike a deal with her."

Vallance's voice slices through the speaker: "Banner day for the NCA, I'd say. I'll just check. Yes, here we go . . . NCA have been pressuring her to speak up about Teddy but to no avail."

"Maybe we'd have better luck," says Moneypenny.

Vallance cuts in: "You're not permitted to work on UK soil. Today—or yesterday, rather—was an exception."

M clears his throat. "Come on, old chap. The BBC bombing was the exception. Most of these attacks are taking place internationally. This is our field. Let us till the earth, ay?"

Vallance says, "The corner of *this* field is forever England, *old chap*. Your field is over the water."

"And who stopped the death count in your field?" snaps M.

"An MI6 agent," says Vallance, "who thought it best to destroy a Nash church in the process, because why only damage *one* symbol when we can see *two* damaged?"

"That agent is now fighting for his life, so watch it."

Moneypenny holds up her hands. "Let's compromise. We'll use our Wild Card. 003 needs something to get her teeth into besides night duty, anyway."

M says, "I told you, Harwood isn't ready. Shrublands *are* insisting . . ."

"It's only one interrogation," says Moneypenny. "Besides, persuasion is what Johanna Harwood does best."

"A delicate job, this."

"I have faith in 003."

M heaves a sigh. "That's usually when they break your heart. All right, Moneypenny. Play the Wild Card."

Three
Wild Card

London

One hundred and sixty-one thousand, six hundred and forty minutes unspent. Forty-one. Forty-two.

Johanna Harwood now wears two watches. Her Hermès watch with its gold and orange horses on the ceramic face remains on her right wrist. It is this watch that was equipped with a simple Morse code emitter, allowing 003 to communicate with Moneypenny while she risked her life, body, and soul as a triple agent, first tortured then "flipped," embedded with Rattenfänger. It was with this watch that she sent the signal to Moneypenny identifying the mole in MI6—Bill Tanner, the trusted Chief of Staff.

That betrayal is the reason Harwood now wears a second watch. A World Time Casio AE1200WHD-1A, with a silver case and a stainless-steel band. A classic of sorts, with a compass and map, though there is nothing too rare about it. Still, this particular Casio is more valuable to Johanna Harwood than any other possession. Sid died wearing it. 009, Aazar Siddig Bashir. Johanna's fiancé. Sid set the timer on the watch running when he and Harwood split up in the tunnels that laddered the hillside in Syria. A fork in the road. Though Tanner committed suicide in isolation, somebody tipped off Mora, the Rattenfänger Colonel, that she and Sid were preparing an ambush. It took, Harwood calculated, another twenty-six minutes for the shot to find him—Sid stepping in front of the bullet meant for 003 and Dr. Nowak, the climate scientist whose safety was the Double Os' mission. Then another five minutes for Sid to bleed to death in Harwood's arms. It was remarkable how rapidly one could lose everything that mattered.

It wasn't until the coroner released 009's effects that Harwood realized the watch was still counting the minutes Sid Bashir would not live. Something was broken, keeping the stopwatch function from resetting every eleven hours, fifty-nine minutes, and fifty-nine seconds. Time continued regardless. She strapped the

Casio to her right forearm, where it slips up and down by fractions.

Now, Harwood unnecessarily presses the button that backlights the digits with a soft orange glow. It is foreign to her to be outside in daylight. Since the death of 009, Harwood has been deemed unfit for active fieldwork by the psychologist at Shrublands. There is nothing wrong with her physically, but it is considered that Sid's death requires the "healing process of time, as 003's loss of 009 represents the loss of not only a colleague but a lover and fiancé—note: this is why intimate relationships between Double O's are *not* recommended, especially as 003 had already been involved with 007, who was 009's mentor . . ." Harwood watched Dr. Kowalczyk write this in the reflection of the steel tissue holder in the therapy room and almost smiled, gripped by an urge to reach across the cheerful carpet and still Dr. Kowalczyk's pen. To tell the psychologist: "I know you mean well, but the bomb has already gone off. Can't you see I'm too broken for time to matter?"

But she knew that if she did that, Dr. Kowalczyk would ask her yet again: "Then why are you still wearing two watches?"

As it happens, time is all she has, as the two watches remind her, joint seconds measuring hours on night duties shopped between outfits as a Wild Card. This is a new initiative—that when not on active duty, Double O's should operate on home soil and learn about their sister organizations by staffing the emergency phone lines across London at night. She is kept from anything where the stakes matter. Kept from protecting the BBC yesterday, standing on her balcony watching smoke spiral from central London, as breaking news came over Sid's green world receiver radio and TVs flashed on in every window. But now she has been thrown onto the steps of a Knightsbridge police station, a Wild Card tossed after a thin lead, told by Moneypenny to get the job done—and by M not to push herself too hard, recovery is a game of patience . . .

Harwood knows she's remained employed only because of Moneypenny's insistence. Following Sid's funeral, M seemed to know what the Shrublands reports would say before Harwood was even processed. He took her to one side at the Barton Hill community center, a gentle hand at her elbow.

"Johanna, you don't have a father, so let me be one for a moment. I did promise Sid I'd walk you down the aisle, after all. You've given everything to your country. What your country owes you now is peace."

Harwood told him: "I don't want peace."

"That's the problem. You and I both know there are invisible wounds worse than what any X-ray could show, no matter what your training as a surgeon might tell you. There are some wounds we never recover from. If I could have any wish for you now, Johanna, it would be a new life. There are too many ghosts in this one. First James. Now Sid."

Harwood removed her arm from his grip. "James is alive. I am going to find him." She waited for a reply. "Don't you believe that?"

M ran red-veined eyes over the heads of the mourners. At last he spoke, but it was as if he forgot who he was speaking to—as if he were speaking to himself, down the decades. "I believe I have attended too many funerals."

When Harwood discovered the numbers 007 carved into the rock face of a cave with iron bars for a door, along with the marks of a struggle as a prisoner was dragged outside, she was seized by the certainty that James Bond was still alive. She demanded MI6 give her the task of finding where Rattenfänger relocated him. But Moneypenny and M both said Q Branch was still applying what they'd learned about Rattenfänger's method for concealing people from satellites to the new intelligence she'd supplied. 003 would be told when there was a trail to follow. The briefing was yet to come, her Hermès watch yet to sing its haunting dots and dashes—for Harwood refused to believe that Tanner had acted alone. Who warned Mora that she and Sid were coming? She spent the seconds, minutes, and hours of night duty imagining Moneypenny briefing her through Morse on another hush-hush mission: to uncover the second mole responsible for Sid's death, and find James Bond. But no orders came.

Now, 003 slips into her jacket and crosses the threshold of the police station, avoiding the unavoidable fact that her hands are shaking. Once, on night duty at MI6, she crossed paths with 000. Conrad Harthrop-Vane asked her cheerfully: "Still rusting here, Harwood? Careful. Get too rusty and you'll crack up."

Well, how about it, Johanna? Are you rusted shut?

Marilyn Aliyeva has recast her surroundings. Someone supplied her with a takeaway tea that wouldn't taste of dust—the tag says Darjeeling—and water rather absurdly in a wineglass most likely kept at the back of a cupboard for Christmas parties. The rim is red with the person of interest's lipstick. She wears fur, which should have been confiscated when she was transferred to general holding. She wears more money than Johanna has ever touched in a whole lifetime. She wears it in her posture and her highlights and her heavy sunglasses. The boarded-up vulnerability tells Harwood to defuse, defer, and then reflect the same trauma back in order to win the subject's confidence—tactics she once could have articulated, but now wades toward uncertainly.

Harwood raises the chipped mug she was given. "Now why didn't I think to order out?" She takes the seat across the table. "I'm told you haven't spoken to anyone for a few days. Neither have I, as it happens, and I'm afraid I'm a little rusty. You might have to start."

"Who are you? You do not look like a policewoman."

Harwood scratches her forehead. "What do I look like?"

"A refugee washed up on the shores of a disaster I want to know nothing about, so spare me your conversational gambits."

Harwood is silent for a moment, and then laughs. There's modeling understanding as an interrogational tactic, and then there's walking into the cell with an open wound. Maybe M's right.

"What is so funny?" says Marilyn.

"Oh, nothing. Only, perhaps you haven't seen yourself in a mirror lately. Or perhaps I'm too much of one."

Marilyn hunches in her fur. "I am not going to talk to any policewoman without my lawyer."

"Your lawyer would tell you to seize the opportunity to get out of a minor mess instead of pushing deeper into the major disaster you're already in. That is, if Teddy wasn't keeping all lawyers from visiting you."

Marilyn stiffens. "What do you know about Teddy?"

"Not as much as I'd like," says Harwood, crossing her legs. "He's your—patron?"

Marilyn Aliyeva throws up her arms. Her bracelets are a wind chime in the wake of a slammed door. "You think he funds me like an art museum? You think I am a prostitute?"

Harwood asks with mild curiosity, "Do you think you're a prostitute?"

"Where are you from? Dark hair, olive skin, English accent—are you only English?"

"Why do you ask?"

"I am wondering how naïve you are, to ask me if I see myself as a whore."

Harwood pulls a file from her bag. "You've spent thirteen million pounds over the course of a decade at Harrods."

Marilyn's coat ripples as she shrugs. "It is very nearby for me, very convenient."

"Twenty-four thousand pounds on tea and coffee. Ten thousand pounds on fruit and vegetables. Thirty-two thousand pounds on chocolates."

"You do not buy these things from your corner shop?"

Harwood smiles. "They don't sell Cartier at my corner shop. Nearly five million on jewelry. Tens of thousands on Disney princess experiences. Teddy Wiltshire calls you his princess, doesn't he?" She drops her smile. "Do you feel like a princess, Ms. Aliyeva?"

Marilyn pulls off her sunglasses and throws them across the table. They fall and clatter at Harwood's feet. "I am not a victim," she says. Her eyes are bruised red and gray.

"Does Mr. Wiltshire feel better after he's hit you?"

Marilyn snorts. "You are as naïve as I thought."

"Do you know why you've been brought to talk to me today?"

No response.

"Here's what I think is happening. Mr. Wiltshire gave you a credit card, to be spent only at Harrods. He gets the bill. He sees everything you buy. Everything you do. He likes it that way. But he's often abroad. With his wife and children. And there are things you want that he wouldn't approve of. So you buy a bag or a coat in Harrods, and you take it to one of the many nearby 'boutiques,' who buy it for cash and resell it. You then have cash to spend that Teddy can't monitor. Some of that cash you stockpile for . . . emergencies. I'm here to tell you, Marilyn, because maybe you've waited so long for it to come knocking you think you're imagining the bang. The emergency is here now."

"There is nothing illegal about selling things from Harrods. All the girlfriends do it."

"Do you know what the Unexplained Wealth Order is?"

Marilyn searches the corners of the room for an answer. "It is not my money."

"It's not Teddy's either. He embezzled it from a Turkmen bank and launders it through fraudulent loans purchasing buildings and businesses around the world that he runs into the ground and sells off."

"Nobody can prove that."

"I would guess Teddy grew more violent around a year ago, when his assets came under scrutiny. He needed to translate his money some other way—to launder it."

"I have no idea about any of that."

"But you know about his interests in art and antiquities, don't you? You buy pieces for him with dirty money."

Marilyn says, "You have a problem in your head. You are making things up."

Harwood clenches her jaw. "You were arguing with the shopkeeper about the price. She said you became aggressive. Are you panicking, Marilyn?"

"Why should I panic?"

"Teddy is in trouble. When his ship goes down, do you think he'll make room for you on the lifeboat next to his wife? He'll drop you overboard first. We can throw you a line."

Marilyn tosses her heavy hair. "If you wish to talk in cliché, here's one. I am mistress of my own fate. I have my own plans."

"Your plans make Teddy laugh; do you see that?"

"He loves me."

"He'll be laughing after he buries you," says Harwood. "I don't mean to be malicious. It's just the way he is. But you don't need me to tell you that." Harwood picks up the sunglasses, closes them, and slides them across the table. "We can help you, if you help us."

Marilyn almost sips from the wineglass of water, then pushes it away, causing a tiny tidal wave.

"We want to know if he's more than a state embezzler. More than just a crook."

"What more? There are only crooks. Big crooks and little crooks."

"Elegantly put. Did Teddy start out in life as a little crook?"

"How should I know?"

"He's been paying your rent for a decade."

"You people have been watching him for a whole year! What does your watching tell you? Nothing that is hard truth, otherwise this NCA would have arrested him."

Harwood opens the file, fanning out surveillance photographs. Teddy dining with his wife at the Connaught. Teddy dining with Marilyn at St. John's. Teddy playing golf. Teddy dropping his daughters off at school. Teddy at the opening of a friend's club. Teddy eating a steak covered in gold foil. "Our watching tells us he's very careful in all ways except one. A truly careful crook would hide his money. Teddy's not the inconspicuous type. He wants to show off. That's why he gave you the card for Harrods rather than a discreet account at a private bank. He wants to display things." She swivels a photograph showing Marilyn naked on her roof garden at a gathering with Teddy and his friends, who are all male, and all dressed. "He wants to display you."

Marilyn considers Harwood straight. "He's earned the right."

Harwood purses her lips. "Do you believe one human being can buy another?"

"I know it."

"So he can do what he likes to you. Until one day you're displayed on a slab in the morgue."

"That won't happen. I can manage him."

Harwood says, "We know he's laundering money through Sotheby's."

"If you could prove that you would have arrested him."

"True." Harwood sits back. "What we can currently prove is that *you're* laundering money through Sotheby's. What's this life that Teddy pays for worth to you, Marilyn? We can give you a whole new one. It might not come with a line of credit at Harrods. But it will come with peace. What would you give not to be afraid anymore? What would you give to sleep well?"

It is one in a series of gambles, and when she delivers it Harwood has no particular faith it will be the one that works. But Marilyn's gaze—which was flitting about the interrogation room like a robin after crumbs—now settles on Harwood side-on, the same robin frozen, staring at the human it realizes has seen it. Marilyn says, "You do not sleep either. Do you?"

Harwood swallows. "Not for a long time."

"Why?"

Harwood picks up the three truest words she can manage. "I lost everything."

"What does it feel like?"

Harwood says, "You tell me."

The gaze remains rigid, an urgent scrutiny. "You could really protect me?"

"Yes."

"But I do not know anything about his past or what he does when he's not with me."

"What *do* you know?"

Marilyn places her hand flat over the photographs. "These pictures show Teddy clothed."

"And?"

"Underneath his clothes, he is covered in tattoos. He doesn't ever swim anywhere people can see. He doesn't even steam at the club. But he won't have the tattoos removed."

"What sort of tattoos?"

"The tattoos of the *vor*. The thieves-in-law."

Harwood doesn't risk breathing. "You're saying Teddy was a member of the thieves-in-law, the mafia that began in the USSR gulag system?"

A fractional nod.

Harwood continues, "But to become a thief-in-law you have to have served prison time, and take an oath to never cooperate with prison guards, police, or any state representative. Teddy ran a state bank."

"I told you," Marilyn says. "There are little crooks. And there are big crooks. Things are not as they used to be. Today, the big crooks run governments. Then they retire from their service, rich and reborn. There's a reason you'll never be able to arrest Teddy, no matter your evidence and your theories. He has the money to buy a new, grand future. The biggest crooks of all are no longer criminals."

Harwood finally breathes. "We can give you that new future. He won't find you."

Marilyn shakes her head. Tears spill over, but her mascara is too high quality to run. "He will. I am a fool. His job is to disappear people. No one can stay hidden from him."

"What do you mean?"

"When he's angry, he tells me he can make me disappear. Make anyone disappear. For good."

Rattenfänger had nearly disappeared her for good when she went undercover. They'd disappeared James. Could Teddy be the magician? "Marilyn—can you describe his tattoos?"

"Why?"

"Russian prison tattoos are a language. They tell the story of a man's crimes. Teddy keeps them hidden because they're as good as a confession—to past misdemeanors, anyway. If a man wears a tattoo of three cats, it means he's a human trafficker. Does Teddy have a tattoo like that?"

Marilyn touches her right hand to her chest. "Yes. Here. They are almost cute, if it weren't for the design around them."

"What design?"

"A moth. A horrible moth."

Unconsciously, Harwood mirrors Marilyn's action, shielding her own heart. The tattoo on Colonel Mora's chest seems to appear before her now, the death's-head hawk moth that flaps over her face whenever she dips too deeply into sleep—she can feel it in the interrogation room, batting any next question back into her mouth, smothering her, and with it Mora's horrible mouth, the bloodied stump of his tongue, just like the Kikimora he was named for, squatting on its victim's chest, sucking out their last breath—their soul.

How about it, Johanna? Are you cracking up?

Four
Property of a Lady

London

The hour of delivery on New Bond Street. A yellow DHL van idles in front of Sotheby's. The tidy entrance of the auction house is flanked by shops whose windows display handbags and crystal ware, projecting a frictionless life. The BBC is only a short walk away. Police with sniffer dogs cluster at the corner. Sotheby's has a humble façade, the blue flag draped over a neat portico, but behind its neighbors' backs it sprawls through most of the block. There is no braggadocio to announce this. Only two small windows, one promising Impressionist paintings, the other timelessness in frosted cursive over sparkling stones. The neat lettering reads *Jewels of Time*. A fifth-generation banker who's suddenly remembered an anniversary stops to study the diamonds.

Joseph Dryden leans against the drainpipe painted the same cream as the building. He wonders, with mild curiosity, if the gray-suited man will notice him, or whether he is just as invisible as the drainpipe, or the deliverymen, all of whom are also Black.

The banker trots inside. He'll purchase a necklace from the luxury division, to be collected by his chauffeur or delivered to Dubai or Paris. Delayed gratification is a dying art.

Dryden turns his attention from the broad-smiling doorman bowing the anxious customer inside to Johanna Harwood, watching as she slips her matte thunder gray Alpine A110S into a spot created by a departing taxi.

When 003 opens the door and rises from the bucket seat, he is struck first by her high-waisted trousers in pale green silk paired with a tight gray cotton T-shirt and a cream linen jacket, realizing he's seen her only in black recently; and then by the purpose in her stride, as Harwood crosses toward him and meets his handshake.

"You don't look too bad," she says. "A little banged up at the edges, maybe."

He laughs. "A high-explosive device will do that to you. But I leave the worrying to Q these days. My body ain't mine to fret about it."

They fall in step, nodding to the doorman.

"If you tell me your body belongs to Queen and country," says Harwood, "I'm going to have to stick you on a recruiting poster."

He shrugs. "Call it duty. Call it Operator's Syndrome. I've given up trying to figure it out."

"I know the feeling."

The foyer possesses the quiet of a first-class lounge. Dryden supplies his name and the receptionist asks them to wait just a moment. They drift toward the adjacent gallery, where a case contains pearls and early Air Jordans.

Harwood says, "There's a black market for trainers these days." At his expression she adds, "Night duty leaves a lot of time for reading. There's even a black market for oil stolen from chip shops."

Dryden says, "During my tours in Afghanistan, everything was for sale. NATO equipment, heroin, oil."

"Still," says Harwood, "I'd rather have the pearls."

He chuckles. "I wouldn't say no to the Jordans. Half the stuff for sale in Afghanistan wouldn't be out of place here. Nineteen seventy-eight, a Soviet archaeologist discovered the Bactrian Hoard out there in the desert. Relics of the Silk Road. Some of the bravest people I ever met were the curators of the National Museum of Afghanistan, who stashed what remained from the Hill of Gold dig and never gave it up to the Taliban. We convinced them it was finally safe to exhibit the national treasure, and they pulled the gold out of the deepest hole in the ground you ever saw. Now we've left them and their country to the Taliban and God knows what'll happen to it all. Or to the curators."

Harwood says, "You know people who are still there?"

"Yeah." Dryden swipes a thumb over his chin. "My interpreter and his family. Doesn't seem to matter how many doors I knock on, I can't get 'em on a plane to London. I used to feel powerful. Maybe it was always an illusion. I've been fighting my entire life, and things only get worse. Now the bad guys think they can kick in *our* doors. They're not wrong."

Harwood says, "Marilyn Aliyeva told me there are crooks everywhere, it's just a matter of scale. In a sense, Marilyn selling coats from Harrods is only a scaled-up version of petty thieves stealing cooking oil. So, what's Teddy Wiltshire's scale?"

That brings animation to Dryden's face. "Difference is, the lads stealing from the chippie are far more likely to be arrested."

Harwood elbows him softly. "So let's see what we can do about that."

He smiles down at her. "Let's."

Moneypenny clears her throat. The agents turn around, finding Moneypenny next to a man in his late fifties she introduces as James Chadwick, the head of clocks and barometers. The tan is surprising because there's something about his deferential squint that suggests he spends most of his time in a temperature-controlled room peering through a magnifying glass.

Chadwick says, "It's a pleasure to meet colleagues of Ms. Moneypenny. If you'll please step this way."

The main auction room is lit by natural spring sunshine, which floods the glass roof of the vaulted ceiling. Decorators are painting the walls jewel green to complement *Jewels of Time*, an exhibition and sale representing a fraction of Lisl Baum's famous collection, which will be installed as soon as the paint dries. The exhibition will show for a fortnight before the auction, when the usual apprehensions—what success will it meet with, how many people shall attend—will not apply. There is every expectation the sale should go well. Once the sale starts, the concentration will be so intense for the auctioneer that there won't be time to think about anything other than the lot at hand, watching for bids from clients in the room, colleagues on the telephones, or online, or the clerk sitting nearby. The pressure will be especially potent for this auction because every lot is of high value. Elation will build in the auctioneer, culminating in a real high once the sale is over, much like an actor when the curtain drops.

Joseph Dryden has never attended an auction and doesn't care to know much about it. What he cares about is 008, now out of surgery, and the stunned silence gripping central London. Chadwick murmurs, "This way please"—and Dryden follows him through a door locked with a keypad and a fingerprint scanner, into a room where jewels blind him. Dryden grins when he sees Ibrahim Suleiman hugging his elbows miserably on a stool in the corner.

Johanna Harwood does take an interest in jewelry and recognizes the significance of the splendor half-unloaded from steel cases. The Württemberg topaz and diamond parure, a Hellenistic gold and turquoise tiara, the Duke of Wellington's watch, a ruby gimmel memento mori ring, diamonds, sapphires, emeralds . . . Moneypenny has drifted to the head of a long bench, where she gazes down at a Fabergé egg on a velvet bed—a gaze that is totally blank. She might appear fixed on the intricate pattern of frosted glass and diamonds, but Harwood knows her mind is examining a different pattern altogether.

James Chadwick says, "Once again, I wish to convey Sotheby's sincere shock and regret at this situation. We offer any and all assistance. The blind man's watch in question is here—this is our secure room. It has been waiting in Collection, but once we learned of its—of the shade it is under, we felt it best to keep it safe here. You are admiring Ms. Baum's collection—it's a little out of my field, but my colleagues in jewelry are really quite excited."

Moneypenny's gaze flickers toward him. "None of the objects we are inquiring after came from or were sold to Lisl Baum, is that right?"

Harwood notices James Chadwick rock on his heels.

"Of course not, ma'am," says Chadwick. "Lisl Baum is the world's foremost—"

Moneypenny holds up a hand. "Yes, I know, thank you. What is the theme of this exhibition? The timelessness of jewelry?"

A polite wag of the head. "Or perhaps it's timeliness. Ms. Baum has long been interested in jewels that represent the passing of history. Objects imbued with time."

"Like the blind man's watch," says Harwood.

"Not sold from Ms. Baum's collection, no." Chadwick reaches for a shelf and brings down a satin box. "A rather beautiful and rare specimen." He passes the box to

Harwood. "As you can see, there are turquoise beads to mark the hours and two beads, known as a Double One, at the twelve, to signify at a touch when one is passing into the morning or afternoon. The face opens—if you see the clasp there, yes, that's it—so that one may feel the watch hand, which in this case is fashioned as an arrow in silver, encrusted with small diamonds, on a light blue enamel face. Set in silver, with a silver chain and pin. The enameled back opens—yes, that's it—you see a gold cover plate and a smaller two-handed watch face. The mechanism cover bears the signature of Abraham-Louis Breguet, of course a most significant horologist, and the inventor of the blind man's watch or tact watch. While it's unlikely the average blind person in the late eighteenth or early nineteenth century could afford such a luxury item, they were popular because it allowed the owner to tell the time simply by touch. It was considered taboo then to consult one's watch in company. Think of that, when my granddaughter spends most of dinner staring at her mobile phone."

"How much did it go for?" asks Harwood.

"One point two million."

Harwood laughs, a nervous reaction alien to her own ears, and carefully closes the box.

Moneypenny says, "You said on the phone that the

blind man's watch was sold by an agent, a Mr. Corso of Crete, representing an unknown owner. Do you deal with Mr. Corso regularly?"

"Yes, and we have of course performed due diligence regarding Mr. Corso, whose background check revealed nothing untoward."

Moneypenny says, "Of course. Thank you, Mr. Chadwick. I realize what I'm about to ask may offend your professional sensibilities, but if you would please give the blind man's watch to my colleague"—she gestures at Ibrahim—"and take him to a quiet workshop, he would appreciate your help with installing a device in the watch."

Chadwick's back stiffens. "*In* the casement?"

Moneypenny remains impassive. "Yes."

"But—" Chadwick tugs a handkerchief from his breast pocket and dabs at his forehead. "Of course. May I ask how large this device is?"

From the corner, Ibrahim pipes up: "Practically invisible."

"And it will not damage the watch in any way?"

"That's right, sir."

James Chadwick shakes his head, thrusts back his shoulders, and tells Ibrahim to follow him to the workshop.

Moneypenny says, "It's a tracking device; that's all

we could manage without its being seen if Wiltshire inspects the watch. 003, I need you to persuade Marilyn Aliyeva to call Wiltshire and tell him she's been released and that Sotheby's have rung her up asking when she's planning to collect the blind man's watch. Sotheby's are insisting she collect it herself. He won't want to send his chauffeur or anyone who can be linked with him, anyway. Once she's recovered the blind man's watch and given it to Wiltshire, we'll get her into the witness protection program."

Harwood says, "He's a people smuggler. At least he used to be. She told me his job is making people disappear." She waits for a reply with the tip of her tongue pressed to her bottom lip, holding Moneypenny's gaze.

She wants to ask whether Moneypenny sees the significance in this. Teddy Wiltshire bears a moth tattoo. If it is the same as Mora's death's-head hawk moth tattoo, it surely means he is affiliated with Rattenfänger. He got his start in life kidnapping people and smuggling them through pipelines into brothels, labor camps, or domestic slavery. Wouldn't it then follow that he was linked to—or even ran—the arm of Rattenfänger that makes people disappear, had disappeared her, had disappeared Bond, the very people who are now holding James in an even darker hole than the cave in Syria? Someone in MI6 knows all this, the second mole. But she says nothing, afraid of being dismissed, afraid of the word "paranoid" that floats over her medical file, ready to be applied at any moment: *"Paranoid just like her schizophrenic father."*

If Moneypenny reads Harwood's mind she gives no clue, saying simply: "You promised Marilyn Aliyeva our protection and I won't let your promises prove false. Trust me, 003."

Harwood clenches her jaw. She gestures to the Fabergé egg. "Do you suppose the tsar and his family saw it coming?"

"If they did, they reacted too slow," says Dryden.

"Strange to think it was only a matter of years between Nicholas commissioning Fabergé and being buried with his entire family."

Moneypenny taps her sunfish brooch. "Are you implying the West is analogous to the tsarist royal family in our current scenario?"

Harwood shrugs. "I can certainly hear a clock ticking."

Moneypenny relents. "Me too. I'm working on a theory. But I don't have enough evidence to commit it to paper yet."

Dryden says, "Try us."

"Q has identified a pattern. Six days prior to terror attacks, objects worth over a million that passed through free ports in Heraklion and Venice are sold at Sotheby's. The agent who sold this blind man's watch lives in Crete. I've been thinking about the *Charlie Hebdo* attack. You remember where the money funding the attack came from?"

"Yes," says Dryden. "Antiquities looted from Syria at the start of the war, transported from the black market to the white market, and sold for a small fortune. The profits paid for guns used to attack the newspaper offices of *Charlie Hebdo*."

Harwood says, "But all sorts of objects must have been sold six days prior to these attacks."

"Yes," says Moneypenny, "and we have no pattern identifying a single origin or even type of object. Only a price tag of over a million, and the free ports, link the objects."

Dryden says, "That's a bigger operation than smuggling antiquities from a single war."

Moneypenny nods. "This is where the theory becomes . . . let's call it abstract. We know all too well that globalization has perhaps been most successful in the criminal world. Global organized crime groups have forged transnational links to share smuggling networks. These networks have four stages, no matter what is being smuggled. First the theft, whether it's an antiquity dug up, diamonds stolen from a shop, even people abducted . . . Oftentimes, in the case of antiquities, it's subsistence looters digging up their own culture in order to feed their families; they receive pennies from the early middlemen, though the antiquity will eventually sell for millions. The second stage sees the early middlemen smuggle an item out of its source country and through transit countries, gaining papers of false provenance along the way. The third stage is the final middleman, a figure known as Janus after the Roman god of doorways, beginnings, endings, and time. Janus has two faces, looking backward and forward as a door does. The Janus is the only person in the chain who can look back at the object's past on the black market and forward to its future on the white market. In a loosely formed and disconnected chain, the Janus alone knows the whole picture. They cross thresholds, equally comfortable buying illicit goods at the border of a war-torn country as they are selling them to major galleries or collectors. The fourth stage in the chain is the buyer: a diamond merchant, a collector, a museum, even a construction company after labor, who will claim to know nothing of the object's or person's origin." Moneypenny leans closer to the ghostly Fabergé egg. "Q has identified a correlation between sales and attacks. What if these Janus figures who cross from black to white markets have formed a group to bankroll terror?"

"The Gray Group," suggests Harwood.

Moneypenny smiles. "That sounds alarming yet bland enough to get an operation green-lit without spooking Government. I'll take it."

Dryden asks, "Is there precedent for these Janus figures to cooperate with one another?"

"In small ways, yes. One Janus might provide a false provenance from a country they specialize in to another Janus. Borrow a bank account. That sort of thing. There's no precedent for cooperation on this scale or to this purpose."

"And the purpose of this Gray Group is to fund terror?" asks Harwood.

Moneypenny draws herself up. "That's my theory. The Gray Group steals and smuggles goods—be they diamonds, antiquities, or even people—through transnational and cooperative pipelines, helping each other out along the way, in order to finance terrorism. Terrorism causes further conflict, creating unstable situations that favor further smuggling. A cycle that pays for itself. Our finance experts suggest the six-day time frame has come about because any longer would attract attention from auditors to the bank accounts being used to transfer the money."

"To what end?"

Moneypenny places a finger at the apex of the Fabergé

egg. "Profit. What if the Gray Group are Rattenfänger's bank, funding its terrorism and semi-legal military activities through theft, smuggling, and more terror? We've never discovered how Rattenfänger is funded. Colonel Mora hasn't so much as whispered in interrogation. What if these Janus figures smuggle and steal and sell and lie, collecting their pretty items and living their pretty lives in the black and the white. Enjoying the gray, while red spills on our streets. For money."

Harwood raises an eyebrow. "What if."

"But it's just a theory."

"It works for me." Harwood turns to Dryden. "We'd better get to Crete, have a conversation with this agent."

Moneypenny raises a hand. "I need you to take care of Marilyn. After that, you'll return to night duty. You've not been cleared by Shrublands for active field-work as a Double O yet."

The wind is knocked from Harwood's chest. She has the urge to meet Dryden's eye, but doesn't, because that would be a call for help and she can't bear to make one. "I'll talk Marilyn through it. Good luck, 004."

But that isn't enough for Dryden, who catches the swinging door and finds Harwood at the lifts. She is staring at the rising numbers on the Art Deco counter.

"Johanna," he says, touching her shoulder.

She turns around with a smile that would be dazzling if it were real. "If you're worried I pocketed the Württemberg topaz, you're absolutely right, and no, I won't split the profits with you."

"It'll suit you better anyway. Listen. What happened last year—you lost Sid, and saved me and Luke in the process. Saved the whole world. You don't deserve to be grounded. Nothing wrong with you I can see. Maybe just a bit banged up around the edges, right? You broke this case for us. M and Moneypenny will see you're fine and you'll get off the bench."

Harwood's voice is lost as the lift dings: "Maybe I'm not fine."

"What?" says Dryden, tilting his left ear toward her as if his implant were failing.

She shakes her head.

"You ever need me," says Dryden, "call and I'll come running."

"See you, Joe."

The doors close as Dryden says, "See you, 003."

Moneypenny greets him with a hand on her hip. "Do I have a mutiny on my hands?"

"No, ma'am. But I can't figure your angle, keeping Harwood out. Especially if it means terminating the bastards who killed 009, injured 008, and abducted 007, not to mention the other Double O's on Rattenfänger's casualty list."

"Who says I have an angle? These objects that are being sold, they're detonators, triggering a bomb that goes off six days later. Get to Crete and make this agent talk. But do it quietly. If this agent sells for the Janus figures, he'll likely have a lot of protection, even surveillance he doesn't know about. So be soft. But by God, Joe, be persuasive. 008 may never walk again. 007 is in one hell or another. Hundreds of people have been maimed or murdered in these attacks. We struck a blow against Rattenfänger when we captured Mora, but evidently, we didn't cut the head off. They're killers for profit. So we have to take away the profit."

Dryden rolls his shoulders. "Yes, ma'am."

"And Dryden—these collectors who think they can dance from black to white and back again with impunity while killing innocent people—I want their heads for *my* collection. Got it?"

"Consider it done."

Five
"Break Him"

London

"Are you proud of yourself?"
On Marilyn Aliyeva's doorstep, Johanna Harwood says, "I'm sorry."

Marilyn's right cheek is newly swollen, the stretched skin the sheen of stewed apricot. She hugs her left arm to her rib cage, lopsided in feathered slippers.

"Can I come in?"

"Do you want to kill me?"

"You think he's watching?"

A one-shouldered shrug.

"Then you'd better let me in as if I'm a concerned friend, hadn't you?"

"Are you?" demands Marilyn.

"Yes."

Marilyn snorts, but lets Harwood follow her to the lift, which climbs through the former factory. Usually, Harwood would suggest taking the stairs. A lift is a warning signal to anyone waiting above. But she doesn't think Marilyn can walk, so she stands with a hand at her elbow, which isn't shrugged off. The lift opens onto the converted penthouse. Syrupy air thickens between bolted shutters and locked windows. The kitchen side is busy with takeaway boxes, rims congealed red and yellow. Marilyn climbs into a director's chair jammed into a corner beneath industrial studio lights from the sixties.

"How about some fresh air?"

Marilyn says nothing.

Harwood opens the shutters, dragging the windows up. The moon is a penny half-stuck in a slot. She shuts it out.

Marilyn reaches with a wince for sunglasses on the nearby mantelpiece. "When Teddy left, do you know what he told me?" Her smile could crack glass. "He told me to play dead."

"Soon he'll take his own advice." Harwood locates a recycling bag. She finishes stacking the dishwasher, then finds two clean cups and presses a tap that produces instant boiling water. "How do you take your tea?"

Marilyn lights a cigarette with a shaking hand. "A slice of lemon."

Harwood leaves the peace offering within Marilyn's reach and sits on the end of a serpentine sofa, positioning her cup on the polished concrete floor, which is speckled with blood: she doesn't have to search for it, there is no clever pattern to divine—only history.

"When I was a little girl," says Marilyn, "my mother told me that once they start, they do not stop. Until you are dead."

"She was right, statistically. You'd better let me take a look at that arm."

"Are you a doctor, too?"

"Yes. Well, a surgeon."

"You can do what you like," says Marilyn. "You already have."

"I'm sorry."

"Twice she is sorry. She persuades me to see Teddy and give him this blind man's watch, without a thought as to what he will do to me as a parting gift. Are you sorry, doubly sorry?"

"Yes."

"Then can you do anything about it, you and your little tax men ruining my life?"

"I've promised to destroy Teddy Wiltshire. I will."

"Promises, promises. You shouldn't make them if

you can't keep them."

"I don't."

A car idles—Marilyn grips the arm of the chair.

Harwood says, "Did he tell you what he intends to do with the blind man's watch?"

"It is a birthday present."

"For his wife?"

"For some whore from Vienna."

Harwood's gaze drifts, recollecting files she read on night duty, and the display at Sotheby's. "You mean Lisl Baum, the jewelry collector? She's considered to have started life as an escort to men like Teddy."

Marilyn sneers. "Like recognizes like, I assure you. But yes, I mean the famous Lisl Baum."

"Do you know how long they've been associated?"

"No."

Harwood studies the blood on the floor. "Turkmenistan is both a source and a transit country for people smuggled into slave labor and prostitution. Perhaps Teddy started there and made his way up, meeting Lisl Baum on the way to the state bank and then a British passport, while she made her way up from mistress to legitimate businesswoman."

"Crime pays," says Marilyn.

Harwood says, "That's a very generous birthday

present for Lisl Baum, even if it was bought with dirty money."

Marilyn waves her good arm. "Teddy likes to be generous."

"Why toward Lisl Baum? Is she his mistress too? Or was she in the past?"

Marilyn laughs, then touches her split lip. "He wishes."

"Have you ever met her?"

"Once. Teddy is very nice to her." Marilyn sits back philosophically. "But Teddy is very nice to everyone."

"Did you get the sense that Teddy was trying to impress Lisl Baum? Or defer to her at all?"

Marilyn considers it. "No. Only to charm her into being impressed by him."

"Then her opinion matters to him?"

"I suppose. Why are you so interested?"

"In order to remove Teddy from your life," says Harwood, "I have to remove the structures that protect him."

Marilyn laughs harshly. "I told you not to make false promises."

Harwood shakes her head. "We have a house for you in Orkney. No Disney princess experiences, but a wide horizon and nothing that goes bump in the night."

Marilyn wavers to her feet. "I do not care if Teddy is at the top of the pyramid or at the bottom carrying rocks on his back. He told me he would make it so that all other men were repulsed by me until he wanted me again. Break him."

Harwood stands up. "I will. Or—we will."

"You are not going to pursue him yourself?"

Harwood brushes the face of Sid's Casio watch under her sleeve. "Let me see that arm."

Six

000

Oman. Two days after the BBC bombing.

Conrad Harthrop-Vane possesses the kind of good looks born from believing one possesses good looks. In reality, his pale skin is so thin it reveals the blue veins beneath like faded Delft china. His upper lip is stuck in a saturnine sneer and his left eyebrow snagged in private amusement. His thick blond hair is so platinum it is almost white. As he cuts through the throng of guests arriving at Al Bustan Palace Ritz-Carlton for a long weekend, he draws keen glances from the women, and envious searches from the men. He is young to possess such assuredness, perhaps mid-thirties. Born to it, the signet ring suggests—this noticed by the single women glancing at his empty marriage finger. But there is also something in the set of his shoulders and the trim strength of his imposing figure that says he might have fought for it, too.

Harthrop-Vane neither observes nor ignores these glances, but takes them quite literally in his stride, as his due, and one that he's scrapped for, fought to get back, wrestled into his arms, and will never relinquish. The sun over the Sea of Oman is cruel and he pulls Versace aviators in gunmetal from his jacket, slipping them on as he approaches a chessboard of deck chairs facing out toward the sea. It is Lisl Baum's fortieth birthday, and she has taken over the hotel. The jewelry empress lies with her back to him beneath a parasol at the center of a coterie of admirers. The queen surrounded by her knights.

He stops behind the striped umbrella, and gently knocks on its stretched cotton. "Fräulein Lisl Baum?"

The conversation drops. Harthrop-Vane first sees a naked thigh emerge, then both of her legs swing down, only partially covered by something gauzy, as she twists around the edge of the parasol to get a view of him.

If her legs stirred him, her smile licks at him, pulling an animal grin out of him and stamping it on his face.

"Hello, pup." Her voice is huskier than he remembers, but just as fun-loving.

He bows.

Lisl Baum laughs and makes shooing signs with her ringed fingers, sparking flashes in the air that magically dispel the witnesses. Conrad Harthrop-Vane sits down on the neighboring deck chair side-on, facing her. His gaze eats up every inch of her sundress until she laughs and taps him on the knee.

"You haven't changed," she says.

"Neither have you," he says.

"Oh, the ravages of time . . ." She casts a mock-despairing hand over her forehead, which Harthrop-Vane catches and kisses.

"Time can't ravish you," he says.

"I said *ravage*."

The grin again. "Either works for me."

"Naughty pup. I saw you were coming as some heiress's date. It's been a lifetime. Sir Emery told me you'd taken up the call of duty for good."

He murmurs, "I try to be useful."

She drops her voice to match his. "I'm sure you do. How attached are you to this date of yours?"

"I'm never attached."

She laughs. "It would break Sir Emery's heart to hear you say that."

"I'll make an exception for the old man."

"You always did. Most people are saddled with a

godfather. You worshipped at his feet, right back to those days in Singapore when you were only a boy."

"He was never officially my godfather."

She ignores this. "Remember that ghastly little bar your father and Sir Emery and Enrico used to visit? I'd pull you all out in the morning and pay the bill—or the fine."

"It wasn't a bar," says Harthrop-Vane equably. "It was a brothel."

"It wasn't!" she says, and then sighs. "Well, perhaps it was. I'd always find you in the waiting room. What did you see, sitting there all those hours, I wonder?"

"It was an education."

"I'll bet. Sir Emery was just Emery then, wasn't he, the dashing spy. And your father the fixer."

"Diplomat."

"Same thing, darling. Bill Tanner, sometimes, too. All trying to get information out of Enrico Colombo, charm it out of him, yank it out of him like fillings at the dentist, suck it out of him like a cheap whore, or have me do it. But I was losing his interest already then . . ." She drifts off, her eyes moving unseeingly over the thick heads of flowering palms. Her attention snaps back to him, like a spotlight. "And there you were in the middle of it all. Growing up. What a fine man you've become."

He finds his voice is thick when he says, "You taught me a thing or two yourself."

She laughs, a sliver of artifice to her ease. "Don't think I've forgotten. I suppose you remember everything. What I was then."

"You were glorious. Still are. You always belonged in the spotlight, not at someone's side."

She sighs, patting down her dress as a breeze threatens. "I suppose you've come to flatter me for my birthday. What does Sir Emery want now?"

"One of your guests is attracting heat."

She peers over the parasol. "Which one?"

"Teddy Wiltshire."

She is totally still for a second, and then sighs. "That old animal. What's he done now?"

"The NCA are investigating him. He's laundering money through purchasing art and antiquities at Sotheby's. Your birthday present is tainted."

"How rude," she comments airily, but her consideration of him is sharp. "Why does that require someone of your . . . talents?"

"There's a crossover with another case." Harthrop-Vane twists his Omega. "Sir Emery said I could let you into the picture, if you think you can help us."

"Haven't I always?"

"MI6 has a theory that art, diamonds, antiquities—

they're being looted, smuggled, and sold to fund terrorism. To fund Rattenfänger."

Lisl Baum flicks invisible dust from his thigh. "There's always a bogeyman under the bed. When I ran around with cops and robbers, it was the drug war everyone fixated on. Now it's terror. I'm glad to be out of it." She hooks a soft finger beneath his chin and raises his face to meet hers. "Do you understand, pup? *Keep me out of it.*"

His sneer turns to a smirk. "Yes, fräulein."

An appreciative hum. "I have to change for the party. Would you escort me to my suite? I may need some help with my buttons."

His smirk stays fixed. "Yes, fräulein."

Afterward, Triple O showers in his own suite. Naked, there is something of a Michelangelo about him: the defined musculature, the careless perfection of his slender ankles, strong legs, curved haunches, the power in his arms. He washes without regard to any of this.

Rather, he thinks of Lisl Baum's body, and how it has changed from when she was in her late twenties and he his late teens, Lisl perhaps seeing something of her own missed adolescence and isolation in him. He let his guard down with her, but of course she left him, too, eventually. But she did teach him some valuable lessons first, that much was true. How to please quickly—in moments similar to this afternoon, snatched-at minutes in a coat check, or the back seat of her Citroën—and how to take one's time. She liked to do it naked in the sunshine, when Enrico and Conrad Harthrop-Vane the First and Sir Emery were off somewhere for "man talk." Then she'd find Triple O, usually hanging around the garage, and hook a finger into his necklace, a medallion of Our Lady of Good Counsel given to him by his mother, leading him to the pool or the rose garden or the dune, whatever bordered the rented house. She wasn't too concerned with privacy, perhaps even got off on exhibiting her "pup" and his enthusiasm—or even on the fear of Enrico finding them. As mistress to a smuggler, her position was tenuous: no marriage vows or children to brandish, no financial independence. Enrico's affection was likely to wander, just like the man before and the man after, probably. Perhaps jealousy would keep him ensnared, and Lisl's affections toward Triple O were all directed at Enrico. Or perhaps Enrico was a lousy lover—Lisl did display a hunger Triple O later learned to call loneliness. Either way, it didn't matter to him back then. Here was a sophisticated woman with curves and a wide mouth like girls in top-shelf magazines, and she wanted to do things to him he could only have fantasized about. All he had to do was ask nicely. He was happy.

Stepping out of the shower and pulling a towel around his hips, Triple O pauses at that. Happy. Had he been happy, back then? After his mother died in that hospice with its awful floral curtains, Conrad was shuttled between international boarding schools. His father operated in the gray zone between trade and government and was unreachable for long periods. Another way to put it—in Sir Emery's words, on one of his many visits to a random school over desultory sticky toffee pudding and milky tea in the tuck room—"Your father's a useful crook. He plays for our side now. You needn't worry about him. I keep an eye." Sir Emery was something in real government, Intelligence in fact, and exploited his boyhood chum's connections and knowledge.

That's how they came to hang about Enrico at the height of the drug war. Conrad was finally fetched from school to be his father's shadow, "learn the family business." He learned all sorts of other lessons about the adult world. Sir Emery wasn't always there to protect him, and his father didn't see what it suited him not to see. He was a groveler, in truth. Sometimes there were bad men around, who took advantage. Conrad learned how to deal with the bad men, once he was big enough. The things the bad men did to him before then are black, memories swaddled in funeral crêpe. The shrink at Shrublands once suggested hypnosis to reveal them. But why go through that? He learned to be a survivor, learned the meaning of power: that was enough.

Sir Emery wasn't there with his watchful eye when Conrad's father, hounded by debts and double deals, committed suicide. His last letter berated Conrad for choosing to waste his time studying marbles and whatever else, the trinkets of boyhood—wasn't it bad enough when Conrad diddled those summers with his nose stuck in *The Book of Why* and whined unless he was taken to the Parthenon or the pyramids? "Here's a question missing from your *Book of Why*"—wrote his father—"Why does my son hate me after all I've done for him? You could be PM, for God's sake. Here's another: Why does my son insist on breaking my heart?"

At the funeral, Sir Emery said he owed it to the old man to take Conrad under his wing. He would soon finish at Cambridge. How would he like to pursue a career in Intelligence, with a view to taking up the Double O mantle himself? Sir Emery was now head of the Double O Section. He'd keep an eye on Conrad, help restore his family pride and dignity. He wouldn't fail him again.

Sir Emery has been true to his word.

At this point, Triple O is tucking his medallion

into his shirt and fastening his tie. He inspects himself in the mirror over the sink. He was ordered here by Moneypenny, following the blind man's watch. MI6 wants to know Wiltshire's movements, and the nature of his connection with Lisl Baum. Moneypenny isn't sure if Wiltshire is a Janus for what she calls the Gray Group—if it exists—or if he has simply strayed across its path. Either way, Teddy Wiltshire is a lead, a rabbit in the crosshairs. Triple O will pursue this end of the pipeline while 004 pursues the other, the agent in Crete. It isn't clear in MI6's records how Lisl Baum went from occupying the position of mistress to crooks, to running a legitimate jewelry empire. When the destination of the blind man's watch became known, Moneypenny told Triple O to *attach himself* to Lisl Baum and tease out the nature of this world-famous collector's relationship to Wiltshire.

So, Sir Emery shared with Moneypenny something—how much?—of those days in the sun. Triple O doesn't mind being pimped for his country. In fact, he enjoys it. He's spent enough time around Sir Emery—and James Bond, for that matter—to learn that trick. Back in her suite, Lisl guided Triple O's tongue down her body with the instruction to "wish her a happy birthday." Afterward, she ran a hand through the stiff waves of his blond hair and told him he was still a good pup; she's glad he hasn't grown selfish like so many men do.

"For instance?" he asked.

She lay with her forearm over her eyes. "HV1, for instance."

He stayed still, his sharp chin digging into her soft thigh. HV1 was his father's nickname, back then. Harthrop-Vane the First. As Sir Emery once remarked, it was worryingly close to HVT: High Value Target. Triple O swallowed. "You were with my father?"

She laughed. "Which one?"

"What do you mean?"

She raised her arm to peer down at him. Her gaze was almost kind. "Both of them, actually. Real and symbolic. HV1 and Sir Emery."

Triple O sneered. "At the same time?"

"Imagine that. No. Enrico sent me to HV1 or Sir Emery's rooms occasionally, to sweeten a deal, or win a secret. Like you're doing now."

"I didn't know that."

"Which part?"

He hummed as he kissed her thigh, her pelvis. "Is that why you left Enrico? Because he shared you around?"

"Yes. Eventually he shared me with the wrong man."

"Who?"

"James Bond."

Triple O sat up. Afternoon sun fell in a blazing slant across his shoulders with the weight of the desert behind it. "What happened?"

She shrugged, her tickling fingers trying to get a second round out of him. "After that, I decided I was tired of Enrico—or any man—feeling he had the right to give out the key to my room."

Harthrop-Vane bared his teeth. "And did 007 make use of that key?"

She tilted her head on the silk pillow. "I think you're jealous."

"Of James Bond?"

"Yes." She glanced down at his lap. "Or maybe it's more than jealousy."

There was a second round: fast, brutal. Midway, she seized his chin and said, "You'd better be thinking of me."

Now, Triple O reaches for his jacket, remembering by its weight that he pocketed his watch earlier. There is a listening device inside. It doesn't stream to Q constantly—that is reserved for 004, whose implant eats up much of Q's bandwidth—but does when he twists the crown, as he did earlier speaking with Lisl under the umbrella.

Triple O takes a last look in the full-length mirror by

the door, which catches a slice of the wardrobe mirror behind him, showing him his face and the back of his head in mise en abyme. He checks his gun, which waits in a chamois shoulder holster beneath his left armpit. He smiles at himself and experiences the sensation of smiling at the back of his own head. Time to be a star.

Seven
Small Disasters

Oman

From the eye of the Sirius—an amphibious plane now climbing over the Al-Hajar range—Al Bustan Palace Ritz-Carlton resembles a diamond-studded watch face, the wings of the hotel loose straps forgotten in folds of bed linen, encased between the glittering Gulf of Oman and the hard, dry foothills of the mountains. As the plane banks, palm trees toss shadows about in the dusk; six illuminated swimming pools wink; and the illusion of diamonds resolves into thousands of arched windows, puncturing the shining sandstone of Al Bustan Palace with light as solid as gold.

On the ground floor, Lisl Baum stands in the spotlight of a five-ton crystal chandelier greeting guests, all of whom have left their suites empty, including Valentin "Teddy" Wiltshire. Eight floors above, Rachel Wolff has never needed long with a safe, and doesn't intend to waste time on this one. The Ritz-Carlton knows better than to provide a digital room safe—a thief would only need dust and fingerprints. A dial safe demands exceptional hearing and an exceptional memory, two skills Wolff puts to use now, blocking from her mind the strains of the orchestra playing below the balcony.

The safe is concealed beneath the vanity table. Rachel spreads her tools on the velvet seat, and makes herself comfortable on the deep carpet. A chaise longue hems her in, blocking a clear line of sight to the bedroom door. But the suite is three thousand square feet—she will hear someone before she sees them, leaving a fragment of her awareness to stray and probe beyond the minute mechanism at her gloved fingertips. No tread in the hallway, no turn of the doorknob, no return of Teddy. And now the moment when the dial trembles before giving in. Rachel smiles, offering a brief prayer, and opens the safe.

Her smile widens.

Ignoring the jewelry, the loose money in different denominations, the gun, and the separate case of bullets—for Valentin Wiltshire is a loving father—she scoops up the small steel case. It rattles softly—she checks the contents with another prayer—and drops it into her over-sized handbag. She rolls up her canvas tool wrap and slips that in too. The orchestra is playing Liszt, and as she re-admits the music to her mind its beauty washes through her with the released tension of a job completed—but it isn't over yet.

It is just as she checks her euphoria that she hears the door to the suite open.

Rachel's excitement plunges with queasy speed into adrenaline she can taste at the back of her throat. She seizes her bag, gauges the distance between the vanity and the balcony, decides she can't chance it, and backs into the walk-in wardrobe, pulling the door closed just seconds before two people enter the bedroom. She shrinks into the soft arms of Valentin Wiltshire's fine silk shirts.

"I couldn't wait"—the rich chords of Wiltshire, too-loud-but-never-told-so.

"Mr. Wiltshire, shouldn't we join the rest of the party?" Rachel would guess from the accent that the second person is a young South Korean woman, edu-cated first in the international schools for diplomats' children, then NYU.

"Call me Teddy. You always used to call me Teddy. I like that about you."

"I don't want to upset Mrs. Wiltshire. Or Jordan."

Jordan Petrov Wiltshire is Teddy's eldest child, recently graduated from NYU.

"You didn't mind at The Plaza. Relax, Eun-Ji. It's a party."

The conversation stops. The sound of hands on fabric, lips on skin, the distracted giggle and *umm* of a woman trying at once to seem like she is enjoying herself so as not to offend, while also hoping to stop what is happening.

"Mr. Wiltshire—"

"Call me Teddy."

"Teddy . . . wait . . ."

The sound of bodies hitting the mattress.

"Didn't you enjoy yourself at The Plaza?"

"Yes, but—"

"So why shouldn't you enjoy yourself now?"

"Wait—no—"

Rachel Wolff holds her breath, waiting for Valentin Wiltshire to hear the word no.

But he never has before.

Rachel searches for a smoke alarm in the ceiling of the walk-in wardrobe, finding its red blink, and then digs a Ronson lighter from the pocket of her black jumpsuit.

She was taught as a child that what distinguished an amateur from a professional was the capacity to manage unexpected situations calmly. Dousing the suite with sprinklers and evacuating the whole party onto the lawn will cut off her escape route and isn't exactly calm, but she can use the panic to her advantage. Most importantly, it will cut off what Wiltshire is doing right now.

Rachel runs her gloved thumb over the wheel, dreading the rasp and click. Nothing happens. She tenses her jaw and flicks it normally. The flame carves a blue hole in the gloom. She raises her hand to the ceiling, while undoing the top three buttons of her jumpsuit and readying the path to the two flat throwing knives harnessed across her bare skin.

"What are you crying about?" asks Wiltshire.

Rachel pauses, lowering the Ronson by an inch.

"This is just a bit of fun, Eun-Ji. Come on, don't cry. We'll go back to the party. There. Go and powder your nose."

Rachel swallows the adrenaline that now threatens to choke her. She dims the flame. Listens to the bend of springs, the click and lock of the bathroom door, the running taps, and Wiltshire releasing something between a growl and a sigh. The springs groan louder, Wiltshire lifting his six-five frame and tired joints and spoiled muscles off the bed. Rachel melts further into the shirts. The door to the walk-in wardrobe opens.

Rachel holds her breath as Wiltshire passes within inches of her. What if he smells the petrol tang of the Ronson? He switches the light on. Rachel closes her eyes, as if that will help—and opens them again. He is inspecting himself in the full-length mirror at the back of the walk-in: the thick head of silver hair, the boxer's nose; the dimpled chin; a grin he flashes now experimentally—they come to Wolff in the slices of visibility betrayed by gaps between hangers. He pulls off his velvet dining jacket, raises his arms, revealing sweat stains. He checks over his shoulder.

Rachel attempts invisibility, shrinking so she can't see Wiltshire in the hope this means he can't see her. A childhood game of hide-and-seek with Marko lances her. All the kids in the neighborhood played, and if you were discovered you joined the seeker. Marko was the seeker, because Marko was always the exception, no matter the game. Rachel was hiding in a wardrobe when he and Katarina came into the bedroom, ostensibly to search for her. When she heard them kissing, Rachel clattered from the wardrobe in tears. Katarina laughed, saying she *knew* it, Rachel was in L-O-V-E. For a split second, rare doubt flashed across Marko's face as Rachel, younger than them both and desperately embarrassed, cried. It was then Marko said, "Don't play if you can't stand to get hurt."

Now, Rachel listens to Wiltshire tut, drag his shirt off, then his vest, both dropping to the floor. The smell of him, like Parmesan rind left in the sun, clogs the space. Another sigh. Wiltshire is pulling open drawers—Rachel imagines he's working out where his valet stowed his vests—as Eun-Ji's speedy footsteps cross the bedroom. Wiltshire chuckles.

And reaches for a new shirt.

Rachel presses herself into the corner, gripping the knife so tightly her knuckles burn. She sees a densely tattooed arm before ducking her face. He selects the closest shirt and pulls it on, dumping himself in an armchair as he transfers his cuff links from the shirt pooled at his boots. But he doesn't notice her shoes amongst his own gleaming pairs. She sees that blue and black ink covers his shoulders too, but daren't reveal herself any further to distinguish a pattern. He works himself back into his jacket, spits in his palm, teases a few stray hairs, draws himself up, and winks at his reflection.

He says, "You win some, you lose some, Teddy boy." Then he leaves.

Rachel Wolff sags against the wall, her hands shaking. She struggles free from the pressing embrace of shirts. Her own reflection makes her jump. Her mascara has run, her mouth paled beneath the Alarm Red lipstick, and her jumpsuit is sagging open, revealing the harness and the red welt where it has rubbed against her rib cage. Her short hair—dyed from brown to platinum blond for this job—stands up at the back. Rachel rolls her neck, relaxing each muscle in her body, and then leans toward the mirror as Wiltshire did, realigning the makeup highlighting her round eyes to create the easygoing glamour of a plus-one here for the view. She shoulders her bag, now a few pounds heavier than it was when she slipped in through the rear entrance and joined the click-clacking flurry of early arrivals debating between a dip in the pool or sundowners on the terrace—the only difference being that Rachel isn't wearing heels.

She waits on the balcony for the orchestra to reach their interval, something they are scheduled to do in three . . . two . . . one—the final shudder of Wagner drifts out to sea. The musicians—all women, flown in from Venice—wear sleeveless black silk jumpsuits with white tie and white Colombina masks. Wolff digs in her bag for her bow tie and mask, then throws a leg over the balcony. Her shoes make no sound on the polished sandstone as she ladders from arched window to window, keeping to the shadows left by arc lights piercing the palm trees. She drops into a crouch, then straightens. Plucking a violin case from a vacated seat, Rachel slips the bag inside. She ties the mask into place.

Rachel is strolling toward the tree line when a crash splits the warm, lazy air.

Eight
Rogues' Gallery

Oman

Conrad Harthrop-Vane shakes hands and kisses cheeks, accepting sly presumptions as one accepts a tall wave standing in the surf. Moneypenny ordered 000 to take on the legend of an arts and antiquities dealer, cobbling together pieces of his own past, as his father would be known to some of the guests. It runs like this: "Harthrop-Vane, old boy! How the devil. What line are you in now? Must be selling *something*. HV1 was always selling something. Terrible shame about—well. Oh, in commodities, are you? Art? That's right—don't I remember you up at Cambridge, reading art or some such? Yes—now let's examine your vintage: you must have run with Tarquin—dated his cousin Binky, you know . . ."

Two men catch his eye in quick succession because they are so different from each other. One reminds him strongly of a warthog, and he is surprised Lisl would invite such a blemish to her party. That alone warrants further curiosity. A short specimen made shorter by his posture: shoulders hunched, neck tucked over a barrel chest. It is a posture that suggests nights hunkering in blacked-out basements or even a trench—the habitual flinch from bombs falling.

But the closer Triple O gets—drifting about the ballroom on Lisl's arm—he sees the beady meanness in the man's stare, the voracious cruelty in his trembling lower lip, salivating after something. Mid-fifties. Head shaved to a gray bullet. A suit cut like a dress uniform. He keeps his hands stiff like spades, shoveling them into his pockets as if bouncing loose shrapnel around in there. He is attended by very few people, and the nearer Triple O gets to his orbit, the more he sees why. The back of Conrad's neck is pricking. This man rings every reptilian alarm bell going.

He whispers to Lisl: "Who's that frightful toad?"

She slaps his arm lightly with her clutch. "Play nice. That's Viktor Babić."

"Bring him here to brighten up the place, did you?"

"In a manner of speaking. He's in diamonds."

"Legitimate?"

"Whyever not? He's made quite a name for himself in Dubai."

"Dubai?"

"The diamond centers of the world have moved on from London, Amsterdam, and New York. It's Dubai, Botswana, and Israel now. You'd better do your homework, pup, if you're going to maintain your cover."

"Can't I just copy yours?" he says, running a finger down the V of her neckline to the diamond clip nestled at the base, a pinwheel design set with round stones. "Birthday present?"

"Van Cleef. A gift from a mutual friend," she says, "in another lifetime."

"Bond," says Harthrop-Vane, dropping his hands. Her wide laughing mouth stings him. "Classier than money on the nightstand, I'll give him that."

"All men are pigs," says Lisl with resignation, "but some are lesser pigs than others."

Before Triple O can respond, his interest is snagged by Babić meeting the eye of his polar opposite with a look of fleeting but real recognition. The man in question has a booming voice, a lion's mane of silver hair, and the tan of a lifelong expat—and indeed there *is* something comically imperial about him in his snow-white suit, his thrust-back shoulders, arm thrown up to point at something in the ceiling so much like Chaplin in *The Great Dictator* it makes Triple O chuckle. The deluded, decaying tyrant—for such is his air—is giving a lecture on the mosaic far above while clutching the hand of a diminutive woman with a gray bob, emerald jewels, and skin like burnt clay. Long-suffering wife.

"And that specimen?"

"Oh, that's only Friedrich Hyde. Bores on, doesn't he? Still, he is a world expert on Arabic art."

"With all this expertise crammed into one room," he drawls, "I don't see how you don't shoot yourself."

"Hush. You'll spoil your legend entirely."

"I'm terrible undercover."

"Not in my experience. Now, here's some entertainment. You'd think it was *his* birthday."

Teddy Wiltshire strides into the ballroom like a conquering hero returning home: shaking hands, tossing off welcomes, his family clustering to his gravity.

"I'll introduce you to your quarry," says Lisl.

Triple O can see what Sir Emery meant. There is a magnetic joviality to Teddy Wiltshire, a promise to provide fun, a vitality taboo in today's polite world. His handshake is testing, then confiding. His grin is packed with gold.

"Fancy I knew your father," he says. Teddy's gaze

locks onto Triple O as if the whole purpose of the evening is for them to meet. "Possible?"

"Possible. He worked out of Turkey for a time. You are . . . ?"

"British." A good-natured laugh. "But a savage underneath. Turkmenistan. Not Turkey, if you know your geography."

"I do."

"Fun winding me up, then?" Wiltshire has a way of speaking that bites off the first few words of the sentence, suggesting there is no need for formalities between friends.

Triple O answers this with a rascal's grin. "Yes, sir. I know all about your illustrious history."

"Do, eh?"

"Who doesn't?"

Teddy glances at Lisl. "Like this one. Where'd you find him?"

"We're old friends."

Teddy grips Triple O's hand again. "Then so are we. Your pa always had a business card, I recall, different title every time, always offering something. You offering?"

"I'm new in the trade. Got out of banking. Too little sleep. I've some friends who know of a few pieces out of Syria. Kabul, too. Of course, it's a tragedy what's happening in Ukraine. Someone should make sure all that craftsmanship and heritage ends up in a museum."

"All those pies, you'll run out of fingers."

"I like to keep my options open."

"I'm always saying that to my son, Jordan"—at this, Teddy glances about, finding Jordan, who is speaking in urgent tones with his girlfriend, grabbing her flighty hands—"you're young, well connected, stay open to opportunity." He refocuses on Triple O. "Just like you. What are you *really* offering, Conrad?"

Triple O licks his upper lip. "Peace of mind."

It is then, unfortunately, that the doors crash in.

In an instinctual switch to flight, freeze, or fight, Rachel Wolff flees, sprinting toward the palms—and she would make it if two shots didn't chop the palms in earthy splinters and make flight impossible. She was already prepared to fight once that night, but in the moment wasted questioning whether she ought now to reach for her knives, or play it like any other musician and hope to see the end of the show, a hand lands on her shoulder.

"Inside."

Rachel grips the violin case, preparing to swing.

"The only useful thing you can do with that right now is play me a tune."

She knows that accent as well as she knows her own voice. The man wears a balaclava, a heavy jacket bulked by a protective vest, and carries a revolver in one hand. An axe hangs from his belt. He is taller than her—it's unusual for Rachel to encounter many people taller than herself, and with Wiltshire this makes two in one evening. He smells of sea salt and mustard seeds. Through the holes of the balaclava she meets eyes the blue of steel that somehow aren't frightening.

"I don't play for free," she says.

A surprised chuckle. "How about for keeps?"

"You can't afford me."

"Give me three minutes." He tugs at her. "Inside."

Rachel hugs the violin case to her body, stumbling as the gunman pushes her over the uneven paving to the doors of the ballroom, which now hang in panels. Two Audis have reversed into them. The second is still occupied by a driver, a woman who remains tensed at the wheel.

The gunman steers Wolff over the wreckage. A few more from the orchestra are pushed inside too—one screams, a shriek that grows shriller, then hoarse, as her panic runs out of air. The gunman's hand slips from Rachel's shoulder. He takes the musician by the arm, advising her to count backward from ten.

Rachel is adding up her own figures. Eight more armed men. Half the gang are pulling jewelry from necks and hands to whimpers and gasps. And half are in the next room smashing the display cases of the hotel shop, the rhythmic cacophony of small disasters. Nine count her escort, ten count the driver.

The numbers and the accent add up to a name. The Chevaliers.

But the Chevaliers are all dead or in hiding. It can't be . . .

Rachel does as she's told, standing against the wall with the orchestra. The pearlescent linen tablecloths and shimmering dresses and winking mosaics all seem to slide toward the focal point of the ballroom: Lisl Baum, whose glittering gold gown, wild ash-blond bob, and tanned laughter lines would usually light up a room, but whose features are now fixed as she removes her black pearl necklace. She casts a questioning look at the man to her left, a tall blond whose careless sneer belongs in the Edwardian wing of the National Portrait Gallery. He relinquishes his Omega so slowly Lisl Baum jogs his elbow.

The greedy palm wants Wiltshire next.

Wiltshire waits with his chin thrust upward and his arms out, protecting his wife, Chelsea, and their two teenage daughters, Virginia and Adelaide, who hide behind him crying. Jordan is hugging Eun-Ji, who appears frozen with shock. Wiltshire's two younger daughters, India and Paris, hug Wiltshire's knees.

The gunman who escorted Rachel inside checks his watch and whistles.

The four men in the shop return to the ballroom, each hoisting a bag over his shoulder. One of them shakes his head.

"All right, everyone," booms Wiltshire. "Let's all stay nice and calm and these clowns will be on their way."

The blue-eyed gunman approaches him.

"Shall I show you a trick, Mr. Wiltshire?"

"That's magicians, not clowns," says Wiltshire lightly. "Not to correct your English, old boy."

The gunman says, "Are you English, comrade? Nobody told me your football club also bought you a passport."

Wiltshire slides his hands into his pockets. "You want to be comrades, you peasant piece of shit? Get over here and suck my—"

He is cut off by Lisl Baum murmuring that he should hold his tongue.

The gunman tilts his head. Then he kneels and beckons to Wiltshire's daughter India with his revolver. "Come here, little girl."

"Let's leave the women and children out of it, hey?"

"Come on. I'll show you a magic trick."

India is five years old and she inches toward the man with the wisdom of a survivor as he says that her tiara is very pretty.

"Ask your daddy why his safe is empty."

India almost topples over as she twists to peer up at Wiltshire.

"It's not empty," says Wiltshire. "Welcome to anything you like. Let's just keep this between men." The smile pinned to his face could have been painted on by a mortician.

The gunman crosses his arms over his bent knee. "Your daddy knows what I'm talking about. He brought something here to give to Ms. Baum for her birthday, but we've checked his room and it's not there. Where is it?"

"It's in the safe I tell you."

Rachel's hands are slick. The violin case threatens to fall.

The thief says sympathetically, "If you ever want to know how much you are worth to your daddy, you have an answer."

Triple O's heart skips a beat.

Wiltshire whispers, "Do you know who you're fucking with, my friend?"

India's voice seems to shake the chandelier above

as she bawls: "You said you were going to show me a magic trick."

The gunman laughs.

Sirens hurl a sudden net over the mountains.

"Watch closely," says the thief. "You and I are going to disappear. If you want your daughter back, Mr. Wiltshire, you'll give me what I want when I call."

The lights turn off. The three minutes are up.

In the second before the room goes black, Harthrop-Vane sees the gunman clutch the child under the armpits: the pinch of cloth in his thickly gloved fingers, the way her cheeks burn red, as if she's just been slapped. Conrad remembers, with awful heat, how his father joked that young Conrad must have Slapped Cheek Syndrome after one of the bad men did something that left him red—how the bad man laughed at HV1's weakness, this unwillingness to protect his own son.

Then it's dark, and Triple O feels as if he's acting in a dream, crossing an unlit stage to pistol-whip the gunman across the face. The masked man yelps. Triple O locks his fingers around the gunman's wrist, forcing the weapon upward—the man pulls the trigger. The bullet strikes the chandelier, a sound like the crack of a glacier. The girl screams, bumping into Triple O's legs. He folds himself over her and drops to the ground as the

five-ton chandelier falls in a shuddering crescendo—
and then twangs and groans on the trembling chain.

Dust settles over Triple O. He can feel the disturbance
of the chandelier swinging just feet overhead. He gathers
the girl up and rolls away as the chain splits and the chandelier explodes with the force of a crystal atom bomb.

Harthrop-Vane shields the girl, shards peppering
his hands and arms.

Mrs. Wiltshire screams for her daughter. India
wriggles away, stumbling toward the sound.

Triple O pushes through the chaos to a spot under
the flight of marble stairs, drawing his phone from his
coat and calling Regent's Park. He barks at whoever
picks up to get Moneypenny on the line.

Her voice clicks through: "What's that racket,
Triple O?"

"Got a problem," he says. "The Chevaliers just performed a smash-and-grab. Target was our object of
interest. The Chevaliers were after the contents of Wiltshire's safe, but came up empty. Must be a second thief.
Chevaliers took my Omega, should be able to listen in.
The tracker on the object will let us know where that's
off to as well."

"Yes, hold on." A pause. "There's interference with
the tracker, Q is working the problem. So, the blind
man's watch was really a gift for Ms. Baum?"

"Seems that way."

"A valuable one. Payoff?"

"Nothing to indicate that. Besides, it would be a stupid one, purchased as a way to launder money."

"True. I doubt the boss at the top of the Gray Group would like that," says Moneypenny. "Then you don't put Baum in the center?"

Triple O raises his eyebrow, which hurts—he pulls crystal from his forehead. "Do you?"

"It was just a thought. Colorful party guests. But there's not a whiff of indiscretion in her holdings. I suppose she's simply maintained an *open mind* when it comes to friends, since her early days as a pilot fish."

"Don't mince your words."

"Spare me your blushes," says Moneypenny. "Here's something from Q now. Yes, we've got audio on the Chevaliers. A lot of angry men. They were after the blind man's watch and they're not keen on disappointment. Ah—they're sweeping the loot for bugs or tracking devices, we might have limited time on this. Wait a moment, we've got a name at least. Marko. And that's all she wrote—dead."

"And the blind man's watch?" says Triple O, hunching as demands fill the lobby, which is caught between the bloodletting of sunset on one side and the hastening dark of the desert on the other. An overlooked cobweb clinging to the bottom of the stairs trails his neck and he twitches.

"Got it—the blind man's watch appears to be heading out to sea."

"Pursue?" says Triple O.

"No point. It's just gone airborne, and with it the second thief."

"What do you want me to do?"

"Play the gallant. Help clear up the mess. And keep your eyes and ears open. After a robbery, people check on the possessions closest to them. I want to know what Teddy Wiltshire checks on."

"Will do."

He ends the call and turns to face the bedlam. What he sees is Lisl Baum standing framed by the shattered door, and Teddy Wiltshire looming over her, his fat fingers gently pawing her cheek.

Rachel sprints for all she is worth, the palm trees clattering above her head, the swimming pools yawning around her. When the ground turns from stone to sand she chucks off her shoes and wriggles down to her midnight bikini, the harness of her throwing knives, and a leather garter. Opening the violin case, she retrieves the bag and straps it to the garter. With a whispered apology to the musician, Rachel tosses the discarded items into a burning firepit. Then she runs headlong into the waves.

She wonders if they've met before, his voice so familiar. She wonders how the Chevaliers knew what was in Wiltshire's safe, and what it means that they are operating outside of their usual territory. Described first in the French press as Chevaliers d'Industrie— men and women who lived by their wits, kind and quick-working thieves who said they had no victims but insurance companies—the Chevaliers were former Yugoslav soldiers who forged a loosely knit network of diamond thieves after the war, hitting jewelry stores and hotels in Paris, London, Madrid, Tokyo. Until the heat from Interpol grew too great and they folded. She wonders what it means that someone is operating with the Chevaliers' methods once again, that they targeted Lisl Baum's party, and Valentin Wiltshire in particular, just like her. Maybe it's a case of *once a Chevalier, always a Chevalier.*

The Sirius is bobbing on the waves, the door to the plane a shuddering yellow portal in the chop. She squeaks over the floats and hauls herself inside, shouting to the pilot: "Go!"

Nine
The Evil Eye

Crete

Crete has many eyes.

004 arrives late by passenger plane, a four-and-a-half-hour journey during which he is acutely aware of how very far he has drifted from the general course of humanity. The mother who swings her eleven-month-old up and down without stopping, demonstrating the flexibility of the double-jointed and the desperate; the aging hostess who defuses a vodka-and-red-wine-fueled row with the deftness of a bomb disposal unit; the brief yet confiding relationships struck up over the aisle that end with satisfied handshakes and choruses of "You have a good holiday now, mate." Dryden has no part in it.

He wonders when this happened, a long look back down years of killing people, and stops looking.

The plane touches down to humid darkness. Palm trees catch the fringe of arc lights. The airport has the feeling of a distant outpost: small, loosely manned. At border control, Dryden glances into the staff offices and notices a framed print of an Orthodox saint hanging over a filing cabinet. He feels the saint's eyes on the back of his neck as he is waved through. Phoebe Taylor, Moneypenny's purple-fringed assistant, arranged a car for him, which Station G has left at rentals. A blue glass medallion painted with an eyeball hangs from the rearview mirror of the white Lotus Elise to ward off the evil eye.

He drives the coastal road with the top down, breathing in foreign fumes—which recede as the traffic grows lighter—replaced by the sweet scent of cypress trees and the flirtation of frangipanis. The waxing moon is heavy and blazing, scrawling a signature in pale ink over the black sea. He's glad not to be arriving in Oman right now for Lisl Baum's birthday party, glad 000 was given the mission to play nice. Let the snake charmer do what he does best, and Dryden will do what he does best.

At last, he feels good. In action. On his own. No

pretense that he is like everyone else. No pretense that the events of winter don't still play on his mind, especially on days when London refuses to give up the grip of the cold, and his body seizes, believing it is back in that cage on the frosted deck of the yacht, the white tiger breathing down his neck, a madman threatening to melt the world, and Luke—Lucky Luke, Dryden's 2ic in the army and the only man he ever truly loved—wavering between good and evil. Luke chose good, ultimately, but the waver cost. They always do.

Luke is now serving time in a prison for terrorists while 004 speeds down the northern flank of Crete with no one around and he can give up the pretense it doesn't hurt—when it does, from top to bottom. He doesn't have to pretend that Luke's refusal to take a phone call from him is something he can just shrug off.

He doesn't have to pretend his faith in his mission is resolute—as the Taliban murder Afghan girls and women for wanting an education; after Dryden gave years of his life and pints of his blood in the earnest belief he could deliver freedom; as the world burns or drowns; as every month a new bomb detonates somewhere—and Joseph Dryden, who has been told since he signed up aged sixteen that he is a vital force for good, begins to question his use and his purpose. Trouble is, he doesn't know how to quit. Unless it's the big quit.

The road curves around the hulking silhouette of a mountain. Dryden drops his shoulders. Action is where he puts his hurt.

Phoebe has reserved a villa across the valley from Mr. Corso's estate. Dryden forces the car up the narrow track to the whitewashed villa, which glows beneath the moon's unreal gaze. The key is in a lockbox. He lets himself in, finds a switch, and is greeted by another pair of eyes, these belonging to the deconstructed face of a saint done in imitation of Picasso. The saint is pointing to the large window, which will have a view onto the target's garden across the valley come morning. In the bedroom, Dryden is greeted by a gloomy painting of a martyr. He takes the painting down and makes it face the wall. He knows so many eyes could be considered, here, a good omen. Warding off evil. But who says he wants to ward it off?

Joseph Dryden wakes to the reassuring song of unfamiliar birds, his alarm clock on so many missions in so many transient billets. It is hot already and his body is grateful for it. Dryden has a warm shower, throws on a linen suit, and strolls down the track to the main road, which promises and delivers an all-in-one kiosk-bakery-café-bar just opening. It isn't yet tourist season. He buys bread and coffee, telling anyone who is curious that he is renting while searching for property to buy.

He carries his spoils back to the villa, a pleasurable line of sweat tickling his nape. He wonders if the baker noticed the frostbite scars on his hands when he paid. Sometimes people do. Sometimes they don't.

Sipping coffee on the terrace, Dryden gazes down onto a grove of olive and fruit trees, whose trunks and branches are painted white midway, bouncing the sun onto the hard soil. Flotillas of bright pink and red flowers. Crazy paving, cracked and made crazier. The pool is empty. Paint pots and tarpaulin gather dust in the shade, the universal symbol of work indefinitely paused. Dryden catches a hard green seed dropping from the branches above. Frostbite or not, his reflexes are just fine. He picks up the pair of binoculars provided by the host for bird-watching. He imagines Ibrahim telling him Carl Zeiss glass remains the best in the world as he trains the binoculars on the estate tucked between folds of the mountain, now brought suddenly and vividly to just beneath his nose.

The only person in sight is the pool boy.

The pool boy's name is Kristos and he is bored. He works for his father, handyman to holiday lets and second homes of executives from candy companies and travel operators, men who run boring companies and bore their wives, who are bored by their children, who are bored by the desperate attempts of their au pairs to provide Fun for the Summer. When this set arrives, Kristos will pick up quick affairs with husband or wife—or even au pair—and accept gifts and sometimes bribes for his troubles. Kristos is saving up with two goals in mind: quit working for his father, and buy a convertible like the one he saw parked outside the usually vacant villa next door to his first job that morning.

Now he is on his third job of the day, Mr. Corso's pool. Mr. Corso sometimes pays Kristos to be a houseboy when he has guests he wants to impress with the "local beauty and color of Crete." Mr. Corso is Corsican but he talks like an American. Sometimes Kristos goes to bed with Mr. Corso's guests; it depends on what Mr. Corso wants. He is connected with important people. Rumor says he is some kind of gangster, some kind of smuggler. He procures and sells things for important people. Mr. Corso sometimes brings in professional girls, too, for the entertainment. He says he can get anything. Mr. Corso started off as an errand boy for his godfather, he says. *And one day you, Kristos, will give the orders instead of following them. For now, undo that top button and go and look romantic . . .*

Kristos drags the green needles and pale olive feathers into the net, then pulls it from the pool in a cascade of water.

"Good morning."

Kristos jumps. A Black man is strolling around the marble edge of the infinity pool. A giant with an easy smile and hands in his pockets. A white linen suit that says money. Calm power that says authority. And a glint that says he's read Kristos just as quickly, if not quicker, and knows a fellow hustler when he meets one.

"Morning," Kristos returns reluctantly, only cautiously prepared to admit the time of day.

Dryden offers his hand and sees the boy—about twenty-one—give a jolt of surprise. "I'm Joe. I've just arrived and I spotted your van. I'm looking for someone to fix my pool."

"Yours is the convertible?"

A nod.

Kristos switches on his inner light, the one that says, I can be anything you want me to be.

"I will give you a business card, wait . . ." He is wearing faded swim shorts, tessellated with the pattern of the evil eye. He digs into the pocket for a ragged wallet.

The card promises repairs, clearance, pools, boat charter.

"You must be busy," says Dryden.

"I can make time for you." This almost comes with a wink.

Dryden laughs, pocketing the card.

As he walks away, Joseph Dryden wonders if this jack-of-all-trades promises luck—or the other thing.

Dryden lets Kristos drive the Lotus that same day, showing him how to take the mountain curves like a pro. He says he sometimes races in rallies and internally chastises himself for the worshipful gaze cast his way. Dryden would usually take more time to develop an asset, but the clock is ticking. A sale could be made anytime, triggering another six-day countdown to hell. The dust kicked up by the tires floats on exhausted air over a Minoan village, whose staggered bones straggle up the hillside, and have done since three thousand years before Christ. The coast drops away on the other side, the sea clear as glass. Spiny broom and yellow oleander create wild borders. Goats watch from the mountainside, poised vertiginously. Over the growl of the engine, Kristos answers Dryden's casual question instantly. Yes, Mr. Corso has many visitors.

"He throws parties," says Kristos. "There is one tonight."

Dryden lounges by the pool in pale blue shorts as Kristos clears out the drain, every now and then stealing a glance at Dryden's body. When a cat missing most of its stuffing throws itself down on the crazy paving and shows Kristos its belly, the pool boy laughs and explains he's taken responsibility for all the neighborhood cats. He digs into his evil eye shorts and reveals a tin of sardines. The cat howls, then gives him a quick rub against the shins before attacking the tin, Kristos batting its head away, trying to remove just one or two sardines before tossing them into the shade.

"Nice of you," says Dryden, "to look after strays."

Kristos gives a shy smile.

"Who looks after you?" says Dryden, hating himself when the smile turns flattering.

"Nobody, Mr. Joe."

"It's just Joe. You said Mr. Corso hires you at his parties sometimes."

Kristos shrugs. "I am working for him tonight, yes. But he doesn't pay much. Sometimes he forgets to pay me at all."

Dryden watches the cat eat the fish to the bone with clever and careful paws. He says, "I think Mr. Corso is someone I can do business with. But I want to get a better sense of his friends first. My watch is sort of special. It records sound. Do you think you could keep it in your pocket while you work the party?"

Kristos says, too quickly: "I can do more than that."

"I don't need you to take any risks. It's nothing important. I just like to know who my friends are."

Kristos leans on his broom, letting the afternoon sun slick his body. "Could you be my friend, Joe?"

Dryden swallows a long-dormant and better-repressed stab of desire before he says, "Absolutely."

Dryden sits by the pool in his shorts with his feet skimming the rising water. Kristos has set it to fill. Around him, the perfume of flowers thickens like a conspiracy. Cicadas argue. The sky is a ribbon drawer in disarray, caught somewhere between sunset and moonrise. He leans back on his palms, wrists straining, bites of pressure. That is the now of him, but in his head, he is across the valley at Mr. Corso's party. The voices of strangers nest and hatch in his skull. He doesn't resist, just reminds himself by the mint cool of the water and the growing numbness in his wrists that he is here, he is himself, he is alone. Meanwhile, the new feature Ibrahim has installed in his watch—it can now transmit sound into his head and MI6 at the same time if it is within a mile of his implant—streams the party: the clink of glasses, shitty Europop, a squeal or a scream, grunts, breaths, whoops, chatter.

"The boss is ready to kill someone, Corso." Accented English.

Aisha's voice cuts into Dryden's head: "Here we go. Marking that as Voice One. No matches."

"The boss cannot blame *me*."

"Labeling that Corso," says Aisha.

"I am only a middleman," continues Corso.

"You have given yourself a promotion, no? You are the guy who fetches and carries *for* the middleman," says Voice One.

"Shut your mouth about that stuff."

"Listen, everybody! Laurent lives in cloud land."

"I told you to shut the fuck up," says Corso. "All I know is I gave the thing over and it went up for sale and then somehow ended up practically back where it started and that wasn't *my* fault. I do my job without attracting attention."

Voice One becomes slippery. "Are you saying the boss made a mistake, uh? Maybe you do really want a promotion."

"Lenski, I've always thought I'd like you better without a tongue. Kristos, I told you to keep the glasses topped up!"

Dryden rolls his wrists. The party wears on with

talk of football and sex amongst the men and holiday plans and power amongst the women.

Dryden says, "Any thoughts, boys and girls?"

Aisha's voice: "I'd like to know what Corso knows about what's going to happen at the *other* end of the pipeline."

"Me too," says Dryden. "I'd have liked to know it before 008 lost the use of his legs for at least a year, too."

Ibrahim says, "Sounds like Wiltshire messed up buying that watch. He put his own money into play, and his fingerprints on a detonator."

"Does that make him the boss of the Gray Group," says Dryden, "above the rules? Or is he chafing at someone else's rules, wanting to *be* the boss?"

"Hold on," says Aisha. "We might have a problem. I thought you told the pool boy to put the watch in his pocket?"

"I did. Cut me back in."

Corso is asking Kristos where he could have got such an expensive watch.

"Shit," says Dryden. The water is climbing his ankles. He promised Kristos he would turn the tap off when the level started to lap the marble lip of the pool.

Kristos says, "I bought it."

Corso says, "I didn't realize you earned so good, cleaning swimming pools."

Laughter.

"I got it in Agios Nikolaos," says Kristos. "My friend has a whole suitcase of them."

Now the laughter turns to howls.

"Kristos," says Mr. Corso, "you've been had."

"Smart kid," says Ibrahim.

"Smart enough," says Dryden.

The water is jostling about Dryden's shins when Kristos appears between the trees. The submerged lights in the pool throw ripples over his sweat-sheened face.

"I did good?" he says.

"Very good," says Dryden, standing up and buttoning his shirt. "Did you recognize anybody at the party? Anyone you've seen before?"

"Yes," says Kristos. "They work in shipping." His straight face cracks into a grin when Dryden raises an eyebrow.

"Can you write down their names and descriptions?"

"I have a good memory."

Dryden is opening the notes app on his phone when the sound of an engine makes him turn his head. All the guests have already left. Twin lights of a car bear down the track from Corso's villa toward the main road, and then cross over, heading for Dryden's villa.

Dryden glances at the villas either side of his, both occupied. He can hear the happy conversations of families above the cicadas. Moneypenny wanted this quiet but persuasive, keeping any interrogation hidden from secret surveillance on Corso. Too many civilians around. Too many witnesses.

Dryden says, "He saw you come here."

"I walked," says Kristos. "I was very careful."

Dryden makes a decision. "Get in the car. You can tell me about the guests on the way."

"Can't I wait for you here?"

"I might not be able to come back." If he learns of another detonator, he'll have to move into action. He doesn't mean he might not be *able* to come back, because he's trained not to entertain defeat. But it occurs to Dryden that, from any other man, his words could easily sound like a very bad omen.

The road corkscrews, popping open views of Agios Nikolaos—the shine of tourist restaurants and a disco clustered around the harbor—before the reassuring pulse-beat of waves recedes and the tarmac drills into the mountains, replacing humidity with a creeping chill.

"I didn't turn off the water," says Kristos. "The pool will flood the garden."

"The flowers could use a drink," says Dryden, glancing at the rearview mirror. The twin stare of Corso's headlights raking him from a respectable distance.

A map glows dimly on the car's dashboard, showing swatches of emptiness. Dryden whips the car around the next bend.

"Where are we going?" asks Kristos.

"Someplace quiet."

"He's following us."

"I know."

"What will he do if he catches us?"

"Nothing."

"You don't know Mr. Corso when he's angry. Once I dropped a bottle and it smashed and the glass caught me and he made me pick it all up with my fingers even though I was already bleeding."

Dryden pulls himself out of his thoughts to turn his most reassuring expression on Kristos. "There's no need to be scared."

"He won't catch us?"

"No, he's going to catch us," says Dryden, shifting gear. "And then he's going to regret a lot of things."

The climb into the mountains is so steep Kristos leans forward in his seat to help the Lotus, making Dryden laugh. The cold of pregnant clouds, bellies scraping the peaks, is getting inside him. But he keeps his window open, the better to hear. The pursuing engine is still coming from below. As he slows for a hairpin bend, gonging surprises him—they are passing two closed tavernas and a craft shop selling painted gourds, which hang from the branches of trees and bang together in the wind. Gong, gong, gong. The headlights catch one painted with the evil eye, then a whole pack of them, hanging like distended eyeballs on shivering strings.

Kristos crosses himself.

"Are you superstitious, Kristos?"

A beat, in which Kristos considers the arrival of a stranger who in a day and a night has thrown his carefully cultivated schemes into chaos. "No," he says.

"Me neither," says Dryden.

"I am not superstitious," says Kristos, turning to see the chasing headlights zigzagging below, "because I know better than to doubt the devil. I simply believe in him."

Dryden is reminded—as he was when Kristos leaned on his mop and asked if they could be friends, his near-naked body radiating brittle confidence and deeper vulnerability—of Luke, who always made room for the devil when they were under fire, and God when they survived. He says, "Have you seen any devils lately?"

"Joe?"

"Any people at Mr. Corso's house who you didn't like to party with. Anyone who scared you."

Kristos picks at his nails. "One man. I never saw him smile, except that time I had to pick up all the glass. He gave me the creeps. He was sort of dead inside."

"Was he there tonight?"

"No."

"Do you know his name?"

"No one ever used it."

"What about his business?"

"I heard him say something about diamonds. He always had a falcon on his wrist. It gave everyone the creeps."

Dryden imagines Q Branch now cross-checking diamond merchants with some rare birds registry. "Anyone else come to mind? Maybe they didn't scare you, just struck you as unusual somehow."

"There was an old man a few months ago who wanted me to take off all my clothes at the Minoan village in a reenactment. That was not usual."

A laugh escapes Dryden for no reason, which he immediately regrets. "Did you?"

Kristos shrugs.

"Right." Dryden checks the rearview mirror. "Do you know their names?"

"These are no-name sorts of people, Joe."

"Could you describe him, the man who wanted you to strip?"

"Very tanned, very white hair, and he sort of ordered people about like he was king. I remember Mr. Corso called him something as a joke, something like Raj. That's like an Indian king, isn't it?"

"Yes."

"But he wasn't Indian. He was English, maybe, or American. He talked a lot about temples and things like that. He was so excited at the Minoan village, digging where you're not allowed, telling me things about my culture I learned in school. His wife was bored."

"I'll bet. You do have a good memory, Kristos. Anyone else?"

Kristos shrugs again. "I don't think so, Joe. Apart from Teddy."

Dryden bumps the car over a crack. "Teddy Wiltshire came here? And he didn't hide his name?"

"He didn't hide anything. Men like him don't. That's who Mr. Corso and his friends were talking about tonight, I think. When he is in the air, they get spooked."

"Men like what?"

"You know. Invincible."

"What makes you think he's invincible?"

"He held Mr. Corso's head under the pool for two minutes and afterward Mr. Corso just laughed like it was a funny joke because Teddy Wiltshire was laughing although Mr. Corso was furious and terrified really. His lips had gone blue."

"And why did Teddy do that?"

"He was just mucking around."

Dryden hums. "He ever try to muck around with you?"

"He likes girls. Once, he tried to force a girl I know to leave the party with him—I saw him pull her into the car."

"Tried?"

"I stopped him."

"How?"

"I flattened his tire while he was distracted. He came back to the party. I showed her the way out the back."

"That was good of you."

Another shrug. "I'm just saving up for a car and a big house somewhere on another island. My father was a farmer up in these mountains. Things stopped growing so we moved to the coast and now we serve tourists and people like Mr. Corso. I don't care how I get what I want, much, when it comes to me. But God has eyes everywhere, Joe."

The plateau seems so unreal after the climb that Dryden checks the map. It is a basin, the flat bottom of an ancient lake perhaps, clasped in the upturned fingers of the peaks.

"Listen," says Kristos. "You can hear the windmills."

"Windmills?"

"We are on the Lasithi Plateau. There were thousands of white windmills here when the Venetians ruled Crete." Kristos says this as if it happened quite recently. "Now, just a few ghosts."

The ghosts are skeletal metal windmills clinging to the edges of properties marked by broken-down fences. They sing painfully in the wind, a feedback loop that chases around Dryden's skull like whispers around the walls of St. Paul's Cathedral. His headlights shock the windmills into being: rusted limbs, once white, now calcified. Money has forgotten this place. Many of the houses checkering the basin—Dryden is cornering the western flank—are shuttered and empty, broken windows stuffed with rags, flags of promise to return. Others are whitewashed defiantly, trailing roses and bougainvillea. Toyota pickups from twenty years ago, once red and now faded salmon, stand loyal. Dryden spears the Lotus through this beautiful graveyard until the road heaves out of the plateau and a sign announces for tourists: *Psychro Cave, Birthplace of Zeus, A Mythic Wonderland.*

Dryden slides to a halt in a forecourt. Orange stands

and a café under a Coca-Cola banner are shut for the night, but a neon sign over a clapboard fence promises a swim park, rides, a mini-Olympia. Beyond the clapboard there is no sign of any of these things, only scaffolding creaking in the wind. Dryden aims the headlights at the stone steps climbing the hillside toward Psychro Cave, and leaves them shining as he gets out of the car, an invitation for Corso to pursue.

"You'll be safer with me," he says. "You'd better come along."

"The pool will be such a mess," says Kristos, tugging at his lower lip. "Junk will be washed back into the drains."

A car growls nearby, churning up gravel.

"Come on," says Dryden. He opens the boot, gets out an L7A2 general-purpose machine gun or GPMG—Kristos stares at him—and slings it over his shoulder. "Let's go."

The headlights reveal a sign painted with a donkey, offering a ride up to the cave for five euros—*Help Us Preserve Our Native Donkeys*. The pen is empty. The path jinks up the mountain on uneven stones; at each turn, they gain a higher vantage over the plateau, toy houses and toy windmills arranged on a card table, the moon an Anglepoise lamp. Steps sound behind them, soft, slow, almost hidden by the noise of night: the chomp of insects, clatter of birds, the mad shot of some creature across the path, the blare of goats or else cattle further off. It is hard to tell what is what. Kristos's breathing is ragged.

"Keep going," says Dryden loudly. "We're almost there."

The steps below hasten. What does Corso fear Dryden is up to? Whatever it is, he's scared enough to follow him—but not scared of Dryden.

A white owl crashes out of the trees and cuts up the black. Dryden can feel the wind from its wing on his cheek. He is pricked all over with gooseflesh. He is dressed for the coast, not the mountains. Cold cobwebs his joints. His aunties said a white owl crossing your path meant death. The owl's eyes were yellow pebbles.

They are nearing the top of the mountain. A concrete block offers a ticket booth for the cave and toilets—locked. Dryden lends his shoulder and the door opens. He checks: the cubicles have bolts.

"Lock yourself in here," he tells Kristos, "and cover your ears."

The path rises toward the mouth of the cave, a freezing blank beneath the overhanging peak of the mountain. Dryden locates a box and throws the switch: emerald spotlights spring up, revealing where steps descend into the cave, a massive spiral of stone so dense and layered it looks like fur—and still deeper, a mesh of stalactites and stalagmites glowing greenly, hiding a tomb of dead water at the well of Zeus's birthplace.

Footsteps approach.

Dryden disappears into the shadows at the mouth of the cave.

Corso arrives out of breath and red in the face: ragefully uncertain. He reaches the entrance to the cave and hesitates, gripping the iron railing over the abyss.

Dryden steps out and taps him on the shoulder. The man's jump—the electricity of fear—races up his arm. Corso spins around. There is a gun in his hand. Dryden knocks it away, grabs the man's tie, and then kicks at the railing, which goes flying into the depths of the cave, clanging off rocks—Corso almost falls after it, his boots losing purchase, until he has only one toe left on solid ground, his whole weight kept from plummeting by Dryden's grip on his tie, stretched taut as a day-old corpse.

Dryden says, "When's the next sale, who are you selling for, and what's the next target?"

"Wh-what?"

Dryden repeats the questions.

"I don't know! They don't tell me!"

"Your type always knows more than it should."

"Wait, pull me up and I'll—OK! OK!—I heard something about a prison! Someone important is there, they want to free him!"

"Where? Who?"

"I don't know!"

Dryden hears a scraping from somewhere behind on the mountainside. "Did you sell a blind man's watch for a diamond merchant you party with? And Teddy Wiltshire bought it when he wasn't supposed to."

"Yes!"

"The diamond merchant's name?"

"Screw you!"

Dryden lets the tie slip by an inch. Corso's scream chases bats from their hiding places, a cold black cloud.

"Do you know what I mean by Janus?" asks Dryden.

"Yes, yes, I know!"

"Is the diamond merchant the Janus behind all this?"

Corso's laugh is hyena-like. "Are you kidding?"

"Then who's in charge? Who's the god of gods, Corso?"

"I don't know! None of us do, outside the top circle!"

"No better place to bare your soul than here, where the god of gods was born. Come on, man. My arm is getting tired."

"I don't know!"

"Guess."

"Mr. Wiltshire throws his weight around—"

Several things happen then simultaneously, which Dryden has to parse into digestible segments. The tie isn't a tie anymore. He holds its narrow tongue and that is all. The cave is roaring, the sound of a train bearing down—or a bullet's echo trapped and inconsolable. Corso isn't there anymore, either. He is simply a scream, then a smack.

Look alive, soldier.

Dryden scrambles, pressing himself against the wall of the cave and out of sight of the entranceway. He peers down through the lattice of rocks at Corso's body. His smashed skull is drowning in a lake of his own blood, made purple by the green spotlights.

A high-pitched whistle cuts the reverberating air. The sniper, trying to call him out. That was one hell of a shot, slicing through the tie, but wasteful. Kill Corso because he is prepared to talk. Fair enough—the Gray Group, surely now proven to be real, could preserve its power only by maintaining absolute silence, and removing those who strayed from that code. But Dryden can't be allowed to live after this, surely? Both problems could have been solved with one bullet, but someone wanted to show off their marksmanship.

"Shot fired," breathes Dryden. "Sniper in the field. Corso dead."

Aisha's voice shivers along his bones: "How assist?"

"Can Q get a visual?"

"Negative, no satellites in range."

"Run checks on prisons that make likely terror targets."

"Already on it."

"All right," said Dryden. "And buy me a nice wreath."

A pause. "Any preferences?"

"Tulips would be nice. Over and out."

"Happy hunting. Over and out."

Dryden draws Corso's pistol to him with an extended foot—a bullet bounces off the rock—and tucks it into his belt. The sniper won't be using night vision because of the green lights. The shot at the tie was a tight one—it came from Dryden's right, threading over the raised shoulder of the cave's exterior, along the oblique angle of the entrance and past Dryden's beating jugular. Dryden swings the machine gun into his grip. He just has to step out into the exposed air, fire at the box clamped to the cave entrance where he threw the switch, dousing the platform. Then turn and spray bullets in the sniper's direction before they can switch to night vision. Easy as Sunday morning.

"Joe?" calls Kristos. "Are you there?"

Shit.

Dryden rises, steps into the open, fires at the circuit breaker box, and in the rushing dark twists to the position of the sniper, squeezes off half a clip, and sprints—return fire scrapes his leg, a slice like a wand of ice—and he falls into Kristos's arms on the path.

"Go!"

The sniper has the high ground and by now the night vision on. What accounts for the moment's pause—is he wounded?

Dryden bundles Kristos into the toilet block, tackling him to the tiles as a bullet pops the window.

"Stay down," hisses Dryden. He forces Corso's pistol into Kristos's hands. "The safety is off. If you have to use it, aim at the torso and keep squeezing. Unless it's me."

"Shouldn't we run?" whispers Kristos. His face is soaked with sweat, maybe tears.

Dryden uses his cuff to dry Kristos's cheeks. "I don't run," he says.

There is an art to being quiet. An art made harder by limping. Dryden tears the sleeve off his jacket and makes a tourniquet beneath the knee. If he were the sniper, he wouldn't want to surrender the high ground at the peak of the mountain; he'd stay put, knowing his quarry had to attempt escape sometime. *But* this depends on how injured, if at all, the sniper is. He might need to retreat for aid. In which case the only way back down is the mountain path toward the plateau. He'd try this through the cover of trees, a wide arc around the ticket booth and toilets, watching for the door to open.

Dryden doesn't use the door. He pulls himself out of the window on the opposite side to the sniper and drops into the shrubbery. Then he begins to edge up the mountainside, keeping to the bushes, his steps light as wishes. He will come at the sniper from the rear, whether he is stationary or on the move. Dryden holds his breath. He listens to his heart slow: steady, untroubled, almost noiseless. His mind is empty but for one purpose, following the grooves of years that say it is a blessing to be empty, to be so purposeful.

He comes upon the sniper's nest from behind, cautiously entering the depression left by the shooter's prone position, storing its dimensions for later. He smells blood, then touches it, a patter on leaves. He waits. The murmur of trees. Infinitesimal whispers of shifting pebbles. Dryden follows the sound—and then stops as something clatters under his shoe. He reaches down. A sniper rifle. He cracks the chamber. Armor-piercing ammunition.

Joseph Dryden searches the area three times before conceding the sniper had some escape route that didn't involve descending to the plateau. How did they get up here in the first place? Parachute perhaps for in-fil, then ex-fil abseiling down the other side of the mountain, the rifle too heavy for whatever injury they sustained? And how did the sniper *know* to come up here? Only MI6 are aware of his location, and as ongoing action it won't have been filed yet, meaning only the people in Regent's Park, perhaps even only the people in Q Branch. Dryden is mulling that over when Moneypenny's voice interrupts his thoughts.

"004?"

Kristos is sitting on the floor outside the toilet block with his head in his hands. Dryden tells him to wait just a minute longer. He raises his phone-with-no-signal to his ear and pretends Moneypenny's voice is emanating from it, moving to the entrance of the cave, which stinks of gunfire.

"Here, ma'am."

"Are you injured?"

"Nothing to write home about."

"Good. Q Branch has hacked into Mr. Corso's car

computer. He makes frequent visits to the free port in Heraklion. There's no hope of being given a warrant. Search his home, phone, and personal computer for the number of his container there. Security is exceptionally tight. You'll also need his fingerprints."

Dryden peers over the edge of the no-railing, down to the darkness that is eating Mr. Corso. "Always carry a penknife, my old man used to say."

"Good advice. You might need some ice, too."

He looks toward the refreshment stands. "I'll see what I can rustle up. Any joy on the target?"

A pause. "Q has calculated likely targets. One of them is Camp X."

Dryden is utterly still. "That's where Luke is."

"Yes, I know," says Moneypenny briskly.

"He never should've been sent there. He didn't know what Paradise was planning."

"We've registered your complaints on that, thank you, 004. It's also where Colonel Mora is held."

Dryden draws a breath through his nostrils. "Free the world's terrorists."

"That's my fear. I'm going to the facility to have a talk with Colonel Mora, but first I'm going to arrange for an outside contractor to assist you. I need you to break into the Heraklion free port and see if you can learn anything from Mr. Corso's container."

"That's a waste of time. I should be assigned to protect Camp X."

"That's for me to judge. We need to know what the next detonator might be, or where it might come from, follow it to the Janus, allow the sale to take place, and follow the profits to the leader of the Gray Group before another six-day cycle has a chance to run down. All right, Joe? I need your head in the game on this."

Dryden grinds his teeth—then stops, remembering it sends static along the line and Moneypenny will hear it. "Yes, ma'am." He checks over his shoulder. "You don't trust our inside contractors?"

"I'm jumping at shadows."

"Well, be careful," says Dryden. "Sometimes they jump back. Will 000 provide me with backup?"

"000 is with Lisl Baum. He's just reported that Teddy Wiltshire has slipped surveillance. I've ordered him to see if he can pick up Wiltshire's scent, and if not, to track the sniper who fired upon you and killed Corso. I need you to do what you do best. Kick down some doors."

"With pleasure."

"Joe, one more thing. Did you tell anyone else you were heading up that mountain?"

"No, ma'am."

"Hmm. Watch your back, OK?"

"Always."

Dryden says goodbye to Kristos in the forecourt. He gives him the keys to the Lotus, taking Corso's Toyota Land Cruiser for himself.

Kristos stares at the keys in his palm. "I can keep it?"

"My advice is to sell it and use the money to do something real," says Dryden. "But I doubt you'll do that."

"No way!"

Dryden chuckles. "One last thing—I don't suppose you ever got a glimpse of any of Mr. Corso's passwords, by accident?"

"By accident?" A grin. "Yes. For his computer. French Connection, one word without any capitals, with threes for e's and zeroes for o's. But if you want to open his safe, I don't know the combination for that. He changed it every week."

"Do you know what he keeps in there?"

"I saw once. Money. A gun. Passports."

"Thanks, Kristos. You've been good luck."

Kristos frowns, weighs the keys in his hand, and then tiptoes to kiss Joe swiftly on the lips. Then he gets in the Lotus and drives away.

Dryden drops into the dead man's seat and closes the door of the Toyota. An evil eye hangs from the dashboard. Lucky Luke fills all of his senses, suddenly, overwhelmingly—the way he used to say: "Don't I bring you luck? Well, don't I?"

At the villa, water from the swimming pool cascades down the hillside, carrying with it olive stones, grass caught and straggled into messy wreaths, the branches of palms, frangipani heads, and the bare skeletons of sardines.

Ten
Night Duty

London

While 000 parties in Oman and 004 hunts down an agent in the smuggling chain in Crete, 003 stands at the open window of her office in the once grand building overlooking Regent's Park. Mostly, the peaceful office suits Harwood: her only contact the cleaner, or another staffer, who might ask if she fancies anything from the kitchen. She says yes or no, hello or goodbye, other people's secrets flowing over her. She is glad not to be observed by people who belong to the day, to avoid entanglement beyond small talk. Tick, tick, tick. The numbers race into infinite space she must occupy without Sid. It is usually just about bearable if no one catches her occupying it, if no one erects a mirror, bouncing her back to herself. But tonight, she wants more.

003 shakes her head—self-pity is a most unattractive quality. Her grandmaman used to say that. She urges the phone to give her something to do. Marilyn Aliyeva is safe, Harwood's job complete. A siren spools. She will be relieved at 6 a.m., when she will, she supposes, return to the Barbican and pretend to get some sleep. She thinks ahead to taking the lift to the twenty-eighth floor of Cromwell Tower, making a cup of tea, watching from the balcony as people blow across bridges and squares below. The stopped bottle that has lodged itself in her upper chest threatens to shatter at the idea. Tick, tick, tick. Are you going to stay frozen here for the rest of the time, Johanna Harwood? Close the curtains on daybreak, lie in bed with Sid's green world receiver on his pillow. He slept to its cycling songs and chatter, and now it is Harwood who skims the surface of sleep on the tide of radio waves, never quite dropping off.

What she needs is a measure of relief. Some comfort. A quantum of solace. But she doesn't know where to find it, nor the man who taught her that phrase.

The phone on Harwood's desk rings.

She says, "Duty office."

"Q Branch."

"Hello, Ibrahim."

"For the files—000 reports that Teddy Wiltshire has vanished in Oman."

Harwood notices that her hand holding the receiver is suddenly very cold.

Ibrahim continues: "And 004 reports that Laurent Corso, the Corsican agent, is dead. 004 is fine. We're recovering the sniper rifle."

"A sniper?"

"Yes. The sniper left their rifle behind, a Lobaev. That cross-checks with the assassin known as Trigger's weapon of choice—note that too. We'll test for fingerprints when Station G sends the package over."

"Anything I can do?"

Ibrahim sounds impatient as he says: "I'm just calling to give you the nightly report."

"Understood. Well, good night, Vienna."

"Excuse me?"

"It's just a—never mind."

She watches the mute phone for a few seconds. Then she lifts the receiver and tells the switchboard she'll be in Records. She types up her report quickly.

The agent Laurent Corso has been assassinated by Trigger, the sniper whose life Bond spared on a night when his introspection got the better of him, just as Harwood's introspection is getting the better of her now.

She checks the time. Quarter past one in the morning. Tick, tick, tick.

Here is a trail, a lifeline to grasp. Trigger was implicated in the mission that ended with Sid's death, her signature detected in the sniper fire that would have killed Felix Leiter were it not for Harwood's surgical skills, ghosts of a life not taken. A fork in the road. Now Trigger has resurfaced. And Harwood won't let her go to ground.

She couldn't save Sid. She will save James. Sid believed that saving one life saved all of humanity. Saving this life will save her own.

The big building possesses the lonely quality Harwood remembers from her university library at night. She filled hours then studying alone in the wake of her father's death. The library lights were on automatic sensors, like those here at Regent's Park. She was alone, and the grid would shut down around her, leaving her spotlit. When she strayed through the library stacks, the spotlight followed her in a series of muffled neon pops, the same that chases her down the corridor now, darkness stretching ahead and closing in behind. The walls murmur with the whir of overheated memories, data seeping from the building to a cold server in some desert. James used to say the Regent's Park building at night gave the sensation of being in a battleship in harbor. Johanna Harwood wonders what battle awaits as she swipes in to Records.

The computer scans her for facial recognition, unmercifully splitting the screen between her ID photo—near-black curly shoulder-length hair and bold eyebrows, high cheekbones, and strong jawline, a soft nose, and hazel eyes that a romantic might, and had, called bronze—and her drained, nocturnal reduction.

Harwood hunches in the seat. She navigates to the file on Trigger. Trigger's long, straight fair hair also falls to her shoulders, but shines, Bond's report observes, like molten gold. Oh brother. Trigger is as tall as Harwood, both hovering around five-nine.

Trigger and Bond met, or rather didn't meet, in Berlin. She was supposed to assassinate a traitor. Bond was supposed to keep her from doing it. Not so much a meet cute as a meet deadly. Bond described her beautiful, pale profile; how she carried the cello disguising her sniper rifle with a careless stride. Bond's spotter, Captain Sender, reported that Bond hesitated when he realized the sniper was the enchanting woman whose easy laughter outside the concert hall had pierced him. He let her get a few shots off before he fired and hit her gun hand. Bond's defense was that he had a long-range, one-sided romance with an unknown enemy agent who had much the same job in her outfit as he had in his, and he'd not been able to murder a woman in cold blood. He noted that she would likely be kicked out of the FSB, no use now as a sniper. He probably took her left hand. At the very least, he scared the living daylights out of her.

Research suggests she fits the profile of two Russian World Championship winners in long-range shooting, named Donskaya and Lomova. Rumor has it she now freelances. The status of her left hand is unknown.

And now she's killed the Corsican agent.

Harwood clicks through Laurent Corso's connections.

When she finds Marc-Ange Draco is Laurent Corso's godfather, she sits back in her chair, triggering the light in the ceiling grid above to flare.

Harwood blinks in its dazzling halo, staring at the photograph of Marc-Ange Draco: the creased face, the wide mouth sunk into folds that deepen when he smiles, caught in the crosshairs of an Interpol photographer. This man with the name of an angel, Marc-Ange Draco, is the head of the Union Corse mafia. He is also James Bond's father-in-law. His daughter, Tracy, was murdered by Ernst Stavro Blofeld, leaving Marc-Ange to outlive his only child, and James a widower who married at ten thirty in the morning and lost Tracy a little after midday—though he told Tracy, cradling her body in the smoking ruins of the car, that they had all the time in the world. When James explained this to Harwood, there were tears in his eyes—the first and only time she ever saw tears in his eyes.

Johanna Harwood scans through the surveillance photographs of Draco again, catching slices of her reflection every time the screen shudders black. What are you then, 003? You've buried your fiancé, and your old lover is missing, presumed dead. What label neatly wraps up your loss for public consumption? None. You belong in the cracks. You belong in the shadow. You always have.

At 6:20 a.m., Harwood isn't on the Underground threading through early commuters and late returners to the Barbican. She is behind the wheel of her Alpine A110S, letting the engine scare the pigeons into mushroom clouds as she rips through Regent's Park, sweeps up Baker Street, and pulls into Wellington Square, parking beneath the plane trees, her favorites because they remind her of Paris.

James Bond lives in the ground-floor flat of a converted Regency house whose white façade, sash windows, elaborate cornicing, and decorative balcony make her think for the first time of a piped wedding cake. Harwood digs her keys out of her bag, finding James's spare set. She tried to return the keys when she broke things off, but James refused, saying she should keep them in case he ever got lonely.

Harwood climbs the five steps to the black front door and lets herself in. As she crosses the threshold, she knows some hidden alarm will signal the intrusion to Moneypenny, who will have rigged the flat, hoping perhaps one day to be alerted to James popping home to pick up a few things—things Moneypenny draped in dustsheets. Harwood drifts past the book-lined sitting room with the bare Empire desk in the broad window, and follows her past self into the bedroom. The white and gold Cole & Son wallpaper, deep red curtains, dark blue linens on the double bed. It is all the same, like James simply stepped out for milk, as the saying goes.

Harwood drops to the mattress. Her knees hurt, as if she's run many miles, and she winces at the comfort of the springs. Her mind suddenly races, deciding what podcast she will summon on her phone to fill the silence, what noise might replace sleep, replace dreams, replace time and her in it. But then she breathes. Slips off her shoes and lifts her legs so she forms a compressed S. There are no framed portraits on Bond's bedside table. Not of Vesper Lynd, or Tracy, or even his parents. Only a clock, an upright brass thing the likes of which you find in hotels. Tick, tick, tick. Harwood watches its second hand wipe clean every degree of its face. Her eyes are closing. All her muscles suddenly tense, warning against deep sleep, warning against solace. Do the sheets smell of James? Does Harwood still smell of Bashir? She lifts her sleeve, watching the Casio hungrily eat the future. James's clock is behind the times, Sid's ahead of them. She smiles at that, and finally surrenders, rocked on the tick tick tick.

When she wakes, it's with a clear mind and a resolution. So you belong in the cracks. You belong in the shadows. Make a deal with them. Ask Marc-Ange to help you save his son-in-law.

Eleven
Cannon

Novi Sad

Rachel Wolff slips through the crowd squeezed between bars and restaurants crammed into colorful Austro-Hungarian houses on narrow Ulica Laze Telečkog. These people would have been in her year at school, probably. If she'd stayed in Serbia after her parents were killed, she'd be hanging with them now. No one recognizes her. All this time she's called herself Serbian. What does it mean, when the only person she knows is the infuriatingly self-possessed woman sipping tea in a neon spotlight, oblivious to the DJ's thumping bass?

Rachel says, "I'll accept a standing ovation."

Moneypenny finishes stirring her tea before clapping slowly.

Leeds, England. Four days earlier. Rachel Wolff was practicing the violin in front of a muted TV repeating footage of the BBC blast when she heard the muffled ding of her grandfather's shop bell between the vibrations of her strings. It was nearly closing time but she knew he would stay open to replace the customer's strap or take a peek at a self-winding mechanism. Clocks and watches were his passion. The shop also sold jewelry, all of it old pieces, but that was by the by to her grandfather. So Rachel was surprised when she heard her grandfather's heavy step on the stairs followed by a lighter tread. She lowered the bow and stood in the evening gold of the tall Victorian window, the needle at the back of her mind pushing red without much reason. She'd been raised suspicious, some might say distrustful. It was a survivor's trait.

"Well come in, come in . . . it's a bit of a tight squeeze I'm afraid, watch out for Rachel's bike—mind you, I'd prefer she stuck to this one instead of that motorcycle, the visions I have of her brains splattered all over the road, and me already losing her mother, you must know about that, the police never discovered . . ."

"Grandpa—" she began, then stopped as a stranger entered the room they simply called "the room" because it contained living room, kitchen, and her pullout bed.

"Penny, from your school, is here," he said. He inclined his head toward the woman, a look of slight confusion on his face. "Above her at school, you were?"

The stranger wore a cream silk shirt tucked into a broad black belt and a high-waisted camel skirt. Curly hair shimmered at her shoulders. She carried a suede satchel. Sheer tights. Camel high heels. On the breast of her shirt a brooch glittered. "Hi," she said. "You might not remember me—my cousin was in your year."

Rachel said nothing.

"I've come because my watch needs a new battery . . ." Rachel's grandfather raised the thing. "And I remembered your surname—Wolff and Granddaughter, it says outside. I thought it'd be fun to say hi."

"You already said hi."

The woman's innocent mouth twitched into a quizzical smile.

"I'll put the new battery in," said Rachel. "Give us a chance to catch up. How is your cousin Dorcas?"

Now the smile was really evident.

Rachel preceded the stranger down the narrow staircase. She dropped the shop counter between them.

"I don't know you," she said.

"Not even Dorcas?"

Rachel wasn't moved. "It's not polite to fool old men."

"It's not polite to break into people's homes and steal their diamonds."

Rachel's hand opened on reflex. She stared down dumbly for a second at the watch. "This is a Nanna Ditzel," she said.

"You know your designers."

Rachel readied the battery, the tools, the magnifying glass. At least, someone did. Her mind was tunneling to a point in childhood when her mother told her what to do if she was ever caught. Bluff it out. That's your job. Her father disagreed. Remove the problem directly but with as little violence as possible, he said. Fear is a better motivator than a weapon.

Rachel looked up into the cool eyes facing her. She couldn't frighten this person.

"Listen, I humored you upstairs for my grandfather's sake. You've either mistaken me for someone or you're some sort of con woman. Either way, I'm happy to replace your battery—which will be three pounds, no cards accepted for anything under a fiver, there's a cash machine around the corner. Then I have to pull down the shutters for the night. I don't want any part in what you're playing."

The woman pulled out her wallet—fine leather, handmade. "As it happens, I have the change."

"Great." Rachel yanked the lamp closer.

The woman bent over a tray of rings. The sparkle of sapphires and rubies played over her face. "Did you steal these, too? It puts your grandfather in danger, if you're fencing from his shop."

"It would," said Rachel, pursing her lips, "if I was a thief. As I'm not . . ."

"Your grandfather moved here from Serbia as a displaced person in 1950, is that right? He was in the camps."

Rachel's mouth turned chalk dry. "Who are you?"

"He brought his father's trade here," continued the woman. "Watchmaker. Married an actress—a very glamorous local girl of German-Jewish extraction who became an actress. He was happy with his cogs and dials while your grandmother appeared on television, even film. Your grandmother died shortly after your mother went missing. Shock, your grandfather says. Your mother was curious about where her father's family came from. She studied Slavic languages and went to Serbia on a year abroad scheme, where she met your father. She'd inherited the acting gene, which was useful to him. He was a diamond thief, an original Chevalier. Each Chevalier cell has a woman. As your mind ran to cons, let's start there. Your mother's job was to con shopkeepers or hoteliers while she carried out the necessary surveillance ahead of the robbery—they had to believe she was a prospective customer with money to spare. She needed nerves of steel and a strong mind. She carried off disguises with the ease of costume changes between scenes. One day she's blond, the next brunette. Fake nails, real pearls. She has a little dog under her arm, or always talks on the phone. The small things that make a person real. She changes identity so much she feels like a doll renamed by a little girl every day."

"How could you know that?" Rachel's voice was a whisper. She remembered her mother sitting at her bedside, telling her urgently: *We must persuade your father it's time to quit, to go back to England. I can't bear it anymore. I am like a doll with a new costume and a new name every day.* But how was she supposed to convince her father of anything? There was always one more job. One last job.

The stranger said, "You've a screw loose."

"Excuse me?"

She pointed at the silver glint in the carpet. Rachel did nothing to pick it up.

"Your mother said those words to us. She wanted a way out. She was afraid."

"Us?"

The woman came closer. She placed her hands on the polished oak, fingers spread. "Your father was a safecracker. He taught you the ear for it, and the mind. He passed on to you the safecracker's particular brand of alertness, too. Your parents were training you."

"It was just playacting."

"I thought you wanted no part in plays?"

"I was a child."

"And now?"

Rachel checked the door at the top of the staircase was still closed. She said hoarsely, "I sometimes . . ."

"Why?"

"It pays."

"Do you need the money?"

"High streets are dying, haven't you heard?"

"Maybe you need the rush. Maybe you were fed adrenaline in the womb. Maybe it's just easier than thinking about the past. Or maybe it's all about the past. One last job—always one last job." The eyes became kind, a shutter opening. "Until your parents didn't come back. The daughter of thieves on a path to self-destruction because she doesn't have any closure for the loss of her parents. That's what our profiler says."

A car honked outside, making Rachel jump.

"Do you know what a cannon is?" asked the woman.

"I wouldn't mind being shot out of one right now."

No polite laugh. "A cannon is a professional thief in the employ of security services, usually hired to steal secrets from opposing outfits. You moved here when you were fourteen, an orphan. We keep watch of the orphans of subjects of interest. They often make good recruits."

"You're a cold bitch, you know that?"

"Yes. It's my job."

"Put that at the top of your résumé, do you?"

"I recruit people with valuable skills who might like to serve their country—instead of going to prison for multiple diamond thefts."

Rachel picked up the screw, tossing it between her palms.

"Safecracking demands high mathematical intelligence, exceptional planning, and paranoia. A good knowledge of explosives, too. All key qualities of a good spy. Your mother hoped we'd take her and your father on. What she had to offer was the emotional intelligence, memory, problem-solving skills, and charisma of the expert con artist. Also key qualities of a good spy. You offer both sets of skills, but you're wasting them and your future on petty crimes. You could be using those skills to serve your country, the country your grandfather made his home as a refugee."

Rachel shifted her jaw from side to side. "I don't

know what you mean by *my* country. I'm Serbian. The UK government hasn't cared for my grandfather, and it doesn't care for me or any of my neighbors."

"I suppose you'd tell me it's terribly old-fashioned to believe we should be the change we want to see in the world."

"I'd tell you to go tug on someone else's heartstrings."

"Well, if all this isn't enough to persuade you, it might interest you to know that this particular mission includes the diamond pipeline your parents went down—and from which they never reemerged."

Rachel straightened. "Those pipelines are different now."

"Your parents were double-crossed, we don't know by whom. I can put you amongst the players. This could be your only chance to win justice for your parents. Or you can leave here in a police car and break your grandfather's heart."

"Not much of a choice," said Rachel.

The woman looked surprised. "I don't recall announcing myself as your fairy godmother."

"Why should I trust you?"

The woman was ready to snap a retort, but then paused. A dog barked on a nearby balcony, hollering its aggression into the hot air. Once it quieted, the woman offered a hand.

"My name is Moneypenny. I work for the British government. I'm here to ask for your help. The attack on the BBC yesterday was funded by the people I want to stop. Will you help me?"

"How?"

"I need you to steal a diamond watch from a gangster. My agent will be present but will not know of your role or intentions. This is strictly off-book. There are reasons for that on my end, and it's nonnegotiable. Chatter says the Chevaliers want the watch. You're going to steal it and use it to partner with them, work your way down the pipeline, and find out who's on the other side. Your mission is to identify the Janus of diamonds, the man who deals from the black market to the white, and whomever they answer to."

"The diamond Janus isn't the target?"

"Not ultimately. I want their boss: the ringleader of this racket for terror. This mission is highly dangerous and if you're caught I won't be coming after you. But if you make it, your country will owe you a blank slate. And your grandfather's business rates will be lowered by the local council. Fair deal?"

Rachel took her hand.

Now, Rachel Wolff pours herself a cup of tea. "When will I enter the diamond pipeline?"

Moneypenny says, "An agent of mine needs your help breaking into a free port in Crete first."

Rachel glances at the neighboring table, where a gang of friends argue in a cloud of cigarette smoke. "You're kidding, right? Those things are worse than banks."

"You can't speak aloud around him. His comms are always open, and no one can know you're involved in this."

"Why's that again?"

"I believe you're familiar with British Sign Language?"

Rachel rolls her eyes at Moneypenny's deflection. "Yes, I took a few modules at university."

"Good. Use that. It's imperative no one hears your voice. I've played this game before and it cost me, but I fear I don't have many other options."

"Shtum it is. I like your brooch—is that a sunfish?"

Gratifying surprise. "Yes. It was a birthday gift from my first chief."

"They had good taste."

"Antiquated, really," says Moneypenny. "But there was something comforting about that."

"Do you get on with your new chief?"

"Hmm? Yes. You know, you'd make a good spy."

"Whatever you say. After the free port, then what?

You said I'd find the people responsible for my parents' deaths." Rachel keeps her composure as she says this, but not without a struggle.

After Moneypenny's visit, Rachel told her grandfather that a friend who worked reviewing hotels had offered her a job and she'd be going away from time to time. She was dumping pasta in a pot as she delivered this lie, her grandfather slumped on the sofa listening to witnesses describe the BBC bombing on the radio. When he said, "I suppose you've run out of hotels to rob here," she lost her grip on the Kilner jar and the whole half-kilo of fusilli splashed into the boiling water.

She didn't dare face him, so she addressed the tea towel she used to dab her scalded hands. "I have a chance to find out what happened to my parents. I have to know."

The voice on the radio described the terrible noise of the shattering glass, and for a moment Rachel thought her grandfather wouldn't reply. But then he said: "Good. Bring the men responsible to justice. Come back here and tell me what happened to my little girl. But remember, Rachel, you are my little girl, too."

"Grandpa . . ."

He held up a finger. "You are worth more than this. Do not sell your virtue to vice, do not sell it to vengeance. Remember, when we read the ten plagues that God gave the Egyptians, you dip your finger into the wineglass and take out a drop for each misery. We celebrate the freedom of Jews around the world, but we do not rejoice in the suffering of our tormentors. Vengeance is not Jewish."

Rachel stuck her smarting hands underneath the cold tap. "I remember reading something about an eye for an eye."

Her grandfather's voice stung. "You know better than that. What do you want to be? A thug, or a thinker? I won't visit you in prison."

The witness on the radio was crying.

Rachel shut off the water. "Then tell me not to go."

"I can tell you nothing. You never listen to me. You feel you must know what happened to your parents. So, you must. But make sure your motivation is justice, Rachel. Justice, not vengeance. Justice, not an excuse to get your kicks as a criminal like your father."

Rachel whispered, "My father was a good man."

But her grandfather pretended not to hear, turning up the radio, where the prime minister's statement was playing again. By the time the mayor of London picked up the baton, Rachel's grandfather's face had gone blank. He had forgotten the whole exchange. She said, "Do you remember my friend Kitty, she reviews hotels for a travel company? She's offered me a job, so I'm going to be away from time to time."

"Wonderful, darling, that's wonderful. Are you listening to this? I told you fascism was coming again. What have I been telling you?"

"It isn't that bad, Grandpa."

"You young people know nothing."

Rachel watched the lump of pasta congeal. Now she watches Moneypenny stir her cup, thanking the waiter for the refill.

Moneypenny says, "There's a good chance you'll find the man responsible for your parents' deaths. But what I want is the identity of the person in charge of the whole racket." She arranges a silver milk jug, a sugar bowl, and a dish for the used tea leaves into a triangle. "So far, evidence suggests there are three Janus operatives involved." Moneypenny raises the sugar. "Diamonds." Then the silver jug. "Antiquities." Then the leaves. "And people. Together, this network of Janus operatives is funding terror. But for a setup like this to work, there has to be someone in charge. A god of gods. A treasurer to terror." Moneypenny clinks the spoon against the teapot. "I want the identity of the boss. Your mission is to find the diamond Janus, and then discover who he reports to."

"And breaking into a free port helps this how?"

"We need to collect fingerprint and particulate evidence from a container. It may point to the source of the next sale, even the identity of the antiquities Janus. Afterward, you'll contact the new Chevalier leader. You'll tell him you can't fence the blind man's watch yourself, and suggest going fifty-fifty. We've identified him as Marko Jovanović."

With the name, the sweat of the crowd and scent of beer and coffee and gibanica wrapped in grease-stained paper all fades. Instead, she can smell the Danube, stirring just a few streets away. So much water under the bridge.

Hello, blue eyes.

Twelve
Talk with the Devil

Location undisclosed

The subterranean cell sits at the bottom of a well ten stories deep, connected to the hexagonal gantry by one retractable bridge. There are no windows. The door never cracks. A steel grille at head height can be opened and shuttered. Moneypenny stands, as she has many times, peering through the bars at the giant hunkered by the desk, half-turned toward the door as if deciding whether or not to answer the summons of a bell. His head is shaven. His gray flannel uniform fails to shrink his scale.

Moneypenny leans a shoulder against the steel. "You don't look surprised to see me again so soon."

Mora smiles widely. His tongue is a chewed-up

scarlet stub that turns Moneypenny's stomach despite her best efforts. "Why talk of the devil when you can talk with him?"

"Are your friends planning to break you out of here, Colonel?"

He scratches his neck. When he speaks, his voice is a hiss, the consonants bleeding. "I don't answer your questions when your drones take to blinding me or drowning me or deafening me. Why would I answer you today?"

"I don't know," says Moneypenny cheerfully. "Why did you answer me last time?"

"I wasn't aware I had."

"The master of interrogation lets something slip without knowing it—somehow I don't quite believe that."

"You flatter me. What did I give away?"

"You've been here a long time with no attempt made to free you. In that period, there have been terror attacks on public institutions, schools, concert halls . . . Rattenfänger hasn't broken its stride for a single second since losing its Colonel. It's almost as if you don't matter. They don't need you. Now there's a supposition they want to liberate you. I wonder if our conversation touched a nerve and Rattenfänger concluded they would be wise to have you either killed or freed. For some reason you're more valuable free."

"An important lesson," says Mora. "Always be more valuable alive than dead. A lesson James knows well."

Moneypenny stills. Electricity shivers through her. She says, as impartially as she can manage, "How is James?"

Mora puts his head back and laughs so hard the chair under him shakes.

Moneypenny feels her ears redden and pulls her curls over them.

Mora wipes his eyes. "Forgive me. I fear you suffer sweet Johanna's ailment. That scoundrel. I don't suppose there's any woman in your service he didn't fuck?"

"Me, as a case in point—not that it matters."

"Doesn't it?" He tuts. "You carry a torch for him. Well, I can tell you James was alive the last time I saw him."

"When was that?"

"We moved him out of the base in Syria when we installed Dr. Nowak there. It seemed prudent. I knew Johanna would not be far behind. I'm sure she found his empty cell."

"Moved him where?"

Mora shrugs. "Who can say? I've been rather cut off from things of late."

"Not for much longer, perhaps."

"Yes." He rises to his full height—he has to stoop

under the ceiling—and rolls his shoulders, a grinding, crunching noise. "Perhaps you're right. Perhaps our most recent conversation touched a nerve and my organization decided it's time to free me, no matter how arduous or costly."

Moneypenny fits her thumbnails together, out of sight; all of the pressure she feels is contained in her hands. "Last time I was here, I asked who makes decisions for Rattenfänger. I reminded you a colonel isn't a king. It's the first time you've answered me. You told me Rattenfänger is a plutocracy. Money is king. I wrote up my report, of course. And now we get wind Rattenfänger wants to break you out. Is that a coincidence?"

A shrug so slow it is more of a stretch.

Moneypenny tries another tack. "Who runs the money?"

He looms closer, then closer still, until she can feel his breath bearing down on her through the grille. "Do you have a guess?"

Moneypenny wants to cover her nose—the fumes from his mouth are as bad as gases she's smelled from dead bodies. But she doesn't, hazarding instead the carefree attitude of a Christmas game of trivia: "Teddy Wiltshire?"

Mora taps his chin. "I don't think I know the fellow."

Moneypenny persists: "Does he run the ring of Janus operatives who fund Rattenfänger—the Gray Group?"

"Imaginative name. What exactly do you think he's *selling*? Guns? Gold? Oil? I suppose it could be anything, really . . ."

Moneypenny frowns. "He doesn't sell. He buys. For his own collections."

"Yes," says Mora, almost encouragingly.

"He runs the Gray Group, but keeps out of it?"

"Not quite."

"What does he sell, then?" asks Moneypenny.

Mora reaches a single finger through the grille. He traces her cheek.

Moneypenny remains motionless as his blunt fingertip trails down her jawline to her throat, over her larynx, toward the open buttons of her shirt. Mora can paralyze or even kill with a few stabs of his finger, targeting nerve endings. His finger nudges her collar this way and that, probing her bones. His shirt is loose, and she sees the tattoo of the death's-head hawk moth over his chest stirring.

Mora whispers, "I can tell you, Ms. Moneypenny, that Teddy Wiltshire would make a small fortune out of you."

"He'd make a fortune out of—because he's still in the people racket. Teddy Wiltshire is the Janus of human trafficking."

"He might even disappear them."

"Then Teddy would know where James is?"

"Now *there's* a thought," he says, caressing her top button. "If only you could ask him. You should improve your surveillance."

"What makes you think we've lost Wiltshire?"

Mora chuckles. "Never play poker, Ms. Moneypenny. You have lost him, and you won't find him."

"Why's that?"

"Teddy can perform miracles. Don't you think he'll perform one on himself? He fucked up, and a lot of important people have had enough of his antics. And once he's gone . . ." He withdraws his finger and blows on his hand as if scattering a dandelion head.

"What makes James more valuable alive than dead?"

"What a heartless question."

Moneypenny breathes out her frustration and elation, the giddy line of an interrogation that tips between success and being played. She wonders if this is how Bill Tanner felt when he was interrogating Mora all those years ago, trying to turn the terrorist, and found himself turned instead. She asks, "So the Gray Group does fund Rattenfänger?"

"Chaos breeds chaos. Loot, steal, blow up, create conflict, displacement, war, instability, poverty, looting . . ."

"To what end?"

"To what end, indeed."

"Does the person who runs the Gray Group run Rattenfänger itself?"

"No. They are simply Rattenfänger's banker. But imagine what they might know about our operations. You may wish to add how very helpful I've proven in your report."

"Why?" says Moneypenny, crossing her arms. "You're hoping you'll get time off for good behavior?"

"I don't expect I'll need it."

Moneypenny says, "So you did answer me in order to trigger panic in Rattenfänger. But that suggests you think Rattenfänger can read MI6's reports. How? Your access to Q was shut down."

"Was it?" Mora turns away, but not before tossing over his shoulder: "Give sweet Johanna my best. Tell her I dream of her. And I hope she still dreams of me . . ."

Moneypenny opens James Bond's front door and pauses on the threshold. The sense of a fresh disturbance strikes her instantly. She does not feel sentiment for the ghostly furniture, the dusty bottles on the shelves. At least, that's what she tells herself. Instead, she searches for what has been touched. James's go bag is missing from the wardrobe. Missing, too, is the bag of Johanna Harwood's belongings that 003 failed to collect after the breakup. And something is here that wasn't here before.

Moneypenny sits down on James's side of the bed and picks up Harwood's Hermès watch. It is as explicit as a note would have been.

Johanna Harwood has gone rogue.

Why? Moneypenny made sure the potential of Mora's prison as a target did not reach Harwood's ears—she logged it herself in a file of active threats above Harwood's access level. But she has wondered how long it would take 003 to boil over. If M thinks this period one of convalescence, Moneypenny knows all they've done is set the water simmering, something that has suited her for reasons she can't quite articulate.

She turns the watch over. Perhaps it's the same reason she's turned to Rachel Wolff for outside help. This doubt—was it confirmed last night by the sniper on the mountain in Crete?—that Tanner acted alone. Perhaps she believed Johanna Harwood would take matters into her own hands if isolated long enough, off the radar and away from intruding eyes. As she is doing now.

Moneypenny pulls out her phone and checks the tracking device on Bashir's Casio watch, but the records show it was disabled after 009 was processed in the morgue. The psychiatrist at Shrublands recommended Moneypenny encourage Harwood to stop wearing it. But that felt to her like asking a believer not to wear a Star of David or a hijab, and that's not the kind of MI6 she is interested in running.

Moneypenny switches on the bedside lamp and holds the Hermès watch next to the old-fashioned alarm clock James once said was good for bludgeoning a man to death if needed. Both clock faces are synchronized. Living the same time. She wonders if James and Johanna are both dreaming the same nightmare.

Sidereal

Thirteen
Beyond the Black Stump

Australia

Anna Petrov joined the farm on a workaway scheme at the height of Australia's summer.

It was pure chance that meant she was not in the hotel room when her husband, Mikhail, was assassinated by Rattenfänger. She and Mikhail had traveled to Sydney for a conference because it was as far away from home as they could get. Mikhail's plan was to buy false passports there. He had the kind of mind that would fix on how things ought to be, and expect reality to follow. So: fake passports. Did he know *how* to buy fake passports? No. But he said they would buy them, and felt secure in his plan. It was Anna who bribed the kitchen porter, who knew someone whose cousin had a friend who could contact a guy who helped out migrants without papers. It was Anna who went to pick up the new identities, because Mikhail was drunk. She called him once she had the passports in her hand, but a strange voice answered after too many rings with a cautious "Yes?" So she fled.

It was the next day at a rest stop when Anna saw the news about the body discovered in the hotel. She watched all the color drain from her face in the smeared reflection of the TV screen over the counter. It would take months for the color to return. She had the false passport and visa. She signed up for the workaway scheme, calling herself a gap-year kid, though she was a decade older; something about the frailty of her bones meant people believed her. She drifted between vineyards, old people's communities, and private tutoring until she found the ranch.

It was perfect, a farm at the end of a long dust track off Highway One, Western Australia. The Greyhound passed once a week with the mail, dropping a sack in the weather-beaten oil drum that served as a postbox. This was the rusted center of Australia. Lush rain forests, parted by railway track and tarmac, played now like a fabricated memory. The farm was called "The Black Stump," a joke another woofer—that was the name for workaways—explained to her. *Beyond the black stump* was slang for middle of nowhere. Exactly where she wanted to be.

Anna had grown up in St. Petersburg. To her, Western Australia may as well have been the flame red of Mars; the ghost gums like petrified sentinels of abandoned explorers on a foreign planet, remnants of Wanderers in the Noon Universe, novels she read secretly as a teenager because they belonged to her brother. At night, she learned new constellations. The Milky Way was like nothing she'd ever seen before: the barrier between this world and the next was paper-tissue thin and heaven showed through in great, generous bursts. A dark shape swam alongside. A sacred emu, she was told.

An astronomer trapped her in conversation once at a dinner party. He talked about sidereal time, measured using Earth's rotation in relation to fixed stars. A sidereal day was four minutes shorter than a solar day. Here beyond the black stump she was out of sync with local time, unmoored, peeling away from the curvature of the Earth, which she could see bending in the desert. She was floating into the throbbing blue sky and the burnt white hole of the sun. Sidereal, side reel, afternoon show at the cinema, ducking out of school. Sideshow, separate from the main event, which was her life as it was supposed to be lived, one of ease and promise. Sideshow freak, watched, not watched over. None of this was meant to happen. Detached. Outside of time. Only sidereal.

Heat warmed her from inside out, a slow thaw. The Black Stump was run by a couple in their seventies with skin hard as the earth. They understood she did not want to talk, and they did not ask questions. She was good with horses—she loved riding as a child—and was soon given the stables as her circumference. Rubbing the animals down, entering their cloud of dust, batting away flies, wiping mud and grit clear, she whispered to them about the spy who loved her. His name was James Bond.

He loved her because he wanted what was inside her husband's head. Then he loved her because of something she stirred in him when she looked up beneath her long lashes and gifted him the secret of her smile.

Did he really love her, or only enjoy her as much as he was capable? Did he truly feel responsibility for her, or was she simply the latest in a long line of women he promised to save? It didn't matter. What mattered was how he held her: as if she was a precious resource he would do anything to defend. Mercenary, yes. But still, it meant she was a treasure to him. She felt safe when he brushed the hair from her face and gently kissed both of her closed eyes. She felt wanted when his gaze hungered after her across a room. She felt listened to when they took a drive and he tilted his head just slightly, murmuring "yes" or "then what?" to her stories about Mikhail. When he said, softer than early rain, "Trust me"—she believed him. When he said, "I'll keep you safe"—she believed him. When he said, "Rattenfänger knows. I'll lead them away from you"—she believed him. When he said, "Go with 009, you can trust him like you trust me"—did she believe him then? What if she and Mikhail had followed that other spy, had boarded the train in Barcelona? Would they both still be alive? Yes. No. Maybe. The horses have no answer. Neither does she.

Now, after months beyond the black stump, it matters less. Color has returned to her cheeks like a revived floodplain. Here in the desert, she is coming alive. She is safe, alone.

Until another woofer arrives, a veteran of many wars for many armies who is now trying to find peace. The owners of the ranch believe Anna and the soldier might help each other come back to life. But the blood saps from Anna's cheeks once again. The man receives too much mail, sends too many letters, calls too many people.

One day, he asks her if she ever had a different surname. It may be chance. It may be fate. It may be nothing at all.

But still she presses her face to the velvet nose of her favorite horse one last time, telling the animal that maybe she was never meant to survive this life. The horse gently presses its head to her neck, trying to keep her riveted to the spot.

The Greyhound is coming. The road is a length of black rope long enough to hang yourself.

PART II
Stolen

Fourteen
"Break and Enter"

Crete

Joseph Dryden answers the knock at the door. The woman standing by the breakfast trolley wears the hotel uniform, and her tan and platinum hair could easily slot her into the twenty-something crowd that works the tourist trade and lives for the beach. In fact, there is nothing to tip him off that she isn't who she purports to be. If you were distracted by female beauty, she would be distractingly beautiful, tall with graceful movements as she wheels the trolley across the blue and white checkerboard tiles, a delicate bone structure that suggests you ought to be gallant and help her out, but beneath that an ineffable impression—a glint in her green eyes, a curve to the wide red lips as she accepts the tip—that while you play the gallant she'll be helping herself to your wallet. There is nothing so unusual in that. But Dryden can sense competence: he is drawn to people who are at the top of their game, and he gets the feeling this woman isn't at the top of hotel portering. So it isn't much of a surprise when she closes the door to the room with her still in it.

He is slightly more surprised when she turns around and signs: "No voices. Moneypenny's orders. I'm here to help you break and enter."

He sizes her up once more, wondering where Moneypenny finds them, and then signs: "The hand is in the cooler."

She signs, "What about his right eyeball?"

Dryden's face falls. He signs, "No one told me we'd need it."

"There's no free port without it. Can we get to the body?"

"It'll be an ugly exhumation, I can tell you that."

She grins suddenly, signing: "Just kidding."

"Oh good," he signs, looking at her dimly. "Everyone loves a kidder."

She winks at him. "My name is Rachel Wolff."

"004."

"Double O—what does that mean?"

Dryden sighed. "That you've killed two people in

the line of duty and been rewarded with the Double O prefix—the license to kill."

Rachel Wolff raises her eyebrow. "You've killed two people?"

"I've killed hundreds of people."

"Oh good," she signs, returning his dim look. "Everyone loves a killer."

Joseph Dryden and Rachel Wolff share his breakfast on the balcony, where the sun blazes off the white marble. Both wear mirrored sunglasses, and watch themselves watch the other over coffee. A breeze that carries the sea plays with the gauzy curtains, tossing shadows.

Eventually, Dryden signs: "So, how will we do it?"

Rachel folds her napkin. She signs, "How would you do it, if I wasn't here?"

A shrug. "Drop into the night manager's house and persuade him he'd like to help me."

"What did he ever do to you—besides oversee what essentially amounts to a tax-free bank without any oversight, whose holdings cross borders with no questions asked on behalf of the mega-wealthy? He's just a guy with a perfectly legal job that probably doesn't pay that well."

"I don't leave *permanent* damage."

"What a slogan."

He smirks. "All right. Got a better idea?"

"Free ports face a security dilemma. There are no records of clientele or content. Privacy is paramount to people who want to store their art or wine collection tax-free and unregistered. That means no security cameras, no facial recognition, not even names. That's where biometrics come in. All the data is air-gapped—it can't be hacked. The main entrance uses a palm scanner, which is more reliable than fingerprints. Once inside, clientele swap their own phones for a tablet, which does two things. First: this free port is known as the Labyrinth, because—well, Crete, but also because of its design. Think M. C. Escher. The layout is meant to disorientate. None of the vaults are numbered. There are no signs. Your tablet guides you to your container."

"You sign well. And second?"

"Gait recognition," signs Rachel.

"After 9/11," signs Dryden, "DARPA poured millions into developing gait recognition as a cornerstone in its Total Information Awareness counterterrorism program—to very little avail. Limp, or carry a duffel bag, or even just jog and you can obstruct or confuse the recognition system."

"Right," signs Wolff. "And there the technology stayed until we all voluntarily started carrying accelerometer sensors in our pockets. Your phone measures your gait. Accelerometer scanners can verify your gait to ninety-nine point four percent accuracy. The Labyrinth staff check your phone's data against their existing data for you. If they don't tally, they feed you to the Minotaur. If they do tally, they give you the tablet, which is loaded with gait biometric data they recorded when you first signed up, and on every visit after that. You start the journey to your vault and if your gait doesn't match what the tablet expects by even one step, the tablet pings the building's alarms."

"I've got Corso's phone," signs Dryden. "We could swap his gait data for mine, right?"

"If he'd never visited the free port before, we could. But the gait information collected by the tablet is stored for comparison next time he visits."

"You said the data is air-gapped. Can we get to the physical computer?"

She shakes her head. "It's inside the building. And to get in you have to pass—"

"The gait recognition sensors. Right. Then I could get through the first gates by using Corso's dismembered hand?"

"Not something you hear much in average conversation, but sure."

He plows on: "But as soon as I'm holding their tablet and take a step forward, the mission is FUBAR."

She frowns.

He signs: "Fucked up beyond all repair."

"I'll remember that one."

"Why not just drop the tablet, then?"

"This is where we run into problem number three," she signs.

"Oh good."

"The Labyrinth uses what the US military calls STORMS, which stands for Sense Through Obstruction Remote Monitoring System, or Someone That Obviously Relishes Military Slang."

Dryden pushes his tongue into the inside of his cheek.

"It's billed as a 'human life form detection system' using advanced penetrating radar. If you move in that building, STORMS senses it by transmitting an advanced electromagnetic waveform through walls and receiving the return waves that bounce off any targets or materials in its path. The electromagnetic waves pick up the radio frequency of the tablet. If you're walking around empty-handed, STORMS senses it and sets off the building's alarms for as long as you're in there with a beating heart."

"FUBAR again."

"Right. But as it happens, FUBAR is what we want."

"How's that?"

"You pull up to the main entrance with dismembered hand in, well, hand. You make it inside. They give you the tablet. You enter the labyrinth and trigger the alarms. Then you evade capture, or engage in hopefully not-so-mortal combat, for exactly forty minutes, triggering the building's alarm system for that entire duration. Then you escape unscathed. Or maybe a little scathed."

Dryden rolls his shoulders. "And while I'm being scathed, what are you doing for those forty minutes?"

"I'll already be in the building. The Labyrinth is climate-controlled and meticulously maintained. Cleaners are given a smaller version of the tablet to carry on their rounds. It's a little less shiny but just as accurate. The service entrance doesn't have a palm reader, only a fingerprint scanner. I've liberated a tablet covered in fingerprints from a cleaner who I can resemble with a few modifications and a stellar performance. The Labyrinth has a week's worth of data on her. I've watched her walk. I can keep it going long enough to get me into the service elevator, at least. After that, the zero point six percent fallibility is likely to have run its course. That's where you come in."

"I set the alarms off, everyone sees there's someone in the building who shouldn't be there, but doesn't look further than me."

"That's the idea. Especially if I can maintain at least eighty percent accuracy, their limit of suspicion. No one will worry about that with you running around. It should take fifteen minutes to get to the vault."

"How do you figure?"

She smiles. "People leave their phones with security. A simple google tells you how long those phones—or the people who own them—averagely stay there. Call it fifteen minutes to reach your vault, ten minutes inside, fifteen minutes to exit through the gift shop. Forty minutes."

"I have the combination for the external door to Corso's vault. Found it scribbled on the paperwork in Corso's house. Not the brightest of dead guys. That said, the Labyrinth provide safes for their clients *inside* the containers, as I understand it. I don't have a combination for the safe, though I dusted the safe at his villa. He changed the combination weekly, so it was mostly a mess, but I picked up a few clusters."

"Did you get it open?"

"That would have taken a wall charge or a gift from Q and I had neither. Safecracking isn't my line."

"Well, 004, this should be the start of a beautiful friendship."

"You can crack it?"

"And take the necessary soil samples and fingerprint

scans from the objects inside in ten minutes, gathering all the evidence you need to discover provenance and the identity of the smugglers, maybe even the identity of the antiquities Janus. Then I leave through the service entrance while you do whatever you do to leave moderately scathed."

"Now it's moderately scathed, I see."

"We'll also need a getaway vehicle. An Audi preferably. And we'll need to know the local police time. My guess is they won't call the police immediately. Too much exposure. But if they hit the alarm, we need to know how soon to expect sirens. A tap on the police station would help."

Dryden holds up a finger. He clears his throat. "Aisha, Ibrahim—you there?"

Rachel Wolff looks around, then back at him with a well-aren't-you-fancy expression, twisting to inspect both of his ears.

He says, "I need to know the average local police response time. And to tap the police radio network."

Aisha's voice slips inside his head: "Working . . . it's twelve minutes. They blame the traffic."

"Of course they do. Thanks, Aisha."

Aisha says, "Anything else we can do for you?"

"That's all."

"Then have a swim for me. Over and out."

Dryden signs to Rachel, "Twelve minutes. Apparently, the traffic is hell."

She signs, "How do you do that? You're not even wearing an earpiece."

"We get all the toys."

She grins. "Maybe being a spy isn't so bad."

Fifteen
The Labyrinth

Crete

Daedalus brought Time to the court of King Minos. As an inventor, he perfected the art of tightly coiling steel into springs, controlling the wheels and chains of incredible mechanisms that could mark the passage of hours with precision. It was Daedalus who designed the Labyrinth to lock up the bastard offspring of Queen Pasiphaë, wife of King Minos, and the beautiful white bull sent by Poseidon. The child was half-bull and half-man. The Minotaur. The Labyrinth was a puzzle of blank walls, dead ends, stairs to nowhere, identical corridors, and symmetrical galleries. The door was always open. Any could enter. None could leave. The design of the passageways fed victims into the stone chamber that caged the Minotaur at the heart of the Labyrinth. In order to save Athens from Minos's fleet, King Aegeus agreed to sacrifice seven Athenian girls and seven Athenian boys to the Minotaur annually. After five years, King Aegeus's son Theseus said enough. Theseus offered himself. It was Daedalus who advised him to carry a ball of string into the Labyrinth, tie one end to the door, and unwind it behind him so that he could find his way out again. When Theseus reached the Minotaur, the tragic creature engaged in a duel because it was the only way Theseus could honorably take his life. He wanted to die. Theseus followed the thread to freedom, taking Princess Ariadne with him. They escaped. For helping the young lovers, King Minos imprisoned Daedalus and his son Icarus. Daedalus improvised bird wings from feathers and candle wax. But his son, famously, would fly too close to the sun.

Joseph Dryden wonders if that is exactly what he is about to do as he eases the Audi to the head of the short queue waiting to enter the Labyrinth. Another school of thought says that Minos's daughter Ariadne asked Daedalus the secret of the Labyrinth and gave Theseus both thread and sword. Dryden hopes Rachel can be his Ariadne. The air smells of salt and rust. The jetty wall of Heraklion port is guarded by the sixteenth-century Venetian Koules fortress. Inside its arm, the shipyard is active with ferries constantly slotting in and out of the passenger docks. But customs takes up most of the port, containers forming a colorful Tetris for satellites. With globalization, maritime transport has been made as frictionless as possible to support trade. Of course, this comes with security trade-offs. Some of the crates and containers will contain drugs and guns. Or desperate people. Revenue from shipping itself is used to fund terrorism, or launder funds for terrorism. But the real dread—considered a high threat since 9/11—is terrorists inserting operatives into the maritime industry who can use cargo to smuggle explosives or even bioweapons into the ports of major cities.

Dryden examines the rusted warehouses over his sunglasses. Despite such security vulnerabilities, the big crime is not housed inside these aging sheds. The big crime is housed inside the blinding complex whose towering steel gates Dryden now edges toward. The Labyrinth is a sprawling building of just one story but more, Dryden anticipates, underground. The exact shape might be named by someone very good at geometry. What Dryden sees is a multifaceted serpentine, every inch painted white. The roof is a raised spine of solar panels. The Labyrinth burns brighter than gold. If you are a smuggler who can pay your way into a free port, this is a temple to crime.

Dryden eases on the brakes, pulling up to a manned sentry point. A guard waves desultorily. A screen on a podium waits for Dryden to hold Corso's dismembered hand an inch above it. The question is how to get the guard to avert his gaze while he does it.

Dryden says, "Aisha, there's a sentry six feet west of my position. Find a phone and call it. Now."

Aisha's voice unfolds inside his skull: "There's having faith in me, and then there's unreasonable demands on my labor."

He buzzes the window down and raises his own hand to the guard.

Dryden reaches out the window.

The phone rings. The guard jumps slightly, turns, and picks it up.

Dryden withdraws his arm, seizes the icy hand from the cool box on the seat beside him, and waves it over the screen. It's like squeezing a bag of kale that has been shoved to the back of a fridge and crystallized. Vein recognition technology reads the dead man's fortune. It isn't good. The screen flashes green.

When the guard turns back to him, Dryden is sitting normally, staring ahead with his own hands at ten and two on the wheel. The barrier rises.

Dryden says to Aisha, "I'll recommend you for a raise."

Aisha replies, "Honey, I earn more than you do."

"I find that worryingly easy to believe."

"I'm still searching, but Q hasn't been able to find a thing on internal security."

Dryden parks the vehicle within twenty feet of the gates. "When in doubt, hit people real hard."

"Hulk smash, I like it."

"I'll take that as a compliment."

"You should, he's the strongest superhero there is. Ibrahim's waiting to test the samples. Good luck."

Dryden's attention settles on the evil eye pendant, which he took from Corso's car to hang in this Audi. "Thanks. Going dark." He presses the combination of buttons on his Commander watch that severs the stream to MI6 without affecting his implant. The link can be turned back on by MI6 but only if Aisha and Ibrahim think his life is under immediate threat. A measure of privacy. Dryden pulls Corso's phone from the glove box and presses it with the dead man's thumb. The screen wakes up. Then he reaches into the glove box and pulls out an IED he assembled from items bought in the local chemist. It can be set off with a tap of his watch. He considers the radio link between the watch and the bomb his own ball of string.

The revolving doors sweep Dryden from the near thirty-degree heat into wintry air conditioning and lighting that makes him raise a hand to shield his face. The needling whine of stressed filaments and fuses bounces inside his ear canal. The STORMS system will already be tracking him. He has switched his gait onto Corso's phone with Aisha's help. For the twelve paces to the curved glass desk, he will appear to be walking in a dead man's shoes.

"Good afternoon, sir," says a cheerful woman from behind the glass desk.

Dryden hands over Corso's phone.

The woman navigates to the free port app. She nods, then reaches beneath the desk to a tray, from which she hands him a tablet, replacing it with the phone.

"Welcome back, sir. Please wear these complimentary sunglasses to protect your eyes, and enjoy your visit."

Dryden accepts the boxy sunglasses, which remind him of the 3D glasses he assembled as a teenager to watch the solar eclipse. He gives his thanks, weighing the tablet, which is sketching a zigzag path between reception and Corso's vault. M. C. Escher all right. Can Dryden even make it across the lobby to the double doors guarded by two armed men before the alarms sound?

One way to find out.

Rachel Wolff stows her bag in the locker of the staff room and takes a last glance at the mirror on the inside of the door. She has colored her eyebrows with white streaks and pouched her cheeks with cotton wool that makes her feel parched. Pale powder and poorly applied lipstick change her skin tone and give the idea of a woman who does her face on the bus. She wears a blond wig that she's stretched until the hair falls lank. Her shoulders roll forward in the stoop of someone whose entire energy is invested in standing up—posture a forgotten idea. The cleaner whose place she is taking received a phone call that her son was injured on a school trip and is now on a ferry to the mainland. The woman walks at a clip, her neck stretched forward, determined to reach some finish line but held at bay by a great gust. Her right foot tilts inward, rolling pressure onto her big toe and callousing her heel. Her left foot splays outward, callousing her little toe. She complains of joint pain. The upward thrust of the earth against these tilted bones crunches her knees. She is a single mother in her late thirties working a minimum pay job and aging before her time. She checks the time on her phone.

OK. Let's go.

Joseph Dryden gets ten paces inside the dazzling corridor before the alarms sound, a deafening wail. Dryden staggers against the marble wall, clutching his head. Groping for the controls on his watch, he turns the volume of his implant down. The doors swing open and the two guards come toward him shouting in Greek, lifting their rifles. The muzzles of the weapons are encased in orange to signify baton rounds.

Don't bring rubber bullets to a street fight.

He comes closer to the men, shouting, "What's happening?"

When one reaches forward to take his tablet, Dryden punches him in the throat with it and catches the falling rifle, which he swings like a club at the other guard's head.

The doors of the service elevator open as the alarms blare. Rachel Wolff wants to press the earpiece deeper into her ear against the din but resists in case anyone appears. She faces a corridor that seems endless. Lights blaze from recesses in the ceiling onto the white marble. Red spots appear in Rachel's vision, making it impossible to anticipate the next turn, or detect how the walls shrink and splay. She pushes the cleaning trolley ahead of her and sets off at a jog. If stopped, she will say she got lost looking for the fire exit. Of course, playing lost in here is pretty easy. She pauses in her tilting run when Dryden's voice crackles through the earpiece. He's connected his implant to her radio device.

"Listen up—two lefts, down two levels, two rights, left right left, up a level, straight ahead sixty paces, on your right."

Rachel repeats it back.

"You've got it. Tossing the tablet away now."

Rachel says, "You know, you sound a little out of breath."

"Screw you."

She laughs. "See you on the other side."

Dryden whips the tablet through the air, striking one of the two guards who've pursued him down to the next level. It hits the man in the head and he collapses like a wet sack. Dryden catches him in his fall and uses him as a shield for the spray of rubber bullets. Then he thrusts the limp body toward the target. The man goes down and Dryden knocks him out with the butt of the rifle. He seizes the phone clipped to the man's belt, which shows a three-dimensional rendering of the entire Labyrinth, where the tablet showed only Corso's vault. The screen is flashing red. Dryden takes a second to absorb the map and then pockets the phone, taking clips from both men's rifles. He hears shouting and sets off sprinting. The corridor is sloping downward and he tries not to think of the Minoan murderers funneled toward the Minotaur before the deal was struck with Aegeus for a diet of innocents. It has been four minutes.

Rachel Wolff has descended to the lower level, bouncing the trolley down the steps, when a door to her left opens in the blinding surface of the wall. A woman in a Barbie pink power suit knocks into Rachel and dashes up the stairs, carrying a painting under her arm. The rats are leaving the sinking ship and carrying their gold with them. Rachel takes the next turn and bowls into a man whose square haircut, sweating lip, and shiny blazer says mid-level management. He seizes her elbow and shouts at her—Rachel only knows a little Greek, but recognizes the word "emergency," and that he is calling her by the name of the cleaner she is impersonating. Small victories. She points the way she needs to go. He shakes his head vehemently, dragging her back the way she's come. Rachel resists his tug, gesturing with one finger that she'll just be one minute, one minute. He gives up— he has bigger problems—shouting one last time that she should leave, before running himself.

Dryden takes the stairs three at a time, spraying rubber bullets over his shoulder. When he reaches the top, he almost leaps out of his skin—but it's only his reflection. The stairs are a dead end, a mirror where he thought there was a door. He turns around. Too many guards to count are piling toward him. He elbows the mirror softly. It gives a little.

He wasn't known as the Door-Kicker in Afghanistan for nothing.

Ten minutes. The trolley is slowing her down and its plausibility lessening by the minute. Rachel parks it, taking the testing kits folded up in a towel. No hope her gait is right now. Sixty paces to go.

The mirror cracks, then smashes. Rubber bullets thud into Dryden's back. He falls into a corridor that seems a replica of the one he's just escaped.

Rachel runs her hands over the marble, searching for the seam that will reveal the door to Corso's vault. Finally she finds it, and pushes. The door sinks deeper by an inch and a touch screen winks to life. Rachel punches the code. The door to the vault swings open.

Now it is a dance. Unarmed combat, no bullets left, just Dryden against half a dozen men in semiprofessional riot gear, their faces protected by visors. Dryden's only protection is the cardboard glasses, which he rips off, scrunches into a point, and jabs under the armpit of the man in front of him, who folds around it. Dryden tears the visor off the guard's face, using it to bludgeon the oncoming man.

Corso's vault is empty apart from the standalone safe, a five-foot-high model made of steel. Too heavy to budge even a millimeter. Too thick to attempt drilling from the front or rear. Diagonal drilling is out, too. Fireproofing rules out burning the lock with a plasma cutter or thermic lance. And blowing it up will destroy the evidence inside. It's what she expected. Given enough time and the right tools, Rachel Wolff would bet on herself to crack any safe in the world. There are a few basic methods. Electronic safes can be cracked with laughable ease by either spraying the electronic keypad with ultraviolet ink and shining a UV flashlight to reveal the fingerprints, or by linking up a device with an app that runs through all possible combinations until finding the right one. All you have to do is wait. Rachel considers this lazy and inelegant but sometimes you have to meet stupid with stupid. On that same level, a surprising number of people never change the standard combination set by the safe makers, or leave the number written down somewhere, as Corso did for the vault door.

This safe demands manipulation of three combination locks. It requires a good ear, not easy when the sheer noise of the alarm is making her feel nauseous. She threads a stethoscope from inside her pinny and drops to her haunches. She played at breaking safes as a child the same way other little girls played house. A skilled safecracker can find the correct combination to any safe simply by listening through a stethoscope as they twist the dial. Her father would make her practice blindfolded while he blasted the Beatles at top volume. Each number in a combination relates to a different wheel located behind the dial. She is listening for the faint click that means the wheel has moved into place. When the correct combination is dialed, the wheel's notches line up and the door will lumber open. Rachel closes her eyes and listens to the whispers over the screams. That was something her mother used to tell her. Her mother believed in signs from the universe. Listen to the whispers so you don't have to hear the screams. What would her mother say the universe had in store for Rachel when Moneypenny walked through the door?

Dryden wipes blood from his face and fights for breath. He clambers over the pile of unconscious limbs and stumbles down a corridor. He finds a door to a vault open. The room is filled with wine racks. Dryden looks up. The Labyrinth is carefully climate-controlled and meticulously cleaned. That takes air conditioning. Clambering up the ladder of the wine rack, he punches the grille in the ceiling. Dryden hauls himself into the ventilation shaft and checks his watch. The ten minutes Wolff needs to crack the safe are nearly up. Then she needs fifteen minutes to leave the building. Time to clear the exit. He presses the combination on his watch, renewing his link with MI6.

Dryden whispers, "Aisha, can you see anyone within a twenty-foot radius of my vehicle in the car park on satellite?"

There is a pause, and then her irate voice whips back: "What the hell is going on there? No, I can't. It's clear. The guard at the gate was pulled into the building in response to whatever chaos you're wreaking."

"Get off the line."

"All right, all right, I'm gone."

He detonates the bomb.

The third combination lock springs, and the door groans open. Rachel tightens her right hand in a small fist of victory, and then swallows as a bath of gold floods her vision. She unfolds the towel bundling the testing kits. Now she has to take fingerprints and particulate samples so that MI6 can analyze where this treasure came from, and whose hands it passed through.

The explosion lifts the Audi six feet into the air and slams it back down. The stench of petrol blooms into the sky. Police cars skid to a halt at the gates, which are now a tangle of steel.

Rachel drops the vials into the pocket of her pinny. All done. She is closing the door when a gleam catches her eye.

It would be the easiest snatch in the world. No one knows what is in the safe. No one will miss it.

If someone was there to witness her resist, and ask her what brought on this sudden bout of virtue, she would feel foolish telling them that by a trick of the light, the fingerprints she pulled appeared blood-red.

Dryden drops into the climate office, where the chair is still spinning from the recent exit of who-ever oversees the precious air. A giant whirring vent cools a long bank of air-gapped computers. Dryden is tempted by the computers but he doesn't have the time. He picks up the chair and jams it in the vent, slipping through the louvers. The smell of sewer and sea rises from far away to greet him.

"Ariadne, come in."

"Cute. I've got the samples and I'm at the service lift but it's been shut down."

"I had to blow the Audi up."

"What?"

"Trust me. Get the doors to the lift open, then pop the service hatch. Climb down to sub-level five then make your way west to the climate office."

"I suppose I'll only be moderately scathed. Then what?"

"We're going swimming."

"You should have told me," she says. "I would've worked on my tan."

He laughs, then grips his ribs, resting inch by bruised inch against the wall.

Sixteen
Le Milieu

Paris

Johanna Harwood is up 125,000 euros at the black-jack table and for the first time in a long time, she can breathe. In the Gare du Nord, she was greeted off the Eurostar by lampposts like wilting snowdrops, and thought: *Immediately, Paris.* Home rushes in like spring rain. Being surrounded by her mother tongue is akin to the moment your eardrums pop on a plane after hours of hermetic silence.

What made blackjack different to other games, Sid said, was that it was based on dependent events: the past affects the probability of what is going to happen next. She is using cash she found in a go bag at the back of James's wardrobe. Harwood figures Bond won't care as long as she wins. What she is waiting for is her winning to attract enough notice that she will be taken seriously. And she has less than a quarter of an hour before it will all be for nothing.

Harwood is playing at an illegal gambling den occupying a cruise ship on the Seine. The floating journey began as the Eiffel Tower was lanced by its double beam of light, traveling on past the golden chocolate wrapper glimmer of the Musée d'Orsay and the Louvre; the ghostly scaffold of Notre-Dame, the memory of fire mixed with the stink of cigar smoke; and now the monolithic torches of the Bibliothèque Nationale de France. Harwood wears a gray chiffon gown split up the side, just about hiding Bond's spare Walther PPK strapped to her thigh. Sid's Casio watch jangles on her wrist with a diamond bracelet. She glances at the time. The police will board from the Quai de Bercy at 4 a.m. It is a routine case that crossed Harwood's desk on night duty because of a connection with illegal gambling dens in London. Everything is connected. Crime has gone cooperative. The gambling den is run by a Corsican, and it is Harwood's intention to save it from the law.

She says, "*Tirer.*" It is a relief to be speaking French again, to be unknown for anything else.

The dealer turns over the cards. The people around her clap. A man who smells of basement gin and too many perfumes tells her she is lucky. Harwood smiles noncommittally. She has twenty-one, but she doesn't think of it as luck. She thinks of it as Sid's gift. The dealer pushes the chips toward her. Each chip is stamped with a golden revolver, the club's logo. The invitation—which Harwood pickpocketed—is too.

A security guard moves to stand on the red-carpeted stairway that leads to fresh air.

The dealer is relieved by a petite woman wearing a white tuxedo. "This table is now closed," she says in French, bringing her hands together. "Congratulations, madame. Let me buy you a drink while we deal with your winnings."

Harwood responds in French that she appreciates the hospitality and follows Marc-Ange Draco's niece Daniella Draco through the crowd and up the stairs to the bar on deck, which is strung with swaying lanterns.

"What will you have?"

Harwood leans with her back to the bar, surveying the crowd, the shrieks of laughter, the low tinny jazz. Turning to smile over her shoulder at the barman, she says, "Vodka martini. Shaken, not stirred."

"Make that two," says Daniella Draco, a small frown now pinching her square nut-brown face. Her hair, cut short, is the color of Riviera sunshine. "You are a new face here, madame."

"I mislaid the old one."

"May I ask who extended you an invitation to our establishment?"

Harwood takes a drink. Memory is a bitter friend. "I stole it."

Daniella Draco pauses over her glass. "Why? You wish to gain access where you do not belong. But you do not strike me as a police officer."

Harwood lets that one pass, to be considered later. "I'm not. But in about"—a glance at the Casio—"twelve minutes you are going to be raided by the police and the money you lost to me will seem like loose change."

Daniella Draco stiffens. "Why are you telling me this?"

"I want to meet with your uncle."

"Does he want to meet you?"

"Tell him it's about his son-in-law."

The frown deepens. "He does not want to meet with you."

Harwood shrugs and finishes the martini. "Eleven minutes."

"Why did you take so much of my money first?"

"To show you I mean business. My money is at stake too."

Daniella's jaw works. Then she hoists herself up on the bar, leans over, and presses a hidden button. A wail interrupts the music. The staff transform from waiters to the fastest set dismantlers on the West End. Harwood watches three croupiers strip down to their shirtsleeves, stuff the night's take into body bags, and toss them into the Seine, before diving after them noiselessly.

Harwood says, "Impressive. But the police are going to board the boat. There's nowhere for you to hide. I can get you out."

"Why should I trust you? You say you are not a police officer. James Bond was the worst kind. He thought he could be a tourist and holiday with us. He thought Le Milieu belonged to him."

"Seven minutes."

Daniella slams her glass down. "What is your plan?"

Harwood reaches into her Hermès Kelly bag and pulls out identification, which names someone who looks a lot like her as a European justice enforcer.

Daniella says, "Get me out of here, and I will rendezvous with you in Nice in two days' time. From there, I can take you to meet my uncle. But you may regret it."

Every fifteen years or so, the authorities in Paris force the Canal Saint-Martin to give up its secrets. First, the water is drained to half a meter deep. Next, city workers make a slow advance with nets, capturing carp and catfish, rehoming eighteen tons to the Seine. Then tractors and police cars arrive: tractors to haul off the detritus, police in case a sawn-off shotgun is found, or a corpse mosaicked with thousands of discarded mussel shells. Or even, as emerged from the mud once, unexploded 75 mm shells from the First World War.

What's left behind tells a story. Once upon a time, it was bicycles old enough to have had messages smuggled in their baskets for the Resistance. Then it was scooters. The last time the canal was drained, it was hundreds of Vélib' hire bikes, stolen and dumped, preserved like mosquitoes in amber. An inventory of the disposable. A ghetto blaster. The rusted chassis of a car. Wheelie suitcases, forever grounded. Paving stones, street signs, police barriers. Two empty safes. Gold pieces. Two wheelchairs. Bottles and cans, thousands of them.

Older residents say bobos are ruining the canal. The bourgeois-bohemians say they're cleaning it up, transforming derelict warehouses into art centers and coffee shops that serve succulents alongside flat whites. The local marine angling association agrees. The water quality has improved: in the eighties, there were only two species of fish in Paris. Now there are thirty-five, swimming in surprisingly good health amongst bathtubs and rolled-up carpets, before being shocked to find themselves relocated by city workers to a higher-rent district. Not that the tenth is exactly cheap any-more. It was, back when there were only two species of fish in Paris, and Johanna Harwood's grandmaman bought a flat in a new concrete apartment block.

Harwood's father was nominally her caretaker, but he was often unstable. Later diagnosed as paranoid schizophrenic, he believed, in one of life's ironies, that spies were after him. Charlie John Harwood would force Johanna to flee with him across the city, some-times even out of it. Her mother, an administrator with Médecins Sans Frontières, was away for work. That is the simple way to put it. The more complex, and more truthful, way to put it is that Harwood's mother, Clar-isse, became pregnant by an older, charming, unwell man when she was too young to know who she wanted to be; and when she discovered a sense of self and di-rection in MSF, she embraced career and travel and left the early mistake behind with her mother and hus-band, who often believed Clarisse was trying to poison him. She promised to take Johanna on the road when she was old enough, preparing her for a future as a sur-geon. When Harwood rejected that career for the life of a spy, her mother stopped speaking to her.

Johanna tells herself she can live with that; her grandmaman was much more like a mother to her anyway, leaving her this apartment when she died with a note in the will that Johanna would always have a home here. In the solicitor's office, Johanna's mother tossed her hair at that, asking what it was supposed to imply, *exactly*.

Harwood thinks this over as she skips past James's key in her bag and claims the long, flat key to the apartment block in Paris. Daniella Draco told Harwood to rendezvous with her in Nice in two days, from where she would be taken to meet the head of the Union Corse. So for now, Harwood slots the key home as if this were any easy Sunday morning and steps into the glass-fronted lobby, where tropical plants gather dust in layers. She climbs the spiral staircase, running her palm over the steel banister, until she reaches the apartment door. It has been years. There are no longer any hanging baskets to catch the sun that will soon pour through the skylight. Harwood pushes in the next key, remembering as she does how tremendously heavy this door seemed to her as a child, as if the occupants of the apartment needed a strong defense against the world. Or to be kept from it.

Harwood steps onto the carpet, and for a moment everything is all right, everything is going to be all right. Her grandmaman is going to appear from the kitchen and pick her up under the armpits, saying Johanna has grown too big for this but doing it anyway, every single day after school, because she knows the importance of constancy. Johanna could never be certain who, or what, would emerge from her father's bedroom. Harwood closes her eyes, remembering that pluck from the ground, the slight dig of her grandmaman's perfect nails and big rings, the smell from the kitchen—then she opens her eyes, struck by a new and foreign smell. Industrial bleach.

The hallway has taken on new furnishings. Gone are the photographs and the escritoire. In their place, a colorful coat rack and a neon sign in cursive handwriting that reads *Home Sweet Home.*

Can she be in the wrong apartment? Harwood looks down at the keys. She edges into the living room. Midnight-blue velvet sofas form a huddle around a rose gold coffee table, on which there is a stack of pamphlets outlining things to do in Paris, and a binder. Harwood picks it up, moving to the windows. Instead of switching on the light, she cracks the curtains and holds the binder up to the coming of the day.

Welcome to Belle Paris Airbnb.

Harwood hears someone laugh with shock—herself.

Her mother is renting Harwood's inheritance out on Airbnb.

Evidently, it will always be many people's home.

Her grandmaman's books are gone, apart from those

with leather bindings, which are displayed attractively on metal shelving squeezed between a monstera and an oversized jar stuffed with fairy lights. She can spot nothing of her father's, until she finds one of his cameras on a shelf with her grandmaman's kitchen implements: a coffee pot, an orange juicer, all, it would seem, kept for their retro value. Harwood gets the camera down, a Nikon FM2n with a Zoom-Nikkor 35–135 mm f/3.5–4.5s lens. Harwood wondered why it was missing from her father's collection in the Barbican, a flat she moved into as a medical student when she discovered her father starving himself up there amongst the birds.

Her bedroom is now a twin room. There is a framed poster of a Georges Simenon book cover printed A3: *Maigret and the Headless Corpse*. The grainy black-and-white photograph shows two men peering over the side of a barge. Harwood remembers being excited to read a book about her home as a teenager, though it was set at a time when the canal still functioned. In the first chapter, two brothers discover a man's arm in the canal, sparking police interest because it isn't the arm of a woman. The bodies of prostitutes were found in the canal all the time. That was still true when Harwood was growing up. Now, she moves the bright curtain to see the canalside park where dealers would ask if she wanted anything on her way home from school, and she brought her pocket money to a homeless man who gifted her his watercolors, which she pinned to her wall. The man is gone now, along with his paintings. So are the benches and shelters where the homeless sought refuge. Now, the green stretches attract families for a picnic, or a game of pétanque and a drink with friends at one of the many surrounding bars.

But this desk was hers. She did her homework here. Harwood sits down on the charmingly rickety chair. She is turning the camera over in her hands when the sound of the front door is followed by her mother's cutting voice. She moves to the threshold of her bedroom, which gives her the long view down the hallway to where her mother stands in a flurry of damp coat, shaking umbrella, dropped bag, tossed beret.

"Johanna! I thought there was a burglar in here!"

"There is. They've set up an Airbnb apartment."

Clarisse tuts, flings her coat at a hook, and strides into the living room, casting about as if to see what Harwood might have broken. With her comes the force of her personality, her will, and her beauty. "You should have called first!" she says. "Look at you, you are a mess, are you in trouble again?"

Harwood comes to sit on the arm of the sofa, cradling the camera in her lap. She says curiously, "When was I in trouble last?"

"There is no need to take my words and twist them, you are always doing that! I only say you look like you lost something."

This perception rocks her enough to correct: "Someone."

Her mother returns sharply: "Yourself?"

"Maybe that too."

"So you have come home to bleed on my carpet."

Harwood remembers the gash on her arm—she forgot that she received a scrape as she urged Daniella through the throng of police, waving her badge. Chastising herself for being taken in by her mother for a moment, lulled into confidence, she then thinks that perhaps her mother's brash bluntness could invite a form of confidence, because she is already so disappointed. Nothing to lose. She says, anyway, "I'll pay the forty-euro cleaning fee."

"All right, all right," says Clarisse, throwing her hands up again. "I turned it into an Airbnb, what did you want me to do? You never visit, never call, never write. You are jealous of the money? You are wearing diamonds!"

"They're not mine."

"Whose are they, then?"

"Property of the British government and forgotten in the wardrobe of an ex-lover."

Clarisse tilts toward her. "This is the man you have lost?"

"Yes. No." Harwood turns to the curtains, wishing she'd opened them all the way. "You should have asked me, about the apartment. It's mine."

"Don't be a child."

Harwood looks around. "You know, I don't think I ever was."

"You've come here to accuse me of being a bad mother?"

"No." Harwood stands up. "I came here for respite."

"And now I am disturbing your peace, I suppose . . ." Clarisse trails away, marching into the kitchen as she mutters about it not being her fault the alarm went off and she thought the place was being robbed.

Harwood follows her, occupying the kitchen threshold now as her mother pours herself a glass of water. "You ought to put an extra lock on," says Harwood. She raises the camera. "This is worth a lot of money, beyond anything else. It shouldn't be out like a cheap ornament."

"*That.*" Clarisse faces her daughter dead-on. "I should have thrown it away years ago. I don't know why I didn't."

"Sentiment?" suggests Harwood.

"For what?"

Harwood knows her responding smile to be crooked,

to be what Dr. Kowalczyk would call anger turned inward, but she does nothing to straighten it out. "Right. My mistake."

"Now you think me heartless, I suppose," says Clarisse, sitting on a stool at the head of a glass table so new it lacks any scratches. The kitchen window never had blinds, and the pearly near-morning touching the chimney pots on the roofs opposite—always the first thing to take on life and color—is unforgiving to her mother's blond hair, illuminating its gray roots; unforgiving to her capacity for evasion, too, chucking her reflection before her across the glass surface. She covers the face of her second self with trembling hands.

Harwood draws up the opposite stool. She places the camera between them, a managed clunk. She realizes how thirsty she is, but feels unable now to leave the frame. "I never thought you were heartless."

"You didn't?"—this, quickly.

"No." Harwood fiddles with the camera strap. "I suppose I thought you were admirable."

"You admired me?" Clarisse touches her left earring, then says, flatly this time: "For what?"

Harwood meets her square in the eyes. "Your coldness. I think I learned that from you. It's proven a valuable asset."

Clarisse's cheeks burn red. "How can you say such things to me?"

"I don't mean to be hurtful. It's only the truth."

"Only!"

"You had a baby with the wrong man at the wrong time. I suppose that made me the wrong baby." Harwood cups her chin, listening to herself from a distance of years away. "A lot of people would have changed the shape of their ambition to fit the space they found themselves in. You didn't do that. You left us. You left me to Papa."

"I never left your father or you."

"Funny. I remember the door closing."

"I always came back!"

"And always left again. Papa wasn't safe."

"Your grandmaman was in charge!"

"She was too old."

"Are you saying that I neglected you? Abandoned you to abuse? You had housing, clothing, food, schoolbooks—*I* paid for all that! Me! Out of *nothing*, I made *something*."

Harwood nods. "You were ruthless. I can only thank you for that."

Clarisse presses the heels of her palms to her face and shrieks. "You learned all the wrong lessons! You were supposed to be better than us. I was denied my education when your father got me pregnant. To *you* nothing was denied. You were going to be a surgeon!"

"I am," says Harwood, watching her mother's knees bounce up and down through the glass of the table. "I recently saved the life of a friend in the field. Severe gunshot wound to the chest. The hospital said it was the finest—"

Now Clarisse covers her ears. "La la la! I do not want to hear this!"

Harwood says again, with a sense of vertigo, "It's only the truth. I'm a Double O. You know that."

Now her mother explodes from her seat, wrenches open the cabinet, remembers she already has a glass, bangs it shut, seizes her glass from the table—finds it to be full—and then for something to do chucks the lot down the plughole. She heaves a sigh, pressing her forehead to the white plastic of the IKEA cabinet door.

Harwood watches all this with her lower lip between her teeth. She is having a vision of her father dismantling the sink, searching, he said, for hidden microphones. Searching for evidence—of what? Dysfunction? Faulty assembly? A disastrous joining of human beings who shouldn't be joined? It was certainly here to be found.

"I'm here investigating Le Milieu," she says.

"Le Milieu, Le Milieu—you talk as if you are an actor in a gangster film!" Still, Clarisse does not turn around.

"Actors in gangster films talk as if they are me."

"You are a criminal now?"

Harwood studies a cheap Picasso print. "People do struggle picturing me as the law."

"You're not. Only its shadow." Clarisse bangs her head softly against the cabinet.

Harwood suddenly recalls a chaperoned school trip to the zoo—how her father wept when he saw the bear in the pit banging its head against the concrete. "Don't do that."

"Why shouldn't I? My daughter is lost."

"I'm right here. I serve my country—"

Clarisse interrupts: "It's not your country."

"—and I do my duty. I deliver justice, the kind grandmaman talked about, the kind that *matters*. I stop bad things happening to good people."

Now, Clarisse turns. "At what cost?"

Harwood flinches—at the question, the understanding behind it, the anguish on her mother's face, wiped so free of fury it is as if she's cleansed her cheeks with cotton wool.

"At all costs."

"To yourself? And those who you love and who

love you?" Her gaze locks onto the lapis lazuli ring on Harwood's engagement finger.

Barely audible: "Yes."

Her mother slaps the table, making Harwood jump.

"It is just what I did not want!" Clarisse shouts. "After what they did to your father!"

Harwood frowns, touches the camera, which was jolted. She says, "That was all in his head, Maman. My life is real. I'm not delusional."

"Neither was he, until they made him that way. He was never ours. He lived a double life, with a double heart."

"What do you mean?"

But Clarisse has jammed her perfectly manicured finger over her lips. "I promised I would never speak of this."

"Speak of what? Was he really"—Harwood's own heart skips a beat—"a spy like me?"

Clarisse shakes her head so vehemently her earrings clatter. "Get out. Take that stupid camera and get out. I cannot bear it. You do not know—you cannot know, unless you quit. *Quit*, Johanna, right now. Or get out."

Harwood rises. Her voice is cool as the Seine in winter when she says, "You get out. It's my house."

Clarisse backs away. Harwood watches the road below, the strip of cobbles, the sedentary canal, keeping its secrets for now. She sees her mother's yellow Alpine A110 Berlinette, the famous rally model of 1962, parked in the dappled light of the silver birch. Then the unmistakable double-barreled glint of binoculars flashing from a balcony across the canal. The binoculars disappear as soon as her attention lands on them.

"Wait," she says. "Did you tell anyone you were coming here?"

"What are you accusing me of now?"

Can it be Moneypenny, or one of René Mathis's boys on the job as a favor to M? Perhaps MI6 put a watch on the Parisian apartment as soon as Harwood went rogue. She should never have come home. It was a foolish mistake, born out of a childish need for comfort. Look where that got her.

"I need to borrow your car," says Harwood.

"You think you can make demands of me?"

Harwood faces her mother. "We're being watched. Go down to the garage and walk out the rear exit. Leave your car keys on the table."

"Everywhere you go, you bring danger! You are cursed, Johanna. You were always a curse. You do not even care to know how I am aging, you do not even ask why I have to rent my maman's home to bobos."

Heat burns through Harwood's chest. She tugs the diamond bracelet from her wrist and chucks it onto the table. "There. Call it a trade. I'll let you know where the car is in twenty-four hours, and it won't have a dent. After that, you won't have to see me again."

"I didn't mean . . ."

The table flares with light. Harwood turns back, catching the double-barreled flash of the binoculars again. "You're right. I grew up with death chasing me, and I know how to outrun it. You don't, because you weren't there. So go. Get out of my home."

A rustle and scrape. The door closes.

Clarisse left the keys on the table, but didn't take the bracelet.

Seventeen
Going to a Funeral

France

Johanna Harwood is impressed. She thought she lost the tail in the outskirts of Paris, but another car appears to pick up her scent in the national forest near Dijon, prompting her to take a detour toward Geneva, where she loses them at the tolls before turning around and taking the mountain road. Wildfire forms a wall of heat at one stretch, every driver slowing to peer up at the wobbling air. A bird of prey hovers against the flames, a dark silhouette. Harwood can feel the heat on her cheek.

Near Avignon, a car with tinted windows spooks her, and she presses her foot down, coaxing the Alpine A110 Berlinette around the steep bends, feeling the rattling earth in the bump of her bones. The rally car is twitchy and you have to really drive it, keeping her awake. Her father's camera is on the seat beside her. Can her mother have been right? All those times her father thought someone was pursuing them . . . Harwood smiles grimly as she checks the rearview mirror for the hundredth time. She sleeps in a lay-by, a few hours when she skips dreams like a pebble over a pond—beneath the surface, her father is dying of starvation, gripping her hand and telling her he's been poisoned. She wakes gasping for breath, checks her mirror, and turns on the engine.

Harwood finally stops at a village near Aix-en-Provence, parking outside a bar tabac. She sits in the shadow of plane trees at a plastic table with an ashtray molded in the shape of mountains. She has just ordered breakfast when another car pulls up. A Peugeot 208 streaked with orange dust. The tall figure who climbs out is wearing a black woolen suit, and sweating. He avoids her, although she's the only person here. He sits three tables away, takes off his fedora, and fans his face.

"You look hot in that suit," she says in French.

"Yes," he says, turning milky eyes on her. "I've been driving in it all night and all morning."

"Why not change?"

"I can't."

"Are you going to a funeral?"

"I'm trying to avoid yours, ma chère."

Harwood sits back as the waiter dumps her croissant and coffee on the table with the bill and demands an order from the newcomer before stalking away. Then she says, "I didn't think the head of the Deuxième carried out simple tails."

René Mathis sighs expansively. "I do not. But you lost my two best men. If you want something done right, as they say in your adopted country . . ." He gets up, removing his coat to reveal sweat stains under his arms, and joins her table.

"Did London send you after me?" asks Harwood, studying the creased face of Bond's oldest ally.

"M is concerned."

Harwood picks at her croissant. "I can't allow you to take me in."

"I am sure you would like me once you got to know me."

That makes Harwood laugh. She watches the long street, where on weekends a market will sell bagged lavender and soaps and garlic and roasted chicken. Now, a woman is opening her shop, draping a wire-frame mannequin in jewelry on the curb, flapping her hands to shift the dust in the dry air.

"I have always been curious to meet you," says Mathis. "I told James once to surround himself with human beings. They are easier to fight for than principles. But I warned him not to become too human himself. We would lose such a wonderful machine. When he met you, I had the sense he was becoming too human again, something I had not thought possible after Vesper and Tracy. It seemed to frighten him."

"Nothing frightens James," says Harwood.

René wags a finger at her. "You know better than that."

The waiter slams Mathis's coffee down with another slip of paper and bangs the door behind him.

"I have a lead," says Harwood carefully.

"On James?"

"But I can't pursue it within the bounds of the law."

He blows out his cheeks. "You worry me. What is this lead?"

"I can't tell you that. If I do, you'll just give it to M, who will put someone else on it."

"Why?"

"You know why."

"MI6 do not think you are fit for duty."

"Yes." Harwood gives him a sidelong look. "Do you have an opinion?"

"I think you appear perfectly in command of yourself, and quite, quite beautiful, if I may add."

"You may not," says Harwood, draining her coffee.

Mathis chuckles, doing the same. "You wish me to say I never found you. But why should I put more stock in my judgment of you than M's psychologists?"

"Because you want to see James again."

He raises an eyebrow streaked with white hair. "She knows how to touch a man's heart, this one. M says you are out of control." His attention narrows on her face. "But you appear completely in control to me. A wonderful machine, in fact."

Harwood swallows at that. She has been told, in so many words and so many times, that what makes her such an asset to the Service is her coldness. She wonders when it happened, this icing over. A capacity to cut off parts of herself to get the job done. Underneath the ice, she doesn't feel herself to be cold. She didn't feel cold with Sid, or with James. She felt alive.

"Do you need any assistance?"

A sparrow pecks at the pastry she has flaked onto the gravel. "Only to be left alone."

Mathis hums thoughtfully. "Somehow, you fill me with absurd faith that you can achieve the impossible and bring James back from the dead."

"He's not dead. I saw the evidence myself."

"You saw numbers carved into a rock." He holds up

a hand. "Do not listen to my cynicism. For once, I will believe in miracles. James always produced them. Why not you, now? Perhaps you will prove me right."

"About what?"

"You are willing to risk everything to save him. It is easier to fight for human beings, after all. But then, maybe I am wrong, too. Maybe you do not need to be a machine to do it." Mathis drops a note on the table to cover both bills. "Good luck, 003."

Eighteen
Brothers

Cyrus

Ibrahim Suleiman says, "I'm seeing more finger-prints than touch a twenty-pound note in its entire lifespan."

"Really?" says Dryden, collapsing into the standard-issue army chair.

Ibrahim has set up shop in the laboratory of the Royal Army Medical Corps hospital on Dhekélia Station, Cyprus, and looks up from his laptop now to raise his eyebrows at Dryden. "No. Your average twenty-pound note is touched two thousand three hundred and twenty-eight times across a decade."

"How do you know these things?"

"I'm gold in a pub quiz."

"I bet."

"The fingerprints you managed to lift from the antiquities in Corso's vault—mysteriously, despite all alarms and seemingly no data from Q, I might add, *if* I was feeling cynical about your story—do however represent a significant number of people's hands, most of them probably strung across the globe. A good percentage of those will never have been fingerprinted. Subsistence looters digging up jewels and statues in order to eat aren't considered important enough to be on anyone's database."

"I don't plan to arrest people who are starving."

"That's why we like you so much. I've sent the prints to Q. We'll know if there are any matches soon. In the meantime, let me introduce you to my portable mass spectrometer for analysis of particulates . . ."

Ibrahim gives a theatrical wave over a machine that appears to Dryden like a not very advanced photocopier. He says dutifully, "Very impressive. I didn't know forensics was one of your many talents."

"Give me a machine and I will learn its language," says Ibrahim, bending over the workbench to organize the samples.

"Like me," suggests Dryden, stretching his legs and interlinking his fingers over his stomach.

"Exactly." A few seconds pass. "I mean . . . not that you're like some kind of freakish human-machine hybrid or anything."

Dryden smirks. "Of course not. Start analyzing, would you?"

A door shuts noisily somewhere and Ibrahim jumps. "You OK?"

"Military bases spook me," says Ibrahim. "Always have."

"You served in the Engineer Corps."

"I was spooked a lot."

Ibrahim begins to do things with the machine Dryden doesn't understand. He gets up, moving to the window. The Princess of Wales's Royal Regiment is drilling on the training field. He remembers postings like this one. Wake up at 6 a.m. and leave the barracks in shorts and squadron T-shirt. Stretch. Jog through fields of wheat or along hard shoulders, carrying a camouflage-patterned rucksack on his back. Use the time to plan his troop's training. That was when he was a troop corporal, pushing for sergeant. He'd follow the same route every day. Learn to recognize traffic patterns and birdsong. Controlling his surroundings achieved order and peace. He studies Ibrahim's reflection in the steel cabinets: the oversized sweater, week's beard growth, scuffed trainers.

Eventually he says, "Did you ever feel like you belonged in the army?"

"I wasn't popular, let's put it that way. Didn't join the football team, didn't go out on the lash. And it was hard for the boys to forget that I'm Iraqi. It was the same for my dad when he was a terp."

Ibrahim's parents were terps—interpreters—for the British Army in Iraq. As locally employed civilians, or LECs, they had been labeled collaborators and targeted by militias. Eventually they were relocated to the UK, where Ibrahim grew up.

"You know what it was like," says Ibrahim. "My dad served three years on the front line as a terp. The average tour of duty for a British soldier was only six months. Without interpreters, you lot couldn't do anything. You need a local patrol interpreter for house searches, interrogations, intel gathering. My dad was a key player in the counterinsurgency strategy to win hearts and minds. He was outside the wire all the time. An IED doesn't know the difference between a terp and a soldier. He wore your uniform, your socks, your shoes, even the same underwear. The only difference was the make of his gun and that when he got blown up or stabbed he didn't have the automatic right to top medical treatment. But he saw you boys as brothers. Even more than that. He and the other

terps were your protectors. He saved a lieutenant from
an ambush once, got stabbed three times in the process.
He thought the soldiers from London—that's how he
referred to you all—were his brothers. And you were
until one of you died in action and then you'd forget he
was on your side. Suddenly the whole base was frosty
toward LECs. He was your brother when you needed
him. Then, we had to fight for resettlement. You see the
same thing happening now. Your old LEC probably got
left behind when the UK withdrew from Afghanistan,
right?"

Dryden tucks his chin into his chest. "M is working
on it."

"Were you close?"

Dryden says, "He's my brother."

Ibrahim nods. "So it goes." He returns to the machine.
"What did your parents say when you joined up?"

"My father became a terp against his father's wishes,
but still he didn't talk to me for weeks. My mother understood. In some ways, she risked even more in her
work as a terp on the base than my father did. She used
to take me with her, sometimes, when I was a little boy.
One time, I was chased through the streets because
they knew who my mother was . . ." Ibrahim trails off,
bending closer to the screen. "Anyway, she understood

dreams. I wanted an education I couldn't access any other way. And now I've got a job I couldn't have dreamt of."

Dryden taps his ear. "You dreamt it into being, I'd say. I'm grateful to you. Brother."

Ibrahim colors. "Yeah. Well." He returns to the data popping up on his laptop. "You might want to hold your breath on gratitude anyway."

"Why's that?"

"I've got to send you into hell. Or as close to it as you'll get. The soil particulates on the antiquities in Corso's vault originate from Afghanistan."

Dryden straightens. "Can you narrow it down to a location?"

"Easy. It's a well-documented archaeological site. The Hill of Gold."

"Infiltrate Taliban-controlled Afghanistan . . ." Dryden returns to frowning at the window.

Ibrahim's laptop dings. "We've got results on one of the fingerprints." Ibrahim claps his hands. "Say hello to Friedrich Hyde, dealer of Arabic art, under long-term investigation by the FBI and Interpol. Neither organization has ever had enough evidence to take him to court. His prints are all over the antiquities."

Dryden rubs his swollen knuckles. "Makes sense. Smugglers favor free ports for meeting with late-stage

A SPY LIKE ME · 243

intermediaries. Medici, that Italian art and antiquities smuggler and dealer, he favored a free port in Switzerland for meetings before he was brought down. The easiest way to stop smuggling long-term is to limit convergence settings, where different actors in the pipeline meet. I should've blown more shit up at the Labyrinth."

"Any other methods, besides property damage?"

"Agent provocateur."

"Is that a come-on?"

A slight smile. "You should be so lucky. I infiltrate Afghanistan, make contact with the curators of the National Museum of Afghanistan, and locate the hidden Hill of Gold hoard. I tag an object with a tracking device and feed it into the hands of the subsistence looters. I follow the object through the pipeline to Friedrich Hyde. We let him sell it, roll him up, and then follow the money to the god of gods, ending the Gray Group."

Ibrahim says hoarsely, "You should be so lucky. Do you know how batshit that plan sounds? And do you know *why* it sounds so batshit? Because it's grade-A batshit. You'll be so far outside the wire, backup will be nonexistent."

"I can find Ahmad, my terp. He'll help me."

"If he's alive, you'd be delivering another death sentence to his door."

"I can get him and his family out."

Ibrahim shakes his head. "That's a death sentence on your own head."

"I told you. He was my brother. I ate with his family. I played with his children. This is my chance. Friedrich Hyde is profiting from Taliban bloodshed and funding further terror. I'm going to end him. I'm going to end them all."

Ibrahim's gaze flicks up and down Dryden's figure. "Yeah, all right. I can help with that. Should we flag the visa for Ahmad's family to Moneypenny, or . . . ?"

Dryden shrugs. "It's easier to seek forgiveness than permission."

Nineteen
The Iron Gate

Serbia

It is here, where Serbia and Romania face each other across water the color of an oxidized Roman coin, that the Danube forms the longest gorge in Europe. The walls mock human plans, wild rock faces lush with fearless shrubs climbing to forest so tall and dense it makes a pinned-on party hat of the sky. The Iron Gate, two towering cliff faces that almost touch across the river, have turned away or crushed adventurers, traders, and conquerors for thousands of years. When Djerdap did welcome people, it accepted them so fiercely it bent them to its way of life. The prehistoric settlements discovered along the banks and plateaus reveal humans who gave up hunting, planted crops, and grew tall as aliens from a pulp comic. They left behind long graves. Today, the Iron Gate is a seldom-frequented spot on a tourist map. In the windows of the visitors' center, the shimmering bodies of butterflies whose season has come and passed gather in gullies.

There isn't anybody at the window today. If there were, they might be curious about the Dufour 61 luxury sailing yacht anchored on the Serbian side, and the tall figure spread out on deck in red trunks whose black hair and broad shoulders glisten from a recent swim. This onlooker might be even more surprised by the appearance of a second person a little way along the bank—a woman with short platinum blond hair wearing a scuba mask and a black bikini, who dives headfirst into the brilliant blue. Next, they would see the figure on deck get to his feet, watch for a moment, and then jump overboard in a neat arrow.

Rachel Wolff first becomes aware that she's drawn Marko from the yacht by his shadow rippling across the riverbed. She runs her hand through the waving seagrass for luck, and jackknifes upward, bursting into sunlight. She pulls off her scuba mask, treading water.

"Do you mind?" says Rachel in Serbo-Croat. "You're blocking my light."

A brief and transparently false expression of remorse passes over his glittering features: a chin you could strike a match on, if you were looking for a cliché; a long, sharp nose that coordinates a face made up of angles; tangled curly black hair somewhere between short and long; and thick eyebrows over slightly hooded eyes, which gleam like blue steel. He treads water easily, his body lean but strong, his shoulders and upper chest showing a smooth tan with faint scars.

"What do you need light for?" he replies in Serbo-Croat.

"I'm looking for pearls."

"You know they're endangered."

Rachel remembers Moneypenny's choices—jail, or face capture and death without rescue. "I sympathize," she says.

"Well, you're not in any danger from me."

"I don't take the pearls, anyway," she says. "I just like finding them."

"It's me who's found the pearl today."

Rachel laughs, splashing him with water. "That's the worst line I've ever heard."

"Really? I was quite pleased with it."

His fingertips touch hers, and then his hand closes on her wrist. He tugs her toward him. His hands slide around her hips, skirting the top of her briefs, and suddenly she is in the circle of his arms while he treads water for the both of them.

"You move quickly," she breathes.

"If I see something I want," he says.

"And what if it doesn't want to be taken?"

"Do you?"

Rachel slips her hands onto his shoulders, then down his biceps to his forearms. She remembers this body so well: where the skin rasped on small hairs, where it was smooth, where the muscle was thick and tensed, where the veins stood out. She tangles her fingers up with his, a small sigh escaping her.

"Can I take that as a yes?"

Rachel traces her thumb over the dimple in his chin. "You don't remember me, do you, Marko?"

Marko's arms stiffen, viselike, around her. The river stirs, buoying them. He forgets to kick his legs so she does it for him, jolting him to life. "I credit myself with never forgetting a beautiful face. I hate to let us both down, but . . ."

"It was a long time ago. We were children. At least, I was."

Marko's shoulders drop. He holds her away from him, then brings his hands back to her waist. "Rachel Petrović, here before me."

"It's Rachel Wolff now."

"You grew up," he says.

"You didn't."

Marko chuckles. "I always thought you wanted me to kiss you. Now you confuse things when we could be doing just that. Maybe *you* don't take what you want, huh?"

"Maybe I don't want you anymore."

He purses his lips, raking an eye over her. "I don't think so. This isn't a coincidence, is it?"

The first shot of plum brandy clears her mind, pushing away the days when Marko's father ran the Chevalier cell that included her parents, and she and Marko learned how to keep secrets. The second hones it. She talks stretched out on a deck chair, wrapped in a white towel. He leans against the mast, one leg folded over the other at the shin, toes pointed, jammed into the floor, like he always did when he was calculating.

"You were the second thief," he says. "Let me guess. The masked violin player I stopped escaping."

"The blind man's watch was in the case."

A snort. "Where is it now?"

"As a child, did I strike you as that stupid?"

He reaches for his sunglasses. "You would have done anything I told you, back then."

"Yes," agrees Rachel, and with a sigh sheds the towel and turns onto her front. She rests her cheek on crossed forearms and peers up at him from beneath her lashes. "Trouble is, you never told me to do anything."

He makes no effort to conceal his searching gaze over the top of his sunglasses. "I was waiting for you to grow up."

"I don't remember you being that gentlemanly."

"Don't play if you can't stand to get hurt."

"Sweetheart, I'm invulnerable."

"Big word."

"Big girl."

A grunt. "Risky, stealing from Teddy Wiltshire. Hard to fence something belonging to a thief-in-law."

"What do you mean?"

"Teddy Wiltshire. He's a thief-in-law, a boss. That's where he started, anyway."

Moneypenny never mentioned that.

"Then why were *you* stealing from him? Wouldn't your diamond Janus think twice before pissing off a thief-in-law?"

"Janus?" He smirks. "Cute." A shrug. "He'll sell anything. Teddy Wiltshire doesn't trouble him."

"Sounds like you know him well," says Rachel.

"Chevaliers don't go anywhere near that end of the pipeline. You know that better than anyone." He runs his tongue over his teeth. "So, Rachel. What's to stop me taking the blind man's watch from you and dumping your body in the Danube?"

Rachel feels the threat of him, the thrill of him, like

electricity. "You don't know where it is, for one thing," she says.

"And for another?"

"The Chevaliers are nonviolent."

"Things change."

She sits up on her elbows. "Yes, they do. Tell me something—did you take that little girl's tiara?"

"It wouldn't have suited me."

She sucks salt from the tip of her little finger. "Maybe things don't change all that much. I don't think you're quite the villain you make out."

"Then you're a fool."

Her expression turns serious. "I hope not, Marko. Because I can't fence the damn thing and I'm prepared to go fifty-fifty with you. But only if I believe I can trust you."

He juts out his lower lip. "What would convince you?"

"First—do you think you can sell it?"

"I know some men who could get it to the man who could."

"That's like saying you've got to see a man about a dog."

"Excuse me?"

"It's an English expression."

He frowns. "I don't think you're using it right."

"Maybe not. I never got a grip on the idioms. It's the dealer I want, not the dog. I'm not prepared to trust the blind man's watch to smugglers and take a smaller cut than it's worth in the bargain. I want to deliver it into the hands of the Janus himself and get the cut it's worth."

"That's not how it works. The smugglers know the routes, and those routes are dangerous. These days the same truck will contain guns, heroin, oil—you name it, it's there."

"Then let us be on it too."

"How well did that work out for your parents?" says Marko, pushing off the mast to stand over her. "They went through the pipeline to meet the man at the end because they wanted a bigger cut. They never came back."

She rolls onto her back. "Who told you that?"

"My father."

"Did he tell you who the Janus was, back then? Is it the same man now?"

"All I know is my father was afraid of the Janus back then, and I don't plan to meet today's Janus, either. There is talk about him."

It is within her gifts to stop the sudden heat rising to her cheeks. Her mother taught her total self-control. The body that acts isn't your own—it belongs to the role. "What kind of talk?"

"He was colonel of a group of paramilitaries in the civil war. A death squad."

Rachel stands up, entering his body heat. "If that were true, he'd be a wanted war criminal, not a diamond dealer accepted in the world's biggest markets."

"Names change. Yours did. Was your father's name not good enough for you?"

"Wolff is my mother's name, and my grandfather's name," she says, too easily, thrown. "He raised me, after . . ."

"You were so angry with your father?"

"Why not?" she snaps. "It was *his* last job. He was a safecracker. He had no business going down the pipeline."

Marko seizes her by the arms. "Exactly! And neither do you! You are just a girl, Rachel. You haven't grown up at all. You still believe in stories. What are you doing, stealing diamonds? You could have a normal life in England!"

"You do it," she says, doing nothing to break his grip. "You couldn't quit, either."

"There is no money here, no jobs, only corruption!"

"You don't look to me like you're struggling. Our parents lived in ordinary houses. You live on a yacht."

"If you think things have improved in Serbia, you have no sense of your own country. You are English now. A country that won't even give us visas, because they believe we are all terrorists."

"Is that what you want—a way out? The blind man's watch would be your biggest-ever score."

He pulls her closer, almost lifting her off the deck. "I know," he hisses. "That's why I wanted it."

"Do you think you can buy another life?"

"Second chances are for dreamers. I'm the best there is at what I do."

"Maybe last week you were."

His sneer becomes a dangerous smirk. "You like the danger, don't you? The danger of me."

"I'm not a kid anymore." She places a flat hand on his chest—the heart of him is still cold from the Danube. "I know what I want. When I see it, I take it. How about you?"

The moment stretches taut between them, a link not loosened by the water breaking around the bow, the clank of rope against metal, birds somewhere, the creak of trees. Then Marko kisses her—hard, angry, hungry—and she returns it with even greater force.

Twenty
The Capu

Corsica

The head of the Union Corse lives in a Napoleonic village protected by mountains rising from the Mediterranean. Johanna Harwood clinks her port over ice against Marc-Ange Draco's glass. The sun is dipping behind the purple pine, fading down the cliff face of pink granite to deepen, here on the stone terrace, to the blue of a magician's robe.

"À votre santé," says Marc-Ange.

Harwood replies the same. A deceptive comfort, this return to her mother tongue, because it had meant no return to her mother.

"Eat, eat," says Marc-Ange. "You are too skinny."

Harwood resists telling him she can do without

comments on her body from men, picking amongst the zucchini beignets and figatellu. It's true, the rich scent of salt and fat is waking her stomach up for what feels like the first time in months.

Marc-Ange grunts his approval. He lights a Gauloise. His walnut face is lined by years of smiling, then years of frowning. The mischief and magnetism Bond adored are still there in his soft brown eyes, but buried, like the last outrageous blaze of autumn on a hillside of winter branches. "I told James to bring you here to Corsica."

Harwood pauses over her plate. "When?"

Marc-Ange shrugs heavy shoulders. "He was good enough to meet with me for a drink on New Year's Day if he was close to France. He and Teresa married on New Year's Day. If not, we spoke on the phone. I always had the feeling it was an awful burden on him, this call to remember. But he did it for me, and never told me to stop calling him my son, though I could see that pained him too."

Harwood sits forward.

"The last I saw him, we met at Harry's Bar in Paris and got drunk together on whisky. I cried like a useless old man and he sat there and listened as he always did and said probably ten words, as he always did. Except this time, he had a little more to say. He was seeing a girl he was serious about. As serious as he was about

Teresa. You. I told him, bring this girl to me, you will only mess it up, James."

Harwood smiles. It hurts.

Marc-Ange flicks his cigarette over the balustrade. "But then, you left him to marry another Double O. A wiser bet for long-term happiness, James said. Still, I see no wedding ring on your finger."

Harwood has to clear her throat before she can speak. "Sid died. He died in the line of duty."

Marc-Ange says, "You do not have good luck with men."

"No. It seems I do not."

He hunches over his drink. "Then we can be unlucky in love and life together." But then the shadow passes. "Still, one cannot be too maudlin sitting across from a beautiful woman on a beautiful night in the world's most beautiful place."

"Anyone would think you brought me here so that you could charm me, instead of me trespassing on your goodwill so that I can charm you."

"Be still my beating heart. Your smile is dangerous, ma chère. You could send an old man to an early grave. But he'd die happy, in your arms."

Harwood's game face flickers momentarily.

Marc-Ange taps his teeth. "I am sorry. That is how he died, this man you left James for?"

An eagle appears overhead. Harwood watches it sway as she says, so matter-of-factly it twists her stomach, "Yes. Sid stepped in front of a bullet meant for me. It was my fault. I held him as he bled to death."

"Did you make Sid step?"

Harwood shakes her head impatiently. "I should have seen it coming. I should have been able to do something. I'm a trauma surgeon. I was a trauma surgeon."

"And now you cannot surgically remove your own broken heart. Do not give me this look. I had a daughter who knew a life of deep pain before she met James. I know the kind of grief that drives a girl to burn the heart out of herself. Teresa did so by living furiously all over the world, by stepping in front of any traffic that might run her down, whether it was South American millionaires or playboys of Dubai, always in and out of scrapes and scandals, until she took her baby daughter from a bad husband and seemed, briefly, like she might be happy. After the baby died, she would have walked into the sea if James hadn't decided to take an interest in a pretty girl who outdrove him."

"He never could resist a woman who passed him at speed."

"Who can? But still, there was perhaps more to his interest. A shared melancholy. Sometimes I have wondered if he did not wish to walk into the sea that night himself, and was stopped by his mission to save Teresa from doing the same. They were lost until they found each other. I am a romantic. Years of banditry will do that to a man."

Banditry—a polite way to put it.

"I recognize that look of being lost in you, ma chère. So lost you have left behind the safety of London and Q Branch and M to throw yourself upon the mercy of the capu of the Union Corse. To what end, he wonders."

Harwood drains her glass. "Your godson, Laurent Corso, has been assassinated."

Marc-Ange's whole demeanor changes in an instant. Where before she faced a concerned father, now he is a general whose response to a casualty is to sneer in the face of the imagined enemy he will soon grind into concrete mix. "By one of your busy Double O's?"

"No. Though a Double O was interrogating him at the time."

"You are very honest. Was it you?"

"No."

"The number?"

"I'm not that honest."

He barks a short laugh. "And who murdered my godson while he was in the capable custody of Her Majesty's Government?"

"Trigger."

Marc-Ange wags his head. "He was not worth the price she charges."

Harwood sits forward. "Have you hired Trigger yourself?"

"Not personally. But I know men who have."

"Her signature was found at the scene. She was also implicated last year in my mission to find the mole in MI6 and locate James. She shot and nearly killed a CIA agent."

"Do you expect me to weep? James is my only up-standing friend. Apart from you. There is a darkness in you both that I cannot help but recognize and like."

"I'm trying to find James. My organization is com-promised. I have to do it alone. But I need help. My target is Teddy Wiltshire, and he's in the wind."

"No one will find Teddy now he has vanished. His specialism is making people melt away. I tried to do business with him, to buy James back, but he would not deal with me. He pretended to know nothing, and I do not have the resources to war with his people. I know you are thinking it would also be bad for business, but you must believe me—where my son is concerned, I do not care for business. I cannot help you find Wiltshire. But you might speak to the one person he helped dis-appear at her request. Trigger."

Harwood says, "He got Trigger out of Russia after she failed in the shoot-out with Bond?"

"Yes, out of Russia and into the shadows, from which she operates as a freelance assassin. You say she killed my godson. If you find her, you might kill her for my honor."

"Do you know where she is?"

"I know where she is said to have killed last, before my godson. The victim was a Double O. It may have been James, I cannot say. The resting place is beyond my reach, and Trigger is not found unless she wants to be. A place known as the End of Everything. I have a blank headstone, next to Teresa's, in my family plot. All this time, I have not been able to bring myself to add the name James Bond. Perhaps you will save me the need. Or carry his body home."

"I'll bring him back alive."

Marc-Ange sighs through his nostrils. "There is that consuming fire. Listen to an old man who has buried his wife and daughter. Blaming yourself is only a bandage. If you say it was your fault, you can live on self-hatred instead of grief. But your fiancé chose to step in front of the bullet. To call his sacrifice anything other than that is to cheapen his heroic deed and his love for you. I do not believe you wish to do either."

She can't speak, so she shakes her head.

"Then we are in agreement. You will mourn him fiercely. But you will not live to die yourself."

Harwood whispers, "I don't know what else to live for."

"That is a much, much longer question, and I hope you have many years ahead of you in which to answer it. For the time being, you already have the answer. Find my son. Find James."

Twenty-One
We Have the Time

Kabul

For Joseph Dryden, flying into what had been Hamid Karzai International Airport feels like coming home. Designed by Soviet engineers, the airport was clobbered in the civil war, then again by US-led airstrikes in 2001. The West poured tens of millions into new concrete, clearing mines and detonating unexploded bombs to establish an international terminal with military bases for the US armed forces, NATO, and the Afghan air force. Landing in Kabul used to mean plugging into the hum of Afghans in business suits and *kameez* crossing paths with military contractors who wore wraparound sunglasses and tattoo sleeves. It meant the despairing envy of aid workers forced to lug books and deflated footballs between checkpoints while the army sailed past. It meant *being in his own time*, an army expression for not going anywhere until the job is done, no matter what's waiting for you back home. To Dryden, life on UK soil was one of wanting to get back here: to Luke, to his team, to his interpreter Ahmad, and back into action.

Only this time, he is wearing the bright blue sweater of a World Food Programme aid worker and the Taliban have dropped the president's name from the airport and taken over security. On the tarmac, Dryden breathes the air deep into his lungs. It tastes different. This isn't the Afghanistan he knew.

Dryden lowers the blue cap on his head. He sets off with ten other aid workers for the walk to the terminal building under the watch of armed men lounging in the back of a rusted pickup. His heart rate is steady as a hangman's drum.

"Remember, 004," says Aisha's voice in his head, "your mission is to find your former interpreter, secure his help in persuading the National Museum of Afghanistan to give you treasure from the Hill of Gold, and feed the treasure into the smuggling pipeline to flush out the antiquities Janus and whoever it is they report to—the identity of the god of gods, Rattenfänger's treasurer.

But all that depends on staying alive in the next ten minutes."

He mutters, "Thanks for the pep talk."

"We've got your back. Even if we are three and a half thousand miles away."

"That's a real comfort."

The countless times Dryden told his team to keep their eyes on a swivel come back to him as, from behind his Ray-Bans, he examines the runway for signs of the exodus he watched helplessly on TV. When the US pulled the plug, Kabul became a traffic jam. Every twenty-four hours the crowd around the airport doubled. Most couldn't even reach the gate. There were bags in every photograph Ahmad sent. Rucksacks, suitcases, plastic bags, schoolbags, all piling up around the airport. Then the blast went off. The suicide bomber had waded into the sewage canal where hundreds of families were waiting knee-deep in water to be processed for travel. Now, Dryden sees a bright pink suitcase toppled off its wheels and eaten by weeds on the tarmac. Swallowing his rising fury is nauseating.

The guards toss out his duffel. Dryden thinks his papers will be rejected, or that the young men scowling at him will recognize his body as one built for endurance and drag him into a room with no light for the

start of what would be a very slow, painful, and ultimately public end. The men laugh at the teddy bears
he's brought, steal the chocolate bars, but wave him on.

At the last checkpoint, a gray-bearded man greets
him. Dryden has shaken hands with the Taliban before,
undercover or striking deals for prisoners. He's never
known an elder's hand to be so brittle, like the bones of
a dead bird. And he will be eating better than most. Afghanistan has reached level four in a food crisis. There
are only five levels. The last is catastrophe and famine.

The elder thanks Dryden and the real aid workers
for recognizing the pain of his people. Dryden manages to smile. The muscles of his face become, in that
moment, foreign to him.

Flanking the elder are two military-aged males, one
missing an eye, the other managing to audibly mash
gum, jaw clicking under the pressure of his resent-
ment. As Dryden shakes the elder's hand, the chewer's
hungry attention latches onto him—to his Garmin
MARQ Commander watch. An alarm goes off in
Dryden's head. It's the high-pitched whine of a bone
saw. If he didn't know any better, he'd think the brain-
computer interface was malfunctioning. But he does
know better. It's the scream of instinct, telling him his
clock is running out.

Twitching his sleeve, Dryden covers the Jacquardweave strap and carbon display. He has learned to think of himself—in Ibrahim's words—as a freakish human-machine hybrid. He never even considered leaving this lifeline behind, though the implant can work without it, unless he severs the connection, as he did in the Labyrinth. There's no indication on the watch that it controls his implant. But it does possess a stealth feature, built-in topographical maps, a kill switch to clear operational data, and jumpmaster capability. In other words, a watch far too expensive for an aid worker, but perfect for a spy.

Luke used to tell new members of the team: *The smartest thing you can do is not be stupid.* So much for that. He's been kept from the theater of war for too long. Now he's going to die center stage.

"Have you been here before?" says the man.

"No," says Dryden.

"Papers."

"My papers have been checked five times already."

The one-eyed guard adjusts his grip on the rifle.

Dryden pulls his passport, visa, and employment record from his pocket. The man chucks the sheaf toward his partner.

"You have the body of a soldier."

"I'm a volunteer fireman, when I'm not on aid missions."

"That's why your hands are burnt?"

Dryden glances at his frostbite. "Yes."

"So much virtue, maybe you are trying to make up for misdeeds. Misdeeds like murdering my countrymen."

"I'm a certified aid worker. It's in my papers."

"Uh-huh."

The one-eyed man begins to rip the sheet on top of the pile.

The Frenchman who sat beside Dryden on the plane purples. "This is outrageous—"

Dryden makes his calculations fast. The chewer obviously wants his watch. He can either lose his papers, his chance to step beyond the airport, *and* his watch or sacrifice the device and hope they overlook its implications. Wringing his hands, he presses the kill switch to clear all data and waves to stop the Frenchman, revealing the watch. The chewer seizes his wrist, closing the gap of dusty tarmac between them.

"Nice," he says. He tries a button, and the watch face is replaced by Dryden's heart rate, which spikes. "You must have great concern for your health."

"Can I have my papers back, please?"

The cold fingers at his wrist squeeze. Dryden's pulse ticks visibly higher. The man murmurs, "What's it worth to you?"

"Take the watch, I don't care. I'm here because it's what my faith demands."

"Your faith?"

Of all the gambles . . . "Yes, brother."

The briefest of scowls. The soldier glances at the elder, who has been watching all this passively, but now waves a hand with a blink that squeezes tears of exhaustion onto his cheeks. The man yanks the watch off Dryden's wrist. Dryden remembers the words of Mullah Omar about America: *They may have the watches. But we have the time.*

The man holds it up to the sun, experimentally pushing buttons. His partner is putting up an argument, but the chewer only laughs, strapping the watch to his wrist and telling the man to give Dryden his papers.

The Frenchman pats Dryden on the back as they clear the last checkpoint.

Dryden says to his shoes, "Aisha?"

"We're here," comes Aisha's voice. "Nice bluff, big guy. You just lost a very expensive piece of government equipment. Not quite as valuable as you, though."

Dryden smiles tightly.

"You won't be able to control the volume now, so there's increased risk you'll become overwhelmed by the din like before," says Ibrahim. "Try to steer clear of any loud bangs."

Dryden mutters, "Good thinking. I'll just ask them to turn down the war."

"The war's over," says Ibrahim. "Remember? We lost."

Riding toward Kabul in a white jeep marked with the WFP logo, Dryden passes blankets and UNHRC tarpaulins propped up on poles, whole makeshift city blocks that house people who lost their jobs when sanctions collapsed the economy overnight. Dryden watches a child chase another down an alley of tents.

When the fumes of the city reach him, it's with the sight of more beggars than he's ever seen in Kabul. It used to be old people and little kids. Now the car crawls past twenty-somethings drifting through the streets with their hands out as if searching for some missing part of themselves. Dryden always thought this generation—kids when Western forces arrived—displayed a will not just to live but to *enjoy* life: party, climb mountains, study, write, dance.

A car horn sounds. Dryden turns, eyeing the technical vehicle as it muscles past, a Nissan pickup truck mounted with an RPG. The shrill note of alarm returns, rattling around his ear canal. The beggars scatter into doorways. Civilians bear the brunt of Taliban violence, which can come from anywhere at any time. Dryden watches the rooftops for shooters.

The convoy inches by a bazaar where mounds of fruit attract flies and whole chickens blacken over oil drums. No one is queuing, no one shouting hello to a friend, no one grabbing lunch. There is enough food. There just isn't any money to pay for it.

The Frenchman—whose jacket bulges with mints, pens, and protein bars—rests a sympathetic hand on Dryden's arm. "This is really your first placement in Afghanistan?"

Dryden turns to him.

"You look *dépossédé*—how do you say . . . bereft?"

Dryden pulls his ear. "I'm just wondering what it was all for."

The Frenchman gives a deliberative grunt. "You and forty million Afghans, my friend."

Dryden's first objective is to find Ahmad and persuade him to facilitate contact with the National Museum of Afghanistan curators. Ahmad is waiting for a visa under the UK's Afghan Relocations and Assistance Policy, meanwhile living under an assumed identity for fear of being targeted by the Taliban for his "collaboration" with Western forces. Dryden spoke with Ahmad on the phone regularly until a month ago, when Ahmad stopped answering. Dryden didn't want to text in case the phone was now in the wrong hands. He has an address for a rented flat but isn't sure what he will find as he climbs the stairs of a bullet-pocked building. It is dinnertime but he can't smell cooking oil from behind any of the doors. Ahmad used to say there were three types of people in Afghanistan: al-Qaeda (the fighters), al-faida (the enriched), and al-gaida (the fucked). This creaking building is a temple to the al-gaida, and Dryden's life is worth far less than the sack of grain over his shoulder. Dryden stops in front of a door so flimsy he wouldn't even need to kick it in, only tap, which he does now, the grip of an ice-cold octopus on his chest. He can hear static from inside, which dims slightly. Then footsteps.

The door opens by two inches. Dryden would know those eyes anywhere, anytime. The color of jade. Compressed by laughter lines that curve from the outer corners and pour down the line of Ahmad's cheekbones to disappear into his short beard. But now the lines are distorted by stamps of sleeplessness. New scars cross the flat nose and high forehead, stretching as recognition and realization hit all at once.

Dryden says, "I've been sent by the WFP, we were

told you couldn't make it to the collection point today because your son is sick."

"That is very kind of you," says Ahmad. "Please come in."

The door closes behind him. He lowers the sack to the floor, where it slumps like a drunk, and toes off his boots. A one-room apartment. Ahmad's eldest child, his son, is standing on the arm of the sofa fiddling with a TV set bracketed to the corner that cycles through hissing snow. Khadija is frozen with one hand on her son's back, helping him balance, and the other arm holding her baby, whose dull gaze does not flicker. The little girl sits on the floor in the corner coloring. She does not stir, but her crayon works faster and harder.

Ahmad turns in a full circle, as if now redrawing a mental map of the room to include Dryden, and then returns to Dryden, landing both hands on his chest with a thud. Knock to see if it's real. He says, "The WFP does not make home visits."

"You always picked holes in my cover stories."

"They always sucked." Ahmad touches the sack. "May Allah bless you. How is this possible?"

When he used to visit Ahmad's home, he'd leave a gift by the door that wouldn't be opened in front of him.

The little boy balancing on the sofa is staring at

Dryden with his mouth open. He threatens to topple and the tableau breaks into life. Khadija rises to stand in front of both children, gripping her baby tighter.

"Captain," she says, and then, "Joe. You shouldn't be here. You are in danger here."

That makes Dryden laugh, a sudden exhalation of absurdity and relief. He places his hand over his heart. "I'm sorry I haven't been able to expedite your visas. I'm trying."

"You came all this way to tell us that?" says Khadija.

"Sort of. I need your help. In return, I can put you and your whole family on an evac to the UK. Your parents too." As Dryden says this, his mouth grows dry and ashy. He used to tell new recruits, *Don't promise these people the impossible—they've heard it all before.*

Ahmad says faintly, "Our parents are dead."

Before Dryden can reply, Khadija says, "What do you mean, in return? We have already helped you. The visa is *in return.*"

"I'm sorry. But if you help me now, I can get you out. I swear."

Ahmad pulls at his beard, a gesture so familiar to Dryden he wants to hug the man. "What is it you need?"

"I've got to make contact with a curator at the National Museum of Afghanistan."

"That is very difficult. They are guarded by the Taliban and watched all the time."

"I know."

"Why must you speak with them?"

The little boy grows bored and twists the knob so that static floods the room, the din of a rattlesnake trapped in a box, or a sphinx whispering *shhhh*.

Dryden says, "I need to borrow something."

"From the museum?"

"From the Bactrian Hoard."

Ahmad scoffs. "Are you kidding me?"

"Unfortunately not. I'm on a mission to stop the looting and smuggling of Afghanistan's cultural heritage."

Khadija throws her hands up in the air. "And you will do this by stealing from us?"

"It's important to my government."

"Your government, your government—why aren't *we* important to your government?"

"I do not understand this, Joe. What about your ear?" Ahmad moves to examine Dryden's skull. "You cannot be a soldier anymore, surely."

"I'm a sort of policeman now."

Khadija hisses, "You mean you are a *spy*? There is enough damage here, my daughter hardly speaks, we do not even have rice or oil, my baby is two years old and looks as if she is only six months, I can't go outside let alone work at the clinic, we have been waiting and waiting and you come here—" Tears change Khadija's face. Even when he brought Ahmad back with multiple stab wounds, Khadija hadn't shown him any sense of her feelings. "Now you arrive finally but not to help us, to take from us, to take my husband. You are not our friend. Your hand is open from here all the way to London."

Dryden rocks on his feet. The saying goes back to the nineteenth century, when Britain controlled foreign policy in Afghanistan. It means *Do whatever you have in your power, I don't care.*

Ahmad turns to stare out the window at the rooftops, where the occasional flag of the Taliban flaps in the wind.

"I tried," says Dryden. "I kicked doors down. I rattled every cage I know. The withdrawal is above my pay grade. But this isn't. My boots are on the ground and I can make this happen. But I need your help to do it. Please. I consider you dear friends. I was honored to be welcomed into your family. I'll be honored to welcome you to Britain. But I can't do it without you." Dryden puts a gentle hand on Ahmad's shoulder. The man is much shorter than him, but the coiled power is still there, though the bones are sharper. "I needed you then. I need you now."

Ahmad does not turn around. "I have needed you, Joseph Dryden."

"I'm here now. I'm here and my life expectancy is getting shorter by the minute. So's yours. Time to gear up. Are you with me?"

There is no answer, but after a long minute filled with static Ahmad pats Dryden's hand.

Twenty-Two
The Tahilwidars

Kabul

There is a plaque at the entrance to the National Museum of Afghanistan that reads: *A Nation Stays Alive When Its Culture Stays Alive*. Located outside the city center in Darulaman, the museum has been occupied, bombed, and looted, the collection repeatedly relocated. In 1989, when the museum became too vulnerable once again, some trunks were carried to the Central Bank vault, others to the Ministry of Information and Culture, while the rest remained beneath the National Museum of Afghanistan. The heavy stone sculptures left behind were lost to looting, then bombs as the roof buckled. The UN bricked the windows, installing a zinc roof and steel doors. Museum staff mopped the floors by the light of kerosene lamps, wrapped in scarves to protect their eyes and mouths from grit. Looters tore the massive schist sculptures off their iron hooks. Locals chopped up Nuristani sculptures for firewood. In the dead grass stretching behind the museum, a locomotive from King Amanullah's railway rusted in the grip of wild and improbable trees. Staff never gave up, returning over years to fish for objects in the debris, writing index cards with shaking hands. Until: 1996. The Taliban were coming.

The Taliban demanded the location of the Bactrian Hoard, the treasure from the Hill of Gold. The tahilwidars—keyholders—never gave up the location, though the Taliban held guns to their heads, arrested them, beat them; dynamited the Bamiyan Buddhas; forced open trunks, tore off wrappings, smashed two thousand objects with hammers, leaving staff once again to sweep, dust, repackage, index. Rumor swirled around Kabul: the Bactrian Hoard had long ago been bombed, looted, sold off, melted down, never saved at all.

But in 2003, the Central Bank declared the trunks intact. The last tahilwidar had broken his key inside the lock of the most important trunk so it could never be opened. A safecracker was called. No one knew if the objects inside would be genuine or even intact, until the archaeologist who first discovered the treasure, Viktor Sarianidi, pointed out a wire repair he'd made with his own hands. The rest of the world saw the treasure first, from Paris to Tokyo. Finally, the government said it was safe, and the collection returned to the Presidential Palace for display. Six months later, the West withdrew and the Taliban retook Afghanistan. The Bactrian Hoard disappeared again. Now, the Taliban are actively seeking the treasure: only this time, they know it exists, know it's intact, and know who to ask. Still, over a year later, the new tahilwidars have kept the keys. And Joseph Dryden plans to ask them to open the door.

Dryden watches the museum through a crack in the boot of Ahmad's cousin's car as the engine quiets and then dies, replaced by the same note of alarm wailing in his head. Maybe his brain-computer interface is malfunctioning. Maybe the soldier at the airport messed it up, fiddling with the watch. Or maybe his mind is playing tricks on him again, making up sounds, like it did after the IED. This sound is a red alert. But usually red alerts are accompanied by running boots. Evacuation. Ahmad is walking the other way. Into the fire. And Dryden is chaperoning him there.

Ahmad's boots land on the dark street. A guard dozes on the statue of a mythical creature at the entrance, head slumped to one side, cradling his rifle loosely.

The noise spilling from Darul Aman Palace opposite, a neoclassical building once gutted by fire and bombs and only recently renovated, doesn't seem to disturb him. Afghans loyal to the Taliban mill around the palace grounds, perhaps reminiscing about using the king's cars for target practice back in the eighties.

Darulaman has always been a particularly dangerous area; in Taliban control right now, tomorrow the palace and the museum might be in the hands of the Islamic State–Khorasan or a splintering Taliban faction, or any number of warlords the Taliban relies on and fights by turns. It might even be targeted by the National Resistance Front in an effort to weaken the Taliban's hold on Kabul. Violence—anywhere, anyone, anytime.

Ahmad hustles toward the museum. The guard sleeps on. Ahmad crosses the lawn and puts his boot on the gravel. The guard jumps to his feet, aiming the rifle at Ahmad's head with a Cheshire cat grin. Dryden clenches the kitchen knife in his fist and holds his breath. Ahmad is armed with a roll of US dollars, which he waves now.

Sweat crawls down Dryden's neck, but the hand on the knife remains dry. The conversation takes place between bowed heads. The cover they decided on is simple. They want to take treasure from the museum. Tell the Taliban that. Ahmad is offering the armed man an upfront cut to leave his post. There is a chance he'll accept this from another Afghan, especially with the wad of banknotes Dryden has provided, though he would never accept it from a foreigner.

Gunfire—Dryden almost bursts from the boot—but it's only the men in the palace grounds firing at the full moon.

The guard lowers his rifle and snatches the bundle. He strides with overt casualness across the road toward his friends.

Dryden counts to ten, then opens the boot, rolls to the ground, and passes through the shadows, catching the museum door as it swings shut behind Ahmad. He squeezes Ahmad's arm. The floors are bare. The sculptures he greeted as friends once are also gone. The museum smells of standing water and grief.

"The guard said there is just one curator here now. He sleeps in the basement." Ahmad tilts his head far to one side, something he used to do when he wanted to crane past reality. "He said they've had no luck but I am welcome to try beating whatever I want out of him. He's tried until his fists were bruised."

Dryden nods, and sees Ahmad smile a little. How well they know each other's body language, whether it is a head tilted to the side, or a nod that means: *I've stored that information but can't process it with this job in front of me, give me until tomorrow;* a form of prayer against trauma that gets into the bones—*give me until tomorrow.*

Dryden says, "Let's go."

The curator swings off the trestle bed, spreading his arms to protect the empty shelves while blinking with bewilderment—who comes down here at night, who comes down here anymore, who knocks?

Dryden raises his open palms. It's the same curator, after all this time. "My name is Joseph Dryden. I was a soldier here. I used to visit the museum. You might remember me."

Ahmad interprets, making that familiar whirring gesture with his index fingers, like he is spinning tongues in the air.

The curator lets out a bellow's breath. He asks what Dryden is doing here.

Dryden wets his lips. "I work for the British government. I need an artifact from the Bactrian Hoard."

Ahmad translates.

The curator's laugh is hard with disbelief.

Dryden says, "I realize what I'm asking. I need the treasure as bait. I'm trying to stop the looting and smuggling. I swear to you I'll keep it safe and return it to Afghanistan when it is safe to do so. I can pay you. I can take you and your family out of here." Words have never been emptier.

The curator scratches his beard, dyed orange with henna. He speaks rapidly.

"He says the Taliban must think he is a gullible fool, sending you to trick him."

Dryden grimaces. "Persuade him it's not a trick. Quickly." He knocks his knuckles into each other as the two men debate. Dryden focuses his hearing on the stairwell. How long will the guard stay away? He doesn't have to imagine what the Taliban will do to him, Ahmad, and the curator if they're discovered—he knows the answer.

Ahmad translates. "He says you know what the tahilwidars have risked to protect Afghanistan's cultural heritage, he would never compromise a piece of it, not for his own safety, not for any money."

"I am trying to help preserve your heritage, too," says Dryden.

The curator snaps in English, "Then where have you been, sir?"

Dryden grips the back of his neck. "Lives depend on this. The looting is funding terror."

"In London," says the curator. "That is what you care about. Not the lives lost to a bomb in my mosque just last week. Not the girls killed for trying to attend school."

"I am as outraged as you, sir, by what's happened."

"I doubt that."

Dryden takes a breath. "You're right. This isn't my home. But it is my war. Please. Let me help."

The curator narrows his eyes. "Now I remember you. You were curious. You wanted to learn."

"I was grateful for the education."

"You believe you can make a difference to the smuggling?"

"I can't promise to end it. But I can promise to destroy the people who profit from it most."

The curator places a hand over his heart. "You promise this to your God?"

"Yes."

The curator shakes his head slowly. "My daughter is in the clinic. She has just had a baby, but she is not well. Her mother visits her. Tomorrow my wife will leave an object at the clinic. But you must swear to your God, Afghans will see it again."

"I swear."

Ahmad says, "My wife is a nurse. She can visit your daughter tomorrow. How can she identify your daughter?"

Dryden knows that Ahmad is avoiding asking her name—for many Afghans it is taboo to utter a woman's name in public.

The curator says, "My wife takes her flowers every day. Poppies." He lurches a little, steadying himself against the nearest shelves. "There are still flowers in Kabul. It is everything else that is dying."

The shelves shudder from left to right, as if the museum is a ship in a storm. Dryden catches the curator under the elbow as the explosion echoes through his skull. Dust rains on his head. His internal alarm is now steam escaping from a kettle about to explode.

Dryden turns to Ahmad. "RPG?"

Ahmad agrees.

Looks like Darulaman will be changing hands before tomorrow.

Dryden draws his knife. "Ex-fil, now. You should come with us, sir."

The curator shakes his head, spreading his arms to shield the trembling shelves.

"An empty building is just that—an empty building. Not worth your life."

The curator's eyes gleam, but he says nothing.

Ahmad asks him if he has a weapon. The answer is no. He turns to Dryden. "We have to get out of here." A glance back to the curator. "My wife will visit your daughter tomorrow. Please, she will be taking a great risk—"

"It will be rewarded. Go now."

Dryden and Ahmad climb to the ground floor. The museum shudders.

Aisha's voice cuts in: "The attack is coming from the north and east. If you exit via the front and return to your vehicle you'll be caught in retaliatory fire from the palace."

"Rear exit," says Dryden, leading Ahmad across the entrance hall, where light from the gunfire ripples like the reflection of water across the marble. Outside, the straggle of trees and flowering mounds of rubble are strobe-lit by the whistling arc of missiles. Dryden weighs the knife in his hand. "Stay low."

Ahmad doesn't need telling.

Dryden leads the dash across a set of formal paths demarcating a dead garden, a cracked fountain, the entrance to a school, as the shouts of victory and rumble of engines come on, and then he is grabbing Ahmad and sending him face-first to the ground, the swing of headlights passing inches over their heads, accompanied by hollers. Dryden crawls on his elbows across the dirt toward the buckled road. A shuttered ice cream shop. A closed university building. A mosque. Dryden risks a glance over his shoulder, where he sees grenades crossing in the air above the museum. The detonations trap him in an echoing well. Violence—everywhere, everybody, every time.

"Keep moving," hisses Ahmad.

Gravel scrapes Dryden's stomach. His yellow belly, he thinks, stuffed with empty promises.

It takes very little persuasion for Khadija to return to the gynecological clinic where she once worked.

The head of the clinic is a woman whose husband has taken their children to Paris while she remains to care for her patients. The day after Kabul fell, she called all her nurses and begged them to come in. Khadija tried—she was scared to walk in the streets, so she took a taxi, but the car was stopped because she was traveling without a man, and the Talib who pulled her out terrified her so much she didn't dare try again. When women took to the streets in protest, she wanted to join her friends, but Ahmad beat his fists against his own temples, begging her to consider what he and the children would do, what he would do, what would happen—*if.* So, she stayed home. She stayed and watched her daughter forget how to speak. She stayed until the distance between their changing addresses and her career at the clinic seemed even greater than the distance between Kabul and London. And now this: navigate the streets so famished she feels insubstantial, and without a companion because her husband is a wanted man; return and find a sick girl with a jar of poppies on her bedside table. *Poppies*. Men are so ridiculously romantic at the worst of times. Go to the clinic and accept some curse of gold, which she will have to smuggle beneath her hijab, praying she is not stopped. There are things far worse than death.

Go there and risk everything—because the soldier she called her friend is back and says he can save her children. She'll do all this and more if it means her children can buckle their seat belts on an airplane and take off, draw pictures of double-decker buses and talk about Paddington Bear and David Beckham, talk talk talk so they don't remember to say goodbye to the hills of Kabul, one last pain on top of every other pain to remember.

Khadija reaches the clinic without being stopped. The poppies are fat, blood-red, a diet of destruction. She hardly glances at the long object wrapped in brown paper waiting beneath the blanket. She tries to avoid the vacant stare of the baby lying on the girl's chest. The head of the clinic calls after her but she says she can't stop, she has to run—run to her children, run with them all the way to London.

It takes very little persuasion because Afghan women know the meaning of courage.

Sidereal

Twenty-Three
Roadkill

Australia

There is a crocodile in the swimming pool.

Anna Petrov watched from the kitchen as it lumbered through the tree line and over the brown lawn, deflating a football. The crocodile zipped across the cracked tiles and plunged into the blue. The overweight Colombian man who ran the house tried to grab her just at that moment, and she decided she preferred crocodiles, taking her tepid glass of water—ice cost extra—into the bludgeoning heat. The crocodile watched her as she approached the pool. The man shouted that she was crazy and slammed the door.

That's how Anna has ended up here, lying on a bare

lounger and eyeing the crocodile over the beaded rim of the glass. It eyes her right back.

Is that really how you ended up here?

She'd never seen so many people stop to watch a sunset as on the evening she arrived in Darwin. Anna joined them on the waterfront, where a loud market offered cold juice; bright food from Indonesia, Vietnam, Thailand; jewelry; Aboriginal art; and knives. A sign painted on a surfboard over a stall read: *ROADKILL BURGERS*. The scent of sizzling crocodile, kangaroo, and buffalo followed her to where she spent dollars she could ill afford on a tarot reading. The Nine of Swords reminded her of Mikhail: a man weeping in bed, blades dangling overhead. The psychic said it meant she was in crisis, living under the strain of terror and self-defeating depression. No kidding. The Tower was next. It frightened her, lightning splitting the white monolith on desperate crags. The psychic said it meant sudden and total change. It could be destruction. It could be liberation. Together, they suggested Anna should turn to a friend for help.

Anna told the psychic she had no friends. The psychic hesitated, and then said she knew someone who gave people shelter, no questions asked, who could hook you up with ID or travel for the right money. She gave Anna the address, with a final thought: "This isn't a lasting solution, though. If you know a higher power, I'd call on it."

The only higher power Anna could think of was James Bond.

That night, Anna barricaded the bedroom door in the no-questions-asked house, where downstairs either a party or a fight was breaking out between members of a drug cartel and an outlaw motorcycle gang. She wrote the letter in careful block letters.

The corporate cleanliness of the British consulate, between the parliament building and Government House, scared her. Anna waited until after 9 a.m. and chose a Bentley in the best parking spot. She slipped the letter beneath the windshield wiper and hurried away, sweating.

Now, Anna watches the crocodile float inch by inch across the dirty pool toward her. Self-destructive behavior is one way to put it.

"I didn't eat you," she says, "so don't eat me."

A British man's cool voice plucks her gooseflesh: "I don't think it works that way."

Anna sits up. He wears a suit belonging to a man who drives a Bentley. He doesn't seem to mind the crocodile. He's not James Bond.

"Are you Anna Petrov?"

She nods.

"We received your note."

A door slams, heavy feet run.

The man smiles mildly. "I suppose I do rather look like the establishment, don't I? Perhaps we'd better relocate."

The crocodile suddenly spins in the water, thrashing and jerking. Water sloshes over the side, carrying a tide of dead flies to Anna's feet as she gets ready to stand—or run, whether from the crocodile or the man in the suit, she's not sure.

"I'm a friend of James's," says the man. "He told me to put you on a plane. He'll meet you in Narva."

Anna swallows on a dry throat. "Not London?"

"We have a safe house in Narva. James wants to do it that way."

"Why?"

"He wants some time alone with you first," the man says confidingly.

Anna feels a flutter in her pulse and tells herself not to be a schoolgirl. "Did he say anything else?"

"He's glad to hear from you," says the man. "He's been worried sick. He wants you to know he meant it when he said he'd protect you."

The relief is too strong to resist. Anna takes the man's hand and lets him lead her away from the crocodile and from houses where she has to barricade herself against a life she was never supposed to lead. It's all been a nightmare, she tells herself. An alternative reality. She took the wrong turn, somewhere. Marrying Mikhail, probably. That's what her parents always said. But it will be all right now. She will find happiness and safety with James.

PART III

Smuggled

A Week's Passage

Twenty-Four
The Living Grave

Afghanistan

The minibus was once painted a jolly mustard, with the English words *We Trust in God* written in blue across the side. Dryden resists taking it as a sign—good or bad—when he pays for the rusting vehicle, which stinks of chicken shit and bounces on rotten springs, but survives the two-hundred-plus-mile journey northwest from tarmac to dusty track, Dryden and Ahmad swapping the wheel, tired eyes gauging the threat of a ten-year-old shepherd with three sheep, lugging a rifle. Khadija tries to keep the children from arguing in the back as they whip past brightly painted chaikhanas without stopping for snacks, murals of abundant rivers and walls decorated using flattened Coke cans hammered inside out with intricate patterns now relics from an immediate yet distant past. Khadija says those other times are like a dream.

The mission objectives are simple. The execution, less so. Locate a subsistence looter at the Hill of Gold and give them the geo-tagged treasure, feeding the item into the smuggling pipeline, then follow it to the antiquities Janus. The Hill of Gold is located just three miles from Shebergh n, the second provincial capital to be retaken by the Taliban. First action is to find a safe place for Khadija to hide with the children in the minibus. This area was always in the grip of strongmen, and Dryden's attention flits between the road and the rearview mirror, passing farmers, forced on foot by drought and floods to seek some alternative in the city to selling their organs or their daughters.

"There," says Ahmad, pointing across the parched oasis to abandoned gas tanks in the scrub.

Dryden nods, off-roading with a lurch and following the broken arrow of a gas pipeline stripped for scrap to the tanks, which look like gigantic golf balls left to weather amongst the weeds. He parks in the shade of two peeling spheres, hiding the minibus from the road. Dryden turns in his seat, giving Khadija a Makarov pistol. She takes it, her mouth set.

The smell of ghostly petrol hits him as he gets out.

Dryden shoulders an AK-47. He tucks the long trea-sure gifted to him by the museum curator into his coat before passing Ahmad the Mosin-Nagant, a five-shot bolt-action rifle made of wood. It was the best he could procure without drawing too much attention.

They proceed on foot over ripples of burnt brown dust.

Ahmad says, "When we spoke on the phone, you told me you were doing government work. I thought you were a clerk. I thought maybe you found peace."

"In times of peace, the warlike man attacks himself. I was going crazy without a mission, crazy not being able to hear or speak normally. The outfit I work for now, they fixed up my head and gave me something to aim at."

"Does Luke still take care of you?"

Dryden lets the euphemism pass gently between them. "Not anymore. He got himself into trouble I couldn't get him out of. He's inside now."

"Inside where?"

"Prison."

Ahmad nods. "Trying to get Luke out of trouble. To get me and my family out of Afghanistan. I do not think you are warlike. I think you cannot live without responsibility to others. That is honorable."

Dryden leads over a trickling riverbed. Flies whine

around his ears. "Maybe, once upon a time. Now, the good fight feels an awful lot like losing the war to me. Nothing I do seems to matter."

"Who says it should?"

"You always did tell me to shrink my ego."

"And you never listened."

Dryden gives Ahmad a hand up the bank to the brown checkerboard of irrigated fields pockmarked by deeper and deeper wells searching for water where none can be found. Disturbed, a rat snake bursts from the stubby grass and darts away, its two-meter body somehow weightless.

"How have you coped with it?" Dryden asks. "Not being able to act, not being able to move heaven and earth to put your family on a plane?"

"Who says I've coped?" A quiet laugh. "It's Khadija who has coped. I've made a friend of despair. Expect nothing and you won't be disappointed when it's what you get."

"You expect nothing from me?"

"There you go again. It's not about you. We will do what we must. We are unlikely to succeed. But it's what we must do."

On the other side of the fields they double-time a dirt road past a closed school and a shuttered petrol station, approaching the ruins of Emshi Tepe as the golden hour burnishes the ancient walled city, whose citadel and palace on an island of green in a barren plain first attracted the Afghan–Soviet archaeology team.

Now it is a dried-out desire path beaten by the footsteps of the hungry and the mercenary, which Dryden and Ahmad follow another five hundred meters to the mound where Viktor Sarianidi, Zemaryalai Tarzi, and Terkesh Khodzhanyazov excavated the necropolis always known by locals as the Hill of Gold.

Q says there's a high statistical probability a subsistence looter will meet smugglers at the site tonight, sifting the pattern of movement around the Hill of Gold caught on satellites in the last six months.

The partitions and scaffolding clinging to the mudbrick terrace and columned hall have partially subsided, the dig ransacked, abandoned, and consumed by shifting earth. Shebergh n hovers on the horizon. Dryden thinks he can see the football stadium on the outskirts of the city, where he, Ahmad, and Khadija will be publicly executed if this does not come off.

He climbs into the tomb after Ahmad as the sun begins its descent, sinking blood-red into the poppies brightening the desert.

Dryden sits with his back against a thick wall of crumbling brick, knees tucked to his chest, keeping his feet from the nearest grave. The discovery of 21,000 gold artifacts lining the tombs of six royal nomads synthesized the Silk Road itself, rolling up the Great Wall of China, the Pamirs, the Kushan Empire, the Levant, and the Mediterranean Sea, revealing ancient Afghanistan's diversity. Chinese-inspired boot buckles, a golden Aphrodite with the wings of a Bactrian deity and an Indian forehead mark, daggers in a Siberian style—the inspiration was global, the workmanship local. Dryden keeps one fist closed around the treasure tucked into his coat. A sword has always been waiting for 004, a sword or a gun or a knife, ready to be wielded by a body designed to do hurt. He is unsure who he is hurting now, and the question yawns around him as the temperature drops.

The stars here are just as bright as they used to be.

It is a short sword or dagger, really, the weapon of the nomads. The blade itself is double-edged iron, mottled and scaled. The guard is smooth gold, the gold-covered shaft studded with turquoise, as is the sheath, gold and turquoise wrapping around leather. The front relief depicts animals devouring one another and being reborn in an unbroken line, the cycle of life and death, what Lucretius called "the living grave." The rear shows the Tree of Life.

Dryden's tired legs stretch toward the grave in front.

Maybe Q was wrong, and he's dragged Ahmad's

family here for nothing. His imagination tells him the tomb is alive with scorpions, but the rustling is probably sand flies or lizards. Probably.

The weapon was found in the fourth tomb with the only man. He had been tall. His head rested on a golden bowl, which itself lay upon a silk cushion. His sword lay beside him with three daggers, two long-distance bows, and a leather-clad seat on folding legs. A throne that traveled. A king of the Silk Road.

Ahmad clutches Dryden's arm. Footfall, getting closer.

The Uzbek tribesman halts, leaving a distance as long as a grave between him and Dryden, who clambers out of the necropolis with his rifle raised. Ahmad outlines the deal rapidly, his words frisked by the wind.

The man spits toward Dryden. "Firangi."

Dryden doesn't need that translated. *Foreigner.* You may be an armed, wealthy Westerner, but you mean less than nothing to me.

Ahmad speeds up. The man waves his arms, telling them to leave.

Aisha's voice cuts in: "004, you've got three vehicles approaching from the west, likely the smugglers coming to meet the looter. And there's movement near the minibus, but we can't get a good picture."

Running out of time.

Dryden tears the wrapping from the sword and stabs it into the hard earth.

The man is silenced, watching the starlight slick the gold. Then he asks Ahmad a question.

"What does he say?" asks Dryden.

"The dialect is difficult—roughly, he wants to know who you think you are conquering."

"Tell him we'll pay him to sell it, and he can keep the profit."

The man listens, then laughs before replying.

"He says he'll take your money. He was planning to give the smugglers gold coins. This will feed his family for months. But he says you should know—the desert doesn't care if you're rich or poor, it will bury you just the same. Ask the king."

Aisha's voice: "Dryden, we're seeing increased movement near the gas tanks, and those smugglers are almost on you."

Dryden leaves the sword in the ground, retreating with his rifle at the ready. He tosses the money down, then tugs at Ahmad's arm. "We've got to go."

"You don't want to keep surveillance—"

"Now."

Ahmad reads Dryden's face. He turns his back on the man, fumbling for his phone, then thinks better of it—if Khadija is hiding, the ringtone could give her away. Ahmad sets off at a run, Dryden behind him.

They have no night vision. The terrain is flat and hard. Dusty sediment kicks up into Dryden's face. The sound of his own pounding boots is interspersed with Aisha and Ibrahim's commentary as they describe the arrival of the smugglers, who draw close to the Hill of Gold and then wait inside the vehicles. The Uzbek tribesman is approaching the smugglers. Ahmad asks if Khadija and the children are in danger, how Dryden knows, what he means when he says he has overwatch, how can that be when he's not wearing an earpiece, what does overwatch show? But MI6 don't have a good enough picture—all Aisha and Ibrahim can tell him is that there is movement building around the gas tanks, nine figures in total. The Uzbek man has handed the sword over. The piezoelectric transmitter hidden in the sheath is working—the smugglers are bugging out with the treasure. A rose blush touches the desert, greeted by birdsong. Dryden and Ahmad cut through patchy forest straggling beside the dry river. The gas tanks are finally in sight.

Ahmad comes to an abrupt stop, Dryden checking behind him.

Nine golden jackals prowl the gigantic golf balls, sniffing the human footsteps, brushing the wheelbase of the minibus. One jumps onto the hood of the vehicle, its elongated body and short snout silhouetted against the rusting paint.

Aisha says, "004, the smugglers are heading west. It's a heavily mined area, they know the route, you don't. If you don't want to lose that sword, you need to pursue, now."

Ahmad slings his wooden rifle around. He aims it a meter over the head of the nearest jackal. The shot warps the air.

The jackals turn as one, fixing pale eyes on Dryden and Ahmad. The jackal on the bus jumps down, pacing forward.

Ahmad fires into the air again, now running forward and shouting. Dryden follows, AK-47 fixed on the lead animal, finger hovering over the trigger.

The jackals scatter. Dust reverberates in the air.

Ahmad tears the door to the minibus open.

Dryden watches, one hand unthinkingly over his heart, as Khadija and Ahmad embrace, Khadija clutching the pistol with white knuckles.

The land that streaks by the windows of the minibus is just what Lucretius said: a living graveyard.

Dryden trails the smugglers' convoy at a distance, sometimes dropping back, sometimes racing to catch up. When they can't avoid passing through a village or town, the people who stare at them are the color of dust, and soon Dryden is too, the windows doing nothing to stop the grit getting into his eyes, between his teeth, inside his clothes.

Sometimes the road is painted with rings of red and white. White means safety. Red means land mines. Dryden has to find a way around, lurching into dry creek beds or reversing for miles. Clashes between the Taliban and local resistance force them to seek shelter as valuable seconds slip through the hourglass and the sword threatens to pass beyond his reach. He can't get involved. He'd expose himself and Ahmad's family. He has to be there to see the Janus accept the sword. Q can surveil from space, but it can't ID a man's face from all the way up there. He has to know who to follow to the god of gods. Khadija tries to shield the children from witnessing the catastrophic fragility of the human body: people shot, burnt, torn apart. The screams in Dryden's head aren't imaginary anymore. Worse than useless, he watches people die.

There has been no rain in Herat for months and Dryden can hardly see through the haze. The minibus is caught up in an endless line of cars and motorbikes trailing to the Iranian consulate. Ahead, the smugglers edge toward a rendezvous. People queuing with all their possessions stuffed into suitcases and plastic bags look petrified, turned to stone and stuck to the spot, as if they have been waiting years for deliverance. Dryden's stomach flips inside out with impotent rage.

The sword changes hands. He thinks the new smugglers will cross the border, but they turn south toward Dasht-e Margo.

Ahmad turns to him. "You know where they're going." It's not a question; it's a statement flat as a terminal prognosis.

"Yes," says Dryden. "The Desert of Death."

Twenty-Five
The End of Everything

Altai Mountains

At the End of Everything there is snow. Johanna Harwood walks the river valley with her gun drawn. The snow is thigh-deep and it rasps as she wades forward. Her breathing is absorbed by the white walls. She spent a day floating in a sensory deprivation tank once as part of her Double O training to withstand torture. This is as white as that was black, as absorbent as that was alienating, and yet somehow just the same. She keeps her eyes on the sky, though it is a white stream just like the river. Icicles beard the trees and ring like wind chimes as a sudden gust breathes down Harwood's neck. Creatures pushed from the snow by global warming form an elephant graveyard in her path. Harwood touches the trunk of a woolly mammoth. She pulls the laminated map from her ski coat and examines the web of mountain passes, following with her gloved finger the thread that leads to Ukok Plateau, where Russia, China, Mongolia, and Kazakhstan meet. The tribes who worship at the holy Buddhist sites and shamanistic altars carved from these rocks know this place as the "End of Everything." She pockets the map. One last push. The head of a saber-toothed beast bares its teeth with her.

It has taken a week to reach this pass where the air grows thinner and the snow coating the towering rocks grows brighter with every step toward the sun, scraping the heavens. First, Marc-Ange Draco arranged a false Turkish passport for her. One slip in her cover and she might as well just wave a flag that reads *Arrest Me, I'm a Western Spy.* She took the long way around, flying from Nice to Shanghai, then catching a connecting plane to Xi'an Xianyang International Airport in Northwest China. Harwood spent a sizable chunk of her winnings from Daniella Draco's gaming tables to secure a cargo plane and a pilot willing to cross the China–Russia border. Passing over the old Silk Road, she was struck by how small the Great Wall looked, a spine of time crumbling into oblivion far from the tourist dollar. Still, when you've got thousands of years of stunning history, who cares about a garden wall. They're just spare bricks.

The plane set down on a farm. When Harwood stepped onto Russian soil, she braced for the bullet from nowhere, the shot that was always waiting to force a Double O's retirement. But only the wind whistled. She bought a banged-up UAZ-469 and drove the uneven Chuisky Highway to the bank of the river Chuya, where she rested at an empty base camp for climbers. A pamphlet told her the highest peak contained the entrance to the afterlife, and that shamans in the Altai Mountains were conductors between the world of the living and those who had moved to a better world. This was a "power place," where the scientifically impossible occurred. There were rumors that Freemasons had built a Moon City in the mountains.

The next day, the car bumping over a dirt road, Harwood's irises expanded as she passed lake after lake, the landscape a Twister mat where every circle was blue—the brilliant light got inside her and cracked something open. A gateway, maybe. She drummed her fingers on the wheel to keep blood pumping through her hands. She reached Tepliy Kluch as the Saylugem Ridge glowed red in the setting sun. Harwood left a stack of coins at a stone altar and stripped off, submerging herself in the twenty-degree hot spring. The muscles around her heart thawed, then kicked, telling her she was still on this side of the gateway, for now. She slept in an empty hut, using her gun as a pillow.

This morning, having driven as far as she could before abandoning the car in a narrow pass, she makes her way into the mountains on foot. Her father's camera hangs around her neck, zipped into the coat, and bangs now against her chest as if shaking its head: no, no, no. Her boots fight for purchase. She slips and her gloved hand catches a rock, the only rock lying above the snow. Steadying herself, Harwood looks over her shoulder at the drop, then at the glistening meteor—for it has to be a celestial body: it is the only rock not covered in snow—lying on a crisp bed. She wonders when it landed. Scraping heaven is right.

"Thank you"—the words of gratitude to the meteorite for holding her steady are whipped from her mouth. Below, a plateau of rolling hills gleams with hundreds of lakes, running from turquoise to bluish-black, bound by veins and arteries of milky rivers. The snow is patchy here, brown grassland waving in the wind. Marc-Ange Draco said that Trigger's last kill was rumored to have been a Double O, slain here and the body said to remain, waiting for burial, at the End of Everything. Had James

Bond never come home because he was shot and killed by the assassin he spared out of compassion? Perhaps those three numbers carved into the cell in Syria were old, or planted there by Mora to unseat Harwood's sense of reality—something, she recognizes with a physician's dispassion, hardly difficult to achieve now she keeps company with ghosts. Or perhaps she'll find some sign of Trigger's path. Perhaps she'll root out the assassin, who will tell her how Teddy Wiltshire makes people disappear. Perhaps she'll lead Harwood to James. This is, after all, a place of miracles.

But what if it's not? What if she finds the remains of James up here in the ice, too late to hold him in his last moments as she had for Sid? The thought knocks her off-balance as she struggles over the rocky earth, the in-finity around her suggesting she could easily take flight, swatted and thrown about in the gale of the world before disappearing into nothingness. The memory of holding Sid in her arms as his blood left him, how he turned from red slick to ice cold in what felt like seconds; the sobs that racked her until she realized he was still here and she didn't want to distress him; telling him M would walk her down the aisle, a glim-mer lighting his eyes, as if he was really watching her approach—and then the glimmer died. The commu-nity center hosted his funeral instead. Sid's father asked her how she knew his son and all she could say was that they had worked together.

They did work together, for although Sid's mind was made of numbers and utilitarian philosophy and hers preoccupied with the body and its meanings, they had worked together.

Harwood is aware of tears freezing on her cheeks and gasps for air. She shakes herself. If you're about to find the body of the other man you love, then you're not going to cry about it. The last thing James Bond would want is the tears of Mary Magdalene, as if he were some fallen saint. If you find his body you'll raise a toast with the flask in your breast pocket and then you'll ask him where he wants to spend eternity, whether you should carry him home to Scotland, or leave him here at the End of Everything, the only place, it strikes her with a small smile, that could ever kill James Bond. For if he is dead and Sid is dead then it really is the end of everything, and Harwood will kill Trigger and then take herself somewhere and leave it there: leave this self she hardly recognizes, and either carry on without it—or not.

The horizon seems never to come. Harwood drinks in the blue-white peaks, time made solid; twisting river valleys, sheer ravines, the green farms far below, the shadow of a yak crossing vast nothingness, the dusty orange of arid desert, the glistening of glacial lakes. The cold reaches for her with a seductive suggestion it could freeze her to this spot, make a statue of her, and all her efforts and all her pains will be over. She can just go to sleep.

Harwood fixes her gaze on a cave across the plateau. If you wanted to shelter, it would be the only spot. Feathers hang on colorful string from the entrance, shivering in the wind. Her steps crunch and creak through the snow, bouncing around the ice walls. The cave meets her with darkness like the ocean floor that turns, as she adjusts, the blue of fine crystal. She stoops, making her way deeper into this frozen vein of the mountain. Toward the back of the cave a shape is gaining outline. An altar formed from rock, on which stubs of candles glisten, fire frozen over. The wind shrieks but her heart is even louder. Harwood tells herself she is a surgeon and a Double O and death is her business. She tells herself her prayers are being answered, she just doesn't know which ones. She takes the last few steps.

It can be read as a crime scene. The floor of the cave is solid blue rock and attempts at building a fire have frozen to the ground. The body lies curled around the glistening remains of petrified coal. It is perfectly preserved by the ice, marbled with snow. It is unclear whether the man decided to die here in this cave that was sacred to someone, or was perhaps brought here and nursed until the inevitable happened. A man over six feet tall with dark hair. His face is obscured by his arm, which he brought up to shield himself, perhaps, or for comfort. A red patch like rust on the floor of a garage spreads from beneath his torso.

Harwood kneels by the body. The clothes are suitable for the mountains. That tells her nothing. The hand held up to the face was strong, the knuckles somewhat swollen from years of damage. The watch on the wrist, encased in an inch of ice, is a Rolex, but she can't read the date or time—the face is shattered. She remembers James telling her about using his Rolex as a cosh once, smashing it in the face of a guard on Piz Gloria when he was trying to escape and warn the world about Blofeld's bioweapons—how upset Q was by his reckless endangerment of government property, back when Q was a person.

She lies down on the glimmering rock floor, forming a closed bracket to the body's open bracket. Cushioning her head on her forearm, she brings herself level with the man, so that she can see his face beneath the shield of his arm.

His brown eyes are open.

Brown.

Relief floods Harwood at a sickening rate, like a river bursting a dam.

It isn't James.

Then the relief turns to adrenaline that hollows her stomach and fills her cheeks with bitter iron.

It's Ventnor. 005. The Double O agent who fell to his death, according to 000. Fell down a ravine, his body hitting the ice. Didn't freeze to death in a cave.

Harwood rolls the body over, a queasy clunk. She touches Ventnor's cheek. He was James's generation. She knew him as someone good for a laugh in the office, his affability cover for efficient deadliness that got him inside and out of worse spots than this one more than once.

Perhaps Ventnor climbed free of the ravine but 000 abandoned hope too soon, not there to lend a hand by tragic chance. Ventnor wouldn't have been able to send a distress signal using his Rolex because it was broken. Maybe it was simply his time, the statutory age of retirement approaching, extinction beckoning. The end every Double O waited for.

But in his eyes, there is a deep black hole of fury. He wasn't resigned.

What Harwood does next is performed by the part

of her that peered through slats in surgical tents when her mother took her as a child on trips with Médecins Sans Frontières. The part of her that wants to understand how people tick, because the mechanisms of her young life were controlled by chaos. She lets it take over as she uses a lighter to thaw the midsection, and then her penknife to make the necessary incisions.

The bullet she removes is the same caliber employed by Trigger; the same caliber she dug from Felix Leiter, the one man she managed to save; the same caliber fired at 004 at the mouth of Zeus's cave.

000 had never said a word about gunfire. He said Ventnor fell to his death.

No sign of abrasions, no trauma from a fall.

For the first time, Harwood regrets being cut off from Regent's Park. She opens the back of Sid's Casio but the location tracking device is gone, something she ought to be grateful for, she reflects, considering Ventnor's fate.

So Triple O is almost exactly what his name suggests— a Double O double agent.

She grits her teeth until her jaw aches as she recalls him laughingly suggesting that she might be cracking up.

It was 000 who shot at Harwood and Felix using Trigger's weapon. It was 000 who shot at Dryden in

Crete. He must have scrambled the geotag on his comms so it appeared he was still in Oman when he reported in to Moneypenny.

What were 005 and 000 doing up here at the End of Everything in the first place? Harwood's skin crawls as she remembers reading the file during her long hours of dogwatch. 000 reported they had been in the Himalayas investigating flora and fauna smuggling, which 005 insisted was part of a much larger crime, after receiving a tip from what he described as twenty-karat-Grade-A-go-all-night-HumInt. In other words, human intelligence gathered from a well-placed informer.

Snow leopards are known as mountain ghosts. Did 005 bring 000 up here hunting for ghosts, not knowing death was watching his six? And was the trade in snow leopards just another tendril of the Gray Group, just another Janus at the end of a pipeline filling Rattenfänger's coffer?

000 named a mountain, named the ice, almost named the place and the crime—was it simply that a lie close to the truth is easier to maintain, or has Harthrop-Vane been laughing at M and Moneypenny's trust in him, granting them the puzzle pieces because he believes they'll never assemble the picture? He used Trigger's

weapon here when he didn't need to, blowing his cover in other killings, because he thinks he's untouchable. The smug son of a bitch is having fun.

Harwood wraps her gloved hand around Ventnor's crooked fingers. What a place to die. Betrayed. Cold, and then colder, life a red thread turning blue. She hopes he wasn't alone, that someone who worshipped at this altar prayed over him, perhaps even offered solace.

"Were you up here looking for snow leopards?" Her whisper carries around the cave.

005 must have witnessed something beyond poachers to invite assassination. The traffic of flora and fauna is not high on MI6's priority list. But for some reason 000 deemed 005 enough of a threat to drop him forever.

What other mountain ghosts wait at the End of Everything?

"Did you see something?" Harwood asks. "Did you see something you weren't supposed to?"

His indignant eyes stare back at her.

The body keeps the score. That was something the psychiatrist told her at Shrublands. The body keeps the score. One's experiences are imprinted on the brain and the heart and the gut and the joints just like eras imprinted on ice.

Harwood leans closer through the crystalline fog of

her own breath to examine 005's fingernails. She undertook a residency in the morgue as part of her medical training. There, she would have taken scrapings and examined the results for particulates that might suggest whether the deceased met with foul play. But here there is no equipment, only what her senses tell her. And her senses tell her that the glittering gray beneath 005's fingernails is not ice. It's meteorite dust.

A plan comes to her, but for it to work she needs the moon. Harwood grips Ventnor's hand tighter.

Light drains from the cave. Harwood uses the lighter, the remains of the candles, and dry leaves and bark kicked to the back of the cave to start a fire, bathing 005 in gold. She isn't sure if he was religious. She isn't sure if she is religious. But she prays nevertheless. Her heart rate slows, needing movement, but she is too tired for that. She remembers lying in bed with Sid in the Barbican, curtains flung open, watching lightning fork the sky. Remembers riding on the back of a motorbike driven by Bond through Tangier, gripping his jacket, breathing in the smell of him, her face buried in his neck. Happiness and complete security sink through her, and she wants nothing more than to lie down next to 005, sleep at this forgotten altar.

Night descends.

Harwood draws herself up. Shakes her head. Pounds

her fists against her thighs and her biceps. Stuffs rations into her dry mouth. Staggers to the opening of the cave.

Under the spotlight of the half-moon, the path of fallen meteors flares iridescent silver against the darkened face of snow that blankets the End of Everything. Her gaze follows the line of meteorites halfway down the Tabyn-Bogdo-Ola Pass: the Five Sacred Peaks, named by Genghis Khan, waves of stone sea frozen under indigo and white caps running down to steep glaciated slopes and further still to black gorges. At the foot waits the entrance to Shambhala, but she isn't going there yet. Not yet.

She knows better than to scale down a mountain at night, but needs the luminous breadcrumbs or she'll never find her way. Of course, Ventnor may have scraped any of these meteors, but it's a clue, the man's last act, maybe even the thing he shouldn't have seen, and she is prepared to walk blind if it means finding her way—has been doing so for months, in fact, so why not a few steps more?

When the sun first leaks over the granite, announcing the tipping point of a new week, Harwood feels it like a bellows in her chest, telling her she is alive. The path of meteors glimmers in and out of her vision. Just ahead is a gigantic glittering dome, half-buried by snow.

She remembers the pamphlet: rumor says Freemasons built a Moon City at the End of Everything—whatever a Moon City is. Either way, she is two hundred yards beyond the perimeter of what appears to be a scientific polar station.

Harwood finds, by a miracle, that her fingers are still working. Your fingers are your livelihood, her mother said when she was training to be a surgeon. Play the piano. Knit. But never, ever play sports. Don't roughhouse with the boys, Johanna. She used to say that when Harwood was a kid. Don't roughhouse with the boys.

Harwood drops behind a rock. She fumbles for her father's camera and presses her eye to the viewfinder. Zooms in. Picks up an armed guard shivering at the entrance.

She knows what 005 witnessed. She knows that guard from the surveillance photographs she showed Marilyn Aliyeva in the interrogation room. He works for Teddy Wiltshire.

There are three possibilities.

Either this is a prison where Teddy Wiltshire keeps high-value prisoners, far away from CCTV cameras and witnesses, and James Bond is inside.

Or, this is Wiltshire's own safe harbor.

Where does a human trafficker disappear to when

the waters get rough and discretion is the better part of tax evasion? Some billionaires go to Dubai, others cast anchor on luxury yachts, others buy islands. This one is the master of disappearing people, so he disappears to the End of Everything.

Or both, and she'll find Teddy and James in Moon City.

Whatever the answer, that's Teddy Wiltshire's guard, and this is Teddy Wiltshire's kingdom, beyond the reach of MI6 and the CIA, where Wiltshire can rest easy in the belief no one will ever track him down.

Johanna Harwood smiles.

He's wrong.

Twenty-Six
The Gap

Europe to Africa to Central America

Felix Leiter says, "When Moneypenny told me she was sending a Double O, I hoped she meant Johanna Harwood."

Triple O says, "I'll try not to take that personally."

"You do that," says Felix encouragingly. "Envy's no good for your skin."

The two men could be mistaken for friends meeting in Gellért Baths, lit by early sun slanting through the stained glass roof. Felix Leiter reclines on the steps descending into the pool, the water up to his waist, his torso wreathed in steam. Conrad Harthrop-Vane leans in light blue shorts against a marble column.

Felix's prosthetic right hand and left leg, from knee to foot, rest on the blue tiles.

"That's why you wanted to meet here?" asks 000. "You were hoping to skinny-dip with 003?"

"I'll have you know I'm wearing trunks."

"Imagine my relief."

Felix Leiter cracks a grin. "Well, come on. Get in. These waters have therapeutic properties."

"I don't need healing."

"Spoken like a true Double O."

Harthrop-Vane raises his arms as if in surrender and rotates slowly on the spot. "No bugs the water will short, no concealed weapons, no ominous markings. Happy?"

"I wouldn't put it past Moneypenny to put the bug in your head."

"Paranoid, are we?"

"Let's just say your outfit hasn't exactly been promoting confidence of late." Felix waves his left hand in the direction of Triple O's shorts. "MI6, that is. Orlebar Brown's swimwear is doing you proud. How'd you hurt your leg?" Felix makes no effort to conceal his study of the bandage wrapped around Harthrop-Vane's calf.

"Falling chandelier. You?"

"Shark," says Felix, a wry smile creasing his hawk-like face. He lifts a straw-colored fringe streaked with gray from eyes the color of ash, revealing a further trace of damage below the hairline. Then Felix taps his scarred chest. "This is my latest. Courtesy of Trigger."

Triple O steps into the water. The steam claims him too. "Moneypenny said you have a lead on Trigger."

After the robbery at Al Bustan Palace Ritz-Carlton and Teddy Wiltshire's disappearance, the rest of the party stayed on for Lisl Baum's birthday over the long weekend. Harthrop-Vane's mission from Moneypenny was to sniff out whether any guests had connections to the Gray Group. He was present for few highlights, and none that pointed to solid leads. The diamond dealer Viktor Babić had a gyrfalcon with him and demonstrated its hunting power in the dunes with an expression that chilled. Friedrich Hyde, the antiquities dealer, tried to persuade the other guests to play Parcheesi as Emperor Akbar intended it, with beautiful women instead of stone pieces. When Hyde told his fuming wife that his was strictly an academic passion, Triple O almost choked on his drink. Conversations consisted of the BBC bombing, the percentage of a kindergarten class that got into the Ivy League, the commodities market, construction for the World Cup. The same bland nothings. It was the world HV1 craved, but its superficiality meant nothing to Triple O. He cared about what lay beneath. Reunited with Lisl Baum,

Triple O remembered the vertigo of loss the day she told him she was going away. Entwining his hand with hers beneath the stars on the beach, he asked whether she'd ever thought of him in the years since.

"Don't get sentimental," she said. "You're only here to use me. Remember?"

It didn't feel that way. Regardless, he got nothing out of it—nothing valuable to MI6, anyway, who were blind to his absence from the party while he dropped in to Crete. After that, Moneypenny directed him to Budapest, where Felix Leiter had been reassigned to head up the American station following the explosives in Berlin the previous year. When 004 discovered the sniper rifle associated with Trigger on the mountaintop in Crete, MI6 flashed an alert to Interpol and the CIA. The American cousins officially said they had no new data on Trigger. Unofficially, Moneypenny was told Felix Leiter had been playing detective, but that Langley had denied him permission to pursue directly or indirectly because his leads were thin and he was being pushed to retire, too many miles on the clock.

Felix says, "If I did have intel on Trigger's whereabouts, what makes you think I'd share it with you?"

Harthrop-Vane shrugs. "Q has given a ninety-five percent probability to Trigger being Rattenfänger's assassin. She's got to be paid somehow. Trigger represents a real and present threat to Double O agents in pursuit of the Gray Group, Rattenfänger's bank, and she may well also point to where the money comes from. Moneypenny wants me to pursue her. And word is you want to run her down as well. You have actionable evidence, but no backup. I'm at your service."

"Lucky me." Felix scratches his chin, eyeing Triple O up and down. "Scuttlebutt has it I'm obsessed with her, that right?"

"She does seem to have a way with men when firing at a distance."

Felix laughs, but his searching gaze does not relent. "You look fit enough to do this solo. Sure you want to ride with an old gun hand who gets winded climbing stairs, since . . . ?" He taps his chest where the sniper would have fully penetrated his heart, were it not for a bulletproof vest and Johanna Harwood.

"003 does neat stitches."

"Next time I'm hoping she'll sign her name. Where is Johanna, anyhow?"

"Off the reservation, as you Americans put it."

"Not anymore. Ain't diplomatic."

"Diplomacy is for other people."

"Aren't you a charmer."

"When I want to be."

Felix snorts. "You're not the first. All right, kid, I could use a young gun. A source told me Trigger was last seen in Tangiers. He said she likes to keep her ears open."

"What does that mean?"

"I guess we'll find out."

It transpires that this tip of North Africa, where the Mediterranean sweeps through the Strait of Gibraltar into the Atlantic, is the best place to keep one's ears open. Driving through the Diplomatic Forest in a silver Mercedes 300 SL Felix borrowed from his contact—a car collector and crook who owed him a favor—shadowed by cork trees and mimosas in fat yellow bloom, the pair follow the coastline, passing Roman and Phoenician ruins punctured by radio masts and pylons. South of Cape Spartel, this stretch benefits from exceptionally clear reception and transmission. Concrete compounds, cracked and weathered, mark where once upon a time America guarded its dishes, the mouthpieces of propaganda penetrating the Iron Curtain.

Felix's source said that Trigger receives her targets via these radio dishes, and that her associate would meet the CIA agent there for a price. Felix parks the car in the shadow of towering antennas. The engine ticks as it cools.

Felix says, "We'll set up there."

Triple O follows him into the shadow of a crumbling fort. "Old-school, receiving instructions over radio," he says.

"Sometimes old-school is the best," says Felix, kneading his chest.

"Does it bother you? Your wound, I mean."

"Something's going to get you eventually. What hurts is knowing it wouldn't have got you back then, when the old school was the new school. It's not that the bad guys have gotten faster. It's that I've gotten slower."

"So why not retire?"

Felix digs his loafers into the grit. "Unfinished business."

"With Trigger?"

"A friend she and I share. It's a good bet she knows where he is, if she's freelancing for Rattenfänger."

"James Bond."

A nod. "What did James make of you, young buck?"

"I don't know if he made anything of me at all."

Felix laughs. "James always knows what'll needle a fella. Why'd you get in this racket? Which of the mice nibbled on your toes?"

Harthrop-Vane checks the view through the empty window belonging to a dead civilization. The beach glistens with Portuguese men-o'-war blown in by the levanter. One way, a fishing port with blue-painted skiffs. The other, emptiness stretching into endless heat haze, beyond which lies Casablanca, two hundred miles south. He says, "Mice?"

"You know," says Felix, "the four reasons a man becomes a spy. Women too, I guess, though they're usually smarter about it than we are. MICE." Felix ticks off the words on his left hand. "*Money.* Debt, one too many mistresses, lavish lifestyle. *Ideology.* Maybe you simply believe your cause is more righteous than your neighbor's. *Compromise.* Maybe you've got some vulnerability that opens you up to blackmail. It's usually sexual or criminal. Once upon a time, both. *Ego.* Primal, howling need. A case officer targeted your susceptibility to intellectual or physical flattery to recruit you. Before you knew it, you were in too deep and there was no way out. You wouldn't even know how to live a normal life if you tried."

Pop-pop-pop.

Harthrop-Vane whips out his gun.

"Steady," says Felix.

A man is walking up the beach, deliberately stamping

on the violent bladders of the Portuguese men-o'-war. Each stamp sounds like a small-caliber pistol. He leaves the sand for the gravel of the ruins. A short man carrying his jacket over his arm, sweat stains oozing over his white shirt, face dark with stubble. He stops at the first dish, giving it a knock which warps and warbles.

"Felix Leiter?"

Felix signals to Harthrop-Vane to stay hidden, then steps out into the scrubby grass separating him from the man by twelve feet.

The man says, "We hear you are searching for Trigger."

"That's right."

"She wants to be left alone."

"She's forfeited that right."

"What did she ever do to you?"

Felix says, "How about we start by you telling me what you are to her."

"This is not American soil. You do not give the orders around here."

"Who does?"

"This." The man's jacket twitches. "Tell your friend to join the party. Throw your weapons down. I have a friend on higher ground, a friend with good aim."

"Trigger?"

The man says nothing. Felix beckons Harthrop-Vane, who joins him. Both men toss guns to the ground.

"Keep your hands where I can see them."

"Sure thing, partner," says Felix. "I only got one hand for you to worry about. No need to get jumpy. Specially on this beautiful day."

"I am glad you like the view. It will be your last."

The man's finger moves as Felix reaches for his concealed weapon, but before he can fire, three loud *pops* shake a stork from the trees, and this time the noise isn't Portuguese men-o'-war.

The man jerks, spins, and flops to the floor in a cloud of disturbed flies.

"Thanks, shamus," says Felix, using the point of his shoe to kick the weapon away from the man's outstretched arm.

"No trouble," says Harthrop-Vane, holstering his backup weapon while scanning the area. No fire comes. "Two-bit outfit. I'd say Trigger was never here at all. Just some people with a grudge against the CIA who thought they could lure you here and leave you with the ruins."

"Guess that answers my question."

"Which question?"

"Quick draw like that," says Felix, considering 000. "I'd place every last chip on ego."

Harthrop-Vane smiles. "How about you? Which mouse gave you a bite?"

"You wanna hear something so goddamn funny it'll make you weep?" says Felix, considering the life slipping out of the man at his feet. "I don't remember."

"**This car** was made for Elvis! Don't shoot me, Leiter! You don't want to get blood on the upholstery."

Felix Leiter regards the pink Cadillac Eldorado, which his source is using as a shield in a yard ringed by vintage automobiles. "All right. Out of respect for The King, I won't shoot you. But he will."

Harthrop-Vane steps forward. "If it belonged to a Beatle, maybe I'd care. As it is . . ." He fires an inch from the man's foot, deflating the front tire.

"OK! OK! I set you up. I was paid for it. What do you want from me, blood loyalty? Trigger doesn't want to know you!"

"Where is she?"

"I've never even met her! She could be dead for all I know!"

"Everybody wants me to think Trigger is a phantom. But I've got scar tissue that says otherwise. You got any ice water around here? It sure is hot." Felix studies the big house beyond the yard, tracing its white walls and stucco roof. "I think I'll just go on inside for some refreshment while my friend refreshes your memory. Your wife home?"

Harthrop-Vane prowls around the car bonnet.

The man hugs his belly. "All right! What is Trigger to me? What are you to me, for that matter? May you kill each other. We collect messages for her, that's all. We send them to an office in Panama."

Felix Leiter has never liked Panama. Never liked the Zonians, as the hangers-on of America's imperial city call themselves; never liked the lawyers greasing the way for offshore banking; never liked the 98 percent of ships whose cargo passes through the Panama Canal unchecked, carrying drugs to Europe. He doesn't like it not because it offends his sensibilities, but because its flagrance shows him everything that is futile, crooked, and cockeyed about his chosen mission in life, and there isn't even a gimcrack façade stuck over it. The link between two continents and two oceans, Panama will always be a site of power for those who can seize it.

Felix thinks this, knowing it's hypocritical, as he waits with his legs on the desk of the office manager due back any minute from lunch. Conrad Harthrop-Vane lounges in the corner, cleaning his gun. When the door in the outer office clicks, the Double O straightens.

Felix offers the surprised manager a conciliatory smile. "Mister, it's your lucky day. I'm here to unburden your soul."

The man, wiry in a linen suit, pulls back thin lips to reveal gold front teeth. He reaches for his phone, then hesitates as Felix continues.

"You've been carrying messages for a wanted assassin. That's the kind of thing that'll haunt a man. If you tell me where she's based, you'll be all the better for it. Name's Trigger."

The office manager opens his collar. "Maybe you don't know," he says. "We own the canal now."

"I don't want your canal. I just want her."

"And in return, you offer me peace of mind? That's what I pay taxes for."

"This is a tax-free zone."

A laugh. "Sure it is. Get out of here, American. You don't scare me. The soundproof shipping container the cartel uses for a torture chamber scares me."

Felix scratches his cheek with his prosthetic. "I can understand how it would. But you see, all I need is your fingerprint to unlock your laptop here, so I can access a log of your messages, and then I'll be out of your way. Lend me a hand."

The office manager's gaze becomes stuck on Felix's prosthetic.

Triple O steps forward. "The gods are asleep and do not watch. Nobody knows we're here. Nobody has to know. You can go on eking out your small existence, with just the touch of a button."

Sweat springs onto the man's face. He studies the gun in Triple O's hand. He nods.

The Darién Gap is 100 miles of impassable mountain jungle, the only break in the 29,000-mile Pan-American Highway from Alaska to Argentina. There are no paths. Nobody sees inside the heart of the jungle, apart from the narco- and people-traffickers, guerrillas and paramilitaries who use it as a smuggling corridor across the border between Panama and Colombia, and Indigenous peoples turning to plantain farming, now that hunting for food has been banned. Felix Leiter follows the guide and 000 at a growing distance. He can't keep up anymore. Getting old. Too many chunks missing. The last SENAFRONT checkpoint was a day back; the Panamanian government knows they've gone inside the jungle, but Felix doubts they care all that much if these two Westerners claiming to be travel writers come back out. The canopy is a stained glass window, every panel a darker green. The air smells of rich damp, though he can't hear or see running water.

Trigger lives in the mountains. The messages were relayed from Colón to Yaviza, received by the guide who now points out a chunga palm tree, warning them not to touch the black spines. He said he'd take them to Trigger for a price.

Felix wonders just how high the price will be.

He won't have to wonder long.

Twenty-Seven
Corridor X

Europe to the Middle East

The diamond trade is a multibillion-dollar global industry based on trust. Deals are struck with a handshake at diamond bourses in free trade zones without oversight. The trade gives a high value to mass ratio: a fortune can be carried across borders legitimately or illegitimately in a suitcase or the hollow head of a doll. Diamonds can be used to pay for arms or buy drugs without any digital fingerprint. Diamonds can be stolen in order to fund further crime, and put to use to launder profit from that crime. For law enforcement focused on what is known as ML/TF—money laundering and terrorist financing—the diamond trade is maddeningly opaque. For smugglers and diamond dealers, it's a gangster's paradise. Attempts at regulation ask diamond bourses to KYC through EDD—Know Your Customer through Enhanced Due Diligence—acronyms like litter shored up against leaks so gaping they pour.

This makes Viktor Babić laugh. Know Your Customer. He knows his customers. They are the world's murderers, rapists, and racketeers, bombers, swindlers, tax evaders, oligarchs, and mob bosses. And he has their money in the palm of his hand. He is the one thing they are afraid of. He likes it that way. He lives on fear the way most people live on oxygen. And soon what he has been campaigning for will come to pass. MI6 are watching. It is too dangerous for Rattenfänger to continue with bank transactions. They will rely on him to ML so they can TF. He just needs more diamonds.

Rachel Wolff has a vague understanding of what purpose stolen and trafficked diamonds are put to, but has spent a lifetime training her mind to admit only certain realities, and has no concept of the diamond Janus's big picture. As she and Marko sail up the Danube, they pass Second World War–era ships pushed from the water by a recent drought, unexploded ordnance floating on the surface with all the innocence of overgrown bladder wrack seaweed. She wonders what else will be pushed to the surface in the coming days.

Being around Marko—even just the salty smell of him—is upsetting the regulation of her mind. Images and sensations from the past erupt in hot flashes: getting high with Marko and his friends and pretending she liked it; watching Marko play basketball, how he used to glance over at her whenever he scored—and how he fouled with abandon, but if a friend fouled him, he'd forget the ball and turn on them, refusing to stop until he made them cry. Rachel's father said Marko didn't have the temperament to become a Chevalier. Too violent. Rachel's mother would point out that the same could be said of Marko's father, the leader of the gang. That was all in the past, Rachel's father said. The Chevaliers are nonviolent. Serbia has been left broken and we are doing what we have to in order to survive, but we don't hurt people. Marko is a good boy, he'll make us all proud one day. Rachel wonders—and she has to decide fast, as Marko steers them into the port of Novi Sad and tells her it's time for a game of show-and-tell. They'll need to give the diamond Janus more than just the blind man's watch if they hope to keep their heads—more to make the deal worth his while and put off suspicion. Marko hasn't yet fenced the rest of the haul from Lisl Baum's birthday party. It is here in the port.

"I'll show you mine if you show me yours," he says, kissing Rachel's naked back in the cabin.

"I thought we already did that part," says Rachel.

"Did we?" He rolls her underneath him. "I must have missed the blind man's watch somewhere. Let me look again . . ."

Rachel laughs as his hands search lower. "I used to fantasize about this. Not that you need your ego stroked."

"Not my ego, no . . ."

"Did you ever think of me that way?"

"Truth?"

"Truth."

"I used to think I'd marry you, if your crush lasted after you graduated from high school."

"And then what?"

"What do you mean?"

"In this imagined future, are we still Chevaliers?"

"I am. You are at home with the children."

She grabs the pillow to smack him, but Marko catches her wrist and presses himself over her. "What, you don't think you'd enjoy waiting for me to come home and surprise you with diamonds?"

She stretches beneath him. "In this fantasy, am I wearing a French maid's apron, by any chance?"

"Give me some credit."

"I will when you earn it."

"All right, how about this," he says, kissing her captured arm. "I propose to you with the Hope Diamond."

"Jean-Baptiste stole the Hope Diamond from the third eye of a Hindu god, and it's been a curse for every thief since." Rachel gives Marko a shove onto his back and straddles his waist. "No, thank you."

Marko drums his fingers on her thighs. "OK, how about the Blue Diamond?"

"No one knows where that is."

"I'm not just a pretty face."

Rachel tilts her head. "That remains to be seen. But I'll accept the Blue Diamond."

"Very generous. Now imagine this. Every day is our own. There's nothing we can't take." His grip on her hips encourages her. "Two steps ahead of Interpol. We live on beluga caviar and only drink champagne raised from shipwrecks and sold at auction for tens of thousands of dollars."

"I can think of duller ways to spend my time," she admits, tangling her fingers with his.

"Me too," he says.

"What else?"

"Anything you want," he says.

"Anything at all?"

"We'll make reservations at the Ritz in Paris and blow them off because we want to go skiing at St. Moritz. We'll be invited to all the best parties and we'll leave wearing all the best jewels."

"What else?"

"Don't stop. That's it. We'll never stop. We'll never catch our breath. We'll burn out together. Take what we want. When we want. Whenever we want. The past won't matter. The future won't matter. We'll have each other. We'll have this."

So many times she wanted to hear words like that from him. A life of freedom, for as long as it lasted. Maybe that's the best someone like her could hope for, anyway. But wouldn't it be fun while it lasted?

Novi Sad was her childhood home, and she longs now to walk along the promenade by the Danube, kept company by the bolt of bright blue trapped between the crenellations of Petrovaradin Fortress and the bruised clouds trying to squeeze out the last of the clear sky, before it breaks into lightning-laced rain.

But they aren't going into town. They are here for the port, which is the second busiest in Serbia, recently bought by the United Arab Emirates, now in the process of renovation. In the language of international shipping, what makes the port so attractive is its location on the left bank of the Danube at the intersection of river Corridor VII and road-rail Corridor X. This algebraic equation results in an epicenter of international communication and transport. Trade has come to this bank of the Danube for hundreds of years because of its connections, and where history waits, the present takes. Roads might change but mountains don't. These routes were used to smuggle food and ammunition by partisans battling the Nazis. They were used to smuggle weaponry during the civil war. And they were co-opted by criminals as soon as the war ended, gangs feeding arms to white markets in France and Belgium and black markets in Syria and Egypt, feeding women and children into the sex trade and men into forced labor in western Europe, heroin from Afghanistan to the Balkans, synthetic drugs into western Europe and the Middle East. The black market superimposed onto the white market, making gray.

As Marko navigates into the port, they feel the swell of *The Albatross*, a new 22.4-meter thruster boat purchased by the UAE to speed up entrance to the port. Rachel points out the name, painted in white on the bright steel.

Marko laughs. "Yes. The Serbian workers at the port were told they could choose the name. Maybe their new masters don't understand irony."

"Just don't shoot at it," says Rachel.

He gives her his devil's grin. "You're bad luck enough, Rachel Wolff."

Five vessels the scale of skyscrapers take up the

eight-hundred-meter quay, but they aren't docking there. Marko brings them into an old jetty, where he calls to laborers smoking in the shadow of corrugated iron, the first in a 44,000-square-meter field of closed warehouses. With a wave, one tosses down his cigarette and comes to catch the rope. The world keeps its white market here: clothes, television sets, bed frames, grain, bananas, halloumi cheese. And Marko keeps a black-market warehouse amongst it all, Rachel following him now down the rusted corridors to a shed that hasn't been given a lick of new paint, a shed with a padlock whose key he wears around his neck. Inside, there is a shipping container, leaking red liquid into the cracking concrete. Marko uses the second key on the chain to open this padlock, and keys a number into the pad—Rachel knows it to be his mother's birthday, derisible sentiment in a professional thief, but one that came in handy.

When the door swings open, Marko freezes, the muscles in his jaw jumping. The blind man's watch sits on its velvet bed on top of the crates. "How did you—" He breaks off, tugging at his necklace. "What's to stop me taking it now and leaving your body in here?"

She puts a hand on one hip and hopes the beat of her jugular isn't obvious. "You tell me."

Outside, gulls make themselves known. Maybe an albatross too.

Marko shakes his head. "You want to know a secret?"

"Always."

"I used to envy you, when we were younger. I wanted to be wild, out of control, dangerous like my father. King of the jungle. I used to imitate him. But you didn't have to pretend to be wild. You just were."

Despite the hammer of her heart, Rachel smiles. "Then why did you call me Mummy's little girl and Daddy's little princess whenever you got the chance?"

"Because I was trying to beat you into a shape I found less threatening." He blinks, as if taken aback to have uttered such words aloud. "Let's go, wild thing. Pick up your treasure and let's go. Before I change my mind."

It takes a diamond the size of a conker to persuade the captain of a ship known for smuggling drugs, guns, and oil to take Marko and Rachel on as well. The ship will travel south to Belgrade, where a container drilled with air holes—inside, Marko and Rachel are provided refreshments by armed men with dead eyes—will join Corridor IV, bound for the Black Sea, and then, slipping through Istanbul, will spill into the Mediterranean and dock at the port of Iskenderun. It will take a further trail of diamonds to keep them alive on the way to the Bazargan–Gurbulak border, and on to the port of Shahid Bahonar in Bandar Abbas, Iran, where they will proceed by RORO (roll-on/roll-off) ferry to the port of Khalid in Sharjah. The passage will take less than a week, a new intermodal trade route that is two-thirds faster than the traditional maritime route via the Suez Canal. Trade is getting smarter. So are criminals. From the port of Khalid they will drive overland to Ras al-Khaimah, and then on to Dubai, where the diamond Janus waits.

Twenty-Eight
The Desert of Death

Afghanistan

The Desert of Death is alive with mirages.

Across the expanse of broken rock and gravel stretching to the border of Iran, ghostly presences feed on Dryden's memory for want of electricity, roads, or water.

He sees armored personnel carriers hovering on the horizon. It's been hours, perhaps days, since he slept. He believes that he is in the phantom vehicle. He watches a fertilizer bomb lift his armored personnel carrier from the road and slam it back down. Inside, the shock wave is a blast thump at the center of his chest; his head is crushed, fracturing the base of his skull and slicing the nerve beneath his right ear. Lucky

Luke is crouching over him, shouting: "Are you good? Are you good?"

But Dryden can't hear him. He can't hear him because he's not in the carrier—there is no carrier. He's driving past poppy fields, feverish rainbows waving in the desert, swollen heads scored and bleeding opium, farmers with sickles scraping the oozing latex under the gaze of men with machine guns, who watch the minibus to make sure it doesn't slow down even for a second.

The smugglers wind across the wastes. Dryden follows.

Luke is riding beside him, telling him to give the stronghold of armed tribesmen camped at the oasis up ahead a wide berth—no, that's Aisha's voice.

The Iran border beckons, the no-man's-land of terrorists, spies, and arms dealers. The day is dimming. The week is dimming, seven days since Dryden boarded the plane to Afghanistan and went outside the wire. The chances of survival are dimming too, if they haven't already gone dark.

Luke says, "You have two vehicles in pursuit."

Dryden rubs salt from his eyes. "Say again?"

Aisha says inside Dryden's head: "You have two vehicles in pursuit and the smugglers are sprinting for the border. They must have twigged and put two bogeys on your backside."

Dryden turns to Ahmad. "Overwatch says we've got company."

Khadija cranes around, but the rearview is clogged with dust.

"There's no cover," says Ahmad, leaning out the window.

Dryden says, "Then we'll make cover."

"Whatever you do," says Ibrahim, voice too loud, probably hugging the microphone, "do it now. Those vehicles are closing fast and you're about to lose the sword over the border."

"That's not going to happen." Dryden can see the vehicles now in the mirror—pickup trucks with mounted guns. "Keep the children down. Ahmad, engage."

Ahmad hangs out the window with his wooden rifle.

The pound of the machine gun replies, nothing to the desert, everything to the rattling minibus as Dryden calls, "Hold on!"—and then wrenches the wheel, drawing a fishhook curve in the salt pan, burning rubber and producing a cloud of dust. The children are screaming.

"On me!"

Dryden swings from the vehicle, AK-47 raised, Ahmad at his shoulder.

The pursing vehicles have barreled into the haze, blind.

Dryden drops to one knee behind the tail of the

minibus, takes aim as the cars nose from the dust, and opens fire.

Shooters spill from the vehicle. The hammer of bullets is deafening. Dryden's body shakes with the impact of the rifle at his shoulder. Three enemy down. Four. Five.

Then the mad spray of the mounted gun, threatening to cut the minibus to ribbons. Dryden's head is the inside of a drum beaten by a mallet. He can't turn the volume down.

He taps Ahmad on the shoulder. Ahmad lays down suppressing fire, impossibly slow. Dryden races into the smoke with his head tucked to his chest. Clambers on top of the vehicle, finds the man at the mounted gun, whose shocked eyes are lighthouses in the gloom, and then the twin lights go out as Dryden does what he's been trained to do.

The gunner is just a kid.

Dryden can't hear anything. It's as if bandages have been stuffed in his ears. His teeth ache.

The patter of blood. Dryden looks down at his red hands.

They take the lead vehicle, which has been provisionally armored with sheet metal. Dryden floors it. The border is a finish line, close enough to taste.

"Almost there," says Ahmad, reaching behind to squeeze his little boy's knee. His daughter has her head between her legs, arms clamped over her ears. "Almost there."

The noise of nearby weapons fire. The indigo sky pops red and white.

Aisha says, "You're driving into a clash between two small unidentified armed forces. One is using a nineteenth-century cannon, the other is equipped with drones."

Dryden checks his mirror. The deep whir of the propeller announces the craft first. Then the big-nosed V-tailed thing appears in the mirror—it will be rigged with a camera and sensors. Dryden wills it to keep flying toward its intended target and ignore him. But whoever is at the controls has seen the armored vehicle, and the drone has sniffed out a new target.

"No, no, no, we're *this close*," says Ahmad, pounding the dashboard.

The drone howls closer.

"Keep the vehicle steady," says Ahmad.

"What are you doing?"

Ahmad climbs past his family into the back of the truck, taking position at the mounted gun and swinging it to pick out the low-flying drone. The din of the gun drowns out the children crying. The shriek of a missile in reply. Dryden swerves, almost topples, regains the earth as Ahmad lurches but holds on.

The border yawns ahead, an invisible line to which Aisha counts down the remaining miles: five—four—three . . .

Dryden's hearing suddenly cuts to a whine so shrill he nearly closes his eyes but doesn't as in the rearview mirror he sees Ahmad punch the air and the drone wobble, then career, before spitting out a last golden arrow.

Ahmad falls.

On the back seat of the vehicle, Khadija keeps her arms around Ahmad's chest, holding him to her. Blood glugs from his leg. Her daughter presses a rag to the wound. The little boy crouches in the footwell, sobbing. The baby is screaming. They cross the border without realizing.

The exchange takes place in the desert. The smugglers are met by a convoy of Jeeps. Dryden watches, concealed by the rocky hills, as Khadija begs him to forget about the sword and drive on to find medical supplies. Headlights pick the actors out from a backcloth of dead stars. At the center there is a tall figure who carries himself regally, his chin thrust out, his shoulders back, his stride long. When he is shown the sword, he grips it by the pommel decorated with a dancing bear and brandishes the blade, making the smuggler leap backward. Dryden recognizes him from the report Q Branch put together on the guests at Lisl Baum's birthday party. It's Friedrich Hyde—the antiquities collector who deals to the world's greatest institutions is Kristos's Englishman, the creep who wanted the pool boy to pose naked in the Minoan village. He doesn't just accept objects covered with dubious dirt—he drives to the Iran–Afghanistan border to buy them himself, because he thinks it will be *fun*. Now Dryden has him in his sights. He'll let Hyde sell the sword and transfer the money to whoever orchestrates the Gray Group and uses the spoils to finance terror. MI6 will identify Rattenfänger's treasurer. But victory has never felt so hollow.

"You promised," says Khadija. "You promised to get us out."

In the emptiness of the desert, Dryden has no false comfort to provide. Will Ahmad make it to Tehran? Will any of them?

The British ambassador in Tehran is surprised to be woken by the news that a Double O is waiting in the lobby with an Afghan locally employed civilian, a woman, and three children. Apparently the Double O refused to take "no" or "wait" for an answer, instead demanding that a doctor attend to the interpreter, and that the family be immediately evacuated to the UK. When asked if this had been cleared by London, the Double O gave an answer not to be repeated in polite circles. The ambassador gets on the phone to M, who requests to speak to his agent. The phone call between M and the Double O lasts long enough for the ambassador to make polite conversation with the interpreter, who is bleeding on the parquet. When the Double O hangs up and returns to the family waiting in the lobby, it is with the military hand signal for advance. The interpreter receives this with a sigh, placing a hand over his heart.

Ahmad whispers what he has to say in Dryden's ear. "I believe now, Joe. So should you."

These words hang in the air of Aisha and Ibrahim's office. Ibrahim leaves the room, keeping his head averted. Aisha gently rocks her fist. Today it counts.

Sidereal

Twenty-Nine
The Nightmare

Europe

As it happens, Anna Petrov delivers herself into Rattenfänger's hands.

The man who said he worked for the British consulate in Darwin gave her a new passport. She would travel to Europe alone, drawing less attention that way, he said. Anna was secretly pleased. It gave her a stronger sense that she was acting under her own agency. She didn't want company. Perhaps he knew that. She flew to Paris. From there, she took trains across Europe, the familiarity of arid fields hodgepodge amidst lush green and checkered by stone farmhouses and Gothic churches making her cry, drawing the concern of ticket conductors and the interest of men tuned in to the frequency of vulnerability.

Though it is Europe on a map, Narva railway station stands in pockmarked Stalinist Corinthian limestone that leaves her shivering. She knows the Estonian city that connects the EU to Russia on NATO's easternmost flank from family holidays. She hurries past the memorial to those deported to gulags in 1941 and 1949.

At Peter Square, she follows a stranger as the door buzzes into the prefab twelve-story high-rise crowned with a water tower that looks like a squashed church organ in brick. She gets out on the twelfth floor, pausing for the view of the baroque Fama bastion, which offers a gallery and shopping center, bordered by high chain-link fences topped with barbed wire. Across the river, more fences guard Russia and Ivangorod Fortress, whose late-medieval castellated walls almost hide from view a Soviet-era housing complex not too dissimilar from this one. The illustration of the Tower on the tarot card returns to her with a lance of dread. She tells herself not to be a silly little girl. A red line is painted across the bridge. There is no traffic, the war in Ukraine ratcheting up tensions.

Anna jumps at a sound—her own teeth rattling. She hurries on to the last apartment, the address she was

given by the consulate man who wasn't afraid of crocodiles. Her first knock is too quiet. She knocks harder.

It's the soldier from the workaway farm who opens
the door. He wears blue rubber gloves.

Estonia is what is known as a destination, source, and
transit country for human trafficking. Most victims are
from Russia, Belarus, Moldova, Ukraine, Bulgaria,
and Estonia itself, forced into sexual exploitation or
labor. Some are migrants smuggled across the border
with Russia, destined for Europe. Anna doesn't know
what direction she is being taken: she is kept blindfolded in the back of a van, and when she is pulled out
by grabbing hands, she is in a warehouse that could be
anywhere. There are other women in the warehouse.
Some are silent—like zombies. Some are wailing. Some
can't breathe for terror. They are pushed and prod-
ded and made to face bright lights and yelled at and
touched and stripped and photographed and laughed at
and knocked down and herded into other vans and it is
a nightmare that is spinning around Anna, it has to be a
nightmare. If there was ever a time for James Bond to
keep his promises, it is now.

But there is no rescue coming.

Another van, another hood. Different men. A road
in mountains. Casual gunfire. Food forced between

her lips. A weak fire. Cold to her bones. Anna grips a burning log in her bare hands and swings it at the face of the nearest man. She makes it several yards into the night before she is tackled to the ground and the man who now smells of roast pig says in bad English that he'll cut her hamstrings next time. No one needs her to be able to stand.

She is tattooed under bright lights with a rusted needle. They show her the tattoo with a mirror. It is a barcode on the back of her neck. For an infinite second, the blood pressure in Anna's head tells her she is dead. But she is not, and this is real.

The other women Anna shares this nightmare with are stamped with barcodes and trafficked into the sex trade. The sale is made on a Tuesday, the same day Johanna Harwood reaches the End of Everything and discovers Ventnor's body. The profit goes to Teddy Wiltshire, who is warned not to make the usual bank transfer to the treasurer because Q is watching his accounts and can crack the coded datasets of money changing hands. Instead, he should send an emissary to Dubai, where the money will be laundered into untraceable diamonds. The six-day countdown is on. On Monday, there will be a terror attack somewhere in the world, but nobody knows it. Not that any of this matters to the women whose lives are commodities to Teddy Wiltshire.

The return of the hood, which smells of her own vomit—at some point she must have vomited. Hands on her body—blackout, whose body?

Then a slap. Water in her face. No hood. Fingers running through her hair, pinching her cheeks. A light. A laptop, the green bead of the camera. A man watching her from the screen. A shirtless man covered in *vor* tattoos. James told her to gather details, so Anna takes in his pugilist face and the painting behind him, which she recognizes as *The Concert* by Johannes Vermeer, stolen in 1990 from the Isabella Stewart Gardner Museum in Boston, where the frame still hangs empty. The man grins and his mouth glints with gold.

"Nearly home, Anna. Your new home. No more running. Could get a good price for you on the open market with the other women. But there are people who have other plans for you. Be grateful for that. Nice warm home, with guards to protect you, and gourmet food and Egyptian cotton and power showers. You're a lucky girl. Those other girls aren't going home. Don't you feel lucky, Anna? Don't you feel grateful?"

A fist on her arm shakes her.

Anna nods.

"Good girl. I'm a gracious man, Anna. Everyone says that about Teddy Wiltshire."

Anna logs the name. She wets her lips. "Are you going to be my host?"

A belly laugh. "No, sadly you aren't joining me. We're going to reunite you with your old lover. See if you can light a fire in him. I'm afraid it's rather gone out of late."

Hope crawls across her skin, raising each hair. She whispers, "James?"

The monster leans so close to the camera he fogs the square containing him with his breath. "That's right, Anna. James is waiting for you."

PART IV

Sold

Six Days Until Detonation

Thirty
Moon City

If local rumor says the Freemasons built a Moon City at the End of Everything, perhaps that's because human imagination insists this is what life on the moon will be like.

The geodesic dome, constructed from a light aluminum frame and triangular panels, was pioneered by Buckminster Fuller and put to use at World's Fairs exporting the American dream. The dome showcased Ford cars and housed radar at the South Pole. Buckminster Fuller saw the geodesic dome as the future of Spaceship Earth, on which we are all astronauts, and it is our responsibility to steer our global home safely on its journey. Unlike other idealists of his time, he looked to the military-industrial complex, whose helicopters could transport frames and panels to the world's least hospitable places. To NASA, Antarctica and outer space were both frontiers, and designers looked from Buckminster Fuller's snow-covered radome to the moon above, sketching dome cities for the future of space colonization. A promise of utopia.

At some point, somebody constructed a geodesic dome in the Altai Mountains. Maybe it was the Freemasons, or some billionaire conspiracy nut, rehearsing for the end times, when they'll leave the rest of us behind to become just another elephant graveyard.

But that time hasn't come yet.

Johanna Harwood has scoped the structure through the lens of her father's camera. There is only one way in, the entrance to the central dome itself: a door with no handle that fronts a short tunnel. Behind the dome, a longer tunnel leads to a tower, topped with a dish filled with snow. Beyond, a helicopter is pinned down beneath netting. The armed guard who appeared at the door scanned the snow with binoculars. Perhaps her presence triggered an alarm. But his examination was desultory and he returned inside as soon as professional dignity allowed, if not a little sooner. It must surely seem impossible to Teddy Wiltshire that anyone will think to hunt for him here, let alone actually find him. And even then, an assault would come with the warning of helicopter rotors. Who would try to take the snow fortress alone and on foot?

Who indeed.

Johanna Harwood has located the generator, and she is prepared to gamble that throwing the switch will draw the guard back outside, opening the door.

Once you've developed a theorem, Sid would say, you have to design a suitable test.

Nothing like real-world conditions.

The assault takes less than ten minutes. Every minute is red.

When the guard cranks the door open, Harwood covers the man's mouth with her gloved hand. Harwood slits his throat with her Opinel and dumps his body in a grave of scarlet snow.

She heaves the door shut behind her. The floor is carpeted, so different from the terrain she's been climbing that she almost wants to kneel and check it's real. Warmth immediately slicks her skin, suckering her clothes to her body. No lights. Harwood lowers her hood but keeps her ski goggles on. She hears shouting deeper within the dome and walks forward with her gun in one hand and the knife in the other.

The next guard is running around the corner into the tunnel and almost knocks her over. Harwood stabs him under the chin, piercing his brain so he makes no noise. She lowers him to the floor and takes his rifle, slinging it over her shoulder.

"What the fuck is happening?"—a shout from deeper inside the dome.

The voice of a man who thinks he's in charge.

The next guard has her in his gunsights when Harwood brings him down with a double tap to the chest and head.

That's when the party really starts.

Harwood steps over his body into the main living space. Moon City was designed to be comfortable, but she doesn't have time to fully compute, in between muzzle flashes, the five armed men taking cover behind the Georgian secretaire chest or the display cases stacked with skulls or *The Concert* by Johannes Vermeer propped on an easel. She dives behind the sofa as shrapnel and wood and metal fragments splinter against her goggles. She empties the rifle and then empties the clip in her gun until the shots are still reverberating in her ears though she isn't firing anymore and neither is anyone else. Harwood stands hesitantly. The smell of blood and smoke fills the air.

Five dead.

Harwood sweeps the next rooms with adrenaline spotting her vision. Crew quarters. Showers. Kitchen. No reinforced doors for cells. No James.

That leaves one room, fronted by a corridor with a leopard skin rug.

She can hear movement behind the closed door.

"I'll blow your fucking head off!"

Harwood draws herself against the wall. The door is wood. She presumes Wiltshire's bedroom suite is inside, and Teddy is holding position there. She doesn't know the layout. She won't be able to coax him out.

Stalemate.

She doesn't have time for stalemates.

Harwood backtracks. She chooses the leanest dead body, a man in his thirties with *vor* prison tattoos covering his face. She grips him in a fireman's hold and carries him over the leopard skin rug. The white tiger Sir Bertram Paradise kept in captivity and used to torture 004 comes briefly to mind, the white tiger that eventually killed Paradise. She wonders if the same Janus in flora and fauna who lured 005 up here sold the tiger to Paradise. There are too many tentacles to the Gray Group. Maybe she can chop one off today.

Harwood heaves the dead man to his feet, keeping one hand on his belt so he doesn't sag, using him as a shield.

Then she kicks in the door.

Teddy Wiltshire's shotgun takes the man's head off. Harwood lets the body drop, surfing it to the floor as she fires from the hip and brings Teddy Wiltshire down.

The bullet strikes Wiltshire in the thigh. He is on the threshold between the bedroom and the bathroom in just his trousers, with a towel over his shoulder and steam at his back. He fires again as he hits the concrete floor, and the shot wings Harwood, but she doesn't drop her gun, firing once more as she slides across the parquet and slams into the four-poster bed. Her second shot pierces his arm, the force slamming him against the concrete bathtub, smacking his head on the lip. Harwood scrambles up, almost slipping on his blood but keeping her balance to kick the shotgun out of his reach and stand astride his jerking legs. She cocks the pistol and presses it to his forehead.

"Marilyn Aliyeva sent me," says Harwood. "She wants you to play dead."

He laughs. "Aren't you a little late?"

Harwood's scalp crawls. He is looking past her to the bed. She takes a swift glance over her shoulder.

Marilyn Aliyeva, Teddy Wiltshire's mistress whom Harwood promised a safe new life, is lying diagonally across the four-poster in a silk dressing gown the color of the Mediterranean on a summer's day. She isn't moving. Some voice lost to the past tells Harwood to remain calm. That triage requires cool and quick assessment. Marilyn's chest is moving. But she is bleeding from the throat. A two-inch slit.

"The first step in any good escape plan," says Teddy, "is to cut loose dead weight."

Harwood stares down at him. The gun weighs a ton. It would be so much lighter with one less bullet.

Triage. Teddy Wiltshire is bleeding from the leg and the arm. Stop the bleeding so you can interrogate him and find James Bond.

Marilyn Aliyeva is bleeding to death. The seconds it will take to stanch Teddy's bleeding could be her last seconds.

"Where's your first aid kit?"

Teddy glances at the mirrored cabinet over the sink.

"I'm a surgeon. If you cooperate I can save your life." Teddy howls when she yanks his bleeding arm and shoves him face-first to the floor. She grabs a towel and binds his arms above the wound, then ties another around his ankles. Then presses a third to his thigh. "Stay there and think healthy thoughts."

Harwood sticks the gun in her belt, gathers all the remaining towels in her arms, and races to the bed.

She is the gentlest she's ever been as she places the white cotton hand towel to Marilyn's throat. She pulls her eyelids back. Glazed and unresponsive. Damn it. Goddamn it. This isn't happening. Harwood elevates Marilyn's head. This is not going to happen. She returns to the cabinet, knocks aside toothpaste and shaving cream, and then tears open the first aid kit, carrying the contents to the four-poster bed. Stamping on Teddy's arm when he grabs for her, Harwood washes her hands, the water as hot as she can bear and hotter.

"This is *not* going to happen."

She has sutured the inner wound by the time Teddy says from the bathroom floor, "You must be Johanna. The woman with the healing hands. I'm told James talks about you all the time."

Harwood almost drops a stitch, but doesn't. Marilyn's pulse is thready.

"Do you know her blood type?"

Teddy laughs.

"She's been your mistress for a decade," says Harwood. "You don't care if she bleeds to death in your bed?"

"What do you think?"

Harwood swears. Sweat pours down her face. "Do you have a field blood transfusion kit on-site?"

"I think so. Blood is probably out of date. Been a while since I had to come up here, and everything was so hurried, didn't bring much in the way of emergency supplies."

"But you had time to abduct a woman whose life you've already . . ." Harwood slows her breathing. "Do you keep records of your men's blood types? Do you know if anyone here is type O negative?"

"I am," says Teddy. "But I hate to tell you this, Dr. Harwood—I'm not feeling too good."

Harwood turns to glare at him. "Don't you fucking die on me!"

"Do something about it."

Harwood shakes her head. Moves on to the next row of stitches. She calls, "Where's James?"

"Hard to remember. You know what it's like . . ." His voice is getting thicker.

"Are you in charge? People, diamonds, antiquities funding terror—are you in charge of it all?"

No answer.

Harwood wipes her mouth with her forearm. Last row. Marilyn needs an immediate transfusion.

"Are you really type O negative?"

Nothing.

"Where's the transfusion kit?"

Nothing.

"Stay with me, Marilyn. Stay with me. God, please, not this time."

Harwood finds clean sheets in the chest and strips them into bandages, which turn red immediately—her own blood. Fuck. She washes her hands again, using the sheets to stop the bleeding from her right arm, and then starts again. As she bandages Marilyn's throat, she sings a nursery rhyme, a favorite of her grandmaman's.

Un crocodile, s'en allant à la guerre
Disait au revoir à ses petits enfants
Traînant ses pieds, ses pieds dans la poussière
Il s'en allait combattre les éléphants

Ah! Les crocrocro, les crocrocro, les crocodiles
Sur les bords du Nil, ils sont partis n'en parlons
plus . . .

Marilyn's pulse steadies. Harwood tries to remember what happens next, after the crocodile leaves the banks of the Nile to go to war with the elephants. But all she remembers is her grandmother brushing her hair from her eyes, which Harwood does for Marilyn now, standing up and drawing a blanket over her.

Harwood finds the transfusion kit in the kitchen,

stuffed in a cupboard with dog food. The blood is no good, but the kit is intact.

Can she trust that Teddy Wiltshire really has the universal blood type, or is he only angling to stay alive? She herself is AB negative, the rarest blood type, with only a one percent chance of matching Marilyn's.

It comes down to hope.

Open up the crocodile's mouth and see what he has for you.

Thirty-One
Choosing Sides

Venice. Wednesday.

Venice seems so far from Afghanistan to Joseph
Dryden that a picture of Hannibal and his elephants
comes to mind. No one in Rome saw them coming. Now,
the plane cruises over those same Alps, white peaks that
cut through an etching plate of sky, scattering clouds
like copper shavings. The sword is in the Mestre free
port, the end result of a solid chain of smugglers linking middlemen at customhouses who reason with themselves that it is only one signature, one turned head, and
what does that matter when it pays medical bills or puts
kids through school? The Gray Group has perfected the
system and Dryden has the sinking sensation, as below

him land turns to lagoons, that he is only a pawn in the game.

Slumped in his seat, Dryden feels old and tired, a war elephant forced to march without warmth or food. *The day you stop operating is the day you die inside.* Luke said that, and Dryden agreed. But Afghanistan has sapped him of his strength. Everything is falling apart, and the teal and terra-cotta geometry unfolding beneath him is a promise of beauty that can only betray.

Moneypenny's voice unfolds in his head. "Are you with us, 004?"

He scratches his cheek. "Y'know, sometimes it's hard to believe Q isn't reading my mind."

"Why?" asks Moneypenny softly. "Aren't you with us?"

"You sound like you're handling glass," Dryden mutters into his cupped hand, glancing at the sleeping businessman across the aisle.

"I know Afghanistan took its toll," says Moneypenny. "Someone oughta pay."

"Be that as it may, I need you to drop your cock and pick up your socks, soldier."

Dryden laughs so hard he has to disguise it as a coughing fit. He rolls his shoulders. "I'm always with you, ma'am. Sit-rep?"

"The object is now stationary at the free port in Mestre."

"Orders?"

"Q will watch the free port. I want you to rendezvous with Triple O. You'll find him with Lisl Baum at the Ca' Giustinian palace tonight. The president of La Biennale is hosting a party. The great and good of the art world are all planning to attend. Triple O believes he has the antiquities Janus, Friedrich Hyde, in his sights. Join forces and track the target. It's likely he'll make the sale before taking the buyer to see the sword. Let the sale take place. Our priority is following the money to the boss. Once the sale has taken place, roll Friedrich Hyde up. But it's imperative he be allowed to make that sale. Don't let anything stop it from taking place, so we can follow the money to the god of gods. Be the bastard's guardian angel, if you have to."

Dryden snorts. "Yes, ma'am. What's our cover at this party?"

"Triple O has established himself as a dealer in the art world dating Ms. Baum."

"Of course he has. Let me guess, you want me to be a waiter?"

"What do you take me for?" says Moneypenny. "There's a room waiting for you at the Gritti Palace. You have the suite below Ms. Baum, and above Friedrich Hyde. Aisha will send over the briefing package. I'm only sorry we haven't got a new watch for you yet. You'll find suitable attire in the wardrobe. Enjoy."

A water taxi carries Dryden into the city of floating dreams. He's never been to Venice before and at first is surprised to find the glamour of the Lido worn and the confection of pink, orange, and yellow buildings on the outer islands dilapidated, bricks crumbling so the houses appear to lift their skirts to reveal long, skinny legs sinking into turquoise depths. But soon the Grand Canal draws him in with its confidence of being the greatest show on earth: bells sounding; gondoliers leaning on a single oar like striped storks; taxis pushing water between them; barges carrying fruits and vegetables; boats stacked with tourists' baggage; garbage barges and ambulance and police launches; and, on the cobbles, crowds that disappear and reappear down narrow *calli* as if at the whim of a painter layering palimpsests; churches and palaces strung with banners that read *Collateral*, signifying exhibitions running adjacent to La Biennale. The choice of word has Dryden picking imagined sand from beneath his fingernails. In his world, collateral means collateral damage, and he asks himself whether he can keep his promises, or whether the sword he's fed to looters will be lost forever and

Afghan heritage will be collateral once again. It isn't just about history. Heritage means a sense of identity. It means a lasting culture. It means tourism and cultural exchange. Money, jobs, industry. Everything Venice possesses. He breathes in the rich salt, and finds it hard to breathe out again.

La Biennale di Venezia dates back to 1895. Every year, the city is transformed into a living gallery, alternating between art and architecture. This season, half a million people will flood through the national pavilions at the Giardini della Biennale and the central exhibition at the Arsenale to see what artists all over the world are imagining right now. The show opens to the public in two days, but first people with club membership will enjoy the previews and the drinks and the prizes. Dryden realizes that, perhaps for the first time in his life, he has club membership too.

While the art at La Biennale isn't for sale, it is the place to be seen for dealers, and much of what is on display will go to Art Basel next, where a handshake in Venice will become a bank transfer. Antiquities dealers get in on the action, too, by framing history through a contemporary lens—Indian dyed silks bought because they resemble Rothko paintings. Every nation from Albania to Zimbabwe is participating, and though sales stop at the door, politics don't. The whole world is here. The whole world is watching.

The sun is setting as the water taxi passes the Palazzo Ducale, a glorious bloody display over the domes and spires, giving the pink walls an even deeper blush. Dryden steps onto land. He squeezes past the discreet entrance to Harry's Bar, over cobbles that advertise extinct airlines in bright mosaic, and emerges onto Piazza San Marco, where the Basilica and the Campanile are thronged with tourists who produce miniature icons in their proffered phones. But he can't maintain this cynical frame, no matter how much he seeks to resist the beauty around him, resents it even, the hunger pains of Ahmad's children haunting him. The lights in the arched windows of the Procuratie Vecchie over the arcade give the impression of a thousand vanity tables, made infinite by the reflection in the herringbone pavement, slick with soapy liquid. Children race around a man wearing torn jeans who waves a gigantic stick over his head, trailing bubbles. Pigeons pick up the sound of danger, perhaps a distant storm, and clap for no visible reason from the redbrick tower of the Campanile, swooping low toward the orchestra muddling a tune to start the evening outside Florian's.

Then the reason for flight becomes clear, as two

bronze figures hammer the bell on the roof of the Torre dell'Orologio. The clock face is blue and gold in a circle of marble. A golden hand with an emblem of the sun points to the hour. At the center of the clock face, the earth hangs in the balance, and the moon slips through its phases, surrounded by winking stars. The hammering is the countdown before a HALO jump pounded out by a sergeant's fist. Dryden strides across the square. You feel like everything is falling apart? His step lifts. Then do something about it.

When Conrad Harthrop-Vane sees Joseph Dryden stalking into the ballroom of the fifteenth-century palace wearing a pale pink linen shirt by Turnbull & Asser with cocktail cuffs, cream trousers, and a purple-and-pink-checked blazer, he does not manage to resist choking. Triple O has elected a gray mohair suit with a black shirt and is irritated to think people will now consider him funereal whereas before he seemed sophisticated. 004 always irks him. A tin man everyone thinks is a dandy lion. Even Lisl Baum's hungry gaze is licking him up.

"I wouldn't bother," says Harthrop-Vane. "He plays for the other team."

She raises a perfect eyebrow. "How do you know?"

Harthrop-Vane gives her his best withering look

and tries to stop the blush threatening his cheeks. Let
her think she is teasing him, making him uncomfort-
able. He doesn't give a fig about any of that. As always
in these moments, Harthrop-Vane draws in a sharp
breath of air through his thin nostrils and holds it, like
cupping treasure in his hands—holds deep inside the
secret that makes all these daily irritations bearable.
004 does play for the other team, because Triple O
plays for the winners. And all the time the Double O
Section rely on Harthrop-Vane like an unloved work-
horse while patting other men on the back—whether
it's the old favoritism for Bond or Moneypenny's worship of 004—all that time, he is delivering real power
to the people who actually matter.

When Sir Emery first introduced Triple O to the
"star" of the Double O Section, James Bond stared
right through him. Harthrop-Vane remembers how Sir
Emery patted James's shoulder to encourage his attention, the same way he patted Triple O's shoulder in the
days of the tuck shop. Triple O was a star at embassy
parties and arms deals as a youth. He'd been a star at
Cambridge even though he attended only half his history of art lectures. He'd been reared smooth, beautiful, charming to the right people, self-complete. He
knew when to talk and when to use his tongue to wish
a gal happy birthday. He knew how to shoot straight

from a distance, how to strangle a man with the sash of a dressing gown or a washing line, how to deliver poison, and how long to hold a head underwater. He knew some of that before he became a Double O and swore loyalty to M and his duty. But he wasn't the star of the Double O Section. James Bond was, his brother-in-arms, as Sir Emery put it. And James Bond stared straight through him. When Bond "disappeared," Triple O believed his quality would finally be seen. But Moneypenny only has time for her war hero.

It had been the richest of ironies when Moneypenny ordered him to find Trigger. She was, in essence, asking him to find himself. And he even went to the jungle to do it, like some gap year kid. The only complication was having Felix Leiter along too. But the cartel took care of that. It was a shame the cartel refused to let him see Trigger, who really did live in the mountains. Perhaps they knew he'd kill her, that her usefulness as his cover had run out. His code words—*The gods are asleep and do not watch*—told them Rattenfänger was behind him, gaining their cooperation. But Rattenfänger was *very* far behind him, and a man had only so much currency alone in the jungle. Still, it all worked out. Moneypenny believed him when he said the search turned up nothing but Leiter wanted to stay down there and keep searching, promising to holler if he needed help. After a respectable amount of time, the cartel would say they'd captured and executed an American spy.

In the meantime, Lisl Baum had invited Triple O to Venice, where Moneypenny wanted him to exploit his intimacy with her to get at Friedrich Hyde. Something he was more than happy to do.

Harthrop-Vane releases the long breath, his attention sweeping the ballroom, taking in the generals and admirals gathered beneath Murano glass chandeliers, the priests and politicians. Tanned men who never experience winter. Women in black with gold belts and brooches. Even the twenty-something boy high off his head wearing dirty boots with a Prada suit and sunglasses clipped into his shirt shouting into the ear of a cocktail girl that he respects people who work but could never do it himself—these are the people who count. His father was never one of them. Not truly. Harthrop-Vane learned as a boy that good and evil are illusions. There's only the powerful and the powerless. Now he is powerful, because the men who truly matter need him.

"What's eating you?" says Lisl. "It isn't me. Is it him? And if so, can I watch?"

"Shut up."

Her grip on his arm stiffens, nails turning to talons. "Excuse me?"

Harthrop-Vane is startled to see the ice in those big eyes, how her shimmering body exposed in the glittering nothing she wears seems to turn hard like armor. He manages a smirk. "I thought you liked it rough."

"You forget your place."

"Care to remind me?"

"I don't know if I care at all."

He finds himself gulping like a damn schoolboy. He rallies hoarsely. "Oh dear, she's displeased, and she's forgotten all my talents."

She shrugs, watching Dryden inch closer to Hyde. "He's awfully interested in Friedrich."

"He's just another Double O."

A glance back at him. "Don't they trust you to get the job done by yourself?"

"He's my backup."

"Really?" She tilts her head, examining Dryden. "Are you sure you're not his?"

Harthrop-Vane snatches a drink from the tray of a passing waiter and downs it without stopping to see what it is.

Lisl Baum laughs. "You're too easy, pup. Come on. Let's get closer to the fireworks."

Dryden watches Lisl Baum float on Triple O's arm toward the target, drifting past Biennale staff elated to have made it to opening day, people who really care about art and the role it can play in the world, unlike Hyde.

He wonders where Ms. Baum fits. For someone supposedly out of the crime business, she still likes the smell of it. Old habits die hard. The briefing package flagged that, while Ms. Baum's criminal past was known, Triple O hasn't discovered anything untoward about her current dealings. No wonder, Dryden reflects. She has him hooked around her little finger.

Now Friedrich Hyde leaps up theatrically and grasps Lisl Baum's hand, pressing a kiss to her diamond, sapphire, and emerald rings.

"You make a man want to put you behind glass, my dear."

Lisl Baum is rigid and Dryden doesn't blame her. The man is a nauseating fool, but he can't be dismissed. If the FBI and Interpol are right, he's been looting temples and striking deals at conflict borders for the better part of thirty years. Once, when an academic confronted him with photographs of a "dig" in India, he thanked her earnestly for reminding him of good times. Hyde never met a consequence in his life he couldn't shrug off. Born with a silver spoon in his mouth, and as yet no one has yanked it out and stuck it in a museum. As yet.

Later, Dryden will think about Triple O's slight limp, which he has failed to register. Dryden learned in the army that you have to trust your teammates and they have to be able to trust you. When Bill Tanner was revealed as a traitor, Dryden understood that Tanner was being blackmailed and attempting to protect his son. It was an impossible decision, but the result was that Tanner chose family over team and the team suffered. Still, Tanner wasn't exactly on the team, not a Double O himself, never had been.

If Joseph Dryden has a blind spot, it is an inability to imagine a Double O might play against the team. And Triple O has just strolled right into that blind spot with a broad matinee smile on his face.

Thirty-Two
The Diamond Janus

Dubai. Wednesday.

There is something wrong with this picture.

A district that houses 100,000 people and 21,000 businesses in eighty-six buildings known as JLT—the Jumeirah Lake Towers—after the three lakes that stay #nofilter blue all year round, an axis for vertical neighborhoods named with the letters of the English alphabet, from Cluster A (residential, hotel, and hotel apartments) to Cluster Z (the last to reach the design stage). In between, there's Cluster T, where you'll find Fortune Executive Tower and 1 Lake Plaza. In winter, you can work out at outdoor gyms. Families enjoy flea markets, carnivals, and cinema under the stars. Friends catch up in Caffè Nero and Pizza Express. After work, it's drinks at Hoxton Bar or McGettigan's. In summer, hypercars shelter beneath solar panel parking shades.

The laborers constructing this skyline, designed for long exposures taken from the Persian Gulf, are invisible. There's only the laconic ambition of those who are already wealthy, realized in Almas Tower, alone on its own artificial island, the desert watching its back. Sixty-eight stories of glass and steel curling like the rolled leaves of a cigar, a temple to commodities, each floor trading in gold, precious stones, tea, coffee, agriculture, base metals, crypto, and cacao. The gold market and diamond bourse alone generate $75 billion US annually. JLT pays no tax. It didn't exist when the century was new, but has become the world's largest growing free zone. Welcome to Dubai, home of expats, concrete, and money.

What's wrong with this picture is hard to put into words. It's a feeling, that's all Rachel Wolff can say. Maybe the same feeling the gods had when they watched Icarus strap on his wax wings. That's how she feels as she repeats Moneypenny's instructions to herself, walking across the world's largest diamond floor on the second story of Almas Tower, jutting over the lake.

Evidence suggests there are three likely Janus operatives involved in this racket. Diamonds. Antiquities.

And people. Together, this network of Janus opera-
tives is funding terror. But for a setup like this to work,
there has to be someone in charge. A god of gods. A
treasurer to terror. I want the identity of the boss. Your
mission is to find the diamond Janus, and then discover
who he reports to.

It sounded simple enough. The smugglers said she
and Marko would find the diamond Janus at the center
of the trading floor. Viktor Babić, the respected dealer.
Air-conditioning leaves her cold, where moments ago
she was boiling from forty-degree heat. Prismatic
shapes cast in steel and suspended from the ceiling
throw illusory gemstones across the gleaming floor.
She passes from the glare of the sun into the membrane
of shadows, following Marko's scuffed heels. He never
learned the art of the con. Never had to. If he had, he
would have bought a new pair of shoes, or at least had
his old ones seen to at the cobblers in Novi Sad. There
is a reason women are the con artists of the Chevaliers.
We spend our days acting in order to survive.

At the secure tables ranged along the wall of windows, men in dark suits and white kanduras squeeze
their eyes against magnifying glasses, weighing rough
stones in their hands. After the examinations, the
actual bidding will take place online. This floor, with
its specialist lights and security that strips the space

even of smell, is about touch: the feel of a stone, the smack of palm against palm, the squeeze on a bicep, the you-won't-regret-it and congratulations. Rachel is surprised to pass a quick-moving huddle of tanned men in yarmulkes, watching them disappear into a glass box with a sign on the door that announces the Israel Diamond Exchange. Her hand moves to her Star of David, exposed by the deep V of her high-waisted white linen jacket, paired with tapered white linen trousers. She wears her hair short and dark and her lipstick scarlet to match her nails, drawing the glances of each man they pass. That's the idea. There are two ways to play this. Visible or invisible. They want to persuade Viktor Babić that they are worth his attention in order to have him sell the blind man's watch—at least, that's what Marko thinks. And they are going to do it by offering him goods Marko stole at gunpoint from his friend's birthday party. Subtlety was several miles back and the off-ramp is closed.

The Star of David is still because she isn't breathing. Her mother told her she needn't worry about exposing herself too much on a job—it isn't you that you are exposing, it's your character. Nobody here can see the real you. Nobody knows you're following the boy you always wanted to trust but never fully could deeper and deeper into the spider's web and now here you are, just a few more paces and you will reach the spider himself, the man the smugglers warned you waited, crouched and poised, legs spinning a trap of silk, at the end of the pipeline. The diamond Janus who may know what happened to your parents, back in the day. Or may, depending on how long he's been operating and whether Viktor Babić is even his real name, be the very thing that happened to your parents. But you can't think about that right now because your job is to get close to the spider, find out if he truly is the diamond Janus, and who he answers to: the leader of the racket that funded the BBC blast. And then you can end him.

Nonviolence is a nice policy. But she isn't feeling nice today.

With that thought, Rachel comes to a halt at Marko's reassuring shoulder—despite all her doubts, she can't help feeling that reassurance as Marko clears his throat, drawing the attention of the man sitting on a black leather sofa framed by the angular shadows of steel diamonds hanging above.

The man looks up and Rachel wants to flinch but her character doesn't.

It isn't that Viktor Babić is physically imposing. If anything, he is stunted, a compressed torso with stubby arms ending in blunt hands, and short legs folded under him on the sofa, making him more and more like a spider in her mind, one that waits in a ball before gradually unfurling to take its prey by surprise. He blinks twice, rapidly, giving the impression of double eyelids, as if he first sees you, then X-rays you. The lights above pick out a sheen of sweat on his shaven skull. The traders around him maintain their distance, as if they know something she and Marko don't. Marko's scuffed shoes have already transgressed the hallowed aura.

Marko says, "Mr. Babić, we were told you were the man to see."

He says nothing.

"We are having trouble finding the right buyer for a beautiful piece."

Rachel wants to kick Marko. Anybody who doesn't just spend their time holding up hotels and boutiques knows you don't front a diamond with adjectives. You don't call it stunning or unique. You don't even call it natural. By definition, a diamond is all of those things.

She slides her hand into her jacket pocket and lets the blind man's watch dangle from her fingertips on the glittering chain.

Viktor Babić twitches. He meets Rachel's eyes. Then, with a torturous passage of time, shifts his focus to Marko. The traders disappear into too-loud peripheral conversations.

Babić speaks. "A man I know purchased that item

for a friend's birthday. It was a showy gesture. This man is like that. Brash. Like you two. Brash as two Audis reversing into a ballroom."

Marko says, "I believe in making an entrance."

Viktor Babić sniffs, sitting forward so that—if he wants to—he could grasp the blind man's watch for himself. He peers up at Rachel.

"What about you?" His voice is a whisper. "What do you believe in?"

"Diamonds," says Rachel.

His laugh rasps her scalp.

"Do you know what they do to thieves in the desert?" he asks.

"We have a lot more than this to offer," says Marko. "We believe we've earned a higher pay grade than the start of the pipeline."

Viktor Babić chooses his words as if picking over a disappointing buffet. "And what makes you think I would enter into such deals? I am a well-respected trader in this city."

Rachel glances around at the studiously turned backs. "So tell us to take the blind man's watch and the rest of what we have and sell it elsewhere."

He strokes his chin, dragging a cracked thumbnail over sparse stubble. "What is your name, little girl? You are . . . familiar, to me."

Some other Rachel clenches her jaw. This one flutters her lashes. "Wolff. Rachel Wolff. But my father's name was Petrović."

He draws his hands down to clap softly. "Names change but stories don't. What a pleasure to meet the child of former friends." His attention shoots to Marko. "And you?"

"Marko Jovanović."

"Yes, of course. You have your father's eyes. He always had luck with women, those blue eyes. You've continued the tradition." He wags his head toward Rachel. "The prodigals. Are you here to solve my problems or create them, I wonder?"

Rachel says, "What's troubling you?"

He is on his feet quickly, paws seizing her elbows, yanking her close so his hard belly pushes into her pelvis. "Too many fucking coincidences. That's what's troubling me, little girl. Do you hunt?"

Rachel gestures with two urgent fingers for Marko to stay out of it. "When the prey is right," she says coolly.

"Good. Tomorrow morning. Diamond House, Emirates Hills. We'll see where you fit on the food chain."

Rachel doesn't let herself shake until they are out of the air-conditioned prison and breathing in the smell of burnt wind and burnt concrete under the palm trees. Then she shakes violently, with Marko's hand on her arm absorbing each spasm—and perhaps trembling on its own too.

"Do you know who we just met?" she asks him.

"Death." Marko urges her to walk alongside the placid lake. "He has the smell of the death squads."

"I wonder what his real name is. Someone must have this fucker on a wanted list."

"You're talking like police. Don't tell me you're so scared you want to call in cavalry from The Hague."

She says nothing, reminding herself in harsh silent words that Marko isn't on her mission from Moneypenny. He is simply of use *to* her mission. But then the skyscrapers towering around sway in her vision and she wonders what on earth she is doing here, what on earth she means by "mission"—this whole thing is only to save her own skin. She isn't some kind of hero. The easiest thing would be to take the money and disappear with Marko. Burn out together.

Then Marko says, "This is what you wanted, remember?"

Her laughter is brittle. "I never did want what was good for me. Got that from my mother, I guess."

"I never wanted to be anything but bad for everyone."

She studies him from beneath her lashes. "Why?"

Marko's blue eyes are brighter than the artificial lake. "If you set out to disappoint people, you can't ever let yourself down."

She moves her hand to his and squeezes. "You know, I wouldn't think any less of you if you didn't let me down, just this once."

His kiss is soft, fleeting, but perhaps the first real kiss they have shared. "I'll consider it."

Thirty-Three
The Double-Blind

Altai Mountains. Thursday. Six hours ahead of Greenwich Mean Time, five hours ahead of Venice.

"Do you know what a double-blind study is?" asks Johanna Harwood.

Teddy Wiltshire wakes with a jolt. Staring around the bedroom, he takes in the blood-spattered floor, the splintered bedpost, the hole in the wall decorated with brain matter. Then, jerking, he realizes he is tied to his own bed—a jerk that threatens to open the stitches Harwood sewed into his thigh and his arm. The jerk also tugs on the bright red tube running from his arm to Marilyn's arm, where she lies on a chaise longue, which Harwood dragged into the bedroom. Marilyn isn't stirring, but she is breathing through a biro in her chest, secured with gaffer tape. He finds Johanna Harwood reclining on his Eames chair at the foot of the bed. The shotgun is in her lap.

"A double-blind study. Do you know what it is?"

"You fucking bitch, stop playing Frankenstein and unplug me."

Harwood sweeps her tongue over her upper lip. "In a double-blind study, patients with a life-threatening disease to which there is no known cure are divided into two groups. Half of the group are given a placebo drug. The other half are given a new drug, something that researchers hope might stop the disease in its tracks. In order to prevent bias, the doctors involved don't know which group has been given the placebo and which group has been given the real drug. Neither do the patients. That's why the study is called a double-blind. But sometimes, a patient given nothing more than a sugar capsule will show improvement, for a time anyway. Do you know why?"

Teddy jerks again, attempting to pull the tube from Marilyn's arm.

Harwood points the shotgun at his crotch.

He sneers at her, but goes still.

She says, "Hope. That's why."

"Until it wears off and the fool snuffs it," he says.

Harwood gives a half-smile. "I've had a difficult year, Teddy."

"Win some, you lose some. That's what I always tell myself. Win some, you lose some, Teddy boy. Right now, I'm down. What do you think I'll do to you when I'm up again?"

Harwood ignores this. "My fiancé died. I guess you heard about that. And I had to save his killer's life so we could interrogate the monster. A monster with a death's-head hawk moth tattoo on his chest, just like yours." She points with the barrel of the gun. As she speaks, she sees calculations passing through Teddy's eyes: no sound of any guards stirring, his value dropping as Marilyn gets the blood she needs. "Although, Sid wasn't my fiancé when Mora shot him. He broke it off after his mentor and my ex-lover went missing in the field." Harwood bounces the gun on her knee. "These work-place romances. They're frowned upon for a reason, I can tell you that." She checks Marilyn's pulse with her spare hand. "There have been long dark nights when I've questioned my purpose as a Double O. What good am I to the Secret Service if I couldn't even save Sid? If I can't find James? But I still had hope. I believed I could find 007. I came to the End of Everything because I believed I might find his body. Instead, I found the body of another Double O, killed by Conrad Harthrop-Vane because he was too close to your safe house."

Teddy Wiltshire's eyes widen. The calculations are even worse now.

"Yes, I know about that. I found 005's body, and then I found Moon City, and in it the man who disappears people. I thought Marilyn was safe in the Orkney Islands, but something brought me here with time left to save her life. All I had was hope that you were telling the truth about your blood type. The wrong sort of blood would have killed her, but I had to gamble on that. I had to have hope. And hope won."

"Pass me a tissue, would you? Can't reach my handkerchief."

Harwood crosses her legs. "Let me tell you what *you* should hope for, Teddy. You should hope that when Marilyn has all the blood she needs from you, I don't let whatever remains in your sorry body flood the parquet before trickling toward the drains in the bathroom. I have a license to kill. And I've never wanted to exercise it more. Except for Mora. What decision I make depends on how you answer my questions. If you give me what I want, I'll medevac you to the nearest hospital. I'll save your life, just like I saved Mora's. You'll probably be remanded to the same hell as him, where you'll be interrogated daily and kept alive on bread and water. But you will be alive."

"You're a sick bitch."

Harwood sighs. "Of course, MI6 will have to judge your family's involvement."

Teddy swallows—she can hear how dry his throat is. "What are you talking about?"

"Your wife profits from your crimes. She's no idiot."

"A wife can't be forced to testify against her husband."

"I wonder if we'd have to force her, if she saw this." Harwood's gaze flicks to Marilyn, back to Teddy. "But this isn't really a matter for the courts, is it? If your wife is considered an accessory to terrorism, she can be renditioned and held in a black site indefinitely. Though I think we'd have a stronger case against your son. Learning the family business."

Teddy's gaze travels upward, as if seeing through the domed building to the sky. "He's never . . ."

"Really? You didn't decide to give him one of the women you traffic for an eighteenth birthday present?"

"How do you . . . ?"

"Just an educated guess, Teddy. So, how about it? Save your skin, save your precious son's skin."

"Why should I believe you?"

Harwood gestures around. "I don't see many other

options. I saved Mora. I know my duty. You're more valuable alive than dead. But only if you cooperate."

Teddy turns his head on the blood-caked pillow, but when he sees Marilyn he looks the other way. "I'll stick you like a pig for this."

"Maybe one day. But not today. Do you traffic people to fund Rattenfänger's terror?"

Teddy Wiltshire closes his eyes. "Yes."

"Do you profit from that terror yourself?"

"Yes."

"Who runs Rattenfänger?"

"People like me."

"No head of the board?"

Teddy growls, a bass rumble that makes Harwood want to turn and check for a snow leopard. She says, "MI6 is on to Rattenfänger's rackets in diamonds and antiquities as well. Who runs the show? Is it the same person who runs *all* of Rattenfänger, or simply Rattenfänger's treasurer?"

"The treasurer. They answer to the board."

"Give me the treasurer's name."

"Nobody knows."

"You must have an idea."

He doesn't say anything, but his color is turning from marble white to glassy blue. Harwood glances at her racing Casio. "Did you mastermind Rattenfänger's trafficking and kidnap scheme? You disappear people for them?"

A whisper: "Yes."

"Did you make James Bond disappear?"

"Yes."

Harwood leans forward. "He's still alive."

". . . Yes."

Harwood murmurs, "Where is he, Teddy? Tell me where he is and I'll take you off the drip. Marilyn has had enough of your blood now. Tell me where to find James."

"He's home."

Teddy speaks so quietly Harwood thinks she misheard him. She stands up, leaning closer to his pale lips. "Which home, Teddy? Scotland?"

She sees his head jerk a fraction before his skull would have made contact with hers and recoils just in time to avoid a knockout blow, but still it shunts a blinding light through her eye sockets. Teddy roars, heaving his body to one side, pulling the tube from Marilyn, who hits the floor with a thud. Blood sprays the air. Teddy seizes the tube and wraps it around Harwood's throat so tight the bite of the rubber crushes her larynx. Harwood elbows back into his gut, then his thigh, finding the wound. He twists, wrestling her onto the bed, and then his full weight is on top of her and he is winding the cord tighter and tighter, laughing in her face. Harwood's good arm is trapped under her ribs, but her wounded arm is free. She pats the sheets frantically for the shotgun. It must have fallen to the floor—but she didn't hear the clatter. She wriggles and bucks and kicks but his weight is too much. She tries to bite him but he rears away, cackling. Purple spots consume her vision. The moth is coming closer. And then she feels the neat row of sutures in his thigh and hammers with her fist. Teddy yelps and reaches to capture her hand, and for a moment his grip on the tube relents.

It gives her an inch—her hand lands on the shotgun. Harwood twists the barrel, finds the trigger, and pulls. Give me an inch and I'll take a life.

Thirty-Four
La Biennale

Venice. Thursday.

The quantum computer suspended beneath the Regent's Park office known simply as "Q" experiences earth from a God's-eye perspective, if "experience" is the right word. Fed constantly updated footage from MI6 satellites, Q knows Venice as a series of qubits. If its artificial intelligence were put to the task of image recognition or even creation, the computer would liken the canal city of Venice to a fish caught on a line cast from Mestre. This fishing line is, in reality, the railway crossing the dead-straight eighteenth-century aquatint into the mouth of the fish-shaped island, which is carved in two by the S-curve of the Grand Canal.

Q marks four players onto this aerial map. Lisl Baum,

Asset, tagged using a location device secreted inside a diamond bracelet gifted by 000. Friedrich Hyde, Target, tagged using a bug dropped into his jacket pocket by the clean-and-press service at 000's behest. Joseph Dryden, 004, Home Team, tracked through his interface. Conrad Harthrop-Vane, 000, Home Team, tag in his new Omega. Designations of enemy or friend were assigned to the players by human elements and Q has no data to disagree. Neither do Aisha or Ibrahim, who swivel in their desk chairs while watching aerial, police, and CCTV images of Venice on their monitors, discussing the development of an ultraprecise atomic optical clock that will soon redefine the unit of time meant by "one second."

Moneypenny—who is standing in the doorway listening to this with one hand in her pocket stroking the face of Johanna's Hermès watch—could not have articulated exactly what she thinks Johanna could add to this moment, only that as she waits for the games to begin, the part of her brain that sifts data makes her wonder where 003 is and what she has discovered out there in the darkness. Could Harwood tell her which Janus—people, diamonds, antiquities—leads the Gray Group, which is Rattenfänger's treasurer? Could she say if it's none of them, and there's someone else, some unseen god of gods pulling the strings?

But Johanna Harwood can't tell anyone what she knows. She can't alert Q Branch that 000 ought to be reassigned as an Active Threat.

When all four parties leave the Gritti, dots clustered where the Grand Canal meets the larger Giudecca Canal, nobody knows that while 004 will be making sure the sale goes ahead, 000 will be watching to make sure it doesn't, and he has backup on hand if he needs to remove Friedrich Hyde and 004 from the board without drawing any suspicion to himself.

Joseph Dryden lets 000 board the water taxi with Lisl Baum and Friedrich Hyde, whose wife has a headache, understandably, and prefers to stay at the hotel. Dryden keeps them in sight as he steps onto the vaporetto, standing at the open window with hands linked behind his back, spray tickling his cheeks. The party alights at the Giardini, Dryden a few minutes behind. He follows the crowds toward the entrance to the Biennale, stone crunching underfoot, trees filling in for spring.

What gives those around 004 away as people with club membership isn't any one background or style. It's how they are dressed, how they walk. Whether it's an oversized tie-dye T-shirt paired with woolen trousers and a quilted jacket, a three-piece suit with matching tie and pocket square, or a brightly printed agbada, the clothes fit perfectly, and lack a single crease. It's as if a costume designer has gone to work, except instead of extras, everyone here is the main character. And these actors don't walk with shoulders hunched against the threatening rain or heads slumped over maps. They glide because they've never had back trouble their whole lives.

Dryden—who is wearing a beige waxed cotton raincoat over a navy polo shirt with tan chinos—wonders if the crowd could identify his stride as military. He's never tried gliding and doesn't bother now, marching past the metal detectors, where Biennale staff read his posture as something official and carry on displaying impressive patience with a peacock claiming to be the prince of somewhere, who naturally hasn't RSVP'd, but expects to be let inside anyway—and is waved through in just a few moments, the staff's frantic check on Wikipedia fading from Dryden's hearing as he enters deeper into the fray of art and politics.

The national pavilions in the Giardini are an architectural parade. As Dryden hesitates at the intersection, he takes in buildings of different eras and styles: Venezuela's svelte brick topped with tall slatted windows like lashes over surprised eyes; the white Nordic pavilion, trees blooming through the airy roof; the roof of a straw hut. Then he catches sight of Friedrich Hyde, head above the crowds and pointing with a wild arm to something notable, Lisl Baum and 000 listening dutifully. They have elected not to head straight into the central exhibition but to start with the national pavilions.

Dryden follows the group into the Swiss pavilion, his nostrils twitching as the smell of ordnance hits him, and the gravel beneath his feet gives way to burnt straw, which covers the floor. Inside, gigantic straw men have been lit ablaze and left to smolder. It's the stench of the armored personnel carrier when he woke up after the explosion, the world swallowed by blaring din. Dryden shrugs this memory off, pushing deeper into the pavilion as the lights switch from red to black and he is suddenly doused in darkness, stranded between the limbs of burning beings. The rustle and tick of burning straw; nervous laughter; whispered confessions and complaints; a stumble and shriek; Triple O's breathing as the agent approaches on soft tiptoe from behind.

Dryden murmurs, "You wanna get the jump on me, you gotta try a lot harder than that."

Harthrop-Vane snorts. "Fuck you. No attempts at contact so far. Maybe you've fingered the wrong man."

Dryden turns his head, finding himself almost cheek to cheek with 000. "That a come-on, Conrad?"

"Don't start something you can't finish, Joseph," says Harthrop-Vane silkily.

Dryden chuckles. "Stay on the bastard all the same, all right?"

"Fine, but you'd better drop back. You'll be seen this close."

"Nobody sees me unless I want them to."

"Is that a fact?"

Dryden doesn't bother replying, simply disappears, so that when the lights rise, Triple O is left blinking at the absent space in front of him, Dryden catching this as he takes the exit with a hum.

It is a game of cat and mouse and dog, only the cat thinks the dog is another cat. Q watches Dryden linger in the doorway to the Nordic pavilion—which is hung with the pelts of reindeer, currently being driven from the land along with the Sámi people—while Friedrich Hyde, Lisl Baum, and Triple O stop outside the Russian pavilion, a miniature Winter Palace shuttered and empty after the artists and curator resigned with the Biennale's support in protest against the invasion of Ukraine.

Rain sputters to life, tiny blasts amidst the gravel, and as Dryden follows the group past the Italianate English country house and across the bridge to the jutting black cliff faces of the Australian pavilion, his brown Palladium leather boots turn bone white in the chalky mud. He's close enough to the trio to catch their gossip, but suddenly it's lost in the wall of sound that is Australia's installation. Dryden hesitates on the ramp climbing the building, reading a sign that warns of "high intensity sound and rapid movement of light." He edges toward the entrance to the chamber, but he can't push through the slab of noise—massive amplification speakers are blasting discordant electric guitar, a signal generator prompting flashing images on gigantic screens. He has no watch. He can't turn it down. The saturated feedback has Dryden gripping his head, retreating outside to gulp gray sky and green canal.

Leaning against the wall beside the speakers, Triple O watches this with a smirk. He beckons Hyde toward him.

Later, Dryden will remember seeing this small gesture but not registering it through the fear that he was about to lose his hearing. He will wonder exactly how Triple O told the antiquities Janus to back off, not to make the sale because MI6 are watching, and how Harthrop-Vane reacted when Friedrich Hyde told him to go to hell, dear boy—for surely this man without consequences must have said something like that, given what happened next. But Triple O, like Hyde, was accustomed to being obeyed, and therefore failed to read the warning signs of a mutiny.

Dryden catches up with them in the café, where the walls are painted with lightning stripes of black and white bounced between mirrors. He sees Hyde check a flip phone that Triple O hasn't reported. When he asks Triple O about it using military hand signals in a mirror, Harthrop-Vane shrugs.

Inside the central pavilion, crowds driven indoors by the rain are so dense Dryden loses visual contact with the target in a room of body horror assembled from pins and cogs. He can't see Triple O either. He turns 360, searching for a glimpse of Harthrop-Vane's dismal black or Friedrich Hyde's Burberry cuffs in the adjacent halls.

He murmurs, "Give me a position on the target."

Aisha's voice comes to him: "Standing with Lisl Baum."

"Where?"

"Southwest of your position. Triple O is standing near them."

That's the bathrooms.

"Why would Hyde queue for the bathroom with Baum while 000 takes a leak? Don't bother answering that. He's given her his coat with the tracking device to hold while he slips away. Alert Triple O I'm pursuing. Over and out."

Dryden swaps his mac for a hi-vis jacket from the cleaning crew station. Nobody in the sculpture courtyard of the central pavilion thinks anything of it when he hoists himself up the wall. It is a short clamber onto the roof of the pavilion, giving him a human-scale taste of Q's vantage point. He spots Hyde's thick white mane in the queue for the vaporetto to the Arsenale, where the central exhibition continues.

"When's the next boat to the Arsenale? Any water taxis around?" he asks.

Aisha says, "Not for another twenty minutes. We see him now on satellite. The boat will take ten minutes to the Arsenale. It's a fifteen-minute journey on foot."

"Looks like I'm running. You've got the map, honey."

Aisha laughs. "I love a man who isn't afraid to ask for directions. Better get going if you want to beat him there. Over and out."

Dryden squares his stance, and jumps.

When Triple O realizes Hyde isn't in the stall and that he left Lisl to hold his coat, he almost calls her a daft bitch. He bites his tongue and sends a message instead to the Rattenfänger unit standing by to serve Hyde his notice. He adds that 004 is acceptable collateral damage.

Dryden runs. He runs through the park, in and out of the shadow of irregular balconies frilly with geranium, through vegetable patches and dogs and over a bridge, the canal beneath him crisscrossed with the reflection of washing lines. Boats sleep tucked under taut covers. The water casts rippling illuminations up the high orange walls. Green shutters blink at him repeatedly. Sudden roof terraces elbow for room, sprawling with wisteria. He runs down an alley that shrinks, barreling toward a dead-end door, above which a marble relief shows saints presenting scrolls to baby Jesus on his mother's lap. Aisha shouts at him to make the left *now*, and a sudden jink reveals a passage under a damp timbered roof, a subterranean world beneath bridges that might only lead to a private door. A city that guards its secrets. He runs through a courtyard dressed with flapping laundry and centered by a broken fountain where kids play football, the ball's echo percussive and bottled. Across a wide street where masses of people tangle under the green awnings spilling from pink buildings and dither outside pale and peeling churches, debating whether to visit this or that collateral exhibition. Plunges down an alley narrower than his shoulders, so that he runs with his fists squeezed in front of his face, and pops free on the bank of a canal, facing the towering walls of the Arsenale, where once upon a time shipbuilders lived from cradle to grave, denied permission to ever leave these walls with their knowledge—knowledge that meant Venice ruled the world, knowledge that meant the difference between victory and the other thing.

The bridge is rattling rusted metal. A barge stacked high with folded cardboard and crates of fruit passes beneath him. It takes another minute to thread the compressed lanes that twist around the Arsenale, until he emerges from an alley hooded by a staircase blinking into sunlight, the rain finally parting, to see the queue building at the entrance to the Arsenale, people in Fendi trainers waiting on the pavestones because a prime minister has arrived. Dryden chuckles as he passes a woman who tells her husband testily, "Well, the bloody prime minister should use another entrance."

He spots Friedrich Hyde at the back of the queue, swaying from foot to foot, red-cheeked. So, still waiting for satisfaction.

It is then Dryden notices two men join the queue behind Hyde. They don't look like men who want to do business. They look like men whose business is the same as Dryden's. Murder in the spring sunshine. Except today it's Dryden's job to save the bad guy.

Dryden clears his throat. "Mr. Hyde!"

The bastard's bewildered blanch is priceless. The two opposition freeze.

Dryden hurries over and puts his arm around Hyde. "We've been waiting for you," he says loudly. "Right this way, sir."

As he leads Hyde to the front of the queue, the woman asks her husband why he hadn't arranged fast-track entry.

"Wait just a minute," says Hyde, "who in the name of . . ."

"You don't need to know my name," says Dryden, "just my role. Rattenfänger sent me to ensure the sale goes ahead."

"Well, tell them to make up their bloody mind, will you! First they tell me not to sell it, too much bloody heat, now you tell me—"

"Yes, sir. The only trouble is that Interpol are in play. I'll clear the way but I'll need your full cooperation. Where are you meeting your buyer?"

"I've had enough of this bloody cloak-and-dagger stuff. Never used to be like this! Used to be plain as day! But between you lot and bloody Interpol it's no fun anymore. I received a text to meet at the Arsenale. He said he'd find me."

Oh joy.

They've reached the front of the queue, where Dryden places a hand on the arm of the young man with enamel heart-shaped earrings checking tickets. 004 produces his most charming smile, along with his best Italian. "Another for VIP entry."

A worried check of the paper. "I don't have anything . . ."

Dryden leans closer. "This is the Duke of Wessex. I was told he should come straight through. He didn't RSVP."

"They never do. Um . . . yes, OK, go ahead . . ."

Dryden gives him a clap on the bicep and ushers Hyde through the ancient doors, glancing back at the two fuming military-aged operatives waiting at the back of the queue. There's club membership, and then there's walking with confidence. He'll always take the latter.

The central exhibition occupies the vast Corderie, a building over three hundred meters long with a wooden Palladian roof held up by two rows of columns in crumbling masonry. Dryden tells Friedrich

Hyde that he'll be watching, and then drops into the background, scanning for the enemy, and Hyde's contact, who might be spooked by Dryden's too-close presence. The noise in the cavernous brick space is almost too dense for his interface to pick through.

He spots the first of Rattenfänger's operatives snaking between potbellied ceramics that nearly touch the loft. His coat is bulging—Dryden isn't the only one who can skip a metal detector, clearly—and a swastika tattoo creeps above his collar. Dryden squeezes through the crowd, keeping his head down. When he taps the operative on his right shoulder, the man turns that way, helping the wrench of Dryden's hands as he snaps the man's neck. Dryden catches the body under sagging arms.

The great pot wobbles but Dryden steadies it with his shoulder.

He carries the dead man to a mosaicked bench where he tells the teenager fanning herself with the Biennale map: "Excuse my friend, he's in a dead faint."

She yawns and ignores him.

Dryden locates the next operative in a room where rain is falling from the ceiling into a mirrored trough. The operative sees Dryden in the reflection, and catches his oncoming hand with a grin.

"He told me you'd want to dance," the man hisses,

accent central European, no visible tattoos, hands red with eczema.

"My dance card is full," says Dryden. He slips free of the wrist hold, and would have stabbed a punch into the man's throat, but his arm is blocked by the operative's forearm.

It is a dance, and a tight one, held in close quarters as the rain spills over their shoulders and neither man blinks and the crowd streams heedlessly around them, until Dryden breaks the operative's trigger finger.

"Who told Rattenfänger to warn Hyde off?" he asks.

"Who told you that you get to live today?" says the operative, stamping on Dryden's boot.

Dryden grins. "I don't need permission. I do my breathing all on my own now. How about you? This paycheck worth dying for? I've already killed one of you."

A blur and the man's hands are free, and glinting with a knife. The hubbub of the room is swelling, a large group pushing through. Dryden takes the most direct route possible and headbutts the operative with all of his might. The man drops unconscious in the puddle. He will drown in three inches of water before anyone notices him.

Dryden finds Hyde in a room printed with black-and-white text that exhorts its audience to *Please Care*.

Hyde appears blind to this, because he is checking his phone.

"What is it?" asks Dryden.

Hyde jumps. "He won't just bloody well meet me here! Says they've heard it's not safe and they're bloody skittish, insists on doing the deal at the Conservatorio di Musica Benedetto Marcello. Almost not worth being in the game anymore."

Dryden clicks his tongue in sympathy. "Almost. Come on. Let's get going."

The exit is beyond a room that is rich with damp earth. Plants are growing in the dim light. A growing installation. His hand on Hyde's elbow, Dryden can't slow down, but he breathes it all in. This beauty, the beauty of life, worth fighting for.

Thirty-Five
Stop the Clocks

Altai Mountains. Thursday. Six hours ahead of Greenwich Mean Time, five hours ahead of Venice.

Fifteen minutes before a bullet is fired through the library window of the Conservatorio di Musica Benedetto Marcello in Venice and over four thousand miles away, Johanna Harwood pushes the corpse of Teddy Wiltshire off her. There is a hole through Wiltshire's torso, like a blind spot on the sun, seeping red. Sitting up, she wipes his blood from her face. Her throat burns. She was so close to finding out where James was being kept prisoner. Harwood sets her feet on the floor. Her head is pounding. Muscles trembling. Wound in her arm leaking. Ears ringing. She gets her arms around

Marilyn Aliyeva, lifting her onto the chaise longue. Marilyn's pulse is faint, but hanging on.

The walls and the floor change places as Harwood staggers down the hall and through the central room, which is still hazy with gunfire and reeks of a butcher's shop. She struggles into her coat and leans her shoulder to the door at the main entrance, now so much heavier. Cold air revives her like a slap to the face. She pushes through the snow, slipping on glaciated rock before righting herself. Very little light in the sky. She tracks around the dome toward where the helicopter waits. She will check the engines and get ready for takeoff, then return for Marilyn. There is no hospital marked on the laminated map. She'll have to risk going into Gorno-Altaysk.

Harwood stops. The netting that covered the helicopter is flapping loose. The helicopter is gone.

Harwood's stomach drops, blood and air failing her. Who could have taken it? How did she miss an extra man? She came to the End of Everything, only to overlook the one thing that would ultimately matter—the means to get Marilyn off this mountain and to a hospital before she goes into shock, the means to communicate with MI6 and warn them about Triple O, the means to continue her search for James, who is "home," but which home, and in what state, she is now helpless to discover.

She can hear her teeth chattering and clamps her jaw tightly. Not now. Not yet. Defeat isn't an option.

The words of Joseph Dryden come back to her. *You ever need me, call and I'll come running.*

Harwood races to the generator. She throws the power back on—but the lever jams. Rust and cold have conspired to lock it into place. She tries three times before giving up with a yell. She can't turn the power on.

Find a phone.

Harwood has to keep one hand out for balance as she searches the dome. Not even a radio. No phones in any of the dead men's pockets. But there is a laptop, set up in front of the stolen Vermeer. Harwood takes a bottle of whisky from the cabinet and carries the laptop to the bedroom, checking on Marilyn's pulse once more before collapsing into the Eames chair. The laptop wants a facial scan. Harwood holds it over Wiltshire's corpse. He is still warm, but gone. Luckily computers don't read souls. She is in.

Harwood takes a hit of whisky. Her throat sears, then softens.

There is a router listed, grayed out. No Wi-Fi—she can't use the laptop to make a call. Harwood remembers the dish on the roof—satellite Internet. The modem isn't working because of the power outage.

She is about to go and inspect the modem when she

notices a folder labeled "Accounts" on the desktop. It contains spreadsheets. Harwood opens the most recently modified. The document lists the sale of "teddy bears." One hundred were sold on Tuesday—that was two days ago. It took this year's profits to one million. If Teddy is the Janus of human trafficking, that means he just hit the threshold for money useful to the cause, and the six-day countdown began yesterday. In five days' time there will be a terror attack somewhere. But the column listing transfers has no data. He made the money, but didn't digitally transfer it to the treasurer. Did that mean that he really was the man in charge?

Harwood rubs her eyes. There is a folder of photographs with the spreadsheet. She opens the pictures, a cascade that clogs her throat with bile. Images of women's necks, men's hands shoving their heads forward so that the camera can get a good look at the barcodes tattooed onto their red skin.

If Teddy Wiltshire was the treasurer, and if he knew where James was, and if she had been able to win more information from him that might have saved lives—even with all those factors, Harwood is violently glad in this moment to have killed him.

Harwood fixes on Wiltshire, lying supine across the bed, emptier by the second. "You win some, you lose some, Teddy boy."

Harwood is about to close the laptop and search for the modem when something about the most recent photograph grasps her attention. The shape of the slender neck, perhaps, or the heavy gloss of the hair. Another image comes to mind. A surveillance photograph taken from behind a couple at a party. The man had his arm around the woman's waist. He was making a speech, his other arm raised, a circle of people listening. It wasn't a glamorous party—a cheap wine and peanuts affair, hosted in a corridor of some university building. The woman was staring at the floor. That was what triggered Harwood's memory—the slight bump of her nape, the way her hair fell as she perhaps wished herself anywhere but here. Perhaps wished herself in the arms of James Bond, with whom she was having an affair, as James tried to get information from her about her husband's climate research. MI6 believed Mikhail was sitting on a secret, and indeed it wouldn't be so long after that photograph was taken that Mikhail claimed he wanted to defect from Russia to the UK.

Anna and Mikhail Petrov, taken before Mikhail died and Anna disappeared.

And this is a photograph of Anna Petrov's neck, tattooed with a barcode.

Harwood gazes at the wall, not seeing the sheer concrete, but instead seeing a story. Mikhail was an expert in geoengineering. Last year, Sir Bertram Paradise stole quantum computing technology from Dr. Zofia Nowak as part of his plan to melt the ice caps and sell off new trade routes to the highest bidders using geoengineering technology. He was backed by Rattenfänger. So wasn't it also highly likely Sir Bertram took the geoengineering device from Mikhail Petrov, who told James in a passing remark once that his funding didn't come from the Russian state? It must have come from Rattenfänger. When it appeared that Mikhail was going to blow the whistle on Paradise to MI6, Rattenfänger must have acted. He was assassinated in a Sydney hotel room. Anna went missing. And now she has been captured—if Harwood is right—by Rattenfänger, but not killed instantly, trafficked instead. For what? If Teddy wasn't lying, and James is still alive, it can only mean Rattenfänger wants something from him that he hasn't yet given up. What better lever of persuasion than a woman James Bond swore to protect?

Harwood loops her father's camera over her head, and checks the number of exposures remaining. Just one. She focuses on the screen image of the barcode tattoo and takes the shot. Then she closes the laptop.

Marilyn is paler, but the tube in her chest still whistles quietly with air. A power place, where the impossible can happen.

The router is on a shelf beneath the skulls. Its lights are dead. The modem is on the desk, also dead. Harwood searches the drawers for a battery backup, then the shelving, the utility room, the men's bunk room. Nothing. She lets out a stream of swear words aimed at Teddy Wiltshire for being the world's worst survivalist. Returning to the laptop, she takes the thing to the desk and sets it down beside the modem, then fetches the toolbox from the utility room.

Harwood wipes sweat from her forehead, streaking blood there instead. For a surgeon, what she does next is deplorably messy. It could generously be described as a Heath Robinson contraption, an English phrase she learned not through the cartoonist's drawings of implausibly complex machinery held together by duct tape and string, but in her training for MI6, where she was taught about the mammoth machine used to crack German codes in the Second World War, dubbed the Heath Robinson by the women who operated its wires and pulleys. First, she turns the laptop on its side. It is imperative the laptop remain on while she takes the back off and identifies the 11.1-volt battery. One indelicate movement and the laptop could crash, with no guarantee of waking up again. She works with her lower lip caught between her teeth. She can hear her mother's voice, telling her she'll ruin her surgeon's hands if she roughhouses with the boys. But her hands aren't shaking as she cuts and strips the wires, threading them to the modem, now also spilling its guts. She touches the copper nerves together. The modem lights up.

Kneeling in front of the crooked laptop, Harwood tilts her head—still no signal. She turns around to find the router remains dark. Damn it. She needs more voltage to boost the signal. But too much will overload the system. She casts around the room. Everything electric is plugged into the mains. No remotes. No cameras. Harwood puts her head in her hands—then sits up, eyes fixed on Sid's Casio on her wrist. The battery would be three volts. Just right.

But if she takes the battery out, the minutes will stop counting. She will stop the clocks. Sid's time will run out.

There has to be another watch in this place. She finds one on the wrist of a man she sprayed with bullets, but the battery is cracked. She finds another on Teddy Wiltshire's wrist, but it is self-winding. She is running her hands through her hair, trying to think of another way, when she hears Marilyn's slow breaths getting slower.

Harwood returns to the desk, slipping the watch from her wrist, where a ghostly impression remains, an imprint of the sun's absence. The watch says she is fifteen hours and twenty minutes into this day without Sid. She selects the smallest screwdriver, and removes the back of the watch. The battery is a full stop that she pries loose from its sentence. Time stops.

Harwood connects the wires to the three-volt power source.

The router gleams.

The laptop is connected.

Harwood opens FaceTime, navigating with a ghost's touch so as not to disturb the precarious connection. She taps in Joseph Dryden's phone number. The phone rings once, twice—then Dryden's calm "Hello?" reaches her at the End of Everything and Johanna Harwood smiles, disturbing the muscles of her face. It makes her realize her cheeks are wet with tears.

She says, "Go dark."

Dryden says, "Aisha, cut the stream." A beat. "Do it." Another beat. "*Do it.*" Then Dryden says, "I'm dark. You OK? You sound—"

Harwood interrupts him: "I need your help. Ex-fil from the radome south of Ukok, Altai Mountains. MI6 can't know. Completely closed loop."

"I'm too far out—but we can trust Tiger Tanaka."

The head of the Japanese Secret Service, and James's friend, who saved Dryden's life last year. Harwood agrees.

"You got damage?" asks Dryden.

"Civilian collateral. Not much time."

Harwood can hear thumps and muffled bangs.

Dryden says, "I read you."

Harwood swallows, keeping her throat wet enough to speak—the motion sears. "Wiltshire is selling human beings. He hit a million two days ago, but no bank transfer. A bogey has left my position. If the money makes it to the treasurer, there will be an attack in five days' time."

"Understood. We're attempting to ID the treasurer now."

Harwood gets to her feet. "Joe—are you with Triple O?"

"He's inbound—"

She stands over the laptop as she barks: "Take cover."

"What?"

"You're in immediate danger, he's—"

A smash, a pop, and then the line goes dead.

Harwood calls: "Joe? Dryden? 004?"

Nothing. Her connection is still good. Harwood is retyping the number when the battery dies, and the laptop cuts to black.

Did he hear the warning?

Harwood looks down at the dead watch in her hand.

The only sound beyond the ringing in her own ears comes from the bedroom: Marilyn's muted, agonized breaths through the tube, and the patter of blood from Wiltshire's chest running across the bed and dripping down the sheets onto the parquet. She presses the Casio to her forehead.

Thirty-Six
Agent Down

Venice. Thursday.

A short time before Johanna Harwood places her call, clouds gather over the internal dock of the Arsenale, making a menacing silhouette of the old hydraulic crane dipping its beak toward the darkening pool. Joseph Dryden flips his collar, hustling Friedrich Hyde past the people queuing at the coffee stand wondering whether they ought to take shelter. Approaching the colonnaded shipyards, Dryden sees that a screen has been erected across the arches, playing footage of spectral jellyfish, engrossing a crowd—apart from two military-aged males who have their backs to the video, and are facing him and Hyde directly. Both wear wraparound sunglasses, though the sun has vanished. Both wear earpieces. Both—Dryden can see in the bulge of their jackets—are carrying. Blocking the exit. Which likely means two more are bringing up the rear, blocking the entrance.

Caught.

Or they would be if Venice wasn't a city on the water.

Tucked into the shipyard is a blue-and-white-striped speedboat with back-slanted italics reading *POLIZIA*. The speed limit on the Grand Canal and other smaller central canals is between five and seven kilometers an hour. Police can go up to forty kilometers per hour without anyone blinking.

There is a single officer standing at the rear of the boat watching the jellyfish footage, probably waiting for his partner to return with coffee.

The police boat is equidistant between Dryden and Hyde and the enemy combatants.

"Walk forward," says Dryden. "Act as if we're going to walk through the shipyards and head for the exit."

"Aren't we?" asks Hyde, mopping his forehead with a polka-dot handkerchief.

When they reach the boat, Dryden delves into his pocket for his wallet, opening it to a card describing him as something generic in international law enforcement. He gestures to the policeman, who is fresh-faced enough that Dryden feels guilty when he steps down into the boat and knocks the man out with a single punch. The officer drops to the deck. Dryden drags him into the cabin, and then checks to see how many people noticed what he just did. Nobody has. The crowd is still watching the jellyfish.

"I love art," says Dryden, before seizing Hyde by his tie and pulling him into the boat.

The opposition sharpens.

Dryden starts the motor, arcing the boat around and gunning into the dock, before completing another swivel to aim at the Canale dei Marani and flooring it past six pairs of gigantic arms reaching across the embankments to form bridges. Dryden doesn't know that the hands crossing fingers represent hope, but still it snags his attention as the police boat bursts past the guard tower blossoming with wild shrubbery, and spills into the waters. He turns the siren on.

"Tell Triple O I'm heading for the Conservatorio di Musica Benedetto Marcello," he says.

"Copy that," says Aisha. "It looks on satellite like you just stole a police boat. You haven't just stolen a police boat, right?"

"The technical term is TWOC," says Dryden. "Keep an ear on police radio, all right? This one just stopped working, mysteriously." He delivers a kick to the unit. He doesn't feel like talking.

"Rattenfänger know how to take without owner's consent, too. You've got a boat in pursuit. Over and out."

The enemy are pursuing in a gleaming water taxi.

"Tie the policeman's wrists in case he wakes up," says Dryden. "And move him into the recovery position. Hey! Look alive!"

Friedrich Hyde purples. "I think you forget yourself, boy."

Dryden spins the boat into the Canale di San Nicolò, passing the crook of the Lido where a scattering of cracked stucco villas and empty restaurants face the canal. "Maybe sometimes," he says. "But not today. So do as I say and then keep your head down while I save your worthless life."

"I won't tolerate this, any of it. You people are all brutes! This whole relationship is predicated on mutual benefit. I'm not some zealot for the cause. If I'm not seeing returns, I'd rather go it alone. No one's going to stop me making a living. We've been generations in antiquities, you know. Generations."

Decades of self-confidence and impunity enable the antiquities dealer to meet Dryden's gaze for a few moments longer than most, perhaps, but as the Mediterranean sun battles with rain, casting the snow-globe silhouette of San Giorgio Maggiore into strong shade and eye-squinting light, and then the wailing of the police siren parts the throng of the Grand Canal, Friedrich Hyde blinks and does as he's told.

The opposition aren't put off by the linear vaporetti lines, or the transverse gondola routes connected by the shouts of gondoliers to passing colleagues, or the stolid perseverance of delivery boats pulling up to hotels and restaurants to unload crates and spill the contents of tomb-sized fridges. Dryden pushes the engine past forty kilometers an hour as Aisha's voice competes with the siren to tell him that the police officer's pal finally got his coffee and is trying to contact his partner over radio. The sun is winning, polishing the Grand Canal so bright the passing palaces are reversed in its glass. Spray catches Dryden's face. He shakes his head, grinning.

Ponte dell'Accademia looms ahead, announcing itself by the noise of souvenir vendors and clamor of tourists lining up to take photographs, their boots a shuttlecock echo.

"Turn right!" shouts Aisha.

Dryden spins the wheel, racing down the narrow Rio dell'Orso on a wave of surf that buoys the waiting gondolas. A young gondolier in a striped shirt slouched over his phone sits up to swear at Dryden, who calls an apology as he grabs Hyde by the scruff of his neck and climbs onto the cobbles. The snarl of an engine means the opposition have just turned into the canal. Dryden gets a glimpse of a busy square centered by a green-hooded Louis Vuitton stand selling maps of Venice. People from all across the world move in gentle gangs, opening to greet friends and closing back up again, a blur of high fashion and Biennale totes soundtracked by quarreling dogs and the clink of orange glasses beneath Aperol Spritz awnings.

The blackened façade of the Conservatorio di Musica Benedetto Marcello suggests a reclusive existence, but the building is open as a collateral event for the Biennale. As Dryden pushes Hyde through the heavy doors, that word *collateral* gets its fingers around his throat. Who or what will be collateral damage today? The cool quiet of the courtyard is a momentary relief, the dark stone and heavy columns carrying a monastic quality.

"Where does your buyer want to meet?"

"The library."

"You couldn't just do this over text?" mutters Dryden, dragging Hyde to take cover behind the line of columns.

"A man's handshake is very important," says Hyde,

peering around the column at the two Rattenfänger operatives who enter and hold position, checking their surroundings.

"Finally, something we agree on," says Dryden. "Wait here."

Dryden strolls toward the two men, who immediately fan out to form a triangle with him. Their shared look, hidden by wraparound sunglasses but signaled by the slight jerk of a chin, tells Dryden it's about to start.

Delayed violence is almost as bad as delayed gratification, or perhaps it's the same thing if you're like Dryden. Either way, 004 welcomes the first punch, which he blocks with his forearm while sending an elbow crashing into the chest of the second attacker, who is wearing Kevlar under his shirt. The impact reverberates up Dryden's arm. He uses its force, turning to swing a right at the first attacker, who ducks the blow just in time, Dryden feeling the brush of hair on his knuckles. He follows with a swiping leg that lifts the man from the ground. The second operative jumps him from behind. He jerks back with his head, catching the man in the mouth, breaking a tooth.

Dryden twists, bear-hugs the man, and dumps him onto the cobbles. But the first operative has recovered and tackles Dryden against the naked brick wall. Dryden tenses his stomach as the blows come. Part of training to be a boxer is training to be a punching bag, and Dryden blocks what he can and doesn't sweat what he can't. An orchestra in an open-windowed room above is trying to get something together. The discordant piano is a beautiful racket, occasionally joined by a virtuous horn. Dryden drops a shoulder, weaves, grabs the man by the collar, and slams him into the wall, stamping on his face when he drops. He looks up into the muzzle of the opposition's gun. Dryden doesn't hesitate—he launches himself at the man. The bullet breaks a window and the music stops, replaced by growing sirens. Dryden seizes the man's gun hand and wrenches, once, twice, until the wrist breaks. He knocks the man out with a right hook to the temple.

Dryden steps over the mess, hauls Hyde from his hiding place, and shoves him through the glass doors, across the checkered floor and up the stairs against the flow of panicking people. Chandeliers stir in the commotion. He forces Hyde through an open-air hall displaying sculptures and into the deserted library.

The buyer is waiting in the shadows of the bookshelves. His suit says money. His tan says desert. He doesn't have the appearance of a museum or gallery buyer. There's no way he can claim the sword doesn't have soil on it, or some other bullshit, or that he presumed the whole thing to be innocent—he's making a deal in what's disconcertingly close to a siege. That doesn't seem to bother him. His stubble and short back and sides say military background. Dryden would bet arms dealer, a two-bit warlord who wants to wave the sword under the nose of his rivals. When he sees Hyde, the buyer barks a stream of Italian expletives.

Dryden catches his breath. "Now or never," he tells Hyde.

The antiquities Janus is a man transformed, pulling the envelope of photographs and certificates of provenance from his pocket with a flourish. "You know this piece *redefines* the word *rare*—this is your one opportunity to own *history*. This will not come to the market again."

Dryden puts his weight behind a mammoth oak table and pushes it against the door.

"I don't want to put this on display and be called a liar," says the buyer. "You swear to its origins?"

"Took it from the towelheads myself," says Hyde.

Dryden curls his lip, shoving a filing cabinet on its side.

The sweaty slap of hands.

"I'll transfer the money now, but this is the last time I meet you in person. You're a dinosaur who doesn't know what an asteroid sounds like, do you know that?"

Hyde tuts. He holds his phone out. "Just your thumbprint. No time like the present, old chap."

Where the hell is Triple O? The boots of the police shake the building. At this rate, he'll have to declare himself and start an international incident.

A moving shadow catches Dryden's eye in the windows across the courtyard.

The buyer presses his thumb to Hyde's screen.

"That's it," murmurs Dryden. "Clock's ticking. Six days until it goes boom, funded by my own looting."

"On it," says Aisha. "Now all we need is for Hyde to make that transaction to the treasurer and we'll follow it."

Something is ringing. It takes a second for Dryden to understand it's his phone, he's so used to the voices of MI6 living inside his head. He pulls it from his coat. Number unknown.

"Hello?"

"Go dark."

The voice of Johanna Harwood.

Dryden doesn't hesitate. He says, "Aisha, cut the stream." She argues, then relents. "I'm dark. You OK? You sound—"

Johanna Harwood says, "I need your help. Ex-fil from the radome south of Ukok, Altai Mountains. MI6 can't know. Completely closed loop."

"I'm too far out—but we can trust Tiger Tanaka."

"Copy that."

"You got damage?" asks Dryden.

"Civilian collateral. Not much time."

Dryden's gaze drifts to the windows. There is always collateral damage. "I read you."

"Wiltshire is selling human beings. He hit a million two days ago, but no bank transfer. A bogey has left my position. If the money makes it to the treasurer, there will be an attack in five days' time."

"Understood. We're attempting to ID the treasurer now."

"Joe—are you with Triple O?"

"He's inbound—"

"Take cover."

"What?"

"You're in immediate danger, he's—"

A bullet fired from the opposite window whistles through the shattering glass.

Conrad Harthrop-Vane examines Dryden's inert body through the scope of his sniper rifle for a fleeting moment, half-obscured by a bookshelf, before repositioning his sights on Friedrich Hyde, curling his finger around the trigger, and taking the antiquity dealer's head off. He watches the buyer escape out a door at the back of the library. Let him pick up the blasted sword and get arrested, he doesn't know anything, and the money will never make it to the treasurer now. No transaction, no leads. MI6 will think no attack can now take place. A consolation prize, even if they didn't get the identity of the Gray Group ringleader. Of course, the action will still unfold in five days' time. Teddy Wiltshire saw to that with his flesh market.

Harthrop-Vane stashes the sniper rifle in its case. It is the same model Trigger preferred. He leaves it by the window, pulling the gloves from his hands and stuffing them into his pockets as he exits the gallery, joining the tide of people bottling the hall. The mark of a hero, he has heard, is running into danger while other people run away. He runs toward the library now, getting his ID out of his wallet and waving it at the police who bar his way. His phone is vibrating in his pocket. The police seize his arm when he reaches for it, shoving him against the wall.

"Polizia internazionale!" he shouts. "Polizia internazionale!"

The bullet strikes Dryden center mass.

He hits the floor, skull bouncing off the marble. The ceiling is painted with a mural of clouds, which storm in his vision. He clamps a hand to his chest as a second shot whangs the air. Dryden lifts his phone. It is as heavy as an armored car. He can't breathe. He can't feel his legs. He opens his contacts, scrolls to TT, and presses dial. His chest is tighter than the inside of a tank. His hand is wet.

Tiger Tanaka answers, "Dryden-san. Tell me you are visiting Tokyo and seek my hospitality."

"Airlift," says Dryden. "Radome south of Ukok, Altai Mountains. Black ops."

A rustling pause. "Are you in trouble?"

"003. I promised . . ."

"I do not know 003. I owe them no favors, certainly not ordering my pilots to invade Chinese air space, even if I did happen to have a surveillance plane in the area. Now I mention it, I do not owe you a favor. In fact, you owe me one."

"She and Bond . . ." Dryden gasps as a sledgehammer seems to swing for his chest.

A cough. "I see. I will take care of it, Dryden-san. Are you sure you're not in trouble, my friend?"

Dryden hits end call, dropping the phone. The buyer is gone. Going for the sword. He has to stop them. Dryden rolls onto his side, gets an elbow under himself, and pushes. He almost makes it to his feet before crashing into a chair and sprawling across the floor. Another pounding. Another pound of flesh.

Joseph Dryden can see the light at the end of the tunnel. He is walking on sand. He can hear the sea. And the voice of Luke Luck. Peace settles over him. Shore leave.

It takes another ten minutes for the police to relent, and even then, they won't let Harthrop-Vane into the library. He has a view through the battered door, though, and watches as the paramedics struggle to lift Joseph Dryden into a body bag, his corpse heavy and awkward as a sandbag soaked by a storm. All that stalwart strength means nothing now. Harthrop-Vane hears a paramedic say it was a shot to center mass. His phone keeps buzzing. He answers as the body is carried down the marble stairs.

"000, report," says Moneypenny.

Her voice is constricted. Harthrop-Vane wants to tell her this is why it's prudent not to play favorites. You might lose your best toy. She already lost Bond, after all. But he doesn't say that, of course. He puts panic and fury into his words as he tells her, "Two shots fired from the top floor. Bloody police won't let me do my job. Shooter could be anywhere by now. I've been telling them to drop a cordon around Venice and they kindly reminded me we're on an island where every citizen owns a boat. Incompetents."

"Calm down," says Moneypenny, "and report. Police radio is telling Aisha there are two men down."

"Yes. Hyde and 004."

"Then he's—" She doesn't finish.

"I'm afraid so, ma'am. I couldn't get to him. The police are sieging the building. He was killed on impact. 004 is dead."

Thirty-Seven
The Telegram

London. Thursday.

Phoebe Taylor rises from her desk as Moneypenny strides in, checking to slam her fist into the wall, bringing down a framed print of Regent's Park in the rain.

"It can't be true?"

Moneypenny tugs her shirt straight with a harsh jerk. "Call M. I'm going to Vauxhall."

Aisha locks the door to the bathroom stall and sinks to the floor, banging her hip against the toilet bowl. She can't breathe. A sob expands in her chest like a balloon—when it bursts, she buries her head between her knees, interlacing her fingers in her dreads, keeping the sound of shock trapped there, a silent scream.

Ibrahim blinks—the action, if it can be called action, seems to take years, his eyelids closing over a scene: the last time he shook Joseph Dryden's hand. He kept secret his delight at being called brother by this man he admired dearly. He can't explain why, only regret it.

When Moneypenny tells M what has happened, he twists in his chair to gaze out at the Thames. His voice is distant as he says, "We'll have to notify the next of kin."

"His mother," says Moneypenny.

M nods. "It used to be telegrams. My father died after peace had been declared. Absurd, in many ways. I was just a baby, of course, but my eldest brother told the story often. The knock at the door. The angel of death. That's what telegram boys were called. My mother tipped the boy ten shillings for his trouble. Years later, I asked her why. You know what she said?" He turns a weak smile on her. "'It must have been wretched for the poor lad. Simply wretched.'"

"I don't think Mrs. Dryden will give us ten shillings for this, sir."

Thirty-Eight
Shambhala

Darkness to light. Altai Mountains. Six hours ahead of Greenwich Mean Time, five hours ahead of Venice.

It is an act of faith. Johanna Harwood doesn't know why Dryden's line went dead. Perhaps it was the lap top battery. Perhaps it was live fire. Either way, she can't proceed on foot with Marilyn, and she can't leave her here to die. What she's left with is the belief that no matter the obstacles, Joseph Dryden doesn't leave a teammate stranded with civilian wounded. So she waits, sitting at Marilyn's side with Sid's blank Casio squeezed tightly in one fist.

She is thinking about the word *home*. Teddy Wiltshire said that James was home. She knows he isn't in

London or Scotland. Both CCTV collections have been scoured using the de-masking technology developed by Aisha to combat Rattenfänger's disappearing trick. Besides, the truth is that James was never at home in the UK. He always felt there was something alien and un-English about him. He was a difficult man to cover up. Something a bit cold and dangerous in that face. Appears too fit, too ready for combat. Stands too straight. To even the most casual observer, his presence said death had made a friend of him. This didn't bother James. Abroad was what mattered. But he wasn't in Jamaica, either, his adopted home. Felix Leiter had personally turned the island inside out.

Maybe Wiltshire didn't mean James's home. Wiltshire's own home was Tite Street, London, served a search warrant by the NCA, who found all manner of incriminating evidence for tax evasion, but no James Bond. Where was Wiltshire's home originally? The files didn't say. Where did he consider home?

Harwood touches her cold fingers to Marilyn's head. Temperature rising.

Marilyn might know.

Harwood asks the shamans who guard the gateway for one last favor, one last scientific impossibility. Yes, she could possibly force Marilyn awake and put the question to her, most likely throwing her into full-blown fever and shock. But, just as Johanna Harwood took up a license to kill, she swore the Hippocratic oath to do no harm and help all. Somewhere between these two poles lies the knowledge that she can't jeopardize an innocent person to save James Bond. And nor would he accept such a means of salvation. So she asks the shamans a last favor. Let Marilyn wake up before help arrives. And God, please, let help come soon.

Her faith is repaid by the roar of an engine. Harwood scrambles to the door, peering into the night sky as the fighter jet descends. She recognizes the outline of the Kawasaki RC-2, a Japanese reconnaissance plane.

Harwood presses her hands together. Thanks, Joe.

She returns to Marilyn with the ice wind at her back. Marilyn's eyes are open.

Harwood kneels at her side, checking her pulse. "Marilyn? Try not to speak. There's a tube breathing for you in your chest. You're going to be OK. Help is here."

Marilyn's eyes read a whole history in Harwood's face. Tears slip free, before her gaze flits across the room, landing on Teddy's corpse. Her satisfaction is centuries old.

"Marilyn, listen to me. Where does Teddy call home?" She finds pen and paper on the bedside table, and works her hand around Marilyn's, the pen gripped in both of their fingers. "I told you that I lost everything. This is my last chance to get something back."

Marilyn's fingers move. The letters are blurred hieroglyphs but Harwood knows the story they tell.

St. Petersburg.

She kisses Marilyn on the forehead.

A choice faces her now. Wait here and greet Tiger Tanaka's men, perhaps Tanaka himself. Be the spy who came in from the cold. Hand over the evidence she has gathered. Trust the system.

Harwood's inner compass spins.

Maybe she is paranoid. Maybe Triple O is the last leak. Maybe the system has her best interests at heart.

Harwood shakes her head, slowly, without realizing it.

No system has ever had her best interests at heart. No system ever had Sid's best interests at heart. Even James, the son of the system, was betrayed by it.

Harwood picks up her camera and slings it round her neck. Tucks a fully loaded pistol in her belt and pockets a further two clips and provisions from the utility room in a duffel bag. She strokes Marilyn's hand a last time, and goes out into the cold.

Dawn light gilds the pass down the Five Saints as Harwood reaches the foot of Tabyn-Bogdo-Ola. The narrow fissure branches between the glowing rock faces, and she hesitates, lifting her ski goggles. She is about to reach for her map when the shadows in the right-hand branch move. Harwood freezes. The snow leopard paces forward, blocking the path, its eyes locking with hers. Harwood remembers, as each muscle in her body locks, that locals say the entrance to Shambhala lies at the foot of Tabyn-Bogdo-Ola. Harwood can count the snow leopard's ribs. The creature's lips pull back. She could draw her gun—would probably make it before the animal leaps. Instead, Harwood gradually shows her empty hands. Relaxes her limbs. The snow leopard's breath fogs the air between them. Then, with a swish of its tail, the big cat turns away and leaps into the mountains. Harwood sags, raising her hands to her face—realizing her left hand isn't empty. Sid's watch is tangled with her gloved fingers. She wipes a thumb over the frosted glass. The sun flares in her hand. She kneels and buries the watch between the footsteps of the mountain ghost at the entrance to Shambhala. Then she brushes snow from her knees and takes the left-hand turn, descending toward the rippling grassland.

Sidereal

Thirty-Nine
Coercion

Location unknown. Time and day unknown.

Anna Petrov watches the woman in the mirror. It isn't her, whoever it is. This woman agrees dumbly to strip, to be measured, to be manhandled into dresses and blouses and skirts, to have her hair pulled with a comb, her face made up with powders and inks. This woman smiles when she is told to smile because it may never happen and it could be worse, though it's already happened and it couldn't be worse. This woman agrees to eat and doesn't vomit the food back up. This woman doesn't question where she is or when she is or what she is. This woman agrees that it's important she greet James looking desirable. This woman agrees to reignite her intimacy with the spy—whatever he wants, whatever hungers he has developed in captivity, she will meet. And then she'll ask him, sweetly and softly, to give Rattenfänger what *they* want. It's only something small. One solitary scrap of information. After that they'll both be freed. Make him care again. Reawaken his senses. His thirst for life. His protective instincts. Don't think of it as coercion. You're saving him from his own stubbornness. The woman in the mirror takes these instructions docilely. But it isn't Anna. Anna is eyeing the seamstress's pins. Anna is watching the knife be cleared with the rest of the cutlery and dishes. Anna won't be used. She's done. She can't take any more. She won't let James love her. She won't let him save her. She's not here anymore.

PART V

Detonation

Three Days Until Detonation

Forty
The Hunt

Dubai. Friday.

"Falconry has been a tradition here for four thousand years," says Viktor Babić, standing on the upper level of his garden. Chained to a podium next to him is a gyrfalcon, edging from foot to foot on its bar. "The Bedouin caught falcons on their migration path over the Middle East to Africa and trained them to hunt food. At the end of winter, the Bedouin would release their falcons into the wild. I was given this gyrfalcon by a sheikh whose breeder is the best working today. The houbara bustard hunted by the Bedouin is near extinction. Many of my royal friends have had their hunting permits canceled in the name of conservation. My friends are outraged. Not only is this tradition important to cultural heritage, they say, but it's the national sport. I don't see the point in trying to stop the hunts, personally. If the houbara bustard dies out, it's because it couldn't withstand its natural predator. Us."

Rachel Wolff nods sympathetically. Marko, lounging next to her on the rattan sofa, is unreadable behind his sunglasses. The garden is a small Versailles, a series of green-screen grass steps ornamented with fountains whose runoff falls in a gentle water feature to a moat. When they arrived at the Diamond House they were taken to a cloakroom and searched by a houseboy with gold teeth and the bulge of a firearm under his jacket. Every seam of clothing was checked for bugs, every item of jewelry, loose pocket change confiscated, their phones smashed. For the first time, Rachel was glad Moneypenny said she shouldn't carry a mode of communication. She was also glad she'd left the blind man's watch—which still contained a tracking device—in the JLT diamond vault, which was entirely operated by robotics. No human ever entered. It was, perhaps, the only safe she couldn't crack.

Now, Viktor Babić strokes his stomach. "But I try not to let politics worry me. There's always new prey. If you build parks and skyscrapers in the desert, pests will come. The sheer amount of pigeon shit that corrodes roofs, windows, car paint—it's a disaster for the hotels. Diseases get inside air-conditioning systems, infecting whole buildings. The design of lampposts here makes for perfect nests. The pigeons just tear out the wires and breed inside. So, the hotels employ falconers to fill the sky with predators. The falcons simply circuit the city. It's illegal to kill pigeons here." A waxy smile. "I call this girl Kimberley, after our friendly diamond certification scheme." He pats the bird. "She's just recently come out of the molting chamber. We change her feathers under artificial light, so she's not scorched by the sun as we approach summer. I've attached a camera to her collar, so I can see what she sees. I'd never hunted with a falcon before coming here, but once you start, it's addictive. In an urban environment, you lose line of sight with the bird entirely. It's the most challenging terrain for a hunter."

Rachel says, "What did you hunt before pigeons?"

Viktor Babić gives her a look that raises the hair on her arms.

"I've trained Kimberley differently from other falconers. Kimberley kills the pests but doesn't eat them. She brings them to me. It took hours of teaching, but she knows I'll give her better food than pigeons if she brings me the little corpses. I use them to feed the other birds I'm training."

"What does she eat?" asks Marko, spreading his arms on the back of the sofa.

"Liars and traitors."

Rachel shrugs off Marko's nervous touch at her shoulder and stands, approaching the bird, which twitches, its speckled white wings shivering. "She's beautiful."

Viktor Babić puts one hand on Rachel's elbow. Clammy, despite the heat. "Would you like me to feed you pigeon?"

Rachel sounds like she's having the time of her life when she laughs and says, "I'm vegetarian, but thanks for the offer."

That earns a chuckle. "As talented as her mother, this one."

"Did you fence diamonds for my parents, too?" asks Rachel.

At that moment, a butler appears with a tray of mint juleps. Viktor Babić waits until the glasses have been placed noiselessly on the mosaicked coffee table and the bearer has disappeared with a bow. Then he says, "I haven't said I'm fencing them for you, yet. Put your right arm out. I don't believe in gloves. What's life without pain?"

Marko stands up, but Rachel waves him off, extending her bare arm.

Viktor Babić jerks the thin lead. The gyrfalcon hops, sinking its talons into Rachel's arm.

She bites the inside of her cheek to keep from yelling. The bird whips its head toward her, though the hood is still on.

"Maybe you do belong at the top of the food chain," says Babić.

Blood drips onto the tiles.

"Do you know what happened to your mother and father, little girl?"

Rachel squeezes her fists. "I know they never came home."

"Yes, that's what I heard. Shame. We could have gone on to great things. Those days, my office was a dim basement in Amsterdam. Perhaps you and I can complete the circle."

Marko says, "Hard to crack safes if her arm doesn't work."

With a cold laugh, Viktor Babić unhooks the thin chain, and tugs the leather hood free from the gyrfalcon.

Rachel flinches as the bird tenses. She manages not to raise her arms in defense when it leaps into the air, wings expanding in her face—and then the gyrfalcon is gone.

Babić's hand on the small of her back forces her to watch the tablet on the coffee table. The screen shows the concrete outline of the city from above, crossing from the suburbs to the dense shoreline, the brilliant border of the sea surging and retreating as the gyrfalcon swoops in circles. And then the plummeting dive, glass towers shredded in the sky as the predator whistles toward a flock of pigeons gripping the railing of a private beach belonging to a hotel built on an artificial palm-tree-shaped archipelago. The pigeons take off with just seconds to spare. Now it's a chase, the pigeons bulleting between real palms, completing breakneck turns past balconies, the screen flashing with the burnished furniture of gold suites. The deadly intent of the gyrfalcon is matched by the pigeons' desperate impulse to live. Babić's hand, growing warmer, circles her back. Rachel's blood patters on the tiles. When the pigeons clear the screen and the gyrfalcon is left wheeling, Rachel wants to cheer.

"Bad luck," she says.

"That," he says, raking her face with his hooded eyes, "I am still deciding."

He lifts his arm. The bird lands with a thump. Babić chains it to the plinth, jerking on the hood.

They are no longer alone. The butler is leading a young man out of the house and across the lawn toward them. It's Jordan Wiltshire. Teddy Wiltshire's son is clutching a Louis Vuitton duffel bag to his chest. He looks pale under the hard sun, and small without his father.

"Mr. Babić?" Jordan clears his throat, wobbling under the bag.

The butler says the guest insisted on a personal audience.

The diamond Janus flicks the air and the butler retreats.

"What brings you to my house?"

"My father," says Jordan. His voice is hoarse. "My father said I should bring the money to you personally."

Viktor Babić's tongue darts out, licking his lips. "That bag is heavy with banknotes, I presume."

"Yes. MI6 found us at Moon City. My father said a bank transfer wasn't safe, they'd be watching his accounts. He told me you could—" Jordan catches his breath, seeing Rachel and Marko for the first time, his eyes widening at the sight of Rachel's arm.

"These are friends of mine," says Babić. "You can speak freely."

"My father said you could turn the money into diamonds and give them to . . . you know. The boss. He said a Wiltshire doesn't back out of an agreement. He wanted you all to know his priorities."

"Not your safety, I see."

Jordan frowns.

"He didn't tell you to flee arrest. He told you to make sure the money was safe."

Jordan tries to straighten his shoulders, but that risks dropping the bag, which he won't release, though his arms are trembling. "I am his heir."

"He didn't make it, then?"

"Of course he—I only meant, I'm his priority."

"Daddy's safe, then? He contacted you to let you know everything is under control."

Rachel almost feels for Jordan when he whispers, "Not yet."

"You withdrew the money from your father's account."

"Yes," Jordan says eagerly. "It's cleaner this way."

"Where did you make this withdrawal?"

"The Emirates National Bank."

Viktor Babić unhooks the chain. "Here in Dubai?"

"Yes."

"And you didn't think the police might notice that?"

"I . . . I didn't think . . ."

"Evidently. I'd drop the money now, if I were you. It will make it easier to run."

"Run?"

Babić whips the hood free.

"Wait," says Rachel.

Marko says nothing.

Viktor Babić says, "Kill."

"Hang on, wait . . ." Jordan backs away toward the house at first, where he sees the butler waiting in the doorway, then spins and stumbles down the steps to the next level of the garden. He bumps into the stone lip of the fountain, almost falling.

The bird leaps.

Jordan sprints.

He makes it fifty paces before the bird brings him down, blood spraying from his neck.

Viktor Babić turns to Rachel and Marko. "The birds won't do that naturally. You have to train them. It takes a long time."

Jordan is screaming for help.

"Let him go," says Rachel.

Viktor Babić says, "She doesn't have your stomach, son. Open that bag."

Marko pulls the golden zip. "It's full of one-hundred-dollar bills."

Viktor Babić sips his mint julep, relaxing on the sofa with a great sigh. He stretches his legs, watching Jordan jerk on the lawn. In that moment, he can see the future. A friend of a friend in the FBI told Viktor this morning about the messy events in Venice. Hyde was antiquated, just like the muck he dug out of deserts. And Teddy Wiltshire was too loud, baiting the NCA to scrutinize his financial records, drawing heat from

MI6. The solution lies in Viktor's hands, and he plans to leverage it for all it's worth. He was always the man behind the scenes. Invisible. He grew up with nothing, had nothing, before signing up. All the other members have since been tried for international war crimes. Not Viktor. Strategy was his strength. He didn't lead the death squads on the ground, simply told them where to go. That took a lot of planning, which he brought to bear on his reinvention after the breakup of Yugoslavia. Everybody in the Special Forces had business contacts, stretching from West Africa, the home of diamond mines, to Amsterdam, where he set up business first. The Kimberley Process Certification System was supposed to stanch the trade in blood diamonds. It just made trade easier for someone like him. All he had to do was recut the diamonds and forge new certificates of origin, disguising the stolen diamond as a stone recently mined in Sierra Leone. High-value diamonds made it back into the legal trade. Smaller diamonds were the new and improved dollar for the global black market. A pocketful of diamonds buys a boatful of cocaine. There are no forms to complete, as there would be with large-scale cash withdrawals and payments. No one controls diamonds. No one but him.

Babić clasps his hands at the back of his neck. Even with all this hard work, he earns only thirty to forty percent of the diamond's market value. But now Rattenfänger can no longer fund its operations with offshore banking; they need him. If the treasurer wants to make payments so the strike can go ahead on Monday, his terms will have to be met. Rattenfänger won't lose any time, and it will be thanks to him.

But he'll need more diamonds than he has in his reserve. He'll need the blind man's watch, along with some stock for ready laundering.

Jordan has gone quiet. Babić shields his eyes. "Look at that. She hates not catching a pigeon. You can see the frustration."

Rachel has taken the first steps down to the next level of the garden, but stops there. She faces Viktor Babić, a hand to her stomach.

"It seems I do have need of you children," says Babić. "I'll take possession of your stock."

Marko kicks the bag. "We can keep providing you with diamonds. We're the best thieves in the business. But we want a cut of this."

The diamond Janus claps. "Like father, like son. You'll get your cut from the treasurer. I don't need anything more from you."

Rachel climbs the steps. The bird swoops overhead, dropping something red and viscous onto the tiles between them. Rachel steps over it. "Who's the boss?"

"That's not your concern. I'll have your cut sent to you."

It's Rachel's turn to laugh. "I don't think so. You need diamonds. We can give you a steady supply. But only if you take us to the end of the pipeline with you. We won't take our cut secondhand."

His smile is that of a death mask's last thought of mercy. "You are a useful instrument, that's true. But you might regret it."

"Are you expecting heat?" asks Marko uneasily.

"Not anymore. There was a British spy making trouble. But he's dead now."

Rachel rocks on her feet. Unexpected tears threaten and she blinks them back. The urge to flee grabs her. Madness. This is madness. If even Superman can't get the job done, what chance does she have? Marko's shadow falls between them. Her childhood love watches her fixedly. The sound of tearing flesh fills her head. She swallows, and stands her ground.

Forty-One
Repatriation

Airborne. Friday.

Conrad Harthrop-Vane travels with the coffin.

It took a night and a day to deal with the Italian police, military, and intelligence agencies, all of whom threatened to lock Triple O in a cellar with a rising tide until London suitably humbled itself. Harthrop-Vane was eventually allowed his phone back and something to eat, but not to leave the drab government office where he'd been imprisoned. He dialed Regent's Park, pacing the worn carpet.

"It's useless," Moneypenny said. "No more leads to follow. Hyde dead, the sword gone, no sign of Wiltshire."

"There must be something I can chase down," said Harthrop-Vane with such passion he believed, in that moment, that he truly wanted to avenge 004. "Cigarettes, gold, diamonds, pharmaceuticals, girls—anything with a black market could be funding the Gray Group." It occurs to Harthrop-Vane that he is listing goods that Enrico Colombo, Lisl Baum's gangster boyfriend, once smuggled, and that he left off heroin because Enrico never touched the stuff, lecturing Harthrop-Vane on it as a boy. It was that line in the sand, coupled with Enrico's appetite for life and past favors for Britain, that meant James Bond sided with him over his rival Kristatos, a drug runner. Funny, the lines that comfort people.

"That's the problem," said Moneypenny. "Anything and nothing could be a lead. Come on home, Conrad."

It was the only time Moneypenny had ever used his first name. Harthrop-Vane found his cheeks were suddenly hot, as if he'd been caught out doing something he shouldn't.

"Bring Joe back with you."

Triple O sneered. "Yes, ma'am."

But the sneer has gone from his face now. He feels queasy, and tired in his bones. He tells himself it's because he's never liked flying. When the C-17 Globemaster taxied onto the runway, he was taken aback. The Union Jack painted on the side. The bold stencil against the dark green: *ROYAL AIR FORCE*. It isn't guilt. It can't be, because he's either killed or set up for death four Double O's already. Dryden makes five. To his chagrin, Triple O didn't have a hand in Bond's disappearance. The fool was his own bad luck.

But he's never escorted the body back to the UK. He wasn't expecting the RAF, or the C-17 Globemaster, a plane that was a key enabler of the airbridge operation that sustained UK efforts in Afghanistan. Of course, Harthrop-Vane didn't fight in Afghanistan. None of his forefathers had seen war. His great-grandfather was the right age for the Great War but had poor lungs so was relegated to the Home Guard. It put him one foot out of step with the rest of his generation, said Harthrop-Vane's grandfather, who was born too late to be fighting age in the Second World War. The closest HV1 came to heroism was calling himself an agent of the British government, but he was never truly that. Just convenient. Conrad Harthrop-Vane doesn't have medals, like Dryden.

At that thought, his eyes skitter to the coffin tethered to the center of the vast hold, draped in the British flag.

He grips the bench, which rattles with the pressure of the plane as turbulence hits.

It's not your first time in a C-17, pull yourself together.

The first ride was on a humanitarian flight to some

godforsaken corner of the world where he killed a small-time dictator, possibly did a bit of good. Most recently, a C-17 on its way to an allied forward operating base to support French anti-terrorist work in Africa gave him a lift. That's where he killed Donovan and left him to be eaten by insects. It wasn't that he had anything against Donovan, or Ventnor, the Double O before that. Fine chaps, probably. But his mission was to hobble the Double O Section. A war of attrition. It was for a higher cause and he accepted that. His not to reason why. His just to do and take the pat on the back.

Harthrop-Vane draws a breath sharply through his nose. So why are you feeling queasy now?

Because he did have something against 004, just as he did against 007. A horrible feeling that if good and evil did exist, Dryden and Bond were the better men. Harthrop-Vane thinks of Felix Leiter asking him why he became a spy, which mouse nibbled on his toes. MICE: money, ideology, compromise, ego. Would it be fair to say that Dryden joined the army because he was compromised? Arrested on a drug charge as a teenager; a judge gave him a choice between prison or the army. But after that, what drove him through the ranks into Special Forces? Not ego. Dryden could command any situation, Harthrop-Vane admits, but it didn't puff him up. He simply had faith in his body and belief in doing good. Harthrop-Vane's gaze slides away from the coffin. After being injured in Afghanistan, Dryden could have joined civilian life, technically. But there wasn't much chance of that. If his life in the army began with compromise, it was, Harthrop-Vane guesses, partly a different kind of compromise that drove him into the hands of MI6. Operator's Syndrome. A man bred for killing can't quit. But he could have followed Luke Luck, Dryden's paramour in the army, who became a mercenary. Instead, he became a Double O. That was ideology. He believed he could make a difference. Fight the good fight. All those insufferable platitudes.

Entangling his fingers, Harthrop-Vane studies the hollow of his joined hands. For 003, it seems to be ideology as well. She believes in justice. She doesn't want to simply sew up the damage as a surgeon; she wants to fix things before they get broken, he heard her say once. Why? What is the difference between him and 003? Both come from ruptured homes. Neither could save their father. And yet. She keeps trying to save doomed men, and women from them. Rather a paradox. Whereas Harthrop-Vane has clarity. He knows he can't put a bow on his childhood and make it all better.

What is it for 007? Ego? His is certainly big enough.

Or ideology? Harthrop-Vane doesn't think it's patriotism. He heard Bond say once that this "country-right-or-wrong business" was already old-fashioned in 1952 let alone 2022. He said it was better to see things clearly, to know what you're fighting for, rather than hinge your morality on duty or orders. He never simply did what he was told, much to M's frustration at times. He did what had to be done. When Bond went missing in Japan—years back, under the last M—there was an obituary published for him, ending with some long-forgotten lines of literature: "I shall not waste my days in trying to prolong them. I shall use my time." Bond is defined by his purpose. Harthrop-Vane thinks such a philosophy empty. 007 is just a self-winding mechanism, afraid to stop or he'll die. Not Triple O. He can look himself in the mirror. He is prepared to step outside of everybody else's comfort zone. He doesn't need bedtime stories. He acknowledges the world for what it is. Doesn't bolt. That could be his epitaph.

The C-17 meets the earth at RAF Brize Norton. As the ramp shudders to the tarmac, Triple O chastises himself for his relief when he sees that Joseph Dryden's mother is not waiting for the coffin. Next of kin are given the option when it comes to soldiers, and if Dryden had been killed in Afghanistan, he supposes 004's mother would have been here, hunched against the rain. But Dryden's cover has to be maintained—whatever his family thinks 004 did for a living, probably something in international development, something noble. The body will be held under the jurisdiction of the coroner, who will complete an inquest matching the bullet wound to known kills by Trigger.

Triple O steps forward with three men of 99 Squadron to lift the coffin. It's lighter than his father's coffin. Or perhaps he's simply stronger now. He proceeds down the ramp.

Once the coroner is done, they will dress the body in military uniform, if that's what the family want. Dryden's mother will believe she's speaking to a representative of a funeral home that specializes in international repatriation. The body will then be conveyed to the family's funeral home of choice. Harthrop-Vane has a vague picture of Black women in colorful clothes weeping. He's never attended a Black church, and this is some stock image, as two-dimensional as any epitaph for a spy. How little we know one another, even if we're joined in . . . this.

Moneypenny is waiting in the gray rain, her collar turned up, her face blank.

The other three men carrying the coffin salute her. Harthrop-Vane is late, so doesn't try. He slides the coffin into the maw of the hearse.

"I'm sorry," he tells Moneypenny, but he hasn't spoken in hours and it comes out hoarse.

All the same, Moneypenny nods. "So am I."

"He used his time well," says Harthrop-Vane.

Moneypenny tilts her head. "Yes. He did. He was a hero."

Triple O sniffs. A waiting airman passes him an umbrella, which he extends over Moneypenny's head. "Come on," he says. "I'm in need of a drink."

Wrapping her fingers around his arm, her composure slipping briefly, she leans her head against his shoulder. "Me too. We can drink to the end of the Double O Section."

He draws back, sloshing his loafers. "What do you mean?"

"Joe is our seventh dead Double O in as many years. Eight, if you count Bond. Harwood is AWOL. 008 may never walk again. And I've just received word from the CIA. The cartels report killing an American spy in Panama. It's just you and me, Triple O. And I'm all out of moves."

Conrad Harthrop-Vane covers her hand with his, and squeezes.

Forty-Two
Between Two Fires

Dubai. Friday.

The Diamond House is a house of mirrors, as transparent as the purest stone. Viktor Babić insists Rachel and Marko stay as his guests, and after watching the houseboy pick bits of Jordan Wiltshire off the lawn, they politely thank him for the hospitality. There is no such thing as privacy here. The walls are glass, and if they're not, they're hung with gold-framed mirrors or watchful cameras. Rachel and Marko are given separate rooms. Both come with new clothes. Viktor insists, despite the thorough check of each seam, on sending their existing clothes to the dry cleaners in case of any errant blood. They don't come back. Every member of the house team carries a weapon.

Rachel is invited to use the infinity pool and lies on a sun bed, holding her breath as she watches Marko leave with Babić to show him the take from the Ritz and arrange the forged certificates. The diamonds will be used to pay for a terror attack on Monday. A gunman sits on a statue of a dragon, watching her impassively. She hardly releases her breath until Marko returns, and even then, she's not certain whether she has been betrayed. Has Marko entered a side deal with the diamond Janus? There is no indication at dinner, a silent affair stretched over a polished steel table as long as a limousine. It's like eating on a mortician's slab. Babić says they will meet the boss on Sunday—he doesn't say where. Marko stares into his glass of champagne.

She has to know if Marko is still on her side or whether she's truly alone. That night, the shadow of a gunman strobes the gap of light beneath her bedroom door.

Sunday night, they will meet whoever's in charge. The blind man's watch has been sent, along with most of the stash, directly to the "operatives"—but Babić won't make the transfer until he's met with the boss. Then the diamonds will be moved and the attack will go ahead in the early hours of Monday morning. A tight window, if she's to meet the boss before the deal goes through, but Rachel excels at climbing through tight windows. She can only pray support will be there when she needs it. Otherwise, they're delivering diamonds to someone with a plan to blow up another target like the BBC, a prospect that raises Rachel's heartbeat as she watches the shadow of the gunman pass once more, even if she tells herself that she never used to care about events outside her own control, her own private morality of robbing from the rich for a thrill because without that thrill she didn't feel alive.

The chance to be normal was taken from her at birth, she figures. But who wants to be normal? She ought to just run. Get out. Her mind races through escape routes, but the memory of 004, beat-up and bloody but smiling after they hit the Labyrinth, keeps her where she is, despite the inner voice that mocks her, asking, *If Superman is dead, what chance do you have? Just run. Flee.* But she doesn't. Because of a thought she can't quite dismiss as ridiculous. Heroes don't flee. She wasn't born to a normal life. She wasn't born bad, either. Her parents did what they had to in order to survive. And this man Viktor Babić, this man who was perhaps responsible for their deaths, this man who told her human blood is an excellent fertilizer, he's the thing at the end of the pipeline whose shallows she paddles. He's responsible not just for her own private pain. He's responsible for mass death. And she can end him.

She's just not sure if she can do it alone. The gun-man's shadow is gone. Rachel wraps herself in the silk kimono provided and pads across the hallway to Marko's door, turning the crystal handle with her gentlest hand.

He sits up in bed, and the light from the hall falls across his bare chest.

"What are you doing?" he hisses.

Rachel puts a finger to her lips, easing the door shut. Crossing the thick carpet, she grabs his hand and tugs him into the gold bathroom suite. She turns on the power shower, drops her gown, and urges him under the flow. Marko puts his arms around her waist, whispering in her ear, "Didn't know my body was worth dying for."

"Get over yourself," she says against his mouth. "In case the room is bugged. What happened at the vault?"

"We took stock for the certificates," he says, hands sliding down her body. "Why, what do you think happened?"

She says nothing as he presses her to the glass wall of the shower.

"What are we really doing here?" he whispers, lips moving over her chest. "This man might be psychotic, but he means real business. Yet all you do is provoke him about your parents. Can't you let the past go, Rachel?"

"No."

"That's because you don't know the value of the future. You never had to. You were never a true Yugoslav."

"Is that right?" she says, touching her Star of David.

"I don't mean that," he says contemptuously. His grip on her hips hurts. "I mean your mother. You always had an English passport. Yugoslavia had school, food, jobs, holidays, sports, equality. Then it all went away and my parents gave everything to try and earn it back. I do this just to survive. I don't have a soft, fat country to waste away in now, like you."

"You don't know what you're talking about."

He tangles his fingers in her short hair, dragging her into a kiss. When he finally releases her, he breathes, "I know you and I could have any future we want if we deal with this man and then forget all about it. Do you remember when we used to play between two fires?"

The game meant dividing everybody in the neighborhood into two groups. You tried to hit your opponents with a ball to get them out. Marko was always the last man standing.

"I never let you get hit," he says.

"That's not how I remember it," she says, searching his eyes, which are hidden beneath lashes beaded with glistening water.

He catches her hand. "We've both lived lives in between fires. We could have something different now. A real life, together."

Viktor Babić can't hear the conversation over the roar of the shower, which muffles the hidden microphones, but he has a good view of the young lovers through the cameras installed behind the bathroom mirror. He is watching them on the bank of screens in his basement office. He's still most comfortable in basements. There doesn't seem to be anything more to Rachel Wolff's nighttime raid than a sexual appetite he'd like to take advantage of one day. After all, does he really need Marko? The strong arm. Anyone can provide that. It's the girl who has the two most important skills. The con woman and safecracker wrapped into one. As he watches them rattle the glass wall of the shower, he chuckles to himself, thinking of Marko's urgent tones in the car on the way to the vault.

The boy knows that Rachel's mother tried to strike a deal with MI6 for herself and her husband, and that when Marko's father found out he was so furious he took everything from them at gunpoint. They could've fled to London. They didn't need money for that. But Rachel's father didn't want to work for Tony Blair, the man who dropped NATO's bombs on his country. That left one last job, for which they would need a higher percentage. That meant the end of the pipeline. Marko also knew that his father found out and warned the diamond Janus that the woman had been meeting with police. Rachel's parents delivered themselves to death's door without realizing it. Killing them was the easiest of matters, so easy that Viktor had practically forgotten all about it before Rachel announced her true surname. Marko told Viktor that Rachel knew nothing about it, and doesn't need to know.

This boy wants everything. The profit. The girl. Absolution from the sins of the fathers. He doesn't know that peasants who can't rise above petty visions don't get to win. Viktor Babić licks his own fingers, watching Marko do the same to Rachel. Only death wins in the end.

Forty-Three
Into the Mouth of the Bear

Siberia. Saturday.

Beneath the chandeliers of Novosibirsk railway station, Johanna Harwood purchases four tickets so she can have sole occupancy of a second-class four-berth compartment. First class no longer exists. This is common practice for wealthy women traveling long-distance and foreigners, both of which her clothes and passport attest to already. The sallow man behind the glass hesitates, perhaps questioning the presence of a foreigner here the same month the EU delivered its fifth package of sanctions against Russia for its attack on Ukraine. But he waves her on, and Harwood crosses between columns with quick purpose, avoiding the police in combat gear leading muzzled dogs sniffing for weaponry through the chairs where families wait. The train leaves for St. Petersburg in just over an hour. Time enough.

It was easy to steal someone's phone, once upon a time. But now anybody waiting for a train is clutching the device five inches from their face. Harwood goes into a shop off the main concourse selling chargers, SIM cards, and cheap phones. She buys one that just about connects to the Internet, paying cash. New phone in her pocket, Harwood walks down the vaulted length of the station, locating the photo lab the metal plant worker who gave her a lift from Gorno-Altaysk said she'd find tucked into this distant corner. The window is dusty, plastered with posters of Siberia so faded they are simply white as snow. The bell rings as Harwood slips inside. A carousel offers postcards of the station itself, the famous baby-blue façade popping with over-saturation. The man behind the counter, leaning on his elbows over a newspaper, pushes his rimless glasses up his nose to verify her appearance.

Harwood asks in Russian, "How quickly can you develop a roll of thirty-five-millimeter film?"

"An hour."

"Any quicker?"

The man eases from foot to foot. "It depends."

"I want to scan the last negative and take a look on your computer. How much would that cost?"

Another sway. "That is not a service we offer."

Harwood slips five thousand rubles between the folds of his newspaper.

The man clears his throat. "It won't take long. Please, take a seat."

"I'll watch you work," says Harwood, "if it's all the same to you. I've always been interested in photography."

Another thousand.

"How nice," the man says faintly.

The back room has the same chemical smell as the bathroom where her father would develop photographs. Harwood sits on a broken sofa, watching. She remembers the violent distress in her mother's voice as she said, "He lived a double life, with a double heart." Would the film prove her mother right and illustrate her father's life as a spy? *A spy like me?* Clarisse said that whoever his masters were made him delusional. Could that be true? And if it was, why did they do it?

Harwood clutches her empty wrist, considering what it means to be a spy like her—her own double heart, her own double life, in grief and the waking world, in love with two men, an untaken path as a doctor and a half-life as a spy.

"Almost ready."

Harwood draws the phone from her pocket and boots it. She downloads a barcode scanner app.

Human traffickers brand their victims to dehumanize them and advertise their ownership. They don't care that law enforcement recognize these tattoos. A barcode is a common symbol, reflecting, Harwood thinks, Teddy Wiltshire's long and wide reign. It has been speculated that the numbers represent the figure the woman will have to earn to buy her freedom. But Teddy was a banker who flaunted stolen wealth, kept meticulous accounts detailing his crimes, and refused to remove tattoos that chronicled his own rise to power through trafficking, theft, and murder. So, what if the barcode wasn't simply a symbol, but inventory? She isn't sure if anyone in law enforcement has tried to scan a barcode tattoo before—she imagines they have, and for some reason dismissed whatever they found as unintelligible. But if Harwood is right that Anna Petrov is with James, this might be the key, just as the barcode on any package or container tells the story of its destination.

"I can put it onto the computer for you now."

Harwood stands up. "I can do that myself. I just need the last frame."

After hesitating, he applies scissors to the strip. "Use

the flatbed scanner. The Fuji scanner is worth as much as this shop."

"Thank you for your help."

The man looks between her and the computer, an ancient gray cube, and then shrugs. "I will have your other negatives ready at the counter." He returns to the front of the shop.

The scanner hums. The photograph of Anna's nape appears on the screen slowly, stripe by stripe. Harwood goes to check the time on her wrist but she is now without any watch at all. She consults the phone. The train departs in ten minutes. Harwood opens the barcode scanning app and holds it up to the monitor. The beep is so loud she thinks it will draw the shop owner back, but he stays put. A set of numbers appears on the phone screen, which would be useless if you didn't already know the city, but she does, thanks to Marilyn. It's a fragment of a postcode, with a number that could be on a door. Harwood collects the rest of her negatives and thanks the man.

She boards the famous *Rossiya* train at 10:31 a.m., heading westbound on the Trans-Siberian Railway into the mouth of the bear. The train smells of heating run by diesel oil or even coal, the faint memory of rotten cabbage, and burnt plastic, the overhead cables carrying too much electricity. The compartment door has two locks, one a normal bolt and the other a latch that stops the door opening more than an inch, and cannot be released from the outside even by a staff key. Harwood drops both. She stashes her father's camera, gun, and clips in the metal box beneath the lower bunk, and then sits down, breathing out a long sigh of bitter adrenaline. A question remains. What is the implication of Rattenfänger using St. Petersburg as its latest hole to hide people? The terrorist group has struck Russia on more than one occasion.

Harwood's eyes are closing.

Forty-eight hours and two thousand more miles to maintain cover. Two days to St. Petersburg. Two days until she finds out whether James Bond is really still alive.

She drops into a deep, dreamless sleep.

Forty-Four
Call to Arms

London. Saturday.

"I need you."

As Conrad Harthrop-Vane hears those words, he knows he ought to say he's been told to get under the radar and stay there. But the phone call comes while he's watching Lisl Baum's *Jewels of Time* auction at Sotheby's on his phone instead of the dancer on the stage of the members-only strip club where he's drinking in the afternoon, the very hour, in fact, when he should be attending his appointment with the psychiatrist at Shrublands for standard debriefing after losing a colleague in the field. He's been drinking steadily since arriving onto home soil, searching for the buzz he felt last time, when he returned to MI6 after ending Ventnor and everybody believed the bruises on his arms were a result of his trying to save 005. But the buzz doesn't come until he hears those words. *I need you.*

Triple O says, "I'm on my way."

Forty-Five
Standoff

Masdar City. Sunday. One day until detonation.

Dubai at night is brighter than the sun. The streets finally cool down enough for citizens to gather. The city shines with flowing traffic, private yachts and jets coming home and leaving again, the world's largest shopping mall, ski slopes, all built on coral reefs and hundreds of Olympic swimming pools' worth of boiling seawater every day. A post–oil boom city drinking what remains in the barrels. A little over an hour away on the outskirts of Abu Dhabi, Masdar City is what's supposed to come next, when the barrels dry up. Ancient architectural practices meet cutting-edge technology. Buildings powered by solar energy crowd together, casting shade

A SPY LIKE ME • 507

onto streets cooled by a wind tower, meaning residents can go outside in the daytime. Only, there aren't enough people yet. Mainly it's scientists who work in the lab testing future technologies, and the commuting laborers tending the gigantic solar fields and recycling acres of construction waste. That leaves an experimental ghost town on the edge of the desert. Viktor Babić arranges the meeting at a hotel he's invested in at the limits of the project. It's still under construction. No cameras, no residents, no witnesses. Plenty of concrete, timber, and steel due to be crunched, ground, and shredded by impersonal machines that won't care if a corpse or two gets caught up in the mess.

The limousine draws to a stop in a street with a dim entrance to the PRT at one end—the underground electric-powered, driverless Personal Rapid Transport system—and a gigantic tower at the other, which hisses as it funnels wind through a spiral of mist to deliver breeze to those below.

Viktor Babić clicks his fingers at Marko. "Open the trunk."

Rachel follows Marko to the back. He touches her arm, then retrieves a gun from beneath the duffel bags, slipping it into his belt at the small of his back.

"Where did you find that?" she whispers.

A grin. "I'm a thief. Managed to swipe it from the houseboy on the way out. We'll only use it if he turns on us."

Viktor Babić climbs from the limousine, the gyrfalcon gripping his shoulder, chained to his wrist. "Get ready," he says.

His butler, now wearing an AK-103, takes position at the head of the party. The unfinished hotel is silent, the offices empty, the streets ghostly.

Rachel and Marko stand beside Viktor, Marko with the duffel bag of diamonds between his boots. Rachel holds her breath. Viktor said the boss would meet them here: Rattenfänger's treasurer, the leader of the Gray Group. Once she knows their identity, she'll do something—anything—to call off the delivery of the rest of the loot to the terror cell. She realizes, with a sensation of living in a new skin, that it's more important to her to stop the next detonation than it is to find out what happened to her parents.

Another engine bumps over the paving stones. There are no roads here. There aren't supposed to be any cars. The vehicle stops with a snarl. It's as if two predators have crossed paths in the desert.

The limousine headlights pick out a lone figure getting out from behind the steering wheel.

Rachel flinches with surprise.

It's Lisl Baum.

The jewelry collector says, "I do not appreciate being called away from my auction to fly all the way here. We had to stop over twice simply to mask the flight path. You have caused me a great deal of inconvenience."

"You have more important responsibilities than appearing in *Vanity Fair*, treasurer."

Lisl slides her hands into her cashmere coat. "You've grown some balls."

Babić says through gritted teeth, "Only one person here has arranged mass graves."

"*Arranged.*" Lisl shrugs, her necklace of multicolored mixed-cut gemstones set in gold clinking gently. "What do you want, Viktor?"

"Teddy Wiltshire is dead."

"How?"

"MI6."

Rachel sees doubt flicker over Lisl's face.

"His idiot son brought me his takings in cash, which he withdrew from a bank a mile from my house."

"That sounds like a *you* problem."

"Wiltshire's bank accounts are all being watched. The authorities will be aware of the withdrawal. You already lost the profit from that fool Hyde. Rattenfänger is expecting you to deliver payment to the cell for tomorrow's action. They don't like failure."

Lisl purses her lips. "You're not telling me anything I don't already know."

"Then what is your solution? Your own money from the auction, to buy a reprieve for the chaos you've overseen?"

"I suppose you're going to offer me another solution."

"Diamonds. The perfect currency. I have turned Wiltshire's cash into untraceable stones. They're ready to be delivered to the cell. All it takes is a phone call. And I have your end here." He gestures to the bag. "But before I make that phone call, we need to renegotiate my cut going forward."

Lisl sighs. She glances at Rachel. "All men are pigs, don't you think?"

Rachel says, "That remains to be seen."

Lisl laughs. "The optimism of youth. I suppose you want a cut of my auction, Viktor."

"Yes."

Lisl considers Rachel more deeply. "You know, the gangster's girlfriend is always overlooked. I was mistress to criminals who dealt in everything from drugs to women. When I started out, I was one of those girls, sold to the highest bidder. Then I discovered I had a certain *vivacity* and *charm* that lit up any room I was in, and men wanted it in *their* room. That was a taste of power. I put to use everything I learned over the years as counsel and therapist to thugs. Made my way in trade. Until I didn't have to ask dashing spies for diamond clips anymore. I could afford them myself. When I approached Rattenfänger to propose the Gray Group, as MI6 imaginatively have it, I vowed I wouldn't be used anymore. I wouldn't be at anyone's mercy. I won't give power away." Her smile flickers. "But I might *share*, if it means I keep most of my profit and Rattenfänger can put the cell into action. Call your logistics people, Viktor. Tell them to move the diamonds into place."

Rachel inches closer to Marko. He's breathing through his nose, attention fixed on the bag of diamonds.

Viktor Babić plucks his phone from his jacket and dials.

Rachel slams her shoulder into Marko, wrong-footing him, and draws the gun from his belt, squaring her body and pointing it at Viktor Babić's head. "Hang up."

The diamond Janus turns to face her, the phone still clasped to his ear.

The butler aims his machine gun at her.

Babić snarls. "Little girl, your instinct for self-preservation is as lacking as your parents'."

Rachel steadies her breathing. "It was you. You killed them."

Marko hisses her name, telling her to drop it.

Babić says, "Your parents came to me for salvation

because your father didn't trust the British. They never imagined Marko's father would betray them to me. Of course, I couldn't offer my help to anybody on MI6's radar. It wasn't personal. But it wasn't pretty, either."

Rachel's gaze darts to Marko, who is frozen on one knee. His face tells her everything. He knew.

Marko puts a hand out. "Rachel, I didn't tell you because I knew it would only complicate things between us, when it doesn't matter. We were both children."

Lisl snaps her fingers.

A red dot floats across Rachel's vision, settling on her chest. The laser of a sniper rifle.

In that second, Viktor Babić uses his free hand to draw his gun. He levels it at Rachel. "Put the weapon down. You're on your own. Don't think Marko will risk his life to help you."

The distant words of the person on the other end of the phone spool into the eerie quiet of the unliving city: "Hello? Hello? Should we move? I have the cargo ready."

"Hang up the phone," says Rachel, the weapon in her hand unwavering even as her head swims.

The butler snaps at Rachel to surrender.

"Do as he says, Rachel," says Marko. His hand is moving toward his ankle.

"Stay where you are," says Rachel.

He has an ankle holster. He pulls out a snub-nosed revolver. He never told her about that. "Rachel, put it down. You're not losing us a fortune. Use your head. We'll take our cut and walk away."

"Those are blood diamonds," she says.

"No, they're not," he says. "We stole them from rich people!"

"They are," says Rachel. "The bomb just hasn't gone off yet."

"When did you become a hero?"

"When somebody on the side of good asked for my help."

Lisl Baum laughs. "I should have suspected. Money-penny recruited herself a cannon. She's a spy, Viktor, and you showed her my face."

Marko turns red. "You're a spy? A damn *spy!*"

Rachel says, "If you help me, you'll get immunity."

"Only traitors help the law," says Marko, his voice shaking.

Viktor says into the phone, "Move—" and Rachel squeezes the trigger. It's a clean headshot. Viktor is a crumbling column. Her mother taught her that. *Sometimes you can't run, Rachel. Sometimes you have to fight.* She expects to die in that instant, as machine gun fire bounces in terrible echo around the close street, but it's wildfire. The guard has been shot, center mass, his dead finger giving a ghostly tug on the trigger.

Marko saved her.

He rises now, gripping his shoulder. He's been clipped.

The gyrfalcon shrieks and strains at the chain, jerking Viktor Babić's body around.

Lisl Baum says, "Would you pass me that phone?"

"You're kidding me, right?" says Rachel, aiming her gun at the god of gods. The red dot of the sniper rifle shimmers over her chest.

"This can end in one of two ways," says Lisl Baum. "You can both join Viktor in the afterlife. Or you can join me in this life. I could use a couple of good diamond thieves. Viktor was right that we can't use bank transfers anymore. Either way, that delivery is going to be made."

Rachel shakes her head. "I won't be complicit in mass murder."

Lisl Baum clicks her tongue. "I'd say you'll grow out of it, but there won't be time for that. What about you—Marko, was it? Do you want to lower your weapon and pass me that phone? I can make you a very rich man."

Marko swallows. "What do you mean, mass murder?"

Rachel says, "Those diamonds are going to fund a terror attack."

"Bad things happen every day," says Lisl. "Wouldn't you rather they didn't happen to you?"

Marko looks from Lisl to the phone to the bag of diamonds. The red dot draws a heart over Rachel's chest.

"Marko, listen to me," says Rachel. "I worshipped you. You aren't the bad guy. We aren't the villains here."

Marko turns to her. "Toss the gun. Come on, Rachel. This is for your own safety."

Rachel curls her lip. "Don't tell me you're doing this for me. You're just like your father. He betrayed my parents. Now it's your turn. It's not one last job with you. You want the world. And you don't care if I'm in it."

His cheeks burn. "I won't go down for you, that's true. I warned you. I told you what I am. Just let her have the phone. It's not our problem. Quit looking at me like that. Don't play if you can't stand to get hurt."

"Never," says Rachel. She knows there are tears in her eyes because the street glitters the moment she and Marko both fire. She regrets it instantly, but it's too late for regrets, because Marko is lying on the ground, clutching a hand to his torso, which is blooming with roses.

Rachel drops to her knees, covering the wound with one hand, the other still aiming the gun at Lisl.

Marko's chest is the heartbeat of a hare under a fox.

The dot of the sniper rifle blinds her.

Lisl Baum picks up the phone, where the voice at the other end is asking for clarification. She says, "Move them into place. Yes. This is a new voice. But you'll get used to it. Now move." She shoots Rachel a smile. "Thanks, sweetie. You saved me a bullet."

The glare of the sniper rifle settles dead on Rachel's chest. Marko's gone still. Marko's gone. She can't hear anything over the ringing in her ears—or maybe it's the pounding of her blood.

"That was very heroic," says Lisl, touching a hand to Rachel's shoulder. "But I'm afraid there's no one left to help you now."

It is then that Moneypenny exits the subterranean transport network, walking onto the street with her weapon raised. "I wouldn't bet on it."

Lisl barks, "Conrad, fire!"

Moneypenny says, "He's a little busy."

On the rooftop high above, Joseph Dryden presses a gun to the back of Triple O's head and cocks the trigger. "What did I tell you, Triple O? You won't see me unless I want to be seen."

Forty-Six
Rewind

Venice and London. Three days earlier.

Johanna Harwood's voice was distorted.

"Joe—are you with Triple O?"

"He's inbound—"

"Take cover."

"What?"

"You're in immediate danger, he's—"

The line went dead as a bullet pierced the window. It would have killed Joseph Dryden were it not for the fact that when Harwood said the words "take cover," she activated training buried deep in Dryden's brain and he immediately took a step behind the nearest bookshelf. The bullet plowed through the oak, leather, and paper, slowing down so that when it hit the bulletproof vest beneath his clothing, the combination arrested the armor-piercing ammunition enough that it burrowed through the Kevlar and stopped half a centimeter into his chest, bruising his heart.

Dryden hit the floor, skull bouncing off the marble. The ceiling was painted with a mural of clouds, which stormed in his vision. He clamped a hand on his chest as another shot whanged the air. The same training that told him to take cover told him to keep fighting until the last breath. Knock me down seven times, I'll get up eight. Johanna Harwood had just saved his life and now she needed help. Dryden lifted his phone. He heard the conversation through cotton wool. His left arm was tingling.

"Now I mention it, I do not owe you a favor. In fact, you owe me one."

"She and Bond . . ." Dryden gasped as a sledge-hammer seemed to swing for his chest.

"I see. I will take care of it, Dryden-san. Are you sure you're not in trouble, my friend?"

Dryden hit end call, dropping the phone. The buyer was gone. Going for the sword. He had to stop them. Dryden got an elbow under himself and pushed. He almost made it to his feet before crashing into a chair and sprawling across the floor. Another pounding. Another pound of flesh.

He could smell burning. The burning limbs of giant straw men dying in the dark. Dryden clutched his chest.

Bob Simmons, the navy veteran and security officer who operated the lift at Regent's Park, knew as soon as the doors opened on Moneypenny that the worst had happened.

"Q," whispered Moneypenny.

Simmons pressed keys that responded just to his touch. He could see Moneypenny's pulse at her jugular—the force of it was making her brooch jump. He said nothing as the lift dropped through the building, but when the doors opened on the ghostly corridor, he couldn't help but ask: "Who?"

Moneypenny gave him a hasty glance. "004."

Simmons watched her run down the length of the padded white corridor and push through the glass doors. He'd never seen her run before. Simmons cradled the stump of his left arm. He was glad when the doors sighed shut and there was no chance the technicians in Q Branch would see him cry.

Aisha stood up as Moneypenny let the door slam behind her—or it would have, were it not for the cushioning.

"I don't believe it," said Moneypenny.

"000 called it in," said Aisha. "Dryden is down. He's down."

"Show me 004's vitals."

"I cut the stream to his implant."

"Why?"

"He told me to, it's the ethical imperative if he wants privacy—"

"Don't give me ethical imperatives," warned Moneypenny. "Give me 004."

"I can't get him back without proper brain activity."

"Get Triple O on the phone."

Aisha twisted, tapping 000 into the comms. The ringing of his unanswered phone was a chainsaw.

"Why did Joe tell you to cut the stream?" said Moneypenny.

"I thought I heard Harwood's voice."

"Where's Ibrahim?"

"Mestre free port, waiting for the buyer to show up for the sword."

"Does he know?"

"Yes."

Ibrahim blinked—the action, if it could be called action, seemed to take years, his eyelids closing over a scene, the last time he shook Joseph Dryden's hand. In the now, he was in the front seat of a Fiat Panda, parked outside the gates to the Mestre free port, watching the flash of the sword on his phone. He tossed the device aside, and lowered his head to the steering wheel.

At Regent's Park, Aisha's screen suddenly flashed red, casting the color into the sterile room like spilt blood. 004's vitals, near flatline.

"He's back! He's alive!" said Aisha, raising her arms above her head. "He's alive. I'm restoring the link."

"For now," said Moneypenny. "Put me through to the Head of Station I—"

Dryden's voice cut through the speakers. "Aisha? Aisha . . ."

Moneypenny seized Aisha's arm.

"I'm here," said Aisha. "Dryden, your vitals are—"

"Triple O," he said. His voice was so faint it was almost inaudible. "You can't trust . . ."

"Dryden? Are you there? Stay with us."

Dryden's heart stuttered.

Moneypenny's scalp crawled. Her first words when she entered the room bounced back to her. *I don't believe it.* Why was she so ready to believe things weren't as they seemed? Was it simply faith in Joseph Dryden's endurance—or something else?

"I've got Station I," said Aisha.

Moneypenny leaned over the microphone to MI6's man in Venice. "004 is down—you should be receiving the location now. Do whatever it takes to have him declared dead at the scene."

"Yes, ma'am. Is he dead?"

Moneypenny ground out, "Not on my watch."

"Triple O is picking up," said Aisha, her eyes wide.

Moneypenny stabbed the accept button on the console. "000, report."

He sounded out of breath. "Two shots fired from the top floor. Bloody police won't let me do my job. Shooter could be anywhere by now. I've been telling them to drop a cordon around Venice and they kindly reminded me we're on an island where every citizen owns a boat. Incompetents."

"Calm down," said Moneypenny, "and report. Police radio is telling Aisha there are two men down."

"Yes. Hyde and 004."

"Then he's—" Moneypenny broke off as Aisha picked up a second phone to speak with the Head of Station I. Aisha gave Moneypenny a thumbs-up.

"I'm afraid so, ma'am. I couldn't get to him. The police are sieging the building. He was killed on impact. 004 is dead."

Moneypenny hung up, focusing unblinkingly on Q's golden tendrils.

Aisha said, "004 is being taken to the ambulance boat in a body bag. Gunshot to the chest. Seems his vest stopped most of it." The speakers blared, the screen flashing red. "Oh my God, he's going back into heart failure."

"Where you heading, mate?"

Joseph Dryden smiled at the sound of Lucky Luke's voice. Dryden gestured at the light at the end of the tunnel. He was walking on sand. He could hear the sea. "Shore leave, man. My nan is gonna feed me up. You coming?"

"Nah, mate, I can't."

Dryden paused in his step. "Why not?"

"I got shit to do. So do you. Ain't time to rest yet."

Dryden touched Luke's cheek. "Don't you ever get tired? You know we can't win this war."

"Victory in war is made up of individual victories in battle."

"I'm dying, and you're giving me slogans from the side of a bus?"

Luke grinned. He closed his hand over Dryden's. "I never saw you surrender in your life. If we lie down for defeat, we deserve defeat. If we fight, we prove there's something worth saving. And maybe get a different ending."

The wash of sea was growing more distant. There was grief to that recession of peace. But there was also comfort in Luke's voice. And there was fire in Dryden's belly.

Luke asked, "Are you willing to go down without a fight?"

Not today. Not any day.

"He's stable!" said Aisha, sinking into her chair. "He's stable."

Moneypenny's hands were linked in prayer. She felt as if the very molecules in the air of the chamber beneath them were vibrating around Q. She dabbed sweat from her neck with the cuff of her shirt. "Tell the hospital to keep 004's survival dark. Ibrahim's standing by at the free port?"

"Yes."

"Tell him he has my permission to use the sword to run that buyer through."

"I don't think that would be culturally sensitive," said Aisha with a weak smile.

"You're absolutely right. Ibrahim is welcome to use a gun if he prefers."

In the lift, Moneypenny told Bob Simmons that their luck was turning.

"He'll be all right, ma'am?" said Simmons, smiling crookedly.

She nodded.

"If you don't mind my saying so, you don't look entirely relieved."

Moneypenny said only, "If 000 attempts to contact you in security, put him through to me immediately."

Bob Simmons saw that her hands were shaking. "Yes, ma'am."

Phoebe Taylor rose from her desk. Moneypenny punched the wall, bringing down a framed print of Regent's Park in the rain.

"It can't be true?" said Phoebe.

"Call M. I'm going to Vauxhall."

"Dryden's not . . ."

"No," said Moneypenny.

"Then—"

"If you hear from Triple O," said Moneypenny, "tell him I'm in a meeting and can't be reached. Do not give him any further information."

Aisha locked the door to the bathroom stall behind her and sank to the floor. She couldn't breathe. She buried a sob between her knees, interlacing her fingers in her dreads, keeping the sound of shock trapped there. Aisha banged her head back against the partition. One thud, two, three. She laughed, brushing away her tears.

"I swear down, Joe Dryden, if you do that to me again . . ."

Ibrahim knew he was beaming like a fool but he couldn't help it. Then his phone started to beep. The sword was moving. Time to collect an arms dealer.

Ibrahim started his engine.

M said, "It used to be telegrams. My father died after peace had been declared. Absurd, in many ways. I was just a baby, of course, but my eldest brother told the story often. The knock at the door. The angel of death. That's what telegram boys were called. My mother tipped the boy ten shillings for his trouble. Years later, I asked her why. You know what she said? 'It must have been wretched for the poor lad. Simply wretched.'"

"I don't think Mrs. Dryden will give us ten shillings for this, sir."

"She will when 004 knocks on the door. But are you quite sure these theatrics are worth it?" M swapped a pot of pens for a heavy hole puncher on his desk, then straightened a framed photograph, shaking his head. "I simply can't believe, you know I simply cannot believe, that Conrad Harthrop-Vane would betray his Service or his country. I knew his father."

"Yes, sir, I know. I think you mean you can't believe he'd betray *you*."

He flushed. "Well, what if I do mean that? I helped *raise* that boy, and I am telling you there is no possible way that I could miss a single flaw in his character."

Moneypenny leaned forward and stilled M's hands, which were tearing tiny corners from a report on cybersecurity. "It's the people we trust without compromise who compromise us, sir."

"You know, I once said much the same thing to young Sid Bashir about you."

Moneypenny pulled back. "My loyalty to my country was called into question last year and the time wasted gave Bill Tanner a chance to hang himself. Every ounce of my life was trawled through and I didn't object for a second. I won't be questioned now, not when the obvious is staring us in the face."

M got to his feet, then didn't seem to know where to go next. "What about 003? AWOL. Psychologically unstable. You played a dangerous game with her. Maybe Rattenfänger—"

"Sir, if you can't see that Triple O is a clear and present danger to this Service and the security of this country, then you yourself are a danger and should not be in command."

M breathed out through his nose, a long and terrible rattle, like a dying dragon. "All right," he croaked. "All right. Bring Triple O in and tail him. See if he leads you to the treasurer." He slammed his fist down on the desk, knocking the pens over. Behind him, the portrait of Sir Miles Messervy frowned down at them both. "I vouched for that boy. Loved him. Just as I loved Bill Tanner. Rattenfänger is taking everything that's good in this country and screwing it up until it's diseased and rancid. Rattenfänger is a *cancer*. Well, I won't be made a fool of. They think I'm an old man who should've retired long ago, think I'm only sticking around in the vain hope I can bring James home. But if they think that, they don't know me. I was trained by the best. *I am the best.* You watch Conrad like he's a ticking time bomb, do you hear? If he steps an inch out of line, I'm going to nail him by his school tie to the bloody mast, and I won't weep, do you hear? I will not weep."

Moneypenny nodded, hoping to hide in her expression her concern—because M was already weeping; he just didn't know it.

Forty-Seven
Time's Up

Masdar City. Sunday.

In the big picture, the two Double O's are minute figures in the scalloped dip of an undulating roof. One is prone, cradling a sniper rifle, no bigger than a matchstick. The other stands astride the splayed figure and leans down to press a handgun to the sniper's head. The handgun is so small, it almost appears as if the figure is blessing the head of the other with a sacred outstretched hand. The glow of Abu Dhabi casts both in golden shadow. The tableau remains like that for a second, and then the prone figure rolls, and the figure above fires, a pop of red.

Joseph Dryden's shot misses by a fraction, and Triple O scythes his legs out from under him. Dryden falls back against the curve of the office building built from steel to Arabic design. His gun clatters away. He pushes to his feet as Harthrop-Vane swings for him.

In the small picture, Joseph Dryden is boxing his shadow, and his shadow is hitting back. He's gone these rounds before, in the practice ring at Regent's Park. Harthrop-Vane boxed for Eton. Dryden boxed for the army. They often trained together, and Triple O never shied away from targeting the right side of Dryden's skull, where his neural implant was buried. Human preservation tells you to shield your vulnerabilities. But self-preservation has no place in the ring. Boxing is more about getting hurt than hurting. So is being a Double O. Dryden abandons his guard to get in a punch to the gut, sending Harthrop-Vane staggering. The movement tugs at the fresh stitches in Dryden's chest. He puts his hand over the wound.

"You sure you've got the heart for this?" says Triple O.

Moneypenny is holding a gun on Lisl Baum, who relaxes against the bonnet of her Ferrari. She reaches down to adjust her shoe.

"Don't you find, at our age, that your feet hurt at the end of the day?"

Rachel sits back on her haunches, dropping Marko's

limp hand. She's left bright red lipstick smeared on his face from administering CPR. His blue eyes watch nothing.

Moneypenny says, "004 is neutralizing the sniper, a rogue Double O agent. I could use your help."

At Dryden's number, Rachel breathes out hard, winded, and then grins. You can't keep Superman down. She glances at the bag of diamonds. Then reaches for Marko's gun and rises. "She made a call to move the rest of the diamonds to the terrorist cell."

"I know." Moneypenny curls her lip at Lisl. "You're going to stand them down."

"I don't have that power. I'm simply Rattenfänger's treasurer. The strike order is given by somebody far above my pay grade."

"Who?"

A sparkling shrug.

Triple O is too fast, blocking, weaving, advancing. His face is pale with shock. Seen a ghost. But instinct isn't failing him. The fight rises over the snaking roof, falls, rises. The passing lights of planes taking off from the nearby airport throw shadows around them, caught by the solar panels, which briefly turn into blinding mirrors in the dark.

Dryden lands a hit to the jaw, then a hit to the nose.

He seizes Harthrop-Vane by the back of the neck. "Even dead I'm faster than you."

Triple O jabs his knee into Dryden's crotch, which Dryden just about avoids, swerving with his hips. Triple O uses the movement to rain blows on the right side of Dryden's head.

"To think I almost felt sorry!" Triple O spits in Dryden's face. "You're on the losing side, 004, always have been."

There's a jet engine roaring inside Dryden's head. Then the engine is silent. His implant is cutting in and out.

"You should've stayed down," says Harthrop-Vane, landing a boot to Dryden's chest. "This is pathetic. One foot in the grave and you're all Moneypenny has to stop me."

"Yeah?" Dryden grabs Harthrop-Vane by the ankle and twists. "Join me then."

The bone snaps. Harthrop-Vane folds, howling.

Moneypenny pulls her phone from her jacket and dials Regent's Park. "Are you tracking the blind man's watch?"

Lisl, who is inspecting her nails, glances up swiftly.

Aisha says, "Yes, ma'am. The diamonds are now

stationary. Whoever they're paying is in New York. That makes Camp X an unlikely target, but the Rattenfänger TACT prisoners are still locked down as a precaution."

"Keep me apprised," says Moneypenny, hanging up. "Security forces at the prison holding Colonel Mora have been doubled, and they're keeping some beds empty for anyone who comes knocking. Your plan won't work."

Lisl tugs at her necklace. "I can see why James used to speak so highly of you."

"I'm not a girl waiting for her first kiss. I don't spook that easily. But, now you mention James, I'd be curious to hear how you justify the destruction of a man who never did you any harm, and in fact offered to help you."

"Is that what he did?" Lisl raises an eyebrow. "Nothing like a savior complex to get a man going. Let me ask you this. Did James Bond ever once think of me again, after that night?"

"I doubt it."

"So do I. Which is why I'm not losing any sleep."

"What about engineering a profiteering racket that destroys lives? Stealing artifacts from war zones and using them to prolong the war. Trafficking women and girls into slavery. Does any of that keep you up at night?"

"I don't make the rules." Lisl glances at her diamond-encrusted watch. "It's your world. I just live in it. Very comfortably."

Dryden lands on Triple O's chest, following up with a headbutt to Harthrop-Vane's already bloody nose. "Not so pretty now, Double O Nothing." He grips Triple O by his perfectly blond forelock and slams his head against the steel-sheeted roof. "I trusted you. We all trusted you. You're our brother! You were supposed to have our backs!"

"Your *brothers* don't come to good ends, Joseph. Just ask Luke."

Dryden seizes up. "What are you talking about?"

Harthrop-Vane uses the pause to land another punch over Dryden's heart, dislodging him. Dryden doubles over. Triple O rolls to the side, and drops off the roof.

Lisl says, "You know the story of the two ants in the jar? One red, one black. They won't fight unless someone shakes the jar. Then, the black ant believes the red ant is attacking, and the red ant believes the black ant is attacking. They'll fight to the death. You can either be an ant tearing apart another ant for someone else's amusement, or you can be the hand that shakes the jar. Your precious government used me to get information from gangsters and crooked businessmen. Gangsters and crooked businessmen used me to get information from your government. Dashing Double O's used me simply because I was there and it would have been a waste to pass up the opportunity. I refused to end up a pathetic mistress surviving off scraps from Harrods, or wasting away, hiding somewhere in terror. I was tired of being an ant. I decided to grab a jar for myself."

"I hope you're not expecting sympathy," says Moneypenny, rotating a finger to encompass herself and Rachel. "Stop any woman on the street and ask her if she feels downtrodden, she'll probably say yes, for one reason or another. But most don't resort to terrorism for a pick-me-up."

Lisl throws her arms wide. "Do I look downtrodden?"

Moneypenny says, "No. I'll give you that. You know what you do look like?"

"What's that?"

"In your past life, the only victim was you. Now, you're destroying the lives of people who are just as powerless as you were. All so Rattenfänger get their kicks, and you get a few pretty jewels. You're not in charge here. You're just a puppet shaking a jar."

Lisl checks her watch again. "Are you sure about that?"

Moneypenny's phone buzzes.

Dryden shakes his head. Crawls to the side of the roof. Triple O is on a balcony one level down, kicking in the window. Dryden limps to the access door on the roof, tugging it open. Staggers down the stairs. The cavernous echo of footsteps running up to meet him. He readies his weapon, steadying himself against the banister.

Rachel Wolff slides to a stop on the landing, raising her hands.

"Hey, killer," she says. "Nice to see you."

Dryden laughs. He tries to make it down the stairs but his chest is screaming. Rachel gets an arm around him. "I was hoping we'd cross paths again, kidder."

She says, "And only moderately scathed, too."

"Speak for yourself," he says, but the look in her eyes makes him pause. He holds her hand. "You OK?"

"Heard you might need some backup."

"From you, any day."

Moneypenny answers the phone. It's M. He says, "We have a problem, Penny."

Rachel and Dryden check each empty floor of the office building.

"He must have gone for the underground network," says Dryden. "There are driverless cars down there, they run on magnets."

"Where do they go?"

"All over the city," says Dryden. "And the airport."

"You think he'd leave Lisl Baum to be captured?"

"I think Conrad Harthrop-Vane has only ever cared about precisely one person in his life. Himself." Dryden touches bloody knuckles to the window, smearing the glowing horizon. "Aisha, can you tell if there's movement in the PRT?"

Aisha's voice responds after a minute. "Yes, one PRT is moving in the direction of the airport."

"Can you hack the system and shut it down?"

"I can try. There's an antenna than runs the length of the PRT system, and provides a wireless link between the individual cars and the system computer. If we can get into that . . . Hold on, 004."

"We're heading down there," says Dryden. "Keep me updated."

The lift descends to PRT level. Rachel and Dryden exit onto the concourse, which smells of absolutely nothing. It's like visiting an archaeological site of some great future civilization.

Aisha says, "We've got him! The vehicle is one hundred meters east of your position, heading in the direction of the airport."

Dryden points to the pattern of blood on the floor, where there are no tracks or railway lines, only a smooth pour of concrete over magnets that direct the cars. He and Rachel set off running.

M's voice is urgent. "The CIA have just alerted me to a credible threat of an unknown number of radiological bombs entering the United States via shipping containers."

"How credible?" says Moneypenny.

"Three men on the FBI watch list were arrested for suspicion of cargo theft at the port of LA this morning, and a random inspection at the port of Virginia just half an hour ago discovered a cargo container with air holes, a bed, heater, toilet facilities, a satellite phone, and a laptop, along with an airline mechanic's certificate and airport security passes for JFK in New York. The FBI and the CIA agree these instances give the threat substance. They are ordering the ports of LA and Virginia shut down while they inspect cargo, and are grounding flights at JFK. All shipping carriers have been issued with a twenty-four-hour stand-down order. This is the nightmare, Moneypenny. If a container ship harbored in a major US city is carrying a radiological bomb listed as bloody class-two fireworks, we are facing a mass-death scenario. If twenty-four-hour stand-downs are ordered for multiple US ports, the backlog to worldwide shipping will take another three months to clear, wiping off one hundred billion dollars from the global market and triggering a worldwide economic catastrophe. Global trade relies on maritime transport, which we've made as easy as possible, much to the glee of global crime and terrorism. Now our pigeons are coming home to shit all over the patio."

"Stay behind me," says Dryden.

"Maybe you should stay behind me," says Rachel, watching his blood join the spatter of the rogue agent's.

"I'm fine," says Dryden, focusing on the PRT, which looks like a shuttle pod from *Star Trek*. The tunnel is smooth, no place to hide, no place to shelter. The blood trail does not continue on the other side. Dryden takes a step closer to the vehicle, weapon ready. "Triple O, it's over. Surrender and I'll take you in alive."

Nothing.

Dryden says, "Aisha, are you sure there's no other movement on the PRT network?"

She says, "Nothing."

Dryden motions at Rachel to advance.

The pair round on the glass doors of the pod together. It's empty.

Almost empty.

There's a bomb wired to a Rolex on the seat. The countdown is at 004.

Dryden pushes Rachel aside.

Time's up.

Forty-Eight
The Loss

Masdar City. Sunday.

Moneypenny grips the phone with white knuckles. Lisl Baum watches with a smirk. "How was the threat delivered?"

"Untraceable call to an anonymous tip-off line at the Pentagon."

"Why the warning?"

"Blackmail," says M. "Rattenfänger's list of demands is longer than all my ex-wives' demands put together. But number one is the release of all Rattenfänger TACT detainees from Camp X. The president has personally asked the PM to comply."

"What about refusing to negotiate with terrorists?"

says Moneypenny, grateful as her head pounds for the breeze spiraling down the wind tower.

Lisl Baum drums her ringed fingers on the hood of the car.

"We do not negotiate with terrorists because it might incentivize them. The president's argument—and one hates to agree with a politician, but here one must—is that Rattenfänger have hardly seemed *disincentivized* so far."

"I'm not letting Lisl Baum out of my sight," says Moneypenny. "We've not logged her capture yet, Rattenfänger don't know we have her. She's their treasurer. She knows *everything*."

"We cannot risk a bomb going off in New York or DC. The PM has given the release order, Moneypenny. Ours not to reason why."

Moneypenny hangs up with a stab. She turns to Lisl. "I am to escort you to your plane."

"Thanks," says Lisl, standing and smoothing her dress. "But I prefer my own company. Try not to look so shocked. It's not that the good guys don't always win, Moneypenny. It's that you never win."

The ground shakes. Smoke pours from the entrance-way to the PRT. Moneypenny almost loses her footing.

Lisl Baum smiles. "Case in point."

Triple O walks out of the black cloud. He keeps his gun trained on Moneypenny. "Drop it. You know I'm a faster shot than you are."

Moneypenny's mouth turns sour. She chucks the weapon. "Where's 004? And Wolff?"

"What do you think you're smelling?"

Dizziness shakes her.

Lisl Baum crosses to Viktor Babić's corpse, where the gyrfalcon is still flapping and straining. She unhooks the chain. The bird tentatively hops onto her arm.

Moneypenny's mind races for a way out, a last bet, a last hope. She knows she's searching for something that isn't there to be found. The hero. But the search tells her she's still alive, this minute as Triple O walks toward her she is still alive, so she can still fight.

"I trusted you," she says.

He says softly, "I know." He almost seems sorry.

"Every Double O you jeopardized or killed trusted you. Felix Leiter trusted you."

Again: "I know."

"Kill her," says Lisl.

Triple O blinks, then switches off the safety on his weapon.

Moneypenny says, "I'm more valuable to you alive."

Triple O's finger leaves the trigger.

"Why's that?" says Lisl.

"I've spent my whole life fighting people like you. I have intelligence that can help you."

"And you'll just give it up?" says Lisl.

Moneypenny can hardly breathe for the smell of burning in her throat. "No. But in between the misinformation I feed you, you might be able to glean something useful."

Lisl laughs. "I like a survivor. I suppose you'd make a good present to Colonel Mora, a peace offering after this mess. They can decide what to do with you."

Triple O seizes Moneypenny's wrists. "Well played, ma'am. But you may regret it."

"You're a bastard, you know that?"

Conrad Harthrop-Vane sniffs sharply. "I am a cold, arrogant weapon, in it for ego and power. I am exactly what you recruited. I am all your dreams come true. You just didn't realize they were nightmares."

Moneypenny considers his sneer, undercut by his scarlet cheeks. "Conrad, you don't feature as an *also-ran* in my dreams, or my nightmares. I've got bigger problems, and better people."

He looks around. "Really? Where's the cavalry, Moneypenny? I don't hear them coming. Do you?"

The awful plume of smoke fills her silence.

Rachel's whole body is shaking with the effort, her lungs desperate for oxygen in the burning tunnel, as she drags Joseph Dryden to safety. He's not breathing. No pulse. Rachel tears open his shirt, finding a bulletproof vest. She unbuckles the thing, pulling it off Dryden's limp body. She's about to pump his chest when she sees bandages already covering his heart. Rachel grips Dryden's hand.

"Come on, Superman. Wake up and tell me what to do. I need you." She casts about desperately. "God, tell me what to do."

Forty-Nine
Detonation

Undisclosed location. Early hours of Monday morning.

The door to Colonel Mora's cell opens with the softest of clicks. He savors the sound, and then rises to his full height. Mora stoops as he crosses the threshold. Six of his men wait on the gantry. He recognizes all but one, who moves aside. The man holds a machine gun like a British soldier.

"All the guards are gone!" says a good man Mora knows from his days fighting in Mali. "The doors are wide fucking open."

Mora smiles benevolently. He is about to pass by the unknown sixth figure, when he turns his monumental head to drill down into the new face. "Name?"

"Luke Luck."

Mora's gaze flickers from left to right, reading Luke's history. "Paradise's man."

"He's with us," says the soldier. "I vouch for him, Colonel."

Mora's hand lands on Luke's shoulder. "Let us walk to freedom."

Four months earlier. The long manacles linking Lucky Luke's wrists to his ankles and to the chair clinked as he rose from his seat at the appearance of a woman. Luke sized her up. Navy slim-cut trousers, a crisp white shirt, and a navy blazer with a brooch in the shape of a fish. Teardrop earrings in Bristol blue glass paired with a matching necklace. A briefcase with a numbered lock, which she placed on the floor beside her chair, sitting down without waiting for the door to close. The bolt dropped. The whole effect was one of cool authority. Luke copied her, his chains rattling as he dumped his cuffed hands on the dented steel table.

"Lieutenant Luck, my name is Ms. Moneypenny."

"I haven't been called that in a while."

"Britain is grateful for your service."

"Really?" said Luke, lifting his hands, but then he laughed. "Don't worry, I got no grievances. I went off the path and I'm willing to pay for it. Besides, being inside is pretty similar to the army. I know where my next meal is coming from, know who's going to clothe me, know I've got a roof over my head, I'm told when to eat, sleep, and shit—excuse my language, ma'am. Maybe I need all that. Never been very good at leading myself."

"That's not what Joseph Dryden says."

Luke sat back in his chair. "And here was me thinking you were some kind of therapist."

"No, you didn't."

"No." He grinned. "I didn't." He thumbed his nose and kept his head averted, staring at the floor. "How d'you know Joe?"

"I'm his CO, of a sort."

"I know he's been calling the prison to talk to me, I just . . ."

"He's agitating to have you removed to a Category B therapeutic facility."

Luke snorted. "Never gives up, does he?"

"I don't think he's constitutionally capable of it."

That raised Luke's head. "You're right there. What can I do for you, ma'am? Don't get me wrong, I'm grateful for the company. But I've got a blank wall to stare at and if I dawdle here it might get away."

"I'm told you read the Bible."

Luke said nothing.

"You're in this prison because you were charged under the Terrorism Act as an accomplice of Rattenfänger. Every other prisoner in this wing is also a TACT detainee with ties to Rattenfänger."

"I know. A couple of 'em were on the yacht."

"Yes. They witnessed you switch allegiances."

"Yeah, you could put it like that. I tried to kill 'em."

"I need you to finish the job."

Luke glanced at the door. "Excuse me?"

"Do you want redemption, Luke?"

He narrowed his eyes. "Questions like that from people like you never end well for people like me."

Moneypenny opened her briefcase with a click and pulled out a file. She selected a photograph of a buzzed ape in military uniform without a flag. "This man is Colonel Mora. He's here in isolation. He was the leader of Rattenfänger. I want you to embed yourself with the Rattenfänger detainees here and find out all you can about their operations, and"—she tapped the picture with her nail—"this man in particular. But first, you'll need to remove the detainees who were on the yacht with you so they can't cast any doubts upon your loyalty. It will raise suspicions if I have them transferred. You'll need to make it seem like a fight over something small. Cigarettes, or soap, whatever you think best. The aim of the mission is to make Rattenfänger trust you completely. There may be suspicions in their minds. Mora had a mole in MI6. It's unclear how much Mora may know about your involvement in stopping Paradise. Whatever it takes, you must make yourself indispensable. You have the perfect cover. Invaluable training in Special Forces; left the army and relapsed as a drug addict; radicalized by Paradise. You've already aided and abetted Rattenfänger in an act of global terror. Yes, Paradise turned against Rattenfänger for his own ends, but that's not *your* fault. And you're here, with the harshest sentence possible, in the harshest hell we can deliver. Convince Rattenfänger you're one of them. Only I will know otherwise. You can't have any further contact with Dryden. Convince Rattenfänger you're disgruntled and want revenge. Be my man on the inside."

"Why? What's the mission?"

"Discovering who runs all of Rattenfänger, and ending them. Whatever it takes. You want redemption? *The way of the slothful man is as an hedge of thorns . . .*"

Luke squared his shoulders. ". . . *but the way of the righteous is made plain.*"

Now, Lucky Luke follows the world's worst terrorists to his first taste of fresh air since Paradise's yacht, praying that he'll find a way to stop them before he has to hurt any civilians in this charade; that backup shows up soon, and that when it does, they know he's undercover, embedded with terrorists but not one himself; and—this last a mutter under his breath— "Come on, Joe. Don't leave me hanging."

Fifty
Hope

St. Petersburg. Monday.

It is a beautiful house, painted in pistachio green with dusky pink piping, three stories high and three bays long, with a gabled parapet where smaller windows indicate servant quarters. The street is quiet, tree-lined. The saloon cars all have tinted windows. The third story and servants' floors would have views of the river and the dome of the Hermitage, if the shutters were open. But every window is shuttered, and there are no signs of light. In fact, there would be no signs of life were it not for the six extinguished cigarettes kicked into a tidy pile at the base of the steps leading to the front door. The sentry has a habit. Still, any house could have a sentry, and if the numbers Johanna Harwood gleaned from scanning the barcode weren't the door number plus the last three digits of the postcode, which she could complete coupled with Marilyn's insight, she might walk on by. As it is, hope is at her throat, bewildering, delirious, terrible, ecstatic, life-giving hope. She takes the stairs two at a time and raps on the door.

At first, nothing happens. Then there's the creak of floorboards, and a shuffle of feet. The camera above the door peers at her.

Harwood clears her throat and calls in her best Russian, "I work next door. Somebody here is using our Internet."

Silence. If James is inside, it must be crossing the sentry's mind that he's somehow accessed the Internet. A bolt is released. Then another. A humming sound tells her an electronic alarm has been disabled. The door opens by an inch.

"We are not connected to the Internet," says a man's voice. "You are mistaken."

Harwood puts her foot in the doorjamb. "It's happened three days in a row. It's slowing our connection down."

She can make out a meaty face in the dark of the vestibule. It becomes clearer as the man regards her more closely. "You are not on our list of approved workers for this street."

Before Harwood can concoct an answer to that, a scream sounds from upstairs.

The man looks over his shoulder.

Johanna Harwood slams her shoulder into the door, breaking the chain lock. She grabs the man's arm—he's holding a gun with a silencer—and slams the door shut on his elbow. Harwood catches the falling gun, spins it round, and shoots him in the stomach. He crumples inward, and Harwood steps over his body, dragging him inside and closing the door, which she sees has been padded for soundproofing.

A red-carpeted stairway with a gold banister faces her. To its right, a corridor tunnels deeper into the house, ending in a glass door—which opens now as a guard runs toward her, weapon raised. Harwood reacts without blinking, finishing him with a shot to the head.

Grabbing a key card from the belt of the first dead man, she races up the stairs. She's made it halfway when a hand grabs her by the ankle and she's tripped, tumbling down, smacking her head on the banister. A hand closes over her mouth. Harwood bites down. She smashes the gun barrel into a bald skull. She twists, scrambling up the stairs, only to be dragged down again, the guard covering her body with his as he tries to reach his radio. Harwood wriggles, squeezes, boxes—she will not be stopped now, nothing will stop her now—and with a vicious kick she breaks the man's neck.

Harwood takes the stairs three at a time. The first landing is blocked by a heavy door. She waves the key card and the lock springs open, revealing a mirrored ballroom. Stairs continue on the far side—in the mirrors, she sees a guard hustling up them, and then the reflection is disappearing, the door to the stairs swinging shut. Harwood slides across the parquet, grabbing hold of the door handle and shooting upward. She kills the man with a double tap. A second guard appears and fires down at her.

Harwood ducks, the bullet deafening as it smashes a mirror. Harwood fires from the ground, hitting center mass.

Shots fired. She can hear shots fired from upstairs.

The third story is a smoky gambling den and bedrooms. One more door. One more flash of the key card. Bare stairs leading to the top floor. A door with five bolts and a lock—cursing, Harwood turns back, hurtling down to the dead body on the last stairs, grasping keys from the guard's belt, then returning, nerves a loose livewire.

She slots the key home. The top-floor apartment occupying the former servants' quarters smells of lilies. Harwood advances through a bright living room, lit by cozy lamps, toward an open bedroom door. A pool of blood seeps over the threshold. Too much blood to belong to a living person.

Harwood is shaking. She raises her gun, and moves into the doorway.

There is a dead woman on the bedroom floor. Anna Petrov. Her wrists have been cut. A spur of glass rests in her hand.

A dead guard lies in a battered heap next to her.

Beyond them both, James Bond stands with a gun in his hand.

It's him.

James.

Alive.

She did it. She found him.

Relief slices through her.

The comma of his hair, always falling out of place, is upside down—contorted into a question mark. His face is sheened with sweat. He wears a white shirt rolled to the elbows and an open collar with no tie. His trousers are impeccably steamed and his shoes are polished. No belt, no shoelaces. He is thin, but he hasn't lost any muscle mass. He's seen her. She knows he's seen her because those gray-blue eyes she knows so well—the psychiatrist at Shrublands asked her once, *How would you characterize your relationship with James Bond?*

And she said, *Let's just say, I know him well*—those eyes she loves so deeply are looking right into hers. But there's no warmth to light his taciturn face. The blank mask that comes over him in sleep, cruel even, is here now.

"James," says Johanna Harwood. "It's me."

He raises his weapon. "I know."

James Bond fires.

Acknowledgments

Much like a smuggling chain, there are many people involved in a book's journey from the author's mind to the reader's hands. Thanks to the teams at HarperCollins UK and Netherlands, William Morrow in the US, Roca Editorial in Spain, and Cross Cult in Germany. Thank you to my agent, Sue Armstrong, for everything. Thanks also to Viola Hayden and Jonny Geller. My everlasting gratitude to the Ian Fleming Estate for inviting me to contribute to the canon of one of my favorite authors—and to the whole team at Ian Fleming Publications Ltd. for your faith and encouragement.

The initial spark for *A Spy Like Me* came during the first lockdown, when my sister and I took an online course in antiquities trafficking and art crime led by Dr. Donna Yates, who was kind enough to later meet with me and offer inspiration and guidance. Thanks also to Jonathan Hills at Sotheby's, who provided expertise on watches, let me walk in Ian Fleming and Roger Moore's footsteps, and offered insight into auctions. Thank you to Fedor, who shared his experiences of Afghanistan with me. I wrote the middle of the novel at Greenway, Agatha Christie's house in Devon, where the garret is my home away from home.

My research into the art world took me to the Venice Biennale, and I am forever grateful to the whole Biennale team, from the president to the curator and all the staff who create this unique and awe-inspiring event. Thank you for inviting me into your dream.

If you're curious about the descriptions of the Biennale in *A Spy Like Me*, please do look at the catalog for the incredible *The Milk of Dreams* exhibition curated by Cecilia Alemani in 2022.

The creative process for *A Spy Like Me* was distinct from *Double or Nothing* because I had the chance to meet Bond readers here in the UK and abroad as I was writing. My biggest thanks go to the Bond community for welcoming me. As a lifelong Bond fan, it is the most gratifying outcome of an extraordinary experience. Thank you to everyone who's come to events, chatted in signing queues, and even gifted me beautiful Ian Fleming editions.

This community is creative and uplifting, and I'm grateful to all the podcasts, YouTube shows, fan clubs, and magazines that have hosted me, from The Bond Experience to the James Bond France and GB clubs. I'm honored to walk in the footsteps of the women of Bond, and it's been incredible to meet so many icons from the first days of the franchise at these brilliant gatherings. I feel lucky to have forged friendships and collaborations with so many in the community. Particular thanks and love to David Lowbridge-Ellis from Licence to Queer for all your support.

My heartfelt gratitude to the real-life Johanna Harwood, the first woman to write Bond. Your legacy inspires me. Thank you for letting me use your name.

Finally, thank you to my family and friends for being on this journey with me. To Simon for being my Q. To my father, Craig, for being my world tour guide. To my parents-in-law, Vera and Stephen, for all your love and encouragement. To my mother, Ellie, for reading every draft and being there when I'd literally lost the plot. To my husband, Nick, for being my copilot on this and every adventure. To my sister, Rosie, for walking every step with me, from virtual galleries to Venetian calli and imagined heists.

Thank you.

From Kim, with Love x

Ian Fleming™

Ian Fleming

IAN LANCASTER FLEMING was born in London on May 28, 1908, and was educated at Eton College before spending a formative period studying languages in Europe. His first job was with the Reuters news agency, followed by a brief spell as a stockbroker. On the outbreak of the Second World War he was appointed assistant to the director of naval intelligence, Admiral John Henry Godfrey, where he played a key part in British and Allied espionage operations.

After the war he joined the Kemsley Newspaper Group as foreign manager of the *Sunday Times*, running a network of correspondents who were intimately involved in the Cold War. His first novel, *Casino Royale*, was published in 1953 and introduced James Bond, Special Agent 007, to the world. The first print run sold out within a month. Following this initial success, he published a Bond title every year until his death. His own travels, interests, and wartime experience gave authority to everything he wrote. Raymond Chandler hailed him as "the most forceful and driving writer of thrillers in England." The fifth title, *From Russia, with Love*, was particularly well received, and sales soared when President Kennedy named it as one of his favorite books. The Bond novels have sold more than sixty million copies and inspired a hugely successful film franchise, which began in 1962 with the release of *Dr. No*, starring Sean Connery as 007. The Bond books were written in Jamaica, a country Fleming fell in love with during the war and where he built a house, "Goldeneye." He married Ann Rothermere in 1952. His story about a magical car, written in 1961 for their only child, Caspar, went on to become the well-loved novel and film *Chitty Chitty Bang Bang*. Fleming died of heart failure on August 12, 1964.

www.ianfleming.com

THE JAMES BOND BOOKS

Casino Royale

Live and Let Die

Moonraker

Diamonds Are Forever

From Russia, with Love

Dr. No

Goldfinger

For Your Eyes Only

Thunderball

The Spy Who Loved Me

On Her Majesty's Secret Service

You Only Live Twice

The Man with the Golden Gun

Octopussy and The Living Daylights

NONFICTION

The Diamond Smugglers

Thrilling Cities

CHILDREN'S

Chitty Chitty Bang Bang

HARPER
LARGE PRINT

We hope you enjoyed reading
our new, comfortable print size and found it
an experience you would like to repeat.

Well – you're in luck!

Harper Large Print offers the finest in
fiction and nonfiction books in this same larger
print size and paperback format. Light and easy to read,
Harper Large Print paperbacks are for the book lovers
who want to see what they are reading without strain.

For a full listing of titles and
new releases to come, please visit our website:
www.hc.com

HARPER LARGE PRINT